THE WILDLINGS

BY THE AUTHOR OF
THE VAMPIRE ODYSSEY

SCOTT CIENCIN

On the glistening, blood-soaked streets of Los Angeles, they were branded Wildlings—vampires who killed their own kind. For them, there was only one punishment…

ZEBRA/0-8217-3934-4 (CANADA $5.50) U.S. $4.50

PRAISE FOR *THE VAMPIRE ODYSSEY*

"THE ULTIMATE ART OF THE NOVEL IS THE ART OF STORYTELLING, AND THERE ARE TOO FEW WRITERS TODAY WHO CAN WEAVE A TALE THE READER SIMPLY CANNOT PUT DOWN. SCOTT CIENCIN IS SUCH A STORYTELLER. READ THIS BOOK. YOU WILL NOT ONLY BE DELIGHTED, YOU WILL ALSO BE ENCHANTED."

—Stuart M. Kaminsky, Edgar Award-Winning author of *Death of a Russian Priest*

"IN *THE VAMPIRE ODYSSEY*, SCOTT CIENCIN OFFERS A UNIQUE SLANT ON THE VAMPIRE MYTHOS, AND HE SERVES IT ALL UP IN A DARK STEW OF MYSTERY, HORROR, AND SUSPENSE. BY TURNS DARKLY EROTIC AND BREATHTAKINGLY TENSE, THE BOOK TAKES THE READER ON A WILD TOUR OF SOME OF THE DARKEST, FEAR-FILLED LANDSCAPES OF L.A . . . READ IT, AND ENJOY THE RIDE!"

—Rick Hautala, author of *Dark Silence* and *Cold Whisper*

"THERE IS A WORLD YOU'VE NEVER KNOWN," SAID THE VAMPIRE.

"A world to which you are entitled. Become true to yourself."

The girl stared into his eyes. "I want to. But I'm afraid." She shuddered as he leaned down, kissing her. Twin fiery explosions flared from the pale flesh of her neck. Soon the beating of their hearts was in perfect synch, the rhythm easing until Marissa could once again hear other sounds. She was surprised to hear another pounding, fists on a door, shouting.

"What's that?" Marissa asked groggily.

"A guest," said the vampire, "someone I want you to meet."

She was only vaguely aware of the throbbing pain above her throat, and a new sensation rising up to dominate her: She was starving. Ravenous.

He helped her stand, and together they walked across the floor, grinning at each other as they saw the way the door's wood shuddered under the blows from the other side.

"Open it," he said. "Consider it a coming-out gift."

HAUTALA'S HORROR — HOLD ON
TO YOUR HEAD!

THE WILDLINGS

SCOTT CIENCIN

ZEBRA BOOKS
KENSINGTON PUBLISHING CORP.

ZEBRA BOOKS

are published by

Kensington Publishing Corp.
475 Park Avenue South
New York, NY 10016

First printing: October, 1992

Printed in the United States of America

ACKNOWLEDGEMENTS

This book is dedicated to Denise Resko with love and admiration. May what we have found together grow brighter and stronger each day.

Special thanks to Kendall Morris for technical assistance.

As fall the dews on quenchless sands,

Blood only serves to wash
ambition's hands.

> — Byron
> *Don Juan,* Canto IX, Stanza 59

The appetite for power grows
on what it feeds upon.

> — Polybius, VI. 57.

Prologue

The dancer waited.

Her audience had arrived. Every booth was filled. She didn't need to leave the small cubbyhole her employers had laughingly called a "dressing room" to know this. She could feel their presence, their desire, their fear. The dance room was a stark, ten foot square, with a dozen adjacent booths. Nine were filled with regulars. She was on intimate terms with each man, though she had never spoken a word to any of them. The other three were newcomers. That was good. Her turnover rate was high and new blood was always welcome.

She had been at the Hellfire Club for a little under a month. Before that, she had worked the strip, dancing in smoke-filled bars with low ceilings. The Hellfire Club specialized in upscale sleaze, yuppie porn wrapped in a cloak of literary and pop cultural allusions. It was housed in a renovated church, with high cathedral ceilings and many of the original pews. There was a bar and a dance floor, along with a host of private Dens of Sin and Debauchery. The dancer had been given a guided tour of the Oscar Wilde Room, the Caligula Suite, the Byronic Hall, the deSade Chamber, and the Madonna Plaza, where she would take up residence. Her first night had been slow, but after a few days, she was playing to sellout audiences.

An angry buzz sounded from the wall intercom. "Lilith. The boys are getting restless out there."

"I know," the dancer said in a breathy whisper. She always kept "the boys" waiting. They loved it. Anticipation was everything. She would wait until they were ready to claw at the metal partitions separating them from their glimpse at sexual heaven and hell before she entered through the "thirteenth door"—as it was labeled inside the dance room—and began her routine.

"Lilith, come on."

The dancer smiled. Lilith was not her true name, but it had been a simple matter to convince the management and her coworkers.

"Tell them to keep their pants on," Lilith said with a wicked laugh. The intercom buzzed again, the connection broken.

The dancer sat before a dark wall, applying her makeup. The mirror sat in the corner, under a sheath of black canvas. When she had been lured by the owners of the club, she had made her conditions clear: No mirrors, no cameras. The owners had wanted publicity shots of her, but the dancer had declined. When they attempted to argue, she turned her hard, unyielding gaze on them.

Her eyes were unlike anything they had ever seen before. They constantly changed color, like gasoline running in a violently churning stream. She terrified the little men who had created the Hellfire Club and made

8

them love every second of it. They couldn't get enough of her. No one could.

Checking her outfit, the dancer rose and cracked open the lighting panel next to the door. Her sequence was preprogrammed. She punched in her code and struck ENGAGE.

The dancer opened the door and stepped into the center of the room. White mist flooded into the chamber from the low vents. She lay on the floor, her face lolling to one side, one knee half cocked, exposing the sensual expanse of her lace-gripped thighs, while she ran her other hand casually over her body. A pool of light pierced the darkness and fell upon her.

The metal partitions slid upward and the music began. The dancer's eyes were closed, but she could feel the thunder of a dozen hearts beating like triphammers as the men received their first, veiled look at her. The soundtrack she had selected was not the harsh, vulgar dance mix the owners had attempted to thrust upon her. It was vibrant and lush, sensual and breezy, pulsing and alive with fire and delight — music that conveyed the excitement of lovers waking in each other's arms for the first time. The image caught the dancer's imagination. In her thoughts, she saw a pair of lovers reaching for each other as bright, filtered sunlight washed over them, firing their ardor. The dancer's rising passion was infectious. It quickly spread to her small audience. Her regulars delighted in her languorous motions as she slowly writhed on the floor, raising one leg then the other into the air and running the length of her flesh with her hands.

She could feel their desire coursing through her, sense their needs and wants. Suddenly she was turning, rising, pirouetting gracefully, her thin white gown whipping behind her. The music took on a slightly darker edge. Eyes squeezed shut, the dancer pulled at the white silk scarf tied around her neck. The interest of her audience rose appreciably. She had them. They would follow no matter where she led them, even to the gates of hell and beyond. The thought filled her with excitement and delight.

She twisted and gyrated, small grunts and moans escaped her rich, full lips. Her lush breasts bounced and swayed beneath her thin lace top, and she made a show of loosing the knot securing the scarf in place. It was the only piece of clothing she would actually remove during her dance. Nothing else was necessary. She worked the scarf, somehow releasing a Gordian knot of desire in her breast.

Her emotions flared, invisible waves of force radiating from her to the men who were no longer simply *watching* her, they were actively participating, their desires mixing with her own to create some new, remarkable synthesis. When the scarf finally fell away, the dancer threw her head back and screamed.

An all-encompassing cloud of undiluted, raw sex mushroomed out from her, filling the room, passing through the barriers of glass and flesh to permeate the minds of the men comprising the audience. From somewhere close, she heard the heavy pounding of strong, masculine hands beating against the glass. With an animal hiss, the dancer sank to her knees and threw her head back. Her long hair scraping the floor, the dancer spread her legs and arched her body in a bow as she reached out to the men who had gathered to watch her perform.

Nine of these men knew there was much more to be had than simple entertainment. They knew she was far more than human. The dancer tended to each of them with her usual reserve, invisible tendrils snaking away from her body, passing through the glass separating her from them, and entering their thoughts. But it was the newcomers upon whom she concentrated her full attention.

Each of them saw her the way they wanted to see her. That was her gift. Her power. The delicious surprise of the man closest, Alejandro, made her flesh tingle. She looked at herself through his eyes.

The walls had, impossibly, come crashing down. At first, he had been frightened. Then he realized that he would not be harmed, and he stepped through the rubble that lay between himself and the woman. When the partition had risen and he had seen her, he could not believe her resemblance to his late wife, Naomi. She had chestnut brown hair, full, blood-red lips, and deeply tanned flesh. Her exotic features were set in the same amused, playful expression with which Naomi had regarded him when they first met, in a Hawaiian supermarket. The woman wore his wife's beautiful wedding dress, though it was partially undone and her exquisite figure could be glimpsed beneath.

After the walls fell, the dance room shifted and became their honeymoon suite. Alejandro could no longer deny what he was seeing. This was Naomi. She had come back to him. His life could begin again. He went to her and took her with reckless abandon.

The dancer luxuriated in the sensations she culled from Alejandro's mind. She was experiencing the fantasies of a dozen men at once, soaking up their desire, tasting it, consuming it ravenously. But his was especially sweet. His need extended far beyond the physical. He had experienced a loss so deep that it had wounded his

11

soul. He had been searching for release from his torment. With her, he had found it, at least for a time, and he had released his every inhibition.

Another man. Probing, clawing, hungry for her. She maintained the illusions she had swathed the others within and turned to him. His name was Paul Goldman.

The glass had vanished and he was back in his office. Carrie was there, sitting on the edge of his desk. She wore a tan business suit with a frilly white top. Smiling an invitation, she unbuttoned her blouse and told him that everyone had left, they were alone.

The dancer turned away, disappointed. An office flirtation. She was going to make him work for this one.

Paul clutched at her through the blouse, forcing his tongue into her mouth. She pulled away.

"First we're going to play a little game, honey. . . ."

Smiling, the dancer moved from Paul and went for the last of the new arrivals. She picked herself up and resumed the dance.

"Stephen," she whispered as her movements became sharper, more feral. "Wonderful," she cried as she sifted his memories and found a banquet of delights. "Yes!"

He was a virgin, twenty-two years old and filled with self-loathing, pain, and need. He had suffered through a disturbing childhood, and was given to loneliness and depression. Throughout his life he had been lost to books, fantasies, daydreams, and illusions. Shadows and dust. He was a fairly good-looking boy who had never been taught how to dress, how to act. Lack of confidence and fear were his constant companions.

Lilith probed deeper. The closest he had come to realizing his dream of not being alone was a two-month stretch with a girlfriend who allowed him to feel her up

12

but nothing else. He was about to graduate from college and felt like a loaded gun, the safety off.

The dancer reached deep into his mind. His fear was amazing and powerful. She wanted him more than she had wanted any man who had come to the club before. She wanted him to give himself to her fully, she wanted to possess him.

Poor, sweet, Stephen, she spoke into his mind. *I have just the cure for you. My arms are open, love. Come to me and I can give you everything you've ever dreamed, everything you've ever imagined.*

She felt him respond. For several glorious seconds she consumed his fear and desire, wrapping around him a fantasy in which she became the girl he loved and desired most in school. She seduced him the way he had always dreamt his sweetheart someday would. Reality fell away as she looked into the dreamworld and became a part of it.

Darkness surrounded them. She stood, her hands on his hips. They kissed, tentatively at first, then with her urging and instruction, openmouthed, tongue probing. He felt her breasts through her black turtleneck blouse. She wasn't wearing a bra and her nipples were hard and thrusting. He squeezed her breasts, then suddenly clutched at the nipples, yanking so hard on them it caused her to cry out.

The dancer tensed as a bolt of pain shot through her. Moaning, she opened her eyes. She turned to face the booth where Stephen sat, separated from her by a thick pane of glass. His expression was not that of a man lost in transport to some distant land of sensual fantasy, as the other eleven men had been. His eyes were sharp and alert, he grinned at her maliciously. He mouthed a single word:

13

Dance.

She was powerless to resist the command. The dancer writhed, allowing the changing rhythms of her lush music to dictate her movements. Subtle and elegant, the dancer felt her body flow with the music, her heart thundering as she understood that she moved not of her own accord, but of his.

Dance.

The voice split her consciousness, snaking into her mind with the power, assurance, and venom that only another of her kind could produce. The dancer felt her movements increase. She ignored the music, thrusting and pounding to some unheard rhythm, her motions sexual and vulgar, her body gyrating and shuddering to satisfy the needs of the creature who had so easily entrapped her.

Suddenly, she existed in two worlds at once. In the dance room, her body ground and twisted to Stephen's commands.

But on the psychic landscape, she was in Stephen's arms, trying to push herself away from him. She was powerless. His mouth was on hers, his hands spidering over her body with a vicious familiarity. He was oblivious to the blows she rained upon him. If pain reached him, she could not sense it. Her connection had not been to the true man, in any case. She had fallen into a trap, sailed into the arms of a constructed persona. Struggling, she could not pry herself loose.

"It works both ways, bitch. You reach out and touch someone, they can touch back. Or hadn't you expected to meet up with someone like me, eventually?"

With incredible strength, his hand slid between her legs and clutched her, causing her to scream with agony.

"Sex and death. That's what it's all about, isn't it, little vam-

14

pire? The need for sex, staving off the fear of death. Fear and de-
sire. You control them both, don't you?"

He bore down hard on her. "Don't you!?"

"Yes!" she cried, attempting to force herself away from his
grasp.

On stage, the dancer spun and thrust her body in ex-
hausting, sensual motions. She felt her heart ready to
explode, her flesh dripping with sweat. Somehow, she
protected her true face, the veil had not fallen. The
dancer sensed Stephen's desire to know her true name,
to possess her body and soul. She could not allow that.
She would die first and take him with her before she let
another of their kind make her a slave.

In the dreamworld, a teenaged girl's bedroom formed around
them. A collection of stuffed animals appeared in the corner.
Posters of rock stars and teen idols manifested on the walls. The
back of the dancer's legs were pressed against a bed. She vowed in-
wardly that she would not be forced to lay upon it, Stephen above
her. He had lifted the turtleneck up and was squeezing her bare
breast hard enough to leave bruises.

"I know what you want, little vampire. You want blood.
You've been living off emotions for too long, you want to taste the
wine of violence, don't you?"

The dancer did not waste precious time or energy with protests.
She had one chance of escaping the trap. Squeezing her eyes shut,
she allowed the blood need to overwhelm her.

The dancer faltered in her movements, and fell to the
floor. She rolled several times, reached the closest glass
partition, and kicked at it with inhuman strength. Her
bare foot created a spider's web of cracks on the first
blow, and shattered the glass on the second. The man in
the booth, Alejandro, raised his hands in protest as
shards of razor-sharp glass fell upon him, slicing into his

arms and back as he turned away. The blood scent was incredible. The dancer rose above the sudden hunger swelling in her breast and launched herself across the dance floor at another window.

Her connection to the various dreamworlds each of the remaining eleven men occupied had not been severed. That had been Stephen's mistake. As Alejandro plucked pieces of glass from his flesh in the physical world, he underwent an entirely different trauma in his head.

Naomi was dying. They were trapped in the front seat of the VW. A truck had run them off the road, forcing them to crash through a picket fence. The glass window had shattered and a large sliver was lodged in her throat. She was convulsing, unable to speak, blood pouring out of her wound as she regarded him with wide, terror-filled eyes, eyes that spoke of betrayal and fear, eyes that would haunt him forever.

The dancer was almost in tears. She had not meant to bring this pain to Alejandro. She had hoped Stephen would be driven mad by the man's blood, and would be distracted long enough for the dancer to escape. Putting her own safety at risk, she altered the scenario in Alejandro's mind.

The glass splinter fell from Naomi's neck. It had barely penetrated the skin. Alejandro caught it and threw it through the skeletal remains of the shattered front windshield. Easing himself forward, he clutched Naomi in his arms and held her tight. They laughed and cried with relief and love.

The dancer flinched. Turning, she saw Alejandro laughing with joy. She had no idea if a part of her mind had previously absorbed the details of his wife's demise, if she had subconsciously understood that breaking the window would revisit the tragedy upon him. It was possible. She had been capable of cruelties far more severe than this in the past. But tonight she would rise above it.

Her full attention was sucked back into Stephen's nightmare vista. She felt like a drowning victim who had just broken the surface, only to have the undertow drag her down once again.

He was pressing her against the bed, but that was the only piece of furniture which had remained intact. The walls were bare. The posters and stuffed animals had vanished. He was losing his grip.

"Weak, little vampire. You are so weak," Stephen hissed, but that was not true. The uncommon display of compassion had startled him, causing him to tremble with rage. It was inconceivable *for one of their kind to show such tenderness and restraint. He had been frightened by her, and his fear was all she needed.*

Before she could move on him, Stephen slapped the dancer. She fell away from him, to the bed. As he descended upon her, she raised one leg and kicked at him. Her foot connected with his midsection and he was sent against the far wall, which bubbled and dissolved upon contact. The dancer concentrated and the wall became thick, like drying cement, trapping Stephen within its confines. His hands, knees, and face jutted from the smooth wall. The man screamed in rage, struggling to free himself, his hands stretching into psychic claws he would use to burrow deep into her brain and extract her secrets.

She raked his consciousness with talons of her own. At first, he had wanted to break her will, to make her a broodmare, fulfilling his depraved sexual wants while she cared for the human child he would create with a mortal woman, but she had humiliated and frightened him. He would be satisfied with nothing short of her death.

"Too bad, asshole," she said, raising her hands.

Suddenly, the wall solidified, neatly slicing off the man's head and hands. The dancer withdrew.

Stumbling back, the dancer looked to the booth where Stephen sat. He was slumped over. She couldn't tell if he was dead or not and she had no intention of extending her power to him once again to find out. He had trapped her once, that was enough.

A chorus of dull thuds filled the dance floor, overwhelming the sweet, dreamlike melodies of her specially chosen music. The human men were beating at the glass, expressions of desperation on each of their faces. Only Alejandro did not join them. He turned without looking back and left the booth. Her connection to his mind had already fallen away, but her psychic tendrils were still attached to the remaining patrons. They were entrenched in their fantasy worlds, though the foundations of those worlds were crumbling around them. Somehow, they had sensed the dancer's intent to leave and never return, and they were desperate to hold her.

It works both ways.

Brutally, she severed the threads linking her to the other men. They railed and screamed, but she did not care. The dancer found the door leading to her dressing room and burst through it. She did not pause to collect any of her belongings. The short hallway linking her room to the main body of the club was dimly lit, deserted.

Thank God, she thought. She traversed the maze of empty corridors, well aware of the thundering music from the club's dance floor and private rooms. Bursts of laughter and scraps of conversation sliced into her mind, accompanied by the fierce sensations of desire and fear, the constant companions of those natural pred-

18

ators, both male and female, who stalked their willing prey in places such as this throughout downtown Los Angeles. She found an old black raincoat on a hook near the locked double doors at the rear of the club. Without breaking stride she slipped the coat over her and turned, slamming her back into the door. It burst open, the lock shattering with a metal shriek.

In seconds she was in the back parking lot. A light drizzle fell from the night sky. She broke into a dead run, moving so quickly that the open folds of the raincoat whipped behind her, the wings of some impossible beast.

Her bare feet fell on broken glass and she did not stop. Her lungs ached and her limbs burned in protest and she did not stop. Her heart thundered and threatened to explode and she did not stop.

The back alleyways blurred past her, and suddenly she was on the street, passing a strip of liquor stores, video arcades, strip clubs, and tenements. Youths wearing colors screamed at her to stop, but she ignored them. A young couple appeared before her and she shoved them out of her way. She crossed a street and several cars screeched to a halt, barely avoiding her. A dozen blocks passed. More.

Finally, her inhuman endurance gave out. She collapsed twenty feet from a pay phone, clutching at her chest, gasping for breath. The dancer was only barely aware of her surroundings. Brick buildings. A storefront.

Someone approached.

Trembling, the dancer made it to her knees. Her dark, lustrous hair fell before her face, partially obscuring her stunning features.

"Miss? Are you all right?"

The dancer looked up sharply, the hair falling away from her face. Her blazing eyes nearly blinded the forty-five-year-old wearing a McDonald's hat and uniform. The woman backed away, tears forming in the corners of her eyes.

"I'm sorry, I'm sorry, don't hurt me," the woman cried.

The dancer hissed and looked away. She heard a door open, the woman retreating. The dancer waited a moment, then eyed the pay phone. She had no change. Moving forward on unsteady legs, the dancer entered the fast-food restaurant. The woman who had come out to help her nearly ran when she saw the dancer. Coiling her power, the dancer reached out and soothed the woman, easing her tension.

"I need to make a phone call," the dancer said.

"Sure, sure, we got a phone back here, whenever you're ready. You want anything else?"

"Some coffee, maybe."

"Coming right up. Black?"

"Yeah," the dancer said with a slight, harrowed laugh. "Black."

The woman vanished into the recesses behind the counter. Two other people were present, both employees. Neither paid much attention to the girl. The dancer appreciated it. The coffee arrived and she sipped at it tentatively. The heat settled her and she set the cup on the table as the fear suddenly returned.

You're safe, she reminded herself. *You made it out. He can't hurt you now.*

That knowledge, however, was not enough to keep her hands from trembling as she raised the coffee cup once again.

"Shit," she said, utilizing her full strength to set the cup down without breaking it. She rose from the table and approached the woman behind the counter. Her skin had become pale, though her lips were blood-red. Her eyes practically glowed.

"Whatchu need?" the woman asked.

"That call."

"Sure. Right back here."

"No, I'd rather use the one outside. I need a quarter."

The woman stared at her, reluctant at first. Then the dancer's eyes narrowed, her lips drawing tight to create a frown.

"I said—"

The dancer did not have to continue. The woman struck a series of buttons, popped open the cash register, and plunged her hand into the cash drawer with reckless abandon. She slapped a handful of quarters onto the counter, then backed away. The dancer gingerly selected only one, nodded, then left the restaurant.

Outside, her fingers trembled as she fed the coin into the phone and dialed the familiar number. A voice answered.

"Yeah, I need a cab," the dancer said, and proceeded to give her current address. Street signs were visible on the corner. "There's a McDonald's right there. I'll be waiting inside."

"Name?"

The dancer hesitated. "Lilith."

"And where do you need to go?"

"U.S.C."

"Thank you. We'll have someone there as soon as possible."

"Hurry," the dancer said, hanging up the phone. Paying for the cab would be no problem. She would use her talents to make the driver take the money out of his own pocket, then alter his memories.

The difficulty would come in finding another way to deal with her impulses. "Lilith" would have to disappear.

Pain congealed in her stomach and chest. The blood-need spoke to her.

She would have to find it soon.

The dancer decided to wait inside. She would have a clear view of the corner from there.

Inside the restaurant, the woman who had given her the quarters was standing near the window, looking directly at the dancer, as she performed an aerobic workout. The two other employees flanked her, doing jumping jacks.

"What the fuck?" the dancer whispered.

"In case you thought a human witness would actually dissuade me," a cold, cruel voice said from behind her.

Understanding sliced through her. The dancer did not bother to turn. She leaped forward, breaking into a dead run, but only covered a few yards when she felt someone slam into her from behind, knocking her forward, into the wall. There was a sharp, brittle crack as her forehead struck the concrete. She stumbled back and felt inhumanly strong hands upon her. Her assailant picked her up as if she were a child and dragged her to the service alley running between the restaurant and a run-down tenement. She began to struggle and her captor drove her head into the alley wall three times, leaving her bloody and gasping before he tossed her onto a pile of green trash bags.

You thought you could get away from me, little vampire? Stephen asked in the hazy confines of the dancer's thoughts. *I let you get away. It was too crowded in there. I felt we should have some privacy.*

The dancer looked up and saw a tall man with long hair standing before her. He was silhouetted by the light from the street, she could not see his face. His hands were transforming, becoming razor-sharp talons.

The dancer tried to move, but the vampire lashed out with his power and suddenly she was unable to move. She felt as if an impossible weight had descended upon her, pinning her in place. The vampire gestured with his talon and suddenly the dancer rose into the air, gasping with surprise.

She was flying! The dancer shrugged off the stolen raincoat, heard it flutter to the ground a dozen feet below, and felt her limbs perform a series of dance moves. The vampire lifted himself into the air. He danced with her in midair for a few moments, then moved close and took her face in his hands.

"It's wonderful, isn't it?" he asked.

They were forty feet in the air, performing an oddly beautiful and mannered dance. She had learned this dance once, when she was a child, but she could not remember what it was called.

"Yes," she whispered, hating herself for her words. "Wonderful."

The dancer was terrified, but she was slowly coming to understand that this power could be hers, the vampire meant to share it with her, and her fear was replaced with excitement. She was an Initiate, a half-vampire, and had believed that she would be happy with that, she had not wanted to give up the light. No amount of power would be worth a lifetime in darkness. As the dance went on, she found herself reconsidering her position.

Open yourself to me.

The dancer instinctively refused the intrusion into her mind, but the vampire was insistent. He asked again, and she relented. She felt him ease his consciousness forward and allowed him to sift through her memories. His anticipation was palpable. He withdrew suddenly, shaking his head sadly.

Without warning, he drove his taloned hand into her chest. She felt an explosion of pain, then she was falling. Tumbling gracelessly through the air, the dancer cried out as her body struck the ground, her legs shattering on impact. She lay on her back, watching the vampire descend like an angel. This time she was facing away from the mouth of the alley and she could see him.

Eyes glowing with a reddish fire, the vampire allowed his feet to touch the ground. He bowed with a flourish, as if he expected applause. His wolflike incisors gleamed in the near darkness. His fingers were polished ivory blades.

"I had hoped it would be you," he said with genuine disappointment. "You were the first in a long time to present any real challenge. But you're not the one. I know you can't believe this, but I am truly sorry this dance must come to an end, little vampire.

"Or should I say Felicity? Felicity Turner, born of Mary and Theodore." His tone darkened and he spat his words with contempt, punching each one hard and without a trace of the sorrow that had existed in his voice moments before. "Felicity *Turner,* born in Orange County, nineteen years ago. Felicity Turner, *honors student* at the University of Southern California. Felicity Turner, a girl who just wants to have *fun.* Are you having fun now, *Felicity?*"

Felicity did not answer. She was trying to coil her power, but it seemed just out of reach. The blinding pain in her chest and legs threatened to overwhelm her. She looked down and saw that blood was pouring from the five puncture wounds he had driven into her chest. Her efforts to control her fear failed miserably, though she knew her fear was helping to feed the vampire's rising fury.

"Did your human father actually believe he had sired you? Or did he know the truth? Do any of them know the truth, I wonder? Tell me Felicity, do *you* know?"

Suddenly he was upon her, leaning down and kissing her wounds, smearing her blood on his face. The vampire grasped her hair in one hand, yanking her up to expose her long, delicate throat.

"You can't!" she cried. "You can't! We're the same!"

He laughed. It was a cruel, brittle laugh. "Even if you were right, *it wouldn't matter.*"

The vampire brought his taloned hand around in a swift motion, slashing at her throat. Her head was severed in one, neat blow. A geyser of blood struck his open mouth. The creature surrendered to his own blood frenzy, tearing her body to pieces.

When it was over, the vampire rose and spent several minutes hiding the body. It was an act he performed more out of habit than fear of discovery. Had he been interested in doing a thorough job, he would have found a human and forced the human to take the blame, implanting false memories in the man's head and physical evidence upon his body. A confession, a conviction, and perhaps even an execution would follow. Once that would have amused him, and he would have rested easier knowing that he had concealed his activities. Lately, however, it didn't seem worth the effort.

When he was finished, the vampire stared at the garbage bags containing Felicity's remains. He wiped his mouth on the back of his hand and smiled. "We're *not* the same, little vampire. And now, we never will be."

The creature left the alley without looking back.

Chapter One

"Well, ain't you just something," Nina Chavez said, placing her hands on her hips and pivoting slightly, the sand hot beneath her bare feet.

Dani's smile eased across her face. She lay on a gray Tower University beach towel, her face tilted up to the broiling afternoon sun. Her luminous, gold-flecked eyes were hidden behind her mirrored sunglasses. She pulled one long perfectly tanned leg up and ran her hand down its length.

"You think?" Dani asked.

"Uh-huh."

"You done thunk it?"

Nina shook her head. She was an attractive, full-blooded Spanish girl with jet-black hair, green eyes, and a trim but unspectacular form. "For someone with as much as you've got, hon, you sure need strokin' sometimes."

Dani stretched luxuriously. Her body was amazing and she damn well knew it. Large breasts, a tiny waist, sensational muscle tone. Her features were exotic and beautiful, her strange eyes, strong cheekbones, and blood-red lips framed by wildly flowing brunette hair. Her flesh practically glowed and her face was lit up with her sexy smile. "Well, I don't want to be obnoxious or anything—"

"Fuck you," Nina said as she dove at her friend, grabbing one end of the blanket and uprooting a portable Watchman. She threw the cloth over Dani, rolling her up in it. Dani laughed and struggled, but Nina fought bravely, rolling Dani several times then sitting on her back. Their actions drew the attention of several bemused beachgoers.

"Now, repeat after me," Nina said. "I, Danielle Walthers."

The figure beneath the blanket stopped struggling. A muffled voice proclaimed, "I, Danielle Walthers," then broke into a giggle fit.

"Do solemnly swear—"

"Oh, come on," Dani said, and made a halfhearted effort to free herself. Finally she gave up and muttered the words expected of her: "Do solemnly swear."

"Not to be a complete bitch for an entire day."

Silence. Followed by, "How do you define 'bitch?' "

"Dani—"

Another giggle. "How do you define 'complete?' "

"I'm gonna have to kick your ass," Nina warned, then hopped off Dani long enough for the girl to free herself. Nina leaped on Dani and they fell to the sand, laughing and screaming. They wrestled on the burning sand, Dani fending off Nina's blows. They rolled around, one on top, then the other. Dani laughed so hard she began to cry. Suddenly she looked down and gasped.

"Oh shit, I popped out."

"Well, get it back in."

Dani turned over and shoved herself back in her skimpy bikini.

"That's sad," Nina said, plopping down, holding her stomach as she tried to get her breath. "I'm embarrassed for you. I really am."

"Shut up," Dani said, turning over slowly and looking around to see if anyone had noticed. She gave a slight wave to the dozen or so people who had been watching the cat fight. Shrugged her shoulders. Grinned mischievously. Finally hollered, "Go away!"

They stopped looking. Nina grinned. "At least your momma didn't see that."

Dani sat up, anchoring both arms behind her, and looked farther down the beach. The entire group was still involved in their volleyball game.

Nina nodded at Dani's suit. "That thing could get you arrested in Florida."

Dani looked down. The tiny, violet strips barely covered her ample body. Nina's pink two-piece had underwire supports, a pushup bikini to make her seem more shapely. "We're not in Florida. We're at the sumptuous Venice Beach resort, courtesy of Halpern and Weiss. Move a little to the left, you're blocking my light."

"Crazy white trash bitch," Nina said, crawling over to lay beside Dani.

"Crazy spic. You probably stole the fuckin' radio out of the Karmann Ghia when no one was looking."

"Wasn't worth nothin', I checked."

"Crazy spic," Dani repeated, smiling.

"No, no, *chiquita,* it is you who is *muy loco.*"

Dani sighed. "Do me a favor? If you're going to speak Spanish, speak Spanish. If not, don't give me this sorry-assed anglo-trash pig-Spanish shit, *comprendes, a mi pobre amiga tonta?"*

"That's not bad," Nina admitted. "You've even got the inflection down."

"Second language, where I grew up."

"Tampa, right?"

"Yeah. Lousy part. Crawlin' with goddamned spics."

"Sounds like a happenin' place to me."

"Yeah, it would."

They lay together, enjoying a slight breeze. A shadow passed overhead and Dani frowned. "How am I supposed to work on my tan when that happens?"

"You don't need to work on it, baby. You need to call the American Cancer Society, that's what you need to fuckin' do. You could be their poster babe for skin cancer. I mean, you're out here, what, four, five times a week?"

"Every chance I get. My people have a real high tolerance. It's a bitch for us to get a tan."

"Your people, huh? Well, since you're always raggin' on my people, Miss 'Your People,' just who the fuck are 'your people,' anyway?"

Dani drew a deep breath. She had said too much. Sure, hon. My people. Vampires. Oh, sorry, didn't I mention that before? And by the way, you've got one hell of an appealing neck on you. "Austrian, Roumanian, Pennsylvania Dutch. Typical white trash."

"Typical white trash *bitch*," Nina said.

"Nuh-uh. Typical white trash *beach* bitch."

"Oh yeah, sorry." Nina rolled her shoulders, getting comfortable in the sand. "So, you comin' back to the party or what?"

"I dunno. I'm sure as hell not playing volleyball wearing this. Besides, I'd kick everyone's ass."

"That you would, my fucked-up friend. You do have certain talents, I'll say that much for you."

"Gee, thanks."

"You're still a bitch, though."

Dani was silent.

"Hey, you're supposed to call me a spic."

"I was trying to think of something better. I don't want to be predictable."

"Sweetheart, I've known you what, goin' on six months now? The one thing you're not is predictable."

Dani smiled and patted Nina on the arm. "Thank you, sweetie."

"Don't mention it."

With a sigh, Dani dragged herself to her feet. "I guess I better go put in an appearance. You coming?"

"Every chance I get."

"Nina."

"You go. I'll catch up. This is nice." She dragged the last word out. *Niiiiiccce.*

"I swear to god, you sound like fucking Senior Wences when you do that," Dani said.

"Senior who?"

"Never mind. Just make sure the Watchman comes back with you."

"Okay. What were you watchin', anyway?"

"Nothin', it's all crap."

Nina found the Watchman, shook out the blanket and made herself comfortable as Dani walked away. "Hey, you can get Home Shopping Network on this!"

"Oh, Jesus," Dani groaned, picking up her pace. The sound of Nina's melodic laughter followed her for a time, then was replaced with the typical sounds of a day at the beach: Portable radios and cassettes, the inane whoops and hollers of macho swaggering beach gods, the gossipy blather of the very old and the very young, and the sensuous rush of the waves. It was this last sound that Dani focused on to the exclusion of all else. She drifted to the water and waded in to midthigh. Her mother and the others were down the beach, finishing up their game. It was wonderful to hear her mother laugh.

Dani noticed a pair of women standing waist high in the water thirty yards away and froze. They both had long black hair, though one was taller than the other, and carried herself with a regal bearing. The shorter one stood with her hands on her hips, a knowing grin on her face. She wore a black strapless dress with red trim, cut deep to accentuate her large, well-tanned breasts. Dani knew that dress very well. The taller woman, who had dark, classically sculpted European features, and appeared to be twenty but may well have been ageless, was completely naked. Bloody wounds scarred the flesh of both women.

"Madison," Dani whispered in a tiny voice. "Isabella."

She had known both of these women intimately, and had been responsible for each of their deaths. Their gazes were locked upon Dani. They barely seemed to notice as a wave rose up behind them and crashed down, engulfing them. The wave broke and both women were gone.

"Frisbee alert!" someone called.

Turning with incredible speed, Dani snatched the Frisbee from the air. When the blond-haired thin guy with the nose guard came to retrieve it, Dani issued only a slight shrug to indicate how five, small, finger-sized holes had been driven into it. The Frisbee's side was bent like a pop-top on a soda can. The guy with the nose guard gave a disgruntled and confused, "Uh, yeah, thanks," and ran back to his friends.

Dani looked back to the waters. There was no sign of Madison or Isabella. This had not been the first time she had seen them. Their sudden appearances were always startling at first, but Dani had come to accept the apparitions.

You will be haunted, Mr. Scrooge, by three spirits.

Gee, someone was missing. She thought of the cop she had lured to his death. Hal Jordan. Perhaps his headless body would show up at some point, give the girls someone with whom they could party.

Living with the ghosts of her dead no longer seemed all that unusual to Dani. What they wanted seemed obvious to her. A scene from *An American Werewolf in London,* one of Dani's favorite films, leapt into her mind.

Kill yourself, Jack. Do it before you create more of our kind.

The hero's best friend, dead and rotting, urging the hero to end it before he became a monster and killed again, condemning more innocent souls to walk the earth in limbo.

That was only a movie, of course. In real life, there were no merciful fade-outs at awkward moments, no punchy tag lines to close out scenes. Every day she lived, she ran the risk of her blood rising up and forcing her to seek out others of her kind, others who could once again make her into a god. Nevertheless, she wasn't about to end her life now that she had finally found a way to enjoy it again. She was fairly certain the ghosts were nothing more than her subconscious turning on her power like a movie projector, messing with her perceptions to show her exactly why she needed to keep her dark impulses under control. Unpleasant as it was, Dani could live with it.

She walked a few yards down the beach, then paused as the sun came out again, allowing her to throw her head back and luxuriate in the glorious, fiery rays of the sun as they washed over her, filling her with warmth. There had been a time when she had almost surrendered to the darkness and the cold she had discovered inside herself. These days, she couldn't get enough of the sun.

"That's some hell of a grip you've got."

Dani turned quickly and saw a man who looked as if he had just stepped off the cover of *Playgirl*. He had a muscular physique and deeply tanned, perfectly toned flesh. A patch of tight black ringlets clung to his chest, and he wore an electric blue Italian swimsuit that covered about as much skin as a G-string. His hair was thick, curly and black as midnight, with a touch of premature gray, and he had a mustache. His features were chiseled, but not perfect. It was his eyes—emerald and sparkling—and his mischievous grin that Dani found instantly appealing. He radiated confidence without arrogance.

Nevertheless, this wasn't something she wanted to pursue. "Look, I've got a boyfriend."

She was lying, and they both knew it.

"Yeah, me too," he said.

She laughed. "You've got a boyfriend, too?"

"Yeah, his name's Biff. Big, jealous son of a bitch. He'd probably kick your ass if he knew you were coming on to me."

Dani resisted a smile. It had been close. "How exactly am I coming on to *you?* I'm just standing here."

"You put on a display of brute force. How the hell am I supposed to resist that?"

Dani pursed her lips. "I don't think what you think happened really happened."

"Uh-huh," he said, shaking his head and trying to figure that one out. In a perfect Peter Weller deadpan he said, " 'And no matter where you go — that's where you are.' "

"Buckeroo Banzai!" she cried. "You *know* that film?"

"I think I have it memorized."

Dani growled, low and deep in her throat. "I'm gonna hate myself for this," she said as she held out her hand. "My name's Dani Walthers."

"Ray Brooks. I've seen you out here before." Ray took her hand and leaned in close. "Don't get scared or anything, but we're dangerously close to what they call, 'meeting cute.' "

"Oh? How does that work, exactly?"

"All right. What happens is, you have some freak occurrence. Let's say a fender bender. Guy gets out of the car, he's real pissed, then the girl comes out, she's beautiful. His gonads override his common sense — "

"Hers too."

"Yeah, so to speak."

"Then?"

"Bing-bam-va-voom, to the moon, Alice, it's all over. That's the technical term for it, anyway."

"Really," she said.

"Sure. I'm a film student. Part time. I know these things. Martin Scorsese lectured here last week."

"And he told you about 'bing-bam-va-voom?' "

"Didn't you see *Taxi Driver?* That was the whole point of the movie."

35

"So 'bing-bam-va-voom' is man's primal scream, his ancient ward against alienation and loneliness?"

"Damn, you're good."

She wrinkled up her face and sprouted her best English frostbite accent. "You have *no* idea."

"Jeremy Irons as Claus von Bülow, Barbet Schroeder's *Reversal of Fortune.*"

"Very good," Dani said, genuinely impressed.

"Can I ask you a personal question?"

"That depends."

"The sunglasses. Do you always wear them? I've seen you out here at night, and I saw you once at the Hellfire Club. It seems like you never take them off."

"I like them. And what are you, following me or something?"

"No, you're just so beautiful, you're kind of hard to miss."

"Ooh," she groaned, "and you were doing *so* well."

"This is the part where I should be smart enough to turn around and mention that I'll see you sometime, right?"

"Uh-huh."

"It's really a shame I'm not smarter than I am."

"It really is."

"I also study behavioral science. You'd think I'd know better."

"I thought you were a film major."

"I am. Studying criminology should give me an edge in dealing with studio execs. But like I said, it's part time."

"So what do you do for a living?"

"Harass gorgeous women. If I hang around long enough they usually pay me something to get lost."

Dani smiled. "You're almost saving it. There's still time to do the right thing, Ray. Just turn around and put one foot in front of the other."

"I will if you do me a favor."

"What's that?"

"Would you take off your sunglasses for me?"

Shaking her head, she began to walk away. "You're losing altitude. I think the number four engine's about to blow."

Ray followed her. "I bet you have beautiful eyes, Dani. I bet a man could see the future in those eyes you keep covered up."

Dani slapped her hand against the space below her collarbone. "The engines are gone, all four of them! You're spiraling down, you're in flames, its a nosedive. *Holy shit, I think you're gonna crash!*"

He tapped her on the arm and she spun around abruptly.

"What?"

"How's this? Dinner, a midnight movie, and you never have to take the glasses off."

"Never, huh?"

"No matter what."

"Hmmmm. No matter what, huh? That's interesting. I guess I'll have to just think it over."

"Come on. You wouldn't torture me like that, would you?"

"A girl's got to have some fun," she said as she broke from him, looked down and cried, "boner at two o'clock!"

"Dani, goddamn it," he snarled, looking around to see if anyone had heard. They had. Five guys stood up suddenly and saluted him. "Great."

Dani looked over her shoulder to see him amble past the squad of men who had saluted him. They now applauded.

She turned away and walked down to the volleyball net, where she saw her mother laughing with Edward and Nora Pullman. The other seven or eight people who had come to the beach party were mostly cops, a couple of them women. Samantha always gravitated to cops. Maybe it was because she had been a cop herself once.

At first glance, Sam and Dani could have passed for mother and daughter by birth rather than legal adoption. They were both tall, beautiful brunettes with generous, shapely figures. But Dani's hair was untamed, while her mother's was considerably shorter, set in elegantly styled waves that barely reached her shoulders. Sam's body was harder, more scrupulously maintained, her muscles more richly defined. The manner in which Sam held herself gave the impression of a warrior who would never fully shake their battle stance; she seemed defensive at all times, unwilling to fully relax. Her daughter, on the other hand, appeared totally at ease, though her knowing smiling radiated confidence and power. The most striking difference between them was Dani's strange Gypsy eyes, almost black with glittering streaks of gold. Her mother's eyes, though quite pretty, were unremittingly dark.

Sam had found Dani abandoned next to a garbage dumpster nineteen years ago, when she had been a rookie cop. She had saved Dani's life that day. Last year, Sam had saved not only her daughter's life, but, quite literally, her soul.

Sam was thirty-nine, though she could pass for five or more years less than that. She wore a dark one-piece bathing suit which covered most of her lower back and the scars. She had endured an unending series of operations to regain the use of her legs. Though the doctors had told Sam she would never walk again; today Sam bounced around like a teenager. The steel rods implanted in her back barely slowed her.

"Hi, baby," Sam said as Dani approached.

Dani smiled in return. She couldn't imagine a day when she would be sorry to see the look of unbridled love and warmth that always played on Samantha Walthers's face when her daughter came into her view.

"You missed a great game," Sam said, snatching a towel from a nearby table. She was covered in sweat. "We're heading over to Ed and Nora's for a cookout later. You and Nina going to make it?"

"Probably not," Dani said. "Got some things to do."

"That's too bad." Sam's words could have been used to inflict guilt, but her tender smile precluded any such occurrence.

Dani looked at the Pullmans. Edward was a detective sergeant with the LAPD. He was a big man in his early fifties, with a red, sunburned face and a bright patch of white hair on the top of his head. His wife, Nora, was a slender, good-looking brunette for whom age would always be kind. Their own daughter, only a few years older than Sam, never came to California to see them. Sam had been unofficially adopted by the Pullmans. They noticed Dani and came over, arms around each other like a couple of kids. Dani loved it.

"Hey, kiddo, how's it goin'?" Edward asked.

"Just fine," Dani said, suddenly noticing the looks she was receiving from several of the young cops who had also come to the picnic. She looked away, to the bench which housed the food. The sight of several empty Tupperware containers made her smile. "Everyone liked my pasta?"

"Sure did," Nora said.

Edward nodded. " 'Course, you could feed horseshit to these guys and most of them would kiss your feet, just so long as it was home cooking."

"Thanks a *lot*," Dani said with a laugh, but she knew what he meant. There had been a period when Dani was growing up that Sam spent on undercover, and their "rich diet" had consisted of whatever takeout was cheapest. It was still better than Sam's health food period, however. Come to think of it, even horseshit would have been preferable to another serving of tofu. Then they had gone back to takeout in a hurry. When that became too costly, Dani had learned to cook.

"They're just yanking your chain," Sam said, placing her arm around her daughter. "It was *wonderful*."

"You want the recipe?"

"Get real," Sam said. "What would I do with it?"

Dani hugged her mother. "Would you guys excuse us for a minute? I have to lecture my mother about proper eating habits now that I'm living on campus."

Sam looked at them with puppy-dog sadness. "I have to go make it clear to my daughter no one gives me lectures."

"Come back soon," Edward said. "We're gearing up for another game."

Sam nodded, and together with her daughter, walked to the shoreline. The sun faded once again, lending a grayish, polarized look to the waters on the horizon.

"What's up?" Sam asked.

"Nothing," Dani said. "Do I have to have a reason for

40

wanting some time alone with my mom?"

"No, but you generally do." Sam rubbed her thumb over her fingertips, the universal sign for cold hard cash.

"Ooh, shivers. It's getting cold out here."

They reached the water.

"Seriously," Dani said. "How are you doin'?"

"I'm fine. Are *you* all right? You look like something's the matter. You're all flushed."

"Nothing's the matter. Not really."

"Tell me."

"Would you be horribly weirded out if I told you that there were times when I just want to move back home?"

Sam looked at her in surprise. "You were so adamant about needing space to work things out."

"Well, I've had that."

"Yeah, anytime," Sam said, a bit distractedly.

Dani smiled warmly. "You don't want me back home."

"I didn't say that," Sam said defensively.

Throwing her arms around her mother, Dani hugged the woman tight. "Thank God, I was getting so goddamned worried."

Sam shook her head. "You just wanted to make sure I wasn't sitting next to the phone, pining for you to call."

"Right."

"Where did you learn this shit? No, don't answer that, I don't think I want to know. Anyway, to answer your question, I'm really fine, and I'm going to go home and rent out your *room* as soon as I get there."

"Sorry."

"Seriously, Dani how are you holding up? Are you set okay on money? You need any moral support? Anything going on you want to talk about?"

Dani thought about the appearance of her dead

41

friends on the beach and shook her head. "No, not really. It's hard, you know. But I think I'm doing about as well as can be expected. I just do one day at a time."

"You'll tell me if you need to talk, right? You'll come to me first."

"Sure, who else could I go to? A shrink? I could just see myself on some guy's couch. 'No, really, I *could* fly, honest. And my best friends all turned out to be vampires. And gosh, y'know, I was one, too.' I don't think so."

"Me either."

"I miss flying. The lessons, I mean. I mean, it was my choice to stop, I got fed up with it and walked out, but lately I've been thinking of going back to it."

"That's good. Let me know, I'll set it up."

"Sure," Dani said, looking away. She and her mother walked down the beach in silence. One of the few things Dani had missed unreservedly about her inhuman state had been her ability to fly. A night did not pass when her dreams allowed her to take flight and literally rise above it all.

A sudden recollection snapped into her thoughts: She was standing in the back of the physical therapy room at her mother's rehab, watching a patient she had attempted to befriend try to walk with a prostheses. The man collapsed between the balance bars, broke into tears, and had refused to get up again. He cried out for his wheelchair, but his physical therapist refused to bring it to him.

You gotta come to me if you want this.

The man had laid on the floor and cried. Dani couldn't take any more, and so she helped him back to the wheelchair. The therapist never explained the mistake Dani had made, though his strong disapproval had been evident in his eyes. Dani didn't understand until she saw her own mother go through the same trials. She had been as heartless and cruel in forcing her mother to go on when the woman wanted to quit.

Without the ability to fly, Dani had sometimes felt like a wheelchair-bound cripple. She had returned to the air, protected by a shell of machinery, and had been amazed to rediscover that same, joyous rush. One day, Madison and Isabella had appeared, hovering in the air before her plane. Dani had screamed, lost control. Her teacher had been forced to take command of the flight. That had been the first time the dead women had appeared to her, shaming her into crawling back to her own wheelchair.

Sam touched her daughter's shoulder as they walked. "I shouldn't keep bringing it up, but I know you need help. And I know I can't give you all the help you need, and it kills me sometimes, it really does."

Dani studied her mother's face. The sadness she saw there worried her deeply. Sam was only thirty-nine. Until recently, she could pass for ten years younger. In the last year her age had started to show, the lines at the corners of her eyes and around her mouth deepening from continuous distress, most of which had been Dani's fault. There was something else in her face, something Dani had seen before, on long nights spent at her mother's side in the hospital.

"You've been having the dreams again, haven't you, Mom?"

"What?" Sam asked, startled by her daughter's perceptiveness. Or was it something more? Her daughter possessed incredible power. Had she used it?

Dani shook her head, sensing her mother's concern. "I told you, I wouldn't *look* unless you wanted me to."

43

Sam nodded. Her daughter had the ability to reach inside her head and cull the secrets of her existence from her mind. Sam had allowed it once, when they were locked in the basement of a Malibu beach house, waiting for Dani to make the most important decision of her life.

Sam had let Dani inside her mind then. It was a gesture of honesty and trust, and they shared a wonderful intimacy that had finally persuaded Dani to choose her human mother and her humanity over her vampirism. As Dani turned her back on the vampires who had been attempting to convert her to their ways, she also turned away from her all-encompassing blood-need. But both Sam and Dani knew what Dani had given up, the price she had paid.

"Tell me," Dani said. "Are you having the dreams again?"

"This isn't about me."

Dani nodded. That was about as direct an answer as she could expect. Her mother was indeed suffering the nightmares once more, the dreams of the predators somehow returning from the dead and taking Dani from her, this time with no hope of redemption.

"Dani, I'm serious. For a while there, there was a part of you I didn't even recognize anymore. It's like you were two different people. Some of the things you did —"

"That's over. It's in the past. Forget about it."

Dani looked at her mother. Sam would never forget about the many incidents which had occurred since the dead girls first appeared to Dani. The gang she had taken on when it looked like they were going to kill an innocent man. The three A.M. phone calls. The day she had been stabbed in the hand with an ice pick by a fifteen-year-old street kid, a wound which had left a scar in the back of her hand that would never heal, unlike the four bullet wounds she had received when she had been a full vampire. She had been up and around in an hour after those injuries.

Her mother, as always, had been the one to set her straight: *Batman is a fictional character, Dani. You cannot be Batman. You cannot go around trying to protect the innocents to try and make up for the deaths you caused. It only works that way in the comic books. In real life, no matter how powerful you think you are, you're going to get your ass shot off. I'm sorry to be the one to tell you.*

That lecture, and the ice-pick incident, had been enough to convince her. For a brief time, Dani flirted with the idea of becoming a police officer, but the dead girls had killed the dream, too. How could she trust herself to behave properly in a life or death situation involving others when she couldn't even trust her own perceptions?

Then there had been the matter of the demon, which didn't really exist, of course, no more than the dead girls, anyway. It had enjoyed her nighttime excursions far too much for comfort, it had tweaked her private addiction, her need to take the fear and desire of her victims, to feed from those emotions, and had nearly sent her out of control.

That was over, she told herself firmly.

Sure, until the next time.

Sam gave Dani's shoulder a loving squeeze. "All I'm saying is, you can't keep running away from your problems. We've got to get you help before it's too late."

"Fine. What do you suggest, Mother? An AA meeting? 'Hi, I'm Dani. I used to be a vampire. It's been fourteen months since I had a drink.' Think about it. There aren't support groups for my kind of addiction. I had the power of a god. Do you know what it feels like to lose that?"

"You almost lost *yourself,* Dani. I'm scared for you, honey. I mean, is this how you really feel? Are you sorry you didn't go with them?"

"No!" Dani raised her arm, directing her mother's attention to her deeply tanned flesh. "Nina's right, I'm lucky I don't have skin cancer, the amount of time I spend out in the sun. I mean, it's crazy, but just laying out there on the beach, with nothing to occupy my head, feeling the heat burning through me—Christ, Mom, I was so fucking cold when I was with them. I don't want to go back to that."

"I don't want to lose you, Dani."

"You're not. You're not gonna lose me. I'm telling you, nothing's happened for a long time. It's over. I had to get it out of my system. I'm pretty well aware that if I get shot now, I'm not just going to heal over. I'm not going to do anything stupid, Mom. You've got my word on it. You either have to trust me or not. That's your decision."

They regarded each other in silence. "I trust you. Just promise me you'll let me help if anything bad happens."

"I will, Mommy," Dani said, hugging her mother tight. "Believe me, I will."

They pulled away from each other and Dani looked back to the collection of officers. "So, you're back hanging out with cops."

Sam rolled her eyes. "Yeah, I'm hanging out with cops."

"Are you dating any cops?"

"No, I'm not dating any cops. Even if I was interested in dating anyone, I wouldn't be dating any cops. I learned that a long time ago." Sam hesitated. "And no, I'm not interested in dating anyone right now. I've got a career to start over, and that's taking up all my time."

"Um-hum."

"I've got a new client I've got to see on Monday. Some producer. Richard Sterling."

Dani thought about the name. It didn't mean anything to her. "That sounds promising. Is he cute?"

"Dani."

"Well? Is he?"

"I haven't met him and it wouldn't matter if he was."

"Why's that? You're not dead or anything. Get some joy in your life, Mom. It's the only thing that makes it worth living."

"Yeah," Sam said, smiling broadly. "Maybe you're right."

Dani watched her mother's face carefully. "What?" she asked, half laughing.

"You," Sam said triumphantly. "You actually seem *happy.*"

"Great," Dani said with a frown that did not entirely erase her own grin. "Go and piss me off like that. Go on."

"You doin' okay? Really? School's going all right?"

"Got my grades posted again," Dani said, but there was little satisfaction in her tone.

Sam smiled. "I am really proud of you, y'know."

"I know. Ed and Nora told me you already refer to me as 'my daughter, the doctor.' "

Shrugging sheepishly, Sam grinned. "Sorry."

"No, I like it. It's just a long way off. I've clepped the courses I could, but I'm stuck having to put in the semesters, get the credits. I feel like I've soaked up enough information to go to med school now, but you can't do it that way. And there's more to it than what you learn in books." Dani eyed her mother warily. "By the way, you are keeping up with your outpatient therapy sessions, right?"

"Yes, Doctor Walthers." She laughed. "Don't worry, I can still take care of myself."

Dani frowned. "That's what's so weird about seeing you in a bathing suit."

"What's that?"

"You're not carrying a gun."

Sam angled her head in the direction of the far-off parking lot. "In the car."

Dani stared at her, wondering if she really wanted to know if this was a joke or not. As the waves lapped at her feet, she decided she didn't want to know. They turned and started to walk back to the volleyball nets, where another game was already in progress. Dani stopped dead as she saw Ray Brooks across the net.

"That guy," Dani said. "The one in the bright blue Italian swimsuit. Who is that?"

"One of Ed's guys in homicide. Why? You're not thinking of dating him, are you? You know how I feel about dating cops. I thought I raised you with a little more common sense than that."

"You did," Dani said. "He just looked familiar, that's all. There's no reason to worry."

"Okay," Sam said, trying to mask her suspicion. Then she saw the way the dark-haired man's face lit up as Dani joined the game; Dani's, too. Sam decided that she had every reason to worry.

Chapter Two

Richard Sterling had already been seated when Sam arrived. The hotel restaurant was dimly lit and the lunch crowd had thinned considerably. A glass of white wine sat before the man. He stared into it absently, as if trying to lose himself in its sparkling depths. As Sam approached, he looked up suddenly, a broad smile crossing his handsome, sunburned face.

"Ms. Walthers," he said excitedly as he rose with a boyish enthusiasm and insisted on getting her a chair. Sam was amused and did not resist.

Richard sat down across from her. Sam studied his face and found him to be a highly attractive man. Over the phone, his voice had radiated quiet calm and self-assurance, a rich, melodic blend. In person, it was even more seductive. He had fine hair soaked peroxide blond by the sun, crystal blue eyes, strong, beautifully sculpted features, a square jaw, and an impressive physique emphasized by his expensively tailored suit. When he smiled, his teeth were a brilliant, perfect white, revealing no signs of dental work. He had an intelligent look and a compassionate face; serious, but with a self-effacing smile. His flesh had been burned lobster red. If she was asked to sum up his look for a casting director, she would have said, "William Hurt in *Body Heat*, no mustache."

Damn, she loved that movie.

"I see you've been out in the sun," Sam commented.

He laughed. "I tried to get a California tan in one day. That doesn't work."

"It'll fade. You should be careful though. You can get sunstroke or worse."

"That's why I wanted to meet here. I've been feeling a little weak."

You certainly don't look it, Sam thought, chiding herself for the schoolgirl commentary. "I'm sorry I'm late."

"Not at all. Traffic?"

"Yes." She was lying. The time she had spent with Dani on Saturday had caused many of her old fears to return. She didn't like having her baby live on her own, particularly in an environment where drugs, sex, and alcohol were rampant. Dani seemed stronger than she had ever been before, but Sam worried that what she was seeing was a façade, and beneath it, her baby girl was suffering. That thought had kept her awake most of the night. She fell asleep close to dawn, reaching over to kill her alarm when it went off an hour later, then slept until a telephone solicitation call woke her.

"Ms. Walthers?"

She looked up. She shook her head. "I'm really sorry."

"You seem a little bit distracted."

"I apologize, Mister Sterling."

"Call me Richard."

"I don't think that's—"

"Richard."

"All right."

"May I call you Samantha?"

"God, no," Sam said with a laugh. Richard recoiled slightly, as if he had been struck. Sam leaned forward, fighting an urge to reach across the table and place her hand on his in a comforting gesture. Her fingers came close to brushing his, despite her inner protests. "No, I mean — no one calls me Samantha. It's been 'Sam' all my life. The only time anyone's ever called me 'Samantha' is when I've done something wrong." Her voice changed to that of a Monty Pythonesque English schoolmarm. "Samantha, get *down* here and *explain* yourself."

His smile returned, along with an unexpected sparkle in his eyes. "Sam, then."

She smiled. What was it about this guy? He looked at her as if he could see everything about her at a glance, his smile denoting his pleasure at what he saw.

Perhaps he found her attractive. That was not an unreasonable response. She had dressed to impress; that much was obvious. She wore a long, double-breasted blazer with gold-toned buttons and a V-neckline, a red pleated skirt, rose-colored panty hose, and crimson heels. Removing her black sunglasses, she gave Richard a view of her beautiful dark eyes. He seemed instantly entranced. Sam relaxed, deciding she had fully regained control of the meeting.

The waiter arrived. Sam noticed Richard's white wine, ordered a glass of the same, and said they would need a few minutes before ordering. Nodding, the waiter vanished.

"So what's troubling you, Sam?"

"It's a personal matter. I apologize. Completely unprofessional of me. I can assure you —"

51

"Sam," he said urgently.

She sighed. "It's nothing, really."

Richard angled his head slightly and grinned. "Let me see if I have something straight. I'm going to sign a contract with you, right?"

"That's up to you."

"Well, I am. That means, technically, you're working for me. Right?"

"Uh-huh."

"Then the first thing I want you to do for me is tell me what's on your mind."

Sam smiled despite herself. "You're very sweet. You're a very sweet man."

Richard drew back, seemingly appalled. "God, don't let that get out. I'd be finished in this town."

"You might be right." She looked into his glacier eyes. He wasn't going to let this drop. Tenacious bastard, she thought. But she liked that. "I have a daughter. She's on her own. She's going through some stuff right now. I worry about her. That's it."

Richard shook his head. "You're tough, Sam."

"That's why you hired me, isn't it?"

"Actually, no. I hired you because I always start at the back of the alphabet and work my way forward. Walthers was the last listing."

"Yeah, I get that sometimes."

"And I liked the bit in your ad about 'the woman who answers the phone is *not* the receptionist.'"

"You've got to put some mystery in there. I get tired of the 'gee, you're a woman,' thing."

"So why don't you call yourself Samantha in the ad and avoid the confusion?"

"Because I hate the name. I really do."

"That much?"

"Uh-huh. That much." She smiled warmly. "Don't overanalyze it, okay? The next thing I know you're going to be telling me that I'm trying to deny my femininity, and propel my male self forward so that I don't have to show vulnerability or give trust."

"Jesus. You've been dating L.A. men."

"Yeah, sort of. A couple."

"My assistant could sit down and tell you stories for hours about L.A. men. Believe me, avoid them."

"Your assistant. I don't think I've met her yet."

"Him. Raymond."

"Ah."

"Does that make you uncomfortable?"

"No, not at all." Sam hesitated.

"I'm not gay, if that's what you were wondering."

"I wasn't going to lose any sleep over it, one way or the other."

"You *are* tough," he said, laughing.

"As nails. That's what my kid tells me. I've got a pair of steel rods in my back to prove it."

"That's gotta hurt."

"Hardly notice, most of the time. Gloria Estefan's management company called me about doing some bodyguard work for her, for a stretch. It would have just been for the publicity. We've both been in *People*, we've been through the same operations, and we're both walking around when the doctors said forget about it."

"How limited is your mobility?"

"How limited does it *look?*" Sam asked, her delivery laced with her low, southern drawl that only came out when she was making a pass at a man. The English schoolmarm returned in her head. This is not professional, *Samantha*. She sighed inwardly and absently wondered what this man would be like in bed. She hadn't made love in years.

Down, girl.

The silence hung between them for a moment, an unexpected surge of sexual tension which neither could deny. She had to find a way to restrain her incredible urge to flirt with this man.

Richard said, "I meant, would it in any way interfere with your ability to perform—"

"No," Sam said sharply.

"—your job."

"No."

They both smiled. The voice of the noonday trainer on the ESPN workout show floated into her mind. He talked more than a little like Hans and Franz on "Saturday Night Live."

Und now it is time for da cool down. . . .

"What can I do for you, Mister Sterling?" Sam asked in her most professional voice. She made a show out of catching herself. "I'm sorry. Richard, I meant to say."

"Let's order first," Richard said. "I don't want to be interrupted once I start this. It's not easy for me."

Nodding, Sam looked at the menu. Every item was overpriced.

"My company's paying for it, so don't be shy," Richard said. "Whatever expenses I run up, I can write off later."

With a shrug, Sam closed the menu. "You order, then."

Richard seemed pleased.

Samantha, what are you doing? He's a client. Your only client at the moment.

Be quiet. It's been a long time since I let a man order

for me. I want to enjoy it.

She did. His selections were perfect.

You're completely loosing control of this conversation, the schoolmarm in her head warned.

Shut up. We're not arm wrestling. I'm having a nice, *expensive* lunch with an attractive man, neither of which I've been treated to in a long time.

"I think there's time for your story before our meal arrives. These places are notoriously slow," Sam said, noting that her voice was once again dropping into the slight southern drawl she had acquired from living in Florida, though she had no true accent of her own. She shuddered. *You sound like Jessica Rabbit. Cut it out!*

"I want you to find someone for me."

Sam's heart sank. A girlfriend or wife. "Who?"

"My daughter."

She straightened up, intrigued. Suddenly, all hint of impropriety left her. She had spent most of her life raising her baby girl and had almost lost the child to the darkness infesting Los Angeles. This was a topic that demanded her complete professionalism. Richard Sterling was no longer a man to her, he was a parent in trouble. This changed everything.

"How old is your daughter?"

"Nineteen, or so I gather."

Sam nodded. Dani's age. Then it struck her. "What do you mean, 'or so I gather?'"

"I've never met the girl. I didn't even know she existed until quite recently." He turned to the seat beside him, removed a photograph from the half-open briefcase sitting there, and handed it to Sam. "This is the girl's mother. Elaine Aldridge. I met her twenty years ago. We fell in love and were together for a brief time."

"Why did you split up?"

Richard's face tightened. "It was my fault. I was very young, but that doesn't excuse me for being an idiot. She wanted to get married and have children, I didn't. I was nineteen, I didn't want to be weighed down."

Sam nodded. Ironically, her refusal to entertain the notion of having children had been one of the many causes for her own divorce, twenty years ago. Her views had changed in a heartbeat when she had seen Dani for the first time.

"How did you find out you had a daughter?"

"I was here on business. I have a company that specializes in producing low-budget action films for the foreign market. Karate flicks, shoot 'em ups, erotic thrillers. Whatever sells."

"You're based here in Los Angeles?"

"Actually, no. Rome. If Brigitte Nielson or Carol Alt's in it, I'm probably responsible."

Sam laughed.

"Anyway, I make several trips to the states each year. The current craze is to entice American stars into our productions. It's not hard. Take someone who's minor league here, you can turn them into a megastar over there. Hell, David Hasselhoff from 'Baywatch' and 'Knight Rider' is a big recording star overseas."

"You're kidding."

"Tell me about it. So I was out here, doing meetings with a few soap stars, former series regulars and such, when I ran into Bob Cort. We went to film school together. He dropped out shortly before I did."

"You never finished."

Richard shook his head. "I got a break and went into the industry. Anyway, I'll tell you that story another time, if you like. The important thing is, Bob didn't just 'run into' me at all. He had been following me. We started talking and he told me that he had fallen on hard times.

"Naively, I thought he was looking for a job. I suggested I could fix him up as a P.A. on one of our shoots, see how he does."

"I'm sorry — P.A.?"

Richard smiled warmly. "And you call yourself a native Californian?"

"I wasn't raised here." Sam sipped her drink, camouflaging her widening smile.

"A P.A. is a production assistant."

"I see. Go on."

"He wanted money — one-hundred thousand — but he didn't want to work for it. He thought he could blackmail me with what he knew about Elaine and the baby. He assumed it was my 'dirty little secret' that I didn't want getting out. He couldn't have been more wrong."

"What did he tell you specifically?"

"Not much. My break came right after Elaine and I split up. I was out of the country when the baby came. Cort said she left town right after my daughter was born. He hasn't seen or heard from her since."

A deep, ragged breath escaped Sam. "Richard, I need you to prepare yourself."

"What is it? You don't want to take the case?"

"I may be wasting your time and money. Have you considered the possibility that Cort was lying to you? That there *was* no baby?"

"I've thought about it, sure."

"Did he offer you any proof?"

"None."

"Then what makes you so ready to believe him?"

Richard absently ran his hand through his perfect blond hair. Despite her self-cautions, Sam found the gesture extremely exciting.

"A part of me *wants* to believe him," Richard said with a sigh. "I never thought I'd want to have children. It's not something I found myself actively missing. I mean—I was able to create through my art, if you can call it that. But when Cort told me about Elaine's little girl, something deep inside me woke up, something I hadn't even known was there."

Sam nodded. She understood completely. "But Cort could still be lying."

"I don't think so. He and I were close for a time. I could tell if he wasn't telling the truth."

"Maybe *then* you could have. Twenty years ago. But people change. Things happen."

"You're right, anything's possible. That's why I need your services. I need you to find out the truth."

Sam nodded. "So how did you leave it with him?"

"I gave him money. I let him think it worked. His blackmailing me. What I'm hoping is that I gave him enough to keep him in the background until you finish your investigation and find my daughter for me."

"You could have asked him to prove it. Refused to pay."

"My take on it is that Bob doesn't know any more than he's already told. But that wouldn't have stopped him from getting bookings on 'A Current Affair' and articles in all the tabloids. To be honest, the publicity wouldn't have hurt me at all. But Elaine's kept this a secret for nineteen years. If she wanted me to know, she would have come to me by now. I'm not exactly hard to find.

"No, publicity would make Elaine feel like she's on 'America's Most Wanted.' She would run even farther. Then we never would find her. Or my daughter. God only knows what the girl's been brought up to believe about her father."

"And what if I find out that Elaine never gave birth?"

"I'm telling you, I'm right about this. Cort could never lie to me and pull it off."

"All right. Let's say you're correct. Elaine may have married. Your daughter may believe another man to be her father. You could do a lot of damage to this child."

"We'll worry about that when the time comes." He paused. "I don't want to bring Elaine or my daughter any grief. But the girl has a right to know the truth. And I should have the right to at least see her, even if she doesn't end up finding out who I am. I want to know that she's happy, and healthy, and provided for. She's my child."

Sam thought it over. "My rate is two hundred dollars a day. I'll need a thousand up front."

He nodded, went to the briefcase, and withdrew a checkbook. A gold pen appeared in his hand and he scribbled an amount, signed the check, and handed it to Sam. She was stunned. It was for ten thousand dollars.

"You don't value yourself highly enough," he said.

"All right," she said, "you're serious about this."

"Very." His fingers interlocked and touched his lips. The sleeve of his jacket fell back slightly, revealing his Rolex.

"I have another question." Sam narrowed her gaze. "It doesn't bother you, trusting something so important to a woman investigator?"

"No. Should it?"

She shook her head. "You'd be surprised, some of the attitudes I run into."

"At the risk of sounding sexist, I would think being a woman would be an advantage in this situation. Especially a beautiful one. It's disarming. You could be a neighbor, someone's sister, girlfriend—whatever it takes. That would be especially valuable in a situation like this one. Besides, *la donna e un sesso superiore.*"

"What does that mean?"

"Women are the superior sex."

"You don't spend that much time in the U.S. anymore, do you?"

His expression turned frank and serious. "Sam, I have the utmost confidence in you. You set people at ease, right off the bat. You're drop-dead gorgeous. You're intelligent. You can see around corners, so you're creative in that way. And you obviously know your job. Will you please help me find my daughter?"

Sam felt flush. "I will."

Their meal arrived. As they ate, Richard discussed his current project in development, a low-budget action film to star a female martial arts expert. Paramount was coproducing. Sam had never been particularly impressed with the movie industry, but she was fascinated by Richard's evocative and amusing stories about getting a film off the ground.

They finished with lunch and Richard gave Sam a dossier he had assembled containing all the pertinent facts of the case. She withdrew a standard contract, had him sign it, and gave him a copy along with a receipt for his payment and her card, which gave the number of her answering service.

"They can page me if it's urgent," she said excitedly.

Richard smiled. "I can see you're ready to tear into this one."

"I am, yeah." She stared into his glacier eyes and considered the way he had offhandedly called her beautiful. There had been a few moments when the case wasn't all she had been ready to tear into, and she knew she would have to restrain those feelings if she was going to maintain a professional relationship with this man.

She wondered if she had been alone too long, and was grabbing at the first man who seemed remotely appealing. That was ridiculous. There had been many offers from men, and she had turned them all down. Richard was different, and if she had met him under other circumstances, her personal feelings might be appropriate. For now, they would only get in the way.

"If you have a daughter, I'll find her," Sam promised.

"I know you will," he said as he took her hand and held it perhaps a moment too long. She detached herself and allowed him to lead her out of the restaurant, to the lobby.

When he said goodbye, it was all she could do to keep herself from leaning in and giving him a quick, noncommittal kiss. Instead she nodded, smiled briefly, and exited the hotel.

Chapter Three

It was three-thirty in the afternoon and Dani was in the midst of her anatomy and physiology class. Gerry Laffiter, Professor Owsley's teaching assistant, was lecturing the students on precapillary sphincters. Laffiter was five-six, with a weightlifter's build, a black mustache and beard, and a kind, patient manner. Dani knew from her independent studies that the information Laffiter was handing out as empirical data was obsolete and should have been removed from all textbooks years ago. She had come here hoping to learn about cutting-edge breakthroughs in the medical research field. Instead, she was being coddled with useless information. She vowed inwardly to keep her anger under control, but she knew it wasn't going to be easy.

From the first day Dani had arrived at Tower University, her capacity for self-restraint had existed on a minimalist scale. She had succumbed to what Nina labeled the "Surrender Dorothy!" syndrome: A relatively shy, repressed girl in high school becoming a party-hearty sex-crazed banshee the moment she reaches college. Of course, Nina had no way of knowing the true reasons for Dani's wild behavior; she had not lived through the explosive events that took the lives of Madison and Isabella and she did not have to cope with the aftermath.

Last week, near the end of class, the dead girls had appeared and hopped up on either side of Laffiter's desk. The corpses had begun to touch one another, something they had never done before. The caresses quickly became intimate and soon the girls were kissing, easing themselves back to the desk where they began to moan and perform acts that might have startled an actress in an adult video. Dani had looked away, attempting to dismiss the obscene images of her slain friends, but they had not vanished. She had been forced to run from class and make an embarrassed apology to Laffiter later, citing a nasty case of food poisoning as the reason for her distress.

They had appeared at her dorm countless times. The other students rarely closed their doors, and student etiquette, such as it was, more than allowed other students to look in and strike up conversations with strangers, or to strictly play voyeur. Fridays and Saturdays at the dorm were party nights, and it was rarely necessary to leave the four-story building to find several all-night events to flit between. It had not been an uncommon occurrence for Dani to turn with a drink in her hand and find herself staring into the knowing face of her dead *sister-love,* who would raise her own drink to Dani before being swallowed up by the crowd.

The other day, on the beach, had somehow been the

most jarring visitation to date. The dead girls had done nothing but stare at her with their accusing eyes, but there had been volumes of meaning in their gazes. Dani had been with her closest friends, those she truly loved, and the eyes of the dead women seemed to say, *Don't get close to anyone, Dani. They'll be taken from you and you will have no one to blame but yourself. It doesn't matter if they are human or your kind. Love them and they will die.*

Today, all she had to deal with was a teacher who either knew less or cared less about the subject matter than one of his students. Dani supposed she could find a way to cope.

The class was fairly large, two hundred and thirty students. All Dani had to do was fade into the crowd, not get called on, and everything would be fine. If necessary, she could use her power on the teacher's assistant to dissuade him from singling her out. That would be more trouble than it was worth, however, as she would have to alter the strength of the psychic shields she constantly held in place. Without the shields, she could never walk through a crowded shopping mall, or exist one day in the chaotic swirl of her dorm.

Maximum protection, girls.

She might have smiled at the thought, but Laffiter looked directly at her and called her name.

"Oh shit," she groaned softly. *It's going to be the two samurais on the bridge again. Christ, I really don't need this. Self-control, Dani. Self-control.*

"Not paying attention, Ms. Walthers?" he said in a bright, thoroughly charming voice.

"Is there a reason why I should?" Dani winced at the sound of her own words. Oh damn, that bridge is rickety.

"It sounds like you have something to add to our discussion of precapillary sphincters."

Another student muttered, "A sphincter says what?"

Laffiter looked up. "The desired answer to that question is 'what?' but I saw *Wayne's World* guys."

Laughter ran through the assembled students. Danı forced a pleasant smile and hoped that Laffiter would forget about her and move on to someone else. He returned his gaze to her.

"Ms. Walthers?"

Dani sighed. That first step is a real bitch, even if you are a samurai. She could almost feel the bridge sway beneath her. "Precapillary sphincters do not exist in human beings. The information in our textbooks is out of date."

"On what do you base your argument?"

"There's no argument, that's just how it is. We're paying tuition to be taught bullshit. I'm sitting here waiting for you to tell us that if we cut up the corpses of criminals, sew them back together, then send a few million jolts through them, we can create life."

Laffiter's expression was unreadable. "On what sources of information do you base your argument?"

"*Scientific America*. The *New England Journal of Medicine*. The *Journal of the American Medical Association*. Do you want page and column numbers?"

He did. She gave them to him. He asked if she wanted to explain her theory to the class.

"Fine," Dani snarled. "The blood system branches

out from the aorta to the second, third, and fourth generation arteries. After that, you get down to the arterials and they branch out into the capillaries. It was thought at one time that there were little sphincters that opened into the capillaries and closed again, controlling the blood profusion to the tissues.

"As it turns out, there might be precapillary sphincters in the mesentery tissue of dogs, but even there it's doubtful, despite the way the tissue looks upon examination. For a long time, due to the limitations of light microscopes, the only tissue you could see working capillaries in really well was mesentery tissue — the tissue that holds your intestines in place. It's very thin and transparent and you can clearly see the blood vessels in it. A lot of early research on capillaries was done on dog mesentery tissue and while it *may* be true that there are precapillary sphincters in the mesentery tissue of dogs, it exists nowhere else, certainly not in human beings. The arterials themselves have muscular walls that open and close to perform this function."

Dani waited for Laffiter's expression to change. There were times when she wished that life were more like a movie. In a film, her teacher would have been a consummate asshole and Dani would have been regarded as actually having achieved something by showing him up in front of the class. She would have been a beloved character making a statement; a kooky, crazy kind of gal whom every teenager in the audience would want to emulate.

In a movie, Laffiter would have been staring at her openmouthed and she would have said something cute, like, "Catch flies that way" before she picked up her books and made her grand exit. Or perhaps there would have been a nice merciful cut right there.

This wasn't a movie, and Dani suddenly felt angry at herself. It wasn't Laffiter's fault that he had to teach this crap; he probably knew, as she did, that it wasn't true, and might have even had this exact same conversation with Professor Owsley before the topic came up.

Dani's power as an Initiate allowed her to absorb information at an incredible rate and gave her total retention. She also possessed the creativity necessary to take cold, dead facts and breathe life into them. In high school, she had taken no pleasure in her schoolwork, though it had not been completely laborious for her, either. For a time, when her classes at the university had begun, she had been ravenous to learn and had delighted in drawing lines between areas of information no one had linked previously.

The initial euphoria wore off quickly. She could pick and choose her grade point average in any of her courses. With her power, she could become proficient at anything she chose to explore. There was no challenge, no struggle. She felt like a gambler who had lost his love for the game. After all, what joy was there in playing the odds if you know you are going to win every time?

Just once she wanted to face something and fail miserably. Her misplaced anger and frustration often chose, as it had today, the worst times for self-expression.

Gerry Laffiter stood watching Dani with his strangely angelic smile. His dark eyes twinkled. "May

I see you in my office after class?"

Dani approached the door to the cramped little office Laffiter shared with another teaching assistant. She hesitated before knocking.

I think I'm going to be bounced out on my tanned little ass.
You really think so?
I do, I do!
I mean your ass. It's not so little.

Dani growled inwardly. Even the peanut gallery in her head was giving her shit today. She knocked and Laffiter called for her to come in. His half of the office was covered in foldouts from *Aviation Quarterly*. A photograph of Laffiter with a group of people dressed in fantasy role-playing costumes was tacked to the corkboard. Laffiter was dressed in black robes and he held a staff. His expression was twisted into that of a fighter. She looked away from the photo to the bearded man in blue jeans and a black T-shirt who sat patiently before her, a half-finished cheeseburger poised on the desk before him, above a pile of papers.

Four magazines sat off to the side of his desk. She recognized the issues and swallowed hard.

"You wanted to see me?" Dani said, attempting to hide her fear.

"Sit down," Laffiter said cheerily.

Dani pulled up the other chair and took her seat. His bright attitude worried her terribly. He had barely looked in her direction again, all through class, except on two separate occasions when he delivered his enigmatic smile directly to her then looked away. He had been anticipating this and now he was going to get the full measure of fear from her.

Let him try, the darkness within her whispered. You know what we can do to him.

Dani shuddered. The last thing she wanted to do was utilize her power on this man. She needed to get through this situation without the advantage her gifts afforded her.

"I'm sorry about class today," Dani said awkwardly.

Laffiter smiled his beautific smile. "I didn't ask you here so I could beat you up." He shoved the magazines in her direction. "I looked up the articles you mentioned. You were right."

She waited. "And?"

"That's it, you were right."

She frowned. "I guess I still have something to learn about tact. I lost it in there. I behaved like a jerk. I'm sorry."

"Well, if you learn social graces the way you learn everything else, you shouldn't have a problem. I've been keeping an eye on you, Dani. You're actually passionate. You care about what you learn. You assimilate data, it goes into your pores. That's exciting. But next time you want to point something like this out to me, do it before or after class."

"I really don't know what happened to me. I'm sorry."

He shook his head and made an exasperated sound not unlike that of a tire rapidly losing air. "Come on, stop beating on yourself. I understand your frustration. This course isn't designed for someone like you. Most students are slow learners. The problem is, of course, that even with clepping courses, you have to sit through a lot of classes that might bore you, you have to chalk up the credits. There's no way around that."

"I know."

"I know you do, that's why I'm wondering if what happened today really had anything to do with this course. And if it didn't, I'm wondering what it is that's bothering you?"

She thought of Madison and Isabella. "Nothing. It's just me. It won't happen again."

"I have another question for you."

"All right."

"You're a freshman, but you not only know what you want to major in, you've already picked your specialty. What is it about medical research that interested you in the first place?"

Dani was amazed at how comfortable Laffiter made her feel. "My mother was involved in an accident a little over a year ago. There was a fairly serious spinal injury. We were lucky. She ended up being in the low percentile of victims who regained full mobility. At the time, I wanted to make sure that she had every chance to regain full movement. That meant understanding the injury and the cure. Something happened during those months. I had an epiphany or something. The medical process fascinated me.

"We were lucky that my mother was the exception to the rule. For a while it didn't look like it was going to be that way. There were other victims at the hospital. I got close to some of them, really considered them friends, but when my mom recovered, they pushed me away. How could I understand what they

70

were going through? It was possible that one day my mom and I would be playing racquetball together, going on runs. All that happened, too.

"I guess it really struck me hard that for the majority of those who go through injuries like this, the only treatment seems to be helping them adjust to their new life as a paraplegic or quadriplegic. I decided I want to help people walk again. I mean, I thought about practicing medicine, and my mom would be thrilled, you can't imagine—she had been terrified that I was going to go into criminology or become a cop, like she was."

"So your mom would like to have a doctor in the house?"

"Sure, what parent wouldn't, right?"

"But you decided that wasn't for you."

"No, I don't know. I guess I'm not really comfortable with the idea of patients. I still have a long way to go before I have to make a decision like that, but right now, I'm more interested in getting into medical research. I'd like to help create the means by which victims could be allowed to walk again. The literature's been filled with advances in the study of regeneration and computer-controlled stimulus."

"I'm impressed," Laffiter said, glancing at his watch. "Even so, I'm going to have to cut this short. I've got some work to do before my next class."

Dani rose and squeezed past him, pausing at the door. "A sphincter says what?"

"What?" he said in mock surprise.

She giggled and left, feeling better than she had in weeks.

* * *

The usual madness greeted Dani as she walked across campus. An election was in progress and members of the incumbant party attended classes in togas while those of the opposing monarchy dressed in dapper eighteenth-century clothes. Dani was playfully harassed by members of both parties who seemed to take their positions very seriously, but not seriously enough to keep them from asking for dates.

She arrived at the dorm, a four-story building that looked like a cheap, run-down motel. The lower two floors were coed, the next floor above the "lezbo a-go-go," the all-women floor, and the top floor was the quiet floor. Dani's room, which she shared with Nina, was on the second floor. The residence assistant, a tired young man named Mars, whose first name was not Lars, but he had grudgingly come to accept it, stood behind the front desk. Looking at Dani with sad, red-rimmed eyes, he handed her a folded phone message.

"Not getting a lot of sleep, Lars?"

He shrugged. As R.A.s went, he was pretty lenient. He was a student, like the others, but he was paid to keep things in line, and given free room and board for his trouble. The noise level, the constant screams and crashes, the incessant flow of practical jokes and vandalism were rarely interrupted, except by the occasional visit from the police. Last week, a man they had never seen before arrived at the dorm, proclaimed his love for all mankind, and streaked up and down the halls until the police came to cart him off, dressing him in a sheet first.

The only vice Lars possessed was a low tolerance for marijuana smokers, though he rarely narced anyone. He would knock on doors, tell people to take it outside or put it out when it became excessive — in other words, when an entire floor was buzzed.

Lately, "dissing Lars" had become the favorite pastime of the students. Every night, the R.A. was treated to the sight of floor-to-ceiling furniture piled up in his room. Occasionally, he found a way to snake through it all and find enough floor space for sleep without having to move it all back into the hall.

Dani unfolded the small pink piece of paper and looked at the name and telephone number in surprise. "Do you remember when he called?"

Lars appeared stoned, but Dani knew it was only lack of sleep. "Time is a meaningless concept enforced upon us by the man. Socialist reforms are bullshit."

"That's nice, Lars." Dani turned and walked to the stairs. She rarely took the elevator. In moments she was at the second-floor landing, walking down the long corridor to her room. Six students stood outside someone's door. They were dressed as the press gang from *A Clockwork Orange* with white long johns, cod pieces, and black top hats.

Every two rooms shared a bathroom, which meant that if you wanted to seal someone inside, you had to take a rope and tie it to both doors. The press gang had done exactly that. Frantic banging could he heard from within.

"Let us out, you assholes!" a male hollered.

"I'm sorry," the first boy in the white long johns

called in a voice that was somewhere between Julia Childs and Miss Piggy. His inflection rose at the end of each phrase. "I can't *hear* you."

A stream of obscenities poured from the other side of the door. Dani went past the gang, all of whom removed their hats and placed them over their groins in honor of a lady's presence. One of the hats twitched. She curtsied in return, spreading the wings of her bulky sweatshirt, then went to the end of the hall and entered her room.

Nina lay on her bed, passed out or asleep. Dani scanned the walls, tried to find a single square inch that had not been covered over in photos of hot young studs torn from magazines and motorcycles of every kind, Nina's twin obsessions. Her goal was to one day be made "biker chick of America." One of her magazines actually held such a contest.

Dani sat on her bed, the one near the window, and pulled the phone from her desk. The call was answered on the third ring.

"Homicide. Brooks."

"Well, that has a romantic ring to it," Dani said. She heard movement from across the room and saw Nina dragging herself out of bed. The girl made a hacking sound as if she had just swallowed a hairball and stumbled into the bathroom, where she slammed the door then gave a soft moan at the noise she had just made.

"Dani!" Ray said, his tone immediately transforming from the dispassionate monotone most cops used to answer phones to the warm, sexy voice he had used to try seducing her at the beach. "I'm glad you called."

"My momma raised me to be polite to cops."

"That sounds promising."

Nina emerged from the bathroom, looked at Dani quizzically, and mouthed the word, 'who?' Dani attempted to wave her away, but Nina planted her hands on her hips and raised one eyebrow before mouthing the question again.

"Ray, excuse me, I have to tell my idiot roommate to fuck off." She put the receiver to her chest and gave Nina explicit instructions. Nina shrugged and went to her bed, pulling a biker magazine from beneath her bunk and pretending to be interested in it. Dani raised the receiver once more and said, "Frankly, I'm a little worried about dating someone who carries handcuffs with them."

"Most women are," he replied.

"Do they have reason to be worried?"

"Hey, this is me we're talking about."

"In other words, they have good reason."

"You found me out."

"You're not exactly subtle."

Suddenly, Nina leapt off the bed. "Omigod, it's him, isn't it? The one from Saturday? Mister Bright Blue Speedos?"

"Oh shit," Dani murmured. "Ray, maybe I should call you back. My roommate's still acting like she's eleven."

"Hello!" Nina called, forcing Dani back on the bed as she climbed on and playfully wrestled her for the phone. "Don't let her bullshit you, she hasn't been out on a date in two months!"

"Thanks a fucking lot," Dani said, shoving Nina off

the bed. The woman hit the floor and rolled, laughing. She lifted the receiver again and said, "You still there?"

"Two months, huh?" Ray asked.

"I'm gonna kill that bitch," Dani said, then looked right at Nina and repeated the threat.

"Two months," Ray repeated. He whistled. "Long time."

"Oh for Christ's sake, fine, I'll go out with you."

"Tonight?"

"Sure, let's get it over with."

Nina began to applaud. Dani tried to kick her, but Nina darted out of the way.

Ray said, "How about we meet at the Hellfire Club around seven. That way, if I turn out to be an asshole, you've already got your car, you can just take off."

"I already know you're an asshole. It's my lot in life to surround myself with nothing but assholes."

"Well, I should be no big surprise, then. I'll see you at seven."

"Yeah," she said defeatedly.

"Try to contain your enthusiasm."

"Oh, fuck off."

"Damn, I love aggressive women."

The line went dead. Dani stared at the phone and finally replaced it on the cradle. "Fuck me."

"You're very cute, but I don't go that way."

"He's a cop."

Nina sat up, eyes wide. "You're going out on a date with a cop? Your momma's gonna kick your fucking ass!"

"I know, I know, I know," Dani muttered. "Well, you encouraged me."

"I didn't know he was a cop."

"Well, he is."

"I better get some fucking insurance taken out on you, if I want to make out on this deal. You think about two hundred and fifty thousand would do it?"

"Yeah, any more and people will get suspicious."

"You might as well fuck him," Nina said.

"You say that about everyone I meet."

"Yeah, but this time I mean it. You're gonna be in intensive care after your momma finds out, you should get some while you can."

"Right." Dani frowned and looked to the tiny closet they shared. She wished that she could stop off at the Beverly Hills house first and pick up one of her better outfits, but Sam might be home, and she'd have to explain where she was going.

"You wondering what you're going to wear?" Nina asked.

"Yeah. Pretty stupid, huh? I mean, considering I'm not even excited about this."

"You want my advice?"

Dani shrugged. "Sure."

"It don't matter. I saw the way he was looking at you on the beach. You could wear a tent and he'd get a hard-on."

"Then I guess I better not wear a tent."

Nina's expression softened. "You must have really gotten burnt once in a relationship, huh?"

Dani thought of Bill Yoshino. Before she could reply, the phone rang. Dani snatched it up. "Whores of

Babylon, Bambi speaking. May I have your credit card number please?"

"Dani?"

She winced. "Hi, Mom. Just kidding."

Traffic noise flooded the line. Sam was calling from the cellular phone. "I was wondering if you wanted to get together tonight. Go to a movie or something."

"I thought you had a big case."

"I do. Have dinner with me and I'll tell you all about it."

Dani frowned. "Is something wrong?"

"No," Sam said happily.

"You sound weird."

"I think I maybe met someone."

Stunned, Dani said, "The client."

"Yeah, which isn't really good. Professional conflict of interest and all."

"I understand. Well, you know my feelings on the subject."

"Yes," Sam said drolly, "if it moves, I'm supposed to jump on it."

"Mother!"

Sam laughed. "I'm just in a good mood. What is that, so strange?" Without allowing her daughter the time for a smart-ass reply, Sam asked, "So what do you say? Dinner?"

"I'm kind of tied up tonight."

"I hope you don't mean that literally."

"Jesus, Mom. This guy really got to you, didn't he?"

"I dunno. Maybe."

"I'd love to, but I really have to study," Dani said.

"Oh. All right," Sam said, her conscious effort to

mask the disappointment in her voice evident nonetheless. "You gonna call me sometime, we'll get together?"

"Sure, Mom," Dani said.

"Sure, Mom," Sam repeated.

"I love you," Dani said warmly.

"You'd better." Sam hesitated. "I love you, too."

The line disconnected. Dani lay back on the bed.
Nina walked over, took the receiver from Dani's hand,
and hung it up for her.

"I just lied to my mother."

"Yeah, you sure did."

"I hope this guy's worth it." Dani groaned.

"Worth it? They're never worth it. They are entertaining, though, and sometimes that's enough. I guess
it depends on what you're after."

Dani nodded, her frown deepening.

"So do you know what you're after?"

She sighed and rose up on her elbows. "I don't have
the first fucking idea."

Driving to the club on the highway, Dani felt the
tug of conflicting emotions. Despite the act, she was
excited about the date with Ray. The fact that she had
lied to her mother troubled her terribly. She was
tempted to call her and tell her the truth, but she
didn't want to ruin the evening.

Ahead, the traffic was terrible and the insane drivers were worse than ever. Cars streaked by as if they
were auditioning for the autobahn in Germany, a road
with no speed limit, where people often drove one

hundred miles an hour or faster during a casual jaunt. There had been a time when Dani had been just as reckless on the road, but she had learned the painful and difficult lesson that she would not live forever, as she had seemed to believe when she first picked up her licence.

A red pickup suddenly changed lanes, erupting from her blind spot like a streak of blood then cutting her off. Dani nailed the Karmann Ghia's brakes and narrowly avoided a collision. Fortunately, there was no one behind her.

"Bastard!" she screamed, but the pickup was out of her range, bearing down on the bumper of a station wagon in the next lane over. Dani drew a deep breath, let it out. Looked at the steering wheel, afraid she had pulled it off the column. Everything was fine.

She thought of Nina and a smile came to her. When she had been younger, and living in Tampa, her two best friends had been Jami and Lisa Evans. Their mother, Carlotta, had been a nurse who had helped her mother when Dani had first been brought into the hospital. Sam and Carlotta had been inseparable. The girls had been the same way.

Then a man named Willis and his brother changed their lives forever. They killed Jami and later abducted Dani. Her power had manifested that day for the first time, and the Willis brothers did not survive. Jami and Lisa had been twins, a pair of beautiful Spanish girls. Nina reminded Dani of the way Lisa had been before her sister died: bright, funny, and direct. Dani wondered if she had been drawn to Nina for that reason, if she was trying to replace what had been lost to her.

Ahead, the red pickup was once again causing problems. It was caged in by traffic. There were three lanes and they were all jammed, even the passing lane. The pickup transferred from lane to lane, riding the bumpers of the station wagon, a pale silver van, and a black BMW. It was the BMW which refused to get out of the passing lane. Dani was in the center lane, watching the driver with growing unease. She turned on the radio and cranked the first rock station that came on. It took her a few seconds to identify the group.

Def Leopard, singing about teen angst. Dani punched another station. A news report. She was about to change the channel when the story reached out and grabbed her by the throat:

"The body of nineteen-year-old U.S.C. student Felicity Turner was discovered early this morning in downtown Los Angeles. Though police refused to speculate, the killing appears to be the work of the 'Sorority Slasher,' responsible for no less than six brutal slayings of female university students throughout the state over the last year. The mutilated, headless body was found—"

Dani punched up another station. She had read about the other campus murders and felt she could live without the gory details. The new station was playing classic Van Halen, before the band became Van Hagar. That would do. Eddie Van Halen was letting a tumultuous guitar solo rip through the compact car's speakers when the red pickup decided it was no longer bound by the laws of nature.

Dani watched in horrid fascination as the truck attempted to seize upon a slight opening between the station wagon and the van. The wagon had fallen back slightly, turning the solid wall of vehicles into a marginal V shape. The driver of the red pickup had shot forward, attempting to muscle his way through the crack. He had evidently believed that the driver of the station wagon would do exactly what Dani had done a few minutes earlier, slam on the brakes and let him through. He wasn't worried about the cars bearing down on the station wagon and what a sudden brake at this speed would mean for those behind the family car.

Dani had been lucky when the pickup had done this to her. No one had been directly behind her, despite the crowded road. This time, she was right behind the station wagon. She hadn't been tailgating the other car, but she had been following closely enough to discourage some other asshole from pulling the same routine the pickup had been attempting to perfect.

The driver of the station wagon had apparently considered the long line of vehicles behind him and had visualized a pileup. That, or he was so startled by the driver's audacity and recklessness that he simply failed to react in time. Whatever the case, the station wagon did not brake, and the driver's side of the pickup collided with the station wagon's passenger front end. There was a high scream of metal and the pickup was driven back, into the silver van.

Dani slammed on the brakes. There was nothing else for her to do. Panic seized her. She had read stories where characters experienced car wrecks. From their point of view, the world had slowed to a crawl, slow-motion on a bad cop show. They had time to contemplate their lives, those they would be leaving behind, God only knows what else. Shit, they seemed to have enough time to solve the problems of world hunger and the homeless, the way it happened in stories.

Dani now realized that was a load of crap. She felt the tug of her seat belt, knew there wasn't time to rip it off and somehow leap free of the car. The windows were shut and the air was blowing. She had a vague sense of cars beside her. Turning wouldn't have done any good.

It happened in about four seconds, and they were four seconds of real time, not made-for-TV bullshit time, as she thought of it. She was able to think, *omigod, this is it, this is it, omigod, oh Jesus, omigod, no, omigod—*

Then the crash occurred and there wasn't a damn thing she could do about it.

Chapter Four

"I think maybe there was a reason you were spared. I've seen a lot of these. I've seen worse than this, not very often, but I've seen it. People don't just walk away from something like this unless there's a reason. You religious?"

That's what the emergency medical technician would tell her fifteen minutes later. At the moment of impact, Dani would not have believed she was going to live long enough to hear those or any other words, ever again.

Hours earlier she had boasted that she once possessed the powers of a god. The operative word being "once." Now she was only an Initiate, a being more powerful than any human, but just as vulnerable to injury, unlike the state she had turned her back upon.

During the first second of impact, something occurred within her mind that frightened her even worse than thoughts of her own death. She heard the laughter of the demon, the high, wondrous wail of her blood, from somewhere deep in her mind. A part of her was enjoying this. A terrible, insane part of her was fucking *thrilled* to be going through this experience, it was viewing the entire accident as a chance to live again, to experience life as it was meant to be experienced, on the constant, waiting cusp of imminent death.

The trio of vehicles ahead had formed an H and Dani's car slid into the hollow at the bottom, sandwiching in between the station wagon and the van.

The truck rose before her like a bleeding behemoth, absurd and frightening, a wall of bloodstained metal, though it was only a factory paint job that made the pickup such a vibrant red, nothing more. Dani would have hoped that to be the case, but she had no time to think, only to react.

An old "Ann Landers" column flashed into Dani's mind. The advice columnist had apparently received one too many letters from teenagers who thought driving their parent's cars into trees would be a quick and painless way to end their troubled lives. Landers had written a description of the ten seconds of impact, going into loving, gruesome detail. It had been the last time Dani had read Ann Landers, as it turned out, and she had tried not to think of that wretched column, but even this morning, when she had read the *L.A. Times,* she had avoided the section of the paper where Landers column would have been, had they been running it. She wasn't even sure if they carried it. She didn't want to know, though she never consciously admitted the reason for her aversion until this moment.

It was the part about the steering wheel impaling the victim's chest that burst in Dani's mind as the front end of the Karmann Ghia was crushed against the passenger side of the red pickup. The car's engine was in back, the trunk in the front. The hood bubbled up into scrap immediately upon impact, like an empty beer can on a frat brother's forehead.

Movies, she thought. John Belushi, *Animal House*. Even now, she was thinking about movies. What the hell did that have to say about real life?

Dani was thrown forward, the special over-the-shoulder seat belt her mother had insisted on having installed suddenly biting into her chest, driving the air from her lungs. Dani felt a sudden pain and was certain it was the steering column goring her. She wondered why in the hell she had fought her mother on having an air bag put in.

The Karmann Ghia was spun to a full right angle, slamming the passenger rear of the car into the van. For an instant, all four cars were locked together, fused in some insane way, still moving, spinning, turning. Dani's world became a mad, chaotic assembly of alien sights and sounds. The screams of tearing metal sailed over the bassy, thunderous crashes, deep, horrible groans, and high, strange hisses of dying machinery. Beneath it all, she registered the radio still working, it hadn't even lost its station. Van Halen was rocking steady, nonplussed by all that was happening to Dani.

"Whoa, yeah! Beautiful girl!" the chorus sang.

Diamond Dave wailed, *"I love her! I need her!"*

"Whoa, yeah! Beautiful girl!"

Another vehichle hit the assembly, then another. She was rocked forward, though she somehow managed not to slam her head against the dash. Pain ripped into her chest. She reached forward, grasping at air.

I can't breathe, she thought, I can't! Suddenly she was struggling, panicking, pitching her head from one side to the other, unable to draw air into her lungs. Anything, God, I'll do anything, just let me take a breath, one breath, that's all, let me breathe, please!

Her first breath came and her eyes flashed open with amazement and gratitude. The sun was yanked out of the sky. She wondered why everything was getting so dark. Then she heard and felt the van tip over on top of the Ghia. The roof caved downward and the windshield exploded. Dani ripped the seat belt loose, then jammed her shoulder against the door and pushed. It opened as the passenger side of the car vanished. She pushed hard and the door swung eight inches, then stopped. She twisted her head to see the luggage rack from the top of the van sink down beside her, nearly grazing her arm, where it sat, still as death.

It was over. She was alive.

She looked out over the hood, dimly registering that the pickup now sat on its side, a few yards away. Steam was pouring out of the van's ruptured hood. Her car radio was dead; Van Halen finally silenced.

Dani pictured all the vehicles involved in the accident suddenly exploding into flames, the way they did on television—which was about as realistic as Toonces the Driving Cat on "Saturday Night Live," according to her mother—but Dani didn't want to take any chances. She didn't smell any gasoline vapors, which was a good sign. Nevertheless, she would open the hood of each vehicle and disconnect the batteries, preventing any chance of a spark. Then she would organize people to keep the cars away. Seal it off, the way the police would. Her mom had taught her that. No problem.

Oh, wait. She was going to have to *move* to do all that, wasn't she? That could be a problem. She looked down to make sure her legs hadn't been sliced off. There had been no vast explosions of pain, but then, there usually wasn't with that type of injury, not right away. Nope, everything was there, she was barely even bleeding from the broken glass. She turned to the side and felt a terrific pain in her chest, a sudden fireball that made her gasp in alarm. The sensations subsided the moment she straightened out.

Stupid, stupid, stupid.

God, that hurt.

Police officers went through a "First Responder" course, which focused on basic first aid and taught officers what they should and should not do when arriving at traffic accidents. They were taught to handle several types of injuries. Sam took a refresher course every few years and Dani had attended the last one with her.

Dani knew the best thing she could do was stay still and wait for help to arrive, but she had to get the fuck out of this mess, that's all there was to it. She wasn't going to sit here another second. Pulling her legs up, she half expected to find something broken.

"Working order, boss," she whispered, then carefully climbed forward, through the shattered windshield, over the red hot metal of the Ghia's chassis, to freedom. Lowering herself to the asphalt, Dani felt her legs turn to water and she had to grab hold of the station wagon beside the Ghia to maintain her balance.

Dani stopped dead. A red-haired girl lay in a crumpled heap on the ground before the station wagon. Dani would have thought the girl was dead, but she could hear the child's piteous cries. Drawing a ragged breath, determined to somehow steady herself by will alone, Dani took a few steps in the girl's direction then collapsed to the ground. Unwilling to let this stop her, Dani crawled forward, picking herself up twice then falling again to her knees.

Moments later, at the girl's side, Dani thought she had made a mistake. The child wasn't crying. She wasn't moving at all. Dani reached down and felt for a pulse. The girl was alive, her breathing shallow and irregular. The child's hair wasn't red, it was blond, but it had been streaked red, with blood. She had a pretty face and wore a red and white floral print dress that had been torn in places, revealing bruises.

If this child wasn't crying, who was? she wondered.

Suddenly, she was engulfed by a chorus of wails. Dani cupped her hands over her ears, anxious to blot out the sound, but only a few of the screams were silenced. She looked down at the child and realization seared her. Part of what she heard was real, victims crying out in pain. The rest was a strange, psychic echo of their last cries, mixed with the pain-racked whispers and screams running through the minds of the survivors.

Her power and her hunger flared. The fear on this

89

stretch of highway was greater than any she had ever encountered before. She felt the terror of those who had been hurt, and received a low chorus of apprehension from those safely closing on the accident, but their fear had been tempered with relief that it hadn't been them. Dani's own terror had blocked out her need to consume until this moment, but now it overwhelmed her. She was unable to prevent her silver cord from snaking away from her and reaching into the minds of the victims.

There were seven survivors. Four dead. The demon rose in Dani's mind, triumphant. She smiled, the same dark emotions which had passed through her at the moment of impact racing into her again. The fear of the wounded and the dying would be remarkable.

They would begin with the child.

"NO!" Dani screamed, stumbling back and faltering once again. She fell on her ass and wheezed in pain from her own chest injury.

The little girl's eyes flashed open at the sound of Dani's cry. The child tried to move then gasped as pain barreled through her, accompanied by the most delicious agony Dani could ever imagine.

Dani had never tasted the fear and pain of a child. It was pure and sweet, a white hot blast of undiluted emotion. Strength flooded into Dani's weakened limbs. Her mind went blank and her body buckled in near-sexual bliss. Her last vestiges of resolve were about to be swept away when the child whispered, "Mommy?"

Dani snapped back to awareness. This is not

me, she thought. This is not who and what I am.

Of course it is, the demon whispered in her mind. *Or have you forgotten? I don't really exist. I'm just a projection of what's inside you. And what's inside you now is hunger and need.*

Dani twisted her body to one side, intentionally sending a shock of pain through her system, driving the air from her lungs. Her own fear returned, fear that something had been ruptured inside her, fear that she would spit up blood at any moment, fear that she would die while feeling she had made it. The fear forced the demon to retreat slightly, but it remained at the periphery of her consciousness, waiting to leap upon her in a moment of weakness, anxious to remind her that she was absolutely ravenous and stretched out before her was a feast of apocalyptic proportions. Dani severed her silver thread, silencing the screaming voices in her head.

The tangle of overturned and demolished vehicles loomed before her, a wall of twisted, steaming metal. Enough of a gap had been left in the passing lane for traffic to continue on, though drivers slowed, apparently hoping to see a severed head or two.

Dani shuddered and felt the hunger slam into her at the very thought of blood. The station wagon's front windshield was a red smear, a spiderweb of cracks leading inward to an impact point over the steering column. Sunlight glittered in the grooves of the broken glass.

She heard cars driving by in the passing lane, making a languid circuit of the accident. No one stopped to help.

You can help, she thought. *You're* alive, you can *do* something.

"What can I do?" Dani whispered aloud.

"It hurts," the child said.

Looking down at the girl with the bloodstained hair, Dani saw that the child's leg was twisted under her, broken. Wondering if she could find something in the wreckage to use for a splint, Dani realized she might do more damage by trying to move the child. There could be internal injuries. She noticed the dark circles under the child's eyes. A possible skull fracture.

"Don't move," Dani said sharply, causing the child to freeze. Dani bent low and saw bruising behind the bottom of the ears. More indications of a skull fracture. How in God's name had the child come back to consciousness with this kind of injury?

Dani had read of cases where people on motorcycles had been thrown for a hundred feet and were still wide awake and alert after impact, while others could go two miles an hour, and die from falling over and cracking their heads on a curb. Injuries of this type were unpredictable. The only thing Dani knew for certain was that she had to keep the child calm and still.

The child's eyes were wide with fear. She tried to move again then cried out. The passenger side window of the station wagon was wide open. The girl was small enough to have flown through that opening. It was possible that the child had multiple fractures; if that was true, Dani had to keep her calm and stop her from moving around. The lessons she had learned from the First Responder course and her college studies came back to her. It was good to have cold, dry facts to fasten upon; that way she didn't have to feel.

Who are trying to kid, Dani? Take one look at that face and tell me you don't feel as broken up inside as you think she actually is.

Yeah, she thought, forcing a sudden rush of tears back. She tried to focus strictly on the child's injuries. If she moved around and there were broken bones inside her body, they might lacerate arteries and tear muscles. A great deal of internal damage could be caused by manipulating a break improperly.

That's right, Dani. By the book, all the way. Focus on the facts and you won't feel a goddamned thing.

Christ, this poor kid.

"What happened?" the girl asked.

Dani wasn't sure where to begin. "There was an accident, honey, but everything's going to be fine. Don't try to move, okay?"

"Okay."

Dani touched the girl's cheek and said, "You're going to be fine. What's your name?"

"Hazie," the girl said.

At first, Dani thought the child was slipping into delirium. *Hazy, it's all getting hazy.* But this was California. A name like that was possible. "Hazie?"

"Kids at school called me Witch Hazel. My parents call me Hazie." Hazie paused. "Where's my mommy?"

"I don't know, honey," Dani said, brushing the blood-soaked hair from Hazie's face. The girl did not appear to be cut. Where had the blood come from?

"My mommy," Hazie repeated.

93

"I don't know, baby. I'll find her. You just stay here and don't try to move, okay?"

"I want my mommy," Hazie said, starting to cry.

"I know, honey," Dani said, suddenly realizing how much she sounded like her own mother. The thought made her smile and her expression seemed to calm the child.

"My leg, it really *hurts,*" Hazie said.

Dani felt the first pangs of the child's fear pierce her mind and she struggled to force them away. The hunger welled inside her.

She's terrified, a laughing voice said in Dani's head. *Now ain't that somethin'?*

Desperate to remain in control, Dani squeezed her eyes shut. She had to do something with the hunger, the blood-need that swelled and fought inside her for release. She had to find another way to deal with it, focus it some other way.

"Hurts," Hazie cried.

No, Dani thought. It doesn't. She reached out with her power, bridging the gap between her mind and Hazie's, and numbed the terrible agony the girl had been suffering. The pain was still there, but the child's brain would no longer be able to perceive it. Hazie's body relaxed at once.

The hunger within Dani immediately fled.

"Doesn't hurt," Hazie said, confused.

Dani felt a surge of triumph. "You're going to need to be a big girl, okay? I'm going to find your mommy and then I'll come back. All you need to do is try not to move. Stay still. I'll be right back. Okay?"

The girl nodded. "You come back now, y'hear.

94

Mommy always say that. Thinks it's funny."

Dani leaned down and kissed the child. She was afraid to use her power again, though it would have been simple to ease the child into sleep, preventing her from trying to get up while Dani reconnoitered the scene. But it might be better for her to stay conscious, particularly with the head injury. She could paralyze the girl, leaving her awake, but that would frighten her worse.

Hazie's eyes were strong and determined. She said she wouldn't move, she wasn't going to move. Dani smiled and turned away from her.

Holding onto the side of the station wagon, Dani pulled herself to her feet. She was wobbly, but she knew she would not fall. Walking around to the driver's side of the station wagon, which had been caved in, Dani peered inside and saw a couple in their late thirties.

"Oh, Jesus," Dani whispered. They were dead. The man's head was a bloody pulp. He hadn't been wearing a seat belt. The woman's seat had been thrown all the way back. She was slumped over between the front and back seats, her body twisted at an unnatural angle. Part of her spine jutted from a horrible, bloody wound in her back. Dani turned away and did not look in Hazie's direction.

They were dead, her parents were dead, how in God's name was she going to tell this — what, four-year-old, five-year-old? — that her mom and dad were gone?

A moaning came, this time to Dani's right. She whipped her head around so quickly she brought the screeching pain back from her own chest. Grabbing onto the door for support she straightened herself, then looked at the next car involved in the accident, one of those caught in the chain reaction. It was a white Buick four-door. The windshield was another bloody spider's web. The sun struck it full on, creating a nasty glare. The front end had collapsed. Dani guessed the Buick had struck the station wagon then been hit by another car. There was a green Eldorado behind the Buick. The passenger side door of the white Buick was gone.

Dani wondered if Hazie could have escaped from this car, not the station wagon. She tried to plot out the manner in which Hazie would have been thrown, then gave up. Hazie had been ejected from the wagon, her parents were dead.

The moan came again. Dani took a few steps and the glare receded, allowing her to catch a glimpse of a blond woman sitting behind the wheel of the Buick, alive, but unable to free herself. When Dani was able to make out the word the woman had been repeating like a dark chant in a low key, Dani nearly shouted with joy.

Haiiziiie, the woman moaned. *Haiiziiie*.

It *was* her! *This* woman was Hazie's mother. The girl must have been thrown from the passenger side of the Buick. Everything was going to be all right!

Dani went around to the driver's side of the car and her elation quickly faded. The steering wheel was deformed. The woman's face was covered in blood. Her lips trembled, and several of her teeth were shattered.

She wore a sundress, revealing a pair of bloody knees.

An echo of the accident leapt from the woman's mind, causing Dani to cry out. Suddenly, she *was* this woman, and she was experiencing the moment of impact all over again. Dani felt a terrible pain first in her knees as they struck the dashboard on impact then in her hips as the power of the blow was transferred back. Bone was shattered. Red-hot liquid fire coursed through her lower body as she was thrown forward, against the windshield, her body whipping back, then hurled forward again as another car struck theirs from behind, sending her into the steering wheel.

Dani recoiled from the memory, breathing hard. She looked into the woman's eyes and knew that Hazie's mother was swimming down into shock. The woman was covered in sweat, anxious, restless, trying to somehow detach herself from her seat belt, though her brain would not assist her enough so that she could work the mechanism.

Dani knew that she had to keep the woman from moving around. Reaching out with her power, Dani prepared herself for the horribly intense pain the woman was suffering through. Her preparation wasn't enough, and she was forced to recall her silver thread almost immediately. The woman grabbed Dani's arm and repeated her daughter's name.

"Hazie's safe," Dani said. "She's all right. You've got to calm down. You're injured. If you try to move around, you're gonna hurt yourself worse. Help will be here soon. Just hang on."

The woman's chest worked furiously. Her fingers dug hard enough into Dani's arm to leave bruises.

Dani reached down and pried the woman's hand loose, taking it in both of hers. The woman was determined to twist her way out of the seat, though the belt held her in place. Dani reached out with her power once again and darted back immediately. Making contact with this woman's mind would be as sensible as plunging into a burning building. Dani had gone farther this time, far enough to tell that the woman had suffered some form of spinal injury, accompanied by internal rupturing.

She was dying. The EMTs would arrive too late.

Dani was overwhelmed with her desire to save this woman, whose blood pressure was decreasing rapidly. Her eyes were becoming glassy. She was slipping away into the depths of shock, and she would not emerge again.

"Don't you even think about going anywhere," Dani said, her voice shaky. "You have a daughter who needs you. I know what that's like. You're not going anywhere. I won't let you."

The woman looked at her, wide-eyed and afraid. Dani felt her fear—tempting and delicious—and managed to ignore it. She stared into the brown, doe eyes of Hazie's mother.

What can you do? the woman's eyes seemed to say. What can either of us do? The woman knew her daughter was safe. She could accept her death. There was no other choice. And she was right. What *could* Dani do for her?

Mercy, Dani thought, I can give mercy, I can make her death easier for her. That's all I can do.

Somehow, she was not convinced.

She thought again about the exact manner in which her power worked. She was able to reach into the minds of others and cull memories from them, or implant suggestions, images. If she wanted someone to be afraid, she would sift their memories, learn what frightened them, and make them believe it was happening. If she chose to ignite their desire, she would rely on similar techniques.

The vampires who had taught her how to utilize her gifts had only begun their work when they had been killed. Bill Yoshino had told her that her techniques were crude. Their powers seemed far more highly evolved than her own. Perhaps they had come to realize that the theater of the mind was an interesting, even an entertaining route to provoking the emotions they consumed, but there existed more direct, clean, and efficient ways of accomplishing the same task.

Dani thought of her studies at college.

The exact responses the vampires elicited manifested in the physical range. Fear, desire, rage, calm—all of these states could be traced to chemical roots and they provoked chemical responses. If she could stimulate areas of the brain directly, perhaps she could provoke chemical secretions that would help the woman to hang on long enough for proper help to arrive.

Dani had studied spinal injuries when her mother had sustained similar damage, and she had spent hours listening to lectures from scientists concerning the manner in which information traveled from the brain to the body and back again. Electrochemical impulses. Enzymes.

The more she thought about it, the more frightened

she became. It seemed like science fiction. Impossible. But her power when she had been a full vampire had allowed her to provoke physiological changes in her body.

But she couldn't do that anymore. She had rejected her blood heritage. When she had cut her thumb to the bone six months ago slicing vegetables, Dani had nearly passed out from the lack of blood. The wound had required stitches. How could she turn that power on someone else when she couldn't even make it work on herself?

Maybe you can still do it, she thought suddenly. Maybe you've never *really* tried, because you want so much to be human, and you know you're not. Not entirely. And you never will be.

The voice of her mother returned to Dani: You've always wanted to explore the boundaries of what you really are. You've been afraid, that's all, afraid that the demon would take over, that your hunger and desire would overpower you. As long as you keep thinking of them as separate entities like that, you're giving them power. The demon doesn't exist unless you encourage it to exist. Accept that the thirst and the need are a part of you, and always *will be* a part of you, and you can be their master. There will be a time and a place for them, but it's up to you to dictate when and where that will be. Stop being a slave, Dani. Take control. Do it now or this little girl loses her mother.

I'll do it, Dani thought, and suddenly, intuitive knowledge of where to begin flooded into her mind. It did not help to quell her terror, however, and that was good. Her own fear would banish her hunger. Dani held the woman's hand in both of hers and lowered her head.

"What are you . . . you praying? Are you praying?" the woman said in sudden alarm.

"For both of us," Dani whispered, attempting to steady herself for the shock she was certain she would soon encounter. She eased forward, reaching out with her silver thread, and felt a fiery wave of anguish wash over her. Pain flooded through her body, but she had suffered pain like this before, when she had been shot. Focusing beyond the woman's agony, Dani approached the walls separating her from the woman's surface thoughts, then rose above them, listening to echoes of memory.

The woman's name was Amanda Cross. Hazie was Hazie Cross. Amanda's husband was named Russell Petretski. He was not Hazie's father. Amanda had hopes of becoming an actress and she had not changed her name. There were other memories. Amanda and Russell making love. Taking Hazie to a concert. The day job at Pinelow Industries as a secretary. Acting classes. Working out. A constant stream of auditions. Russell's career crisis at the hospital, where he worked as an orderly.

Dani pulled herself away from these memories. She had to go beyond Amanda's consciousness, but she felt the lure of a comforting, familiar set of words.

"Now I lay me down to sleep. I pray the Lord my soul to keep. . . ."

Amanda was praying. Deep beneath her conscious thoughts, Amanda was reaching out for salvation.

"If I should die—"

Stop it, Dani thought, *you won't die, I won't let you!*

"—before I wake—"

You're to wake again, you have to believe that, have to want to see your little girl grow up. You have to want it!

"I pray the Lord—"

Desperately aware of Amanda's imminent surrender, Dani allowed an array of memories from her *own* life to blanket Amanda's perceptions.

A kaleidoscope of words and images exploded in Amanda's mind. She was able to see Dani grow from an infant to a bright, playful young girl, then to a shy and intensely beautiful woman, and Sam was at her side in each recollection, her expression of pride and unconditional love giving Dani the strength to survive any tragedy, and appreciate every triumph.

The prayer was cut short. Amanda asked, *Who's there?*

Dani froze. She was not prepared for this. Amanda repeated the question, becoming agitated.

God? Is that you?

A laughed escaped Dani. She instantly regretted it.

A woman? God is a woman?

I'm not God, Dani said, realizing she would have no choice but to respond.

Then you're an angel.

No, Dani said sharply, thinking of the vampire she had known who had born that name.

Then who are you?

I'm a friend of your daughter's. She wants to see you again.

I'm hurt real bad.

I know. But you don't have to stay that way. I can help you, but I can't do it alone. You have to work with me. You have to let me in, all the way.

Amanda hesitated. Dani could sense her fear.

So hard, Amanda said.

That's just too Goddamned bad, Dani said, overcome with anger. She reached into Amanda's memories and yanked free the long hours of Hazie's birth, and the sheer joy Amanda felt holding her child for the first time. *It was worth it then, wasn't it?*

Yes, Amanda said, weeping. *YES!*

Suddenly, Amanda was *with* Dani, willing to suffer any pain if there was a chance of seeing her little girl grow to adulthood. They communicated without words, Amanda helping Dani to bring down the final barriers erected by her thoughts, keeping Dani from performing the task which might save the woman.

The familiar mindscape vanished and the enormity of what took its place stunned Dani. She felt as if she had leaped into another reality, which, in a way, she had. The physical world was hers once more. She sat in the Buick, looking at a spider's web of cracks in the glass before her. Someone held her left hand in both of theirs. Though it caused her terrific pain, Dani turned to the left and saw a dark, beautiful young woman with wild brunette hair kneeling outside the white Buick.

The young woman's eyes flickered open. They were dark and flecked with fiery shards of gold. Dani thought she was looking into a mirror as the young woman raised her head. It was Danielle Walthers, holding her hand.

That was impossible. *She* was Danielle Walthers. How could she be looking at herself? How could she be feeling the touch of Danielle Walthers's hands upon hers?

Understanding flooded into her. Dani was *inside* Amanda, looking out through her eyes, looking at her own physical body as if it were a separate entity.

She had looked out the eyes of others before, sampling their perceptions, but this was different. Amanda's shattered, dying body was now her own. In her ignorance, she had somehow pushed her consciousness so far into Amanda's mind that she had become *fused* with Amanda. She felt the woman's pain, and was in command of the woman's physical form.

Dani wondered if Amanda was inside her body, but, to her amazement, Danielle Walthers shook her head from side to side and mouthed the word, "no."

That's not possible, Dani thought, panic seizing her. This is not happening!

But it *was* happening, and Dani had to somehow seize control. Something was inside Danielle Walthers's body, causing it to react independently to Dani's will. Was the demon inside her body? Had her true nature asserted itself, helping to eject her from her body, trapping her in Amanda's bleeding form so that she would die and it could have ascendency? She recalled Isabella's last moments, when her human consciousness had been all but burnt out, and a vicious animalistic mind, the voice of Isabella's bloodthirst, had taken control.

Danielle Walthers's body made the same motion. *No.* Utilizing Amanda's weakened hands, she squeezed the hands of her true body, then willed the dark-haired girl before her to do the same.

"Holy *fuck*," she whispered, the words erupting from

two sets of lips at once. She now existed in both bodies, their nervous systems linked. Her initial panic subsided and she pulled back, trying to find some trace of Amanda's consciousness. The woman had not fled. Her mind was wrapped around Dani's; they were entwined like lovers.

Dani suspected that if she failed, and Amanda died, she might not be able to retreat in time to the safety of her own body. The pain of Amanda's injuries had not lessened.

Hurry, Amanda urged.

Closing her borrowed eyes, Dani trained her power inward. She recalled the movie *Fantastic Voyage,* in which a team of physicians were miniaturized and injected into the bloodstream of a patient to heal him from within. She half expected a phantasmagoric explosion of bizarre sights and sounds similar to those featured in the movie. Any second now, she would be floating through the bloodstream, a vast river of blood, encountering island-sized pulsing organs and monstrous parasites.

Instead, she found herself standing in pitch darkness, thrown into a raging lightning storm of crackling energy. Amanda's brain was sending impulses to provoke the "automatic" functions necessary to maintain her life.

Dani was terrified. She wanted to flee. Suddenly she realized the impulses were not harming her. She raised her hand before her face. Even here, she seemed to have a physical form, but she knew that was only because she willed it to be so. Her body in this place was little more than a reminder that her individual consciousness, her higher self, was separate from the landscape before her. If she allowed this dream body to dissolve away, as she was tempted to, she feared that she would be swept away by the sensuous array of crackling white energy before her.

The longer she concentrated, the easier it became to discern actual patterns in the lightning. Crackling strands of fiery white energy were propelled outward then received back into Amanda's brain.

Dani attempted to expand her perceptions and found that it seemed to be a matter of will alone. She wished to understand where each of the impulses went and suddenly she existed in several realities at once, inside the lightning storm, outside, in Amanda's body, and, somehow, in her own. She would see bursts of light emerge in the storm, then feel a corresponding tingle within her and Amanda's body.

Amanda's blood pressure was sinking.

Her first priority was to arrest and reverse the fall of Amanda's blood pressure. The body normally provided a catecholamine release, an adrenaline-type enzyme, but this had not occurred because of the injured spinal cord. The woman was going into neurogenic shock because the pathways between the brain and the nerves had been interrupted by the injury. Dani's nervous system, however, was functioning perfectly, and they were now fused. The temporary, psychic bridge Dani had forged would have to provide the necessary linkage.

She recalled from her studies the dynamic balance between the sympathetic and parasympathetic systems. The sympathetic speeded up the heart rate and other functions, the parasympathetic held it down; without the parasympathetic to hold the heart in check, it could beat as many as one hundred and ten beats per minute.

The parasympathetic system ran along the vegas nerve, down a sheath in the neck with the carotid artery, unlike the sympathetic, which existed along Amanda's damaged vertebrae. Under healthy conditions, pressure receptors forced the parasympathetic to perform its duties without interruption. But the drop in blood pressure had caused the parasympathetic to ease off, allowing the sympathetic to run rampant, flushing the body with blood from the internal rupturing.

Christ, Dani, think, think!

Bioreceptors in the aorta traveled in the vegas nerve up to the medulla. In the medulla there were cells that controlled the blood pressure. They sent *axons* down to the intermedial cell column in the spinal cord to help regulate the blood pressure, but the damage Amanda suffered had interrupted that activity, dropping her blood pressure.

She needed to stop the internal hemorrhaging by shutting down the peripheral circulation. Then she had to make sure blood was getting to the heart, brain, and kidneys. Without blood, Amanda's kidneys would be blocked, an irreversible event, and without the kidneys, Amanda would die.

The sympathetic system went directly to the adrenal glands. Utilizing her power to bridge the damage on the spinal column, Dani stimulated the release of epinephrine—adrenaline from the adrenal glands. The kidneys were then able to detect the blood pressure loss and act on it. They provided renin, which catalyzed an entire cascade of activities within Amanda's body, eventually causing peripheral vasic constriction: the vessels leaking blood were shut down and the flow of blood was forced back to the body cavity, keeping the core profusion up.

She could suddenly sense that Amanda's condition was stabilizing. The woman was no longer sinking into shock, her blood pressure was rising. Dani released a burst of endorphins, androgynous morphines to flood Amanda's system, kill the pain she had been feeling, and create a temporary high to which Dani had to avoid succumbing.

Dani maintained her symbiotic link with Amanda until the emergency medical technicians arrived. They gently pulled her away from the woman and Dani found that she did not need to be in physical contact with Amanda to continue her connection. Amanda, no longer afraid of dying, allowed Dani to ease herself away as the EMTs assumed her role. As she untangled their conscious minds, Dani saw that Amanda was continuing to fantasize about her daughter's wedding. The man Amanda had chosen for the groom had been pulled from Dani's mind: Ray Brooks.

Dani retreated from Amanda, her dual perceptions fading. She wanted to cry out in triumph, but a sudden wave of loneliness moved through her. She had been terrified of dying while linked to Amanda, but there had been an intimacy in their bonding unlike anything Dani had ever experienced; only her sexual union with Bill Yoshino had come close. Removed from that experience, she felt frightened and alone.

She doubted that Amanda would be sharing her feelings. If the woman had any conscious recollection of what they had shared, it would not be accompanied by the same understanding. Amanda would choose to forget it quickly.

Dani would never forget what had happened. She was about to turn away from the scene when she saw Amanda attempt to climb out of the car. The woman swung her leg out and tried to put pressure on it when the EMT caught her.

"My daughter," she whispered.

"Hazie's fine," Dani said incredulously.

Amanda looked up at her, narrowed her gaze, then allowed the EMT to convince her to lie back and remain still. Dani walked away, to the periphery of the crash, and slumped down next to another demolished car. She watched as Amanda and Hazie were loaded onto stretchers. Hazie caught sight of Dani; she held up her hand and curled her fingers, waving goodbye.

Forcing a smile to cover her growing fear, Dani returned the gesture. Then both mother and child were gone. There were other victims. Dani could feel their suffering, and her resistance to their terror was helped by her own.

Amanda should not have been able to move her legs. It was impossible, but it had happened.

She had read studies about the possibility of nerve regeneration, but that was speculation, as far as she knew. Perhaps she had incorrectly gauged the extent of Amanda's injuries; her spine might have only been bruised, not separated.

Deep down, she knew that wasn't true; she knew she had done more than direct Amanda's body to release enzymes and trigger its own recovery.

Amanda's broken body had been *healed*.

A half hour later, at the hospital, Dani was sitting outside the emergency room, contemplating how she would tell her mother about all that had happened. It was something to help force away thoughts of what was truly upsetting her, the last image she had glimpsed in Amanda's mind. With very little effort, Dani could alter Amanda's image of the grown-up Hazie marrying Ray Brooks by placing herself next to Ray instead.

Marriage. Children. A life like other people. That was not something Dani often contemplated. She barely knew Ray Brooks. She had already put in a call to the Hellfire Club. A bored-sounding waitress had promised to give Ray the message to call Dani at the hospital pay phone—not that Dani said that it was, in fact, a *hospital* pay phone, she had simply left the number. No, Brooks was not the issue. He was a nice guy, he could even be *the* guy, if she were normal.

She was not normal. Perhaps one day she would get married. She might even settle into the human world and get old and fat and grow to hate what she heard on the radio. But she would never have children; not now, not ever. That was one of the many curses of her kind. The males could reproduce. The females were sterile. She had been told that by the vampires, and she had sensed it today, in her dual explorations of

Amanda's body and her own.

Dani had to fight the urge to schedule tests while she was here. She had adopted the scientific method, she would only fully believe she was unable to have children until it had been proven empirically. Not that she wanted children, not that she thought she ever would, but the idea that even the possibility of having children would be denied to her, like so many other things she had believed were her birthright as a human being, was enough to make her want to put her fist through a wall.

"Miss Walthers?"

Dani looked up to see the EMT who had worked on Amanda. He was a large man with ruddy skin, silky black hair, and a hawklike face. Native American, at least partially. Early thirties.

She could tell from his eyes that somehow he knew what she had done. He wasn't quite sure that he believed it, she guessed from his expression, but he *knew*, nonetheless.

"I know I'm supposed to give you a lecture on leaving work like this to the professionals," he said, "but you did something out there, something it's going to take a long time for people to understand.

"I've never believed in miracles before, but then, I've never seen one up close. You're a miracle, child. A miracle on two legs."

"I don't know what you're talking about," Dani said.

"Sure you do. I've heard the stories, but I never thought they were true, that your people were real."

"What stories?"

"On the reservation, where I came from. Some of

them are old stories, passed down. The shamans don't like to admit to them, no one likes competition, you know. But the stories get told anyway. And there are new stories that crop up. People who can heal with a touch. The ones who don't need to perform a *way* to cleanse a person's body and spirit. Mostly it's the kind of thing parents tell their kids to keep 'em entertained. But sometimes, too, you gotta wonder."

Dani rose abruptly. "I need to make a phone call."

The man held out a slip of paper. He urged her to take it. Reluctantly, she did.

"My name's Jimmy Hawkings," he said. "My family name was Hawk Flies Funny, but my parents changed it when we came here. Can't imagine why, huh?"

Dani smiled, despite herself.

"My number's on there, home and at work. If you want to talk sometime, I'll tell you what I know."

"All right," Dani said noncommittally.

Jimmy Hawkings smiled warmly and walked back to his partner, who waited at the end of the corridor. Dani watched as they left together through the automatic doors, which closed again behind them. Then she walked to the pay phone, dropped her quarter into the slot, dialed her mother's number, and prayed that she could get through this conversation without bursting into tears.

Chapter Five

By midafternoon, Sam's excitement had faded and she found herself facing the tedium that so often consumed her work. She had several rituals she performed when taking on a new client, all of which could have been avoided if Sam had not been imbued with a healthy dose of paranoia. Richard's hotel checked out, he was indeed staying there. The bank listed on his check confirmed he had an account with them. Sam made a few more stops then went to the library.

Richard's claims of working in the movie industry were confirmed by several mentions in the trades over the last fifteen years, including *Variety* and the *Hollywood Reporter*. The *Wall Street Journal* and several other financial magazines had mentions of his company, Seventh Heaven Productions.

Richard's personal history checked out, too. He had indeed attended USC until his junior year, when he left to work for Captiva Films. She dug even deeper, and found that he had underplayed his position of importance in the industry. A *Los Angeles Times* article revealed that Richard had been a featured guest at an independent film seminar three years earlier, and his company had endowed several grants to help new filmmakers. He had also established a somewhat prestigious distribution branch to handle domestic arthouse films, the restoration of film classics, and notable foreign releases.

"It's Troma meets Miramax," a detractor was quoted as saying, in a subsequent write-up. "Richard Sterling is trying to *buy* respectability. It has to be earned."

The insult had made Sam angry, and she had to remind herself that although she found Sterling quite attractive, she would not let her personal feelings interfere with her professionalism.

The guy who said that is still an ass, she thought as she folded the old newspaper and set it in the pile beside her. She moved on to her next subject—Elaine May Aldridge. Elaine had been a waitress in a diner which had since been torn down. According to Richard, she had no living relatives, and few friends.

What kind of woman had she been? Sam wondered. The photograph Richard had given her and his description of her life-style had revealed her to be a typical Californian beach girl, pretty face, slender body, limited concerns. Was there anything more to her? There must have been, for Richard to have been taken with her.

Then again, he had only been nineteen at the time and may well have only been into it for the sex.

"Party-hardy, dude," Sam whispered sarcastically. She shook her head and took a deep breath. This was crazy. She was feeling anger and resentment toward a woman she had never met, over a set of circumstances that may or may *not* have occurred. And even if Elaine Aldridge had borne Richard's child in secret then left town without telling him, it didn't make her an evil person, or Richard an immediate saint or martyr. He had freely admitted that things had not gone well for Elaine and himself near the end, and Elaine had been given no reason to believe they would change simply because she was pregnant.

Sam ran the possibilities through her head. Perhaps Elaine had been afraid Richard would try to make her have an abortion. It was even possible that she truly loved him, and didn't want to see him give up his dreams. To Sam, Richard seemed like the type who would have insisted on marrying the girl he had knocked up. She may have been projecting that, of course. There was something else for her to keep in mind, advice she had tried to give Richard: People change. Even if everything she had felt about him from their one, brief meeting was true, that he was a gentle, honorable man, there were no guarantees that he was anything like that twenty years ago.

She wished that she could interview Cort. That would be the quickest and easiest way to get information. Robert Cort, however, had his own agenda, and might not tell the truth, or the whole truth, anyway. Richard had specifically requested that she stay away from Cort, but Sam felt a meeting with the man was inevitable.

Looking up Elaine's name in the newspaper index, Sam was obliged with two references, each dated twenty years earlier. She made notes of the issues and tried for Robert Anthony Cort. Again, two references. She compared the dates and saw they were the same.

The newspapers had been reduced to microfiche. Sam found them, loaded the sheets, and scanned to the proper page. She read the article quickly the first time, then went back and studied it more carefully the second time. Her shock at the words before her faded and she went through the article a third time, picking apart each sentence with cool, analytical detachment.

According to the article, Elaine May Aldridge and Robert Anthony Cort had been killed when Elaine's car had gone out of control as they drove over the infamous Tower Bridge, a popular suicide spot for Tower University students in the sixties. Several witnesses saw the car hit the water and sink, two people trapped inside. Divers found the car, but the doors had been sprung open and the bodies were missing.

They were never recovered. Richard had seen Cort recently. If he had survived, perhaps Elaine had, too.

The second reference was an obituary page. Sam made printouts of each then left the library.

An hour later, she was at the courthouse, checking probate records. Cort had not left a will. His few belongings had been taken by the government. Elaine, however, had drawn up a will naming "Hilary Bartan" of San Diego as her sole heir. The amount of Elaine's estate surprised Sam. Elaine had possessed twenty thousand dollars at the time of her death.

Sam went home and spent the rest of the afternoon on the phone. She called every hospital in San Diego and learned that Hilary Bartan had given birth to a baby girl six months after Elaine Aldridge's fatal crash. There was no mention of the father in the hospital's records.

Checking the address given for Hilary Bartan in the

probate records, Sam learned that it was an apartment complex that was still in existence. Two phone calls later, she was talking to the owner of the complex, a woman in her early sixties who had spent her life running the apartment building. She claimed that she remembered Hilary Bartan. The woman had been pregnant and alone, though a tall, blond, Scandinavian man had come around to see her occasionally.

Sam relayed Richard's description of Robert Anthony Cort to the landlady and she said that sounded right. The woman had a fax machine, and Sam faxed a copy of Elaine's photograph to her.

"Color the hair black as squid piss and that's Hilary," the woman said. "I guarantee it. She left two months after she had the baby."

"What about the blond guy? Did he come around looking for her?"

"Nope. He helped her move."

"Can you tell me what it was about these two that makes you remember them so well?"

"Sure. I had to *ask* her to leave."

"Why was that? Delinquent on her rent?"

"Nuh-uh. The noise. I had my own daughter living here for a time. She had the unit next to Hilary's."

"What kind of noise? Baby noise?"

"No, that would have been fine. It was the fights. The breaking things."

"You mean when the man was over."

"Exactly. I almost had to call the cops one time. After they left, I went through the place and I found this dent in the bedroom wall. It looked as if someone's head had been put through. Hilary's deposit barely covered it."

Sam nodded. "I don't suppose she left a forwarding address?"

"Not hardly."

"How did she pay you? Cash or checks?"

"Cash. I remember because that was something else that was rare."

"Did she have a job?"

"No. She hardly ever left the place. Really kept to herself, though. My daughter, Kimmie, tried to make friends with her, and Hilary wouldn't have none of it."

"I see. And when did she move in?" Sam asked. She wrote down the date the woman gave her. It was a month before Elaine's accident. "Did you see her much that first month?"

"Hardly at all. I thought for a while it was just someplace she and her man friend were using because one of them was married. We get that. Then she drove up one day in this beat-up red 'vette—I noticed because she always drove this gray Duster, and I asked her if she had gotten a new car. I was just being friendly, trying to make conversation. She said the other car died."

Sam pulled out the print of the first article. The car the divers had found was a gray Duster. Excitedly, Sam asked, "Do you think I could talk to your daughter? She may have heard or seen something that would be helpful."

Dead silence.

"Ma'am?"

"Kimmie died. She was stabbed."

Sam allowed a ragged breath to escape her. "I'm so sorry." She wanted to ask the woman about her daughter's death, but she had almost lost her own daughter

118

and she did not want to intrude on the woman's grief.

"Stabbed five times," the woman volunteered. "All in the chest. Like the guy in those horror movies, the one with the glove that had knives over his fingers. I think the people who made those movies saw the newspaper articles on my Kimmie and decided to make some money from it."

"Did they catch the man?"

"No. Bastard's still out there."

The woman had mentioned articles. Sam could get the remaining information from them, if necessary. She looked at her notes. She had written the woman's name down. Norene Bloom.

"Mrs. Bloom—"

"In twenty years you would have thought they'd find something on that bastard. Twenty fucking years!"

Silence again. The soft whisper of ghostlike sobs reaching over the line.

Twenty years, Sam thought, and a flood of questions burst into her mind. The articles, she would learn the rest from them.

"I'm sorry, Mrs.. Bloom. I didn't mean to upset you."

The sobbing went on.

"I'll go. Thank you."

No reply. Sam was gently placing the phone on its cradle when Norene Bloom shouted, "No, don't go!"

"Mrs. Bloom?"

"Norene."

"I'm Sam."

An awkward silence. Finally, Norene asked, "How old are you?"

"Thirty-nine."

"My Kimmie would have been forty this year."

They spoke for another twenty minutes. Sam learned that Kimmie had been murdered six weeks after Hilary Bartan had moved from their complex. There had been no apparent motive and she had been killed in her apartment. The killer had beaten her first. No one had heard her screams. No one had seen the killer arrive or depart. There had been no fingerprints, no hairs, no physical evidence of any kind left in the wake of the killing.

"Everything from around that time is still really clear to me," Norene said. "Like it was happening today."

Sam gave Norene her number and told the woman to call if she needed to talk. Norene thanked her and they hung up.

Immediately Sam was on the line again, dialing her daughter at the university. It was close to five o'clock. They spoke briefly, Sam expertly covering the wellspring of need that had exploded within her. She could still hear the hurt and the emptiness in Norene's voice; if a few things had gone differently fourteen months ago, that could have been her.

The sound of Dani's voice helped to calm Sam. Dani was evasive, brushing off Sam's request that they get together for dinner, blaming it on her need to study. The girl was obviously lying, Sam could always tell. She probably had a hot date she didn't want her mother to know about. Sam had talked about Richard Sterling in less than professional terms, playing up her attraction to the man with hopes of getting Dani to drop her guard and talk about the new man in her life. That tack had not been successful, however, it

120

didn't take much effort for Sam to deduce who Dani would be seeing and why the girl didn't want her mother to know. She recalled the looks that passed between Dani and the washboard-stomach cop on the beach.

"Oh shit, Dani," Sam said to the phone, which had already been hung up in its cradle. The girl was nineteen, an adult, Sam could not force her to do anything. If she were to call Dani back and forbid her to date this man, it would only help to increase the rift between them. Dani had been there when Sam had made the mistake of dating a cop, she had lived through it, she knew the problems. All Sam could hope was that Dani was bright enough to learn from her mother's mistakes. "Yeah, right."

With a sigh, Sam turned her attention to the articles she had copied from the microfiche. There were witnesses to Elaine and Cort's fatal drowning. If Sam's suspicions were correct and Elaine had faked her own death, the witnesses may have been paid off; they may have even helped to stage the "accident." Sam highlighted the three names and looked each of them up in the phone book. None was listed.

She phoned the library back and was delighted to be put through to a highly cooperative reference librarian who looked up all three names in the newspaper index.

All three had died within two years of Elaine's accident. Sam half expected to learn that the killer who had slaughtered Kimmie Bloom with five powerful knife thrusts had also seen to these people, but that didn't appear to be the case. Roy Childress had been struck down by an aneurism. Tammy Lewis had taken her father's shotgun off the rack, cleaned it, loaded it, and blown her own brains out with the weapon. Rachel Levy and her boyfriend Daniel died in an automobile accident. Rachel had been driving late at night and she had swerved into an oncoming lane of traffic; her blood alcohol level was well beyond the acceptable limit.

In the morning, she would go to the Bureau of Vital Statistics and pull the death certificates for each victim, looking for something that might tie their deaths together.

Sam glanced down at the articles once again. The press was easily manipulated. She had learned that fourteen months ago, during the aftermath of her battle with the vampires.

The police and the press would never have believed the truth—that she had shattered a vampire cabal who had been intent on killing her and corrupting the soul of her daughter. So Sam had rearranged the facts to read that she had solved the murders of Mark Smith and his two houseguests, the case she had been sent by Halpern and Weiss to investigate.

According to Sam's statement, a young entrepreneur named Bill Yoshino and several accomplices—in truth, the vampires—had reinvented the infamous Hellfire Club of the eighteenth century with the goal of breaking every law known to God and man. Sam claimed that Smith had paid Yoshino to kill his wife, then, when Smith panicked and it appeared he might tell the police about Yoshino, he and his houseguests were slaughtered by the Hellfire Club. She attributed Yoshino's death to a bombing sponsored by midlevel criminals from whom he had swindled money for a "movie deal," when he actually needed the money to finance his decadent exploits.

Lies, all of it, and of course, the press loved it. They ran with it and Sam was once again getting nation-wide attention, her reputation enhanced. The police could not prove any of it, but the story worked, all the participants were dead, and the file was closed. The idea of the Hellfire Club was so popular that the owner of a string of upscale nightspots opened a club in its honor.

Halpern and Weiss paid Sam's medical expenses, the lease on her car and her house for five years in re-turn for her silence concerning the late Allen Halpern's indiscretions. A quiet parting of the ways took place after the press attention died down, allow-ing Sam to return to the private sector.

Sam frowned and debated on calling Richard. She wondered if everything she said to Dani about Richard had been strictly for the purpose of drawing her daughter out, or if a part of her was actually con-templating an affair with this man. She knew very little about him. He did not wear a wedding ring, but he may have been involved with several women in this country and in Italy, where his company was based.

Did that matter? If all they wanted to do was scratch a mutual itch, they didn't need to sign a for-mal agreement.

Sure, Sam. You believe that.

Suddenly, the phone rang. It was Dani. From the noise in the background it sounded like a pay phone. People were being paged in the background. Doctors. A sudden chill raced through Sam. She glanced at the clock and was surprised to see that almost two and a half hours had passed since she had last talked to her daughter.

"Baby, are you okay?" Sam asked.

"I'm fine. But there *is* something I need to tell you. It's about the Ghia. Or, I should say, what *used* to be the Ghia." Dani's laugh was hollow, forced.

"You're at the hospital."

"I don't have a scratch. They've checked me over. I'm fine."

"How bad was the accident?"

Dani briefly recounted what had occurred, told her how many had died, and how many had been injured. "I would just really like it if you could come get me. I need you, Mommy."

"I'm leaving now."

Dani drew in a sudden breath. It was audible over the line. "This is probably the worst time to tell you, but I met someone. He's a cop."

"Yeah," Sam said, shaking her head and smiling. "Tell me something I don't know."

"Does that mean I'm in for a lecture?"

"Yeah. But not tonight. I'll be right there, baby."

"Mom—do me a favor? Drive safe. Please. I don't know what I'd do if I lost you."

"You won't, baby," Sam said reassuringly. "Believe me, you won't."

They hung up and Sam wondered why her last words to her daughter had felt so much like a lie.

Chapter Six

A night passed since the accident. Dani came home with Sam and spent the night curled up on the couch with her mother gently stroking her hair as they watched B-movies and fell asleep. In the morning, after spending an hour at the beach together, Sam drove Dani to the nearest rental car outfit and picked out a brand new Toyota Camry for her daughter. The previous night, Sam had insisted that Dani get behind the wheel on the drive home from the hospital and all that morning, she made Dani drive. The girl seemed to be fine behind the wheel and that eased Sam's fear to some small extent as she watched her daughter drive away, heading back for campus.

Sam drove to the Bureau of Vital Statistics, pulled the death certificates of the three witnesses to Elaine and Cort's drowning, then Kimmie Bloom's. There was nothing to tie them together, except that they had each come into contact with Elaine. She made several stops that afternoon and a host of phone calls.

Around dinnertime, after Sam spoke to her daughter no less than three times to verify that she was still in one piece, and she had everything she needed, Sam called Richard's hotel, only to learn he was on a film set. She was forced to pass through a gauntlet of difficult people to acquire phone numbers and several less than cooperative production assistants before she was put through to the set, where Richard was summoned to the phone. They spoke briefly and he told her to come out to the shoot, he would have a pass for her waiting at the gate.

It was after eight when Sam pulled her Range Rover into the Hyperion Studios lot. The treatment she received in person was quite different from what she had received on the phone. Her plastic guest badge seemed to grant her the status of visiting royalty, and carry as much weight as a crown and scepter, considering the way people flickered anxious smiles in her direction and downturned their eyes when she approached. They eyed the black briefcase she carried as if it contained employment contracts.

Sam was driven across the lot on a golf cart by an A.D. personally assigned by Richard to greet her and make her welcome. Between the young man's frequent bouts of maddening silence, Sam was able to ascertain that Richard had given his people the impression that Sam would be coproducing his next epic and she should be shown the same reverence they usually reserved for him.

The studio was fairly quiet. Sam wished that she had kept her enthusiasm under control and waited for the following day; she would have enjoyed seeing the backlots in sunlight, with hundreds of people mulling about in costume. That was how she imagined it, anyway.

They passed a series of vast, white, three-story bunkers. The A.D. – a thin young man with a pleasant face who wore torn jeans, an "Empire Strikes Back" T-shirt, a baseball cap, centuries-old tennis shoes, and a three-day stubble — asked, "Are you up on old Hollywood?"

Sam shrugged noncommittally. "Depends."

"You ever hear the one about the dwarfs?"

"I'm not sure I want to," Sam said with a laugh.

"Well, just cut me off if you've heard this one."

"That sounds fair."

"Hollywood, even back in the golden age, was never what you'd expect. Disney hired seven *actual* dwarfs to promote the gala opening of *Snow White*. The problem was, the gentlemen in question got bored waiting for the premiere and they broke open the celebratory champagne several hours early, got stinking drunk, and set up a crap game on the awning above the opening. They mooned half a dozen celebrities before the cops dragged them off."

"Oh," Sam said, nodding. Maybe the story had lost something in the delivery. "Why are you telling me this?"

"I have the feeling you've never worked with Richard before."

Sam decided to maintain the persona Richard had set up for her. "No, this will be the first time."

The A.D. shook his head. "Beware the fucking dwarfs, man. They'll laugh and frolic on camera, then turn around, kick you in the kneecaps, and take a crap on your Beemer."

She nodded, deciding that all the A.D. was trying to tell her was that appearances could not be trusted. That lesson was one she had already learned all too well.

They reached Lot 24. Someone had painted a nine after the large black numbers. Sam didn't get the joke, but this time, she knew enough not to get the A.D. started. They entered through a large metal door and passed through a darkened corridor. A dead man smoking a cigar leapt out before them. Sam issued a slight cry of surprise, then forced herself to relax. It was only an actor in makeup, of course.

The dead man clamped his hand on the A.D.'s shoulder. "Miles, look at this, tell me what you think."

The A.D. sighed in exasperation as the desiccated man took a drag on the cigar and held it. Suddenly, a puff of gray smoke blew from a wound on the side of his neck. Sam noted that he kept one hand in his pocket while creating the effect.

"Do you think that's funny?" the dead man asked, a loose hanging flap of skin flopping with his overblown movements. "I don't think that's funny. Someone ought to tell these people there's a lot more to comedy than physical *shtick*."

"Really?" asked Miles the A.D. "I thought it had a certain Chaplinesque quality."

"Plebeian," the dead man spat as he stormed off.

Miles shook his head. "Theater actors. He blew an audition for the touring company of *Les Miserables* yesterday and he's been in a shitty mood ever since."

Sam was nudged ahead, past several work stations and offices, and soon came to a fairly elaborate soundstage, where a Manhattan penthouse had been recreated, complete with a matte painting of the skyline visible through the picture window.

Sam had watched enough "Behind the Scenes" features on the "E" channel during her recovery to have a decent idea about the look of a film set. The director was shooting single camera, the sound was being recorded independently on reel-to-reel machines, a complex light grid had been assembled above the set on the skeletal rafters, and a collection of production people scrambled across the set like worker bees, anxious to please the director, who looked almost identical to the A.D. who had ushered her to the set.

A large-breasted blonde half in, half out of a negligee was pitching a fit of "artistic temperament" as the director and the woman's costar, an actor Sam was inwardly ashamed to admit she recognized from a soap opera, attempted to mollify her. Richard sat on a director's chair, his name stenciled on the back. He was close to the camera and the black and white video-assist monitors. When he saw Sam, he rose, gave her a light, friendly hug, then motioned for one of his assistants to get a chair for her. Seconds later the chair appeared and they both sat down.

"Love Bites, this one's called," Richard said in a slightly bemused tone. "A 'quirky look at prom queens and cannibals.' "

Sam frowned as she watched the bouncing actress. "You'd think she'd feel a little chill or something," Sam muttered.

"Continuity!" Richard called. "What's with the one tit hanging out?"

A woman wearing round, purple-rimmed glasses checked a series of Polaroids, then embarrassedly said, "You're right. I was just gonna wait until the tiff was over."

As if on cue, the argument dissolved. The director went back to his position near the video-assist banks, close to where Richard and Sam sat. The continuity woman set down the photos and walked up to the actress, yanking her other breast out of her negligee without a word. The actress barely seemed to notice.

Sam rubbed her forehead. The day before, she had been enraged at allegations that the films Richard produced were mindless schlock. At the moment, she felt somewhat foolish.

The director pulled off his baseball cap and ran his hand though his thinning hair. Richard tapped him on the shoulder. He turned.

"Buddy? How's Wilma Jean?"

"Cardinal rule in this fucking business," the director said with a scowl that belied his youthful appearance. "Never hire ex-porn stars or former 'Charlie's Angels.' "

"I hear you."

The director shook his head and went back to his monitor. "Let's get set up and take this fucking thing from the top."

"Can we go somewhere?" Sam asked.

"Sure."

They left the soundstage as action was called. Sam looked over her shoulder and saw the blonde and her co-star kiss and begin a scene that looked like soft-core porn. The man fondled her breasts as she moaned and clawed at him. Sam turned away.

"So—this is what you do?" Sam asked as Richard led her to a small office lined with movie posters, a half-dozen Mr. Coffees, and a pair of recliners. "Sit around and make people nervous with your presence?"

"Uh-huh. Yeah. Great, isn't it?"

"If you say. Of course, the Roman emperors used to have a guy who followed behind them in processions, whispering in their ears, 'Remember, Caesar, you are but a man.' "

Richard laughed. "Point taken. But I wonder what the turnaround rate was in that position."

"I couldn't venture a guess."

"Well, in Hollywood it would be pretty high. If you think I have an ego, you should take some serious meetings at Paramount and Disney someday."

"No thanks."

"Look, we're certainly not making art here. The bottom line is, we can shoot one of these in about six days, for maybe two hundred thousand. Worldwide presales are done, it's part of a package deal. All told, it will make back a million, maybe a million-five. That's a hell of a good profit margin. It adds up to a lot, and sometimes, we get to coventure on some decent, legitimate films. That's where I'd like to be heading full time, but for now, this pays the bills."

"It's exploitation."

"I know."

"I mean, it gives people unrealistic expectations of themselves. You don't know what it's like for women. Every day you're made to feel like you've got to compete with the Wilma Jeans of the world. Men get dignified as they get on in years, women just get old."

Richard nodded.

"I just made a speech, didn't I?"

He nodded again.

"I dunno, it just pisses me off."

"I can tell." He waited, smiling pleasantly.

"And?"

He shrugged. "If I try to defend myself, I'd come off sounding like a capitalist or a Nazi. You know, if I didn't do it, someone else would. I think these movies are fun. Trashy fun, sure, but people aren't —"

Another zombie appeared in the doorway. He shambled back, falling against the door, and held up a tuna fish sandwich reverently. "Brains!" he gurgled. "Brains!"

He jammed the sandwich into his mouth, bits flying to the floor. "Num, num, num."

With a mouthful of tuna he bellowed, "More brains!" then raced after an attractive female production assistant who yelped good-naturedly and ran from him.

"I guess what I'm trying to say is that some of us are never really going to graduate from high school."

Sam threw up her hands. "Okay."

Richard went to the door and closed it. "So what do you have?"

Blinking rapidly, Sam realized that she had nearly forgotten the purpose of her visit. "I have some developments to go over with you."

"Good." He sat beside her. "Do you want some coffee before you get started?"

Eyeing the array of Mr. Coffee machines — two on a slow drip, one having just percolated — she smiled and begged off gracefully. Sleep would be difficult enough tonight. She was too wired about the case.

"Brains!" came a muffled shout from outside.

"Bad mindless zombie," someone else chided. "Bad! Bad!"

A piteous yelping, like a whipped dog. Someone shuffling off, dragging one of his legs.

Richard sighed. "Life is just an audition for some people, I'm beginning to think. Anyway, you were saying."

"I have information about Elaine Aldridge."

"You work fast. I like that."

"You're probably not going to like what I have to say."

132

"Tell me."

Sam set her black briefcase on her lap and removed the article concerning the deaths of Elaine May Aldridge and Robert Anthony Cort.

"This is crap," he said as he read it. "I just saw Cort."

"I know," Sam said, and quickly brought him up to date. She told him about "Hilary Bartan," the deaths of Kimmie Bloom and the three witnesses, and the twenty thousand dollars.

Sam said, "Of course, that was twenty years ago. By today's standards, twenty thousand would be more like—"

"I know. Twenty years ago, you could buy a comic book for one-fifth of what they cost today."

"You read comic books?"

"Sure," he said. "You should see my place in Florence. I've got one entire room devoted to comics."

"My daughter reads them, too. Or she did." Thoughts of the accident raced into Sam's head, making her feel queasy. The idea that she could have lost her child so suddenly, so brutally, had shaken Sam. Only Dani's thoughtful, gentle manner after the accident had served to calm her. Dani had called the hospital four times to check on the condition of the mother and daughter whom she had helped at the accident scene. Both were going to be fine. Sam felt incredibly proud of her daughter, and that feeling had helped to allay the terror that came crashing back whenever she thought about what had almost happened to her baby.

Think about something else, anything else, or you're going to lose it, Sam.

"Where did she get twenty thousand dollars?" Richard asked. "She didn't seem like the kind of girl who would have worked if she didn't have to."

"I don't know. I had to do some real digging, but I found out that according to the bank records, she made the deposit the year before her death and never touched it again. The transfer of funds was to Hilary Bartan—who seems to have vanished from the face of the earth—was handled as a standard inheritance deal."

Richard studied Sam's face. "What is it?"

A ragged breath escaped her. "If I'm right, if Elaine faked her death and assumed a new identity, there had to be a reason. People only go to such extremes if they're desperate, Richard. If they're terrified. So it becomes a question of what scared her."

"Or who."

Sam nodded. "Yeah. Or who."

"Have you considered the possibility that it might have been me she was running from? That maybe everything I've told you is a crock of shit and you're helping some stone-cold bastard find the woman he wronged all those years ago?"

Sam tried not to giggle. "What the hell was that? A speech from one of your movies?"

He smiled. "Yeah. Actually, it was. You do enough of these low-budget flicks and the whole world starts to sound like that."

"You need to pay your writers more. Or get better ones." She shook her head. "I wouldn't even *be* here if I thought that was a possibility. My first question was whether or not Elaine's disappearance was related to the money. There's a couple of ways to go with that.

"She could have withdrawn the money before her death. That might have looked suspicious to investigators. But who would fake their own death and leave twenty thousand dollars behind? That and the witnesses may have been enough to put the police off."

"Wouldn't they have checked into this Hilary Bartan?"

"If there had been reason to be suspicious and if the investigating officer felt there was cause, sure. Apparently, Elaine gambled that they wouldn't bother. With so many pressing cases in front of an officer, something like this isn't going to take precedence.

"That takes us back to the question of where Elaine got the money. If she stole it or embezzled it and the people she took it from wanted it back, leaving it sitting in a bank account wasn't the brightest plan. Willing it to herself in another identity would be even worse, because she would have been leading her pursuers right back to her."

"So there's no answers."

"I don't have any. Not yet. You say that Cort's alive. You've seen him."

"That's right."

"Then we know for certain that he got out of the car—if he was ever in it, that is. Elaine may have died. He may have forced her to write a will leaving her money to Hilary Bartan then killed her. And Hilary Bartan may have been pregnant at exactly the same time as Elaine. Hell, maybe Elaine never was pregnant."

"But the Bloom woman in San Diego identified Elaine from the photograph."

"Yes, she did. It has been twenty years, though. Her memory may not be as good as she thinks it is."

"Do you believe that?"

"No. I think she faked her own death and Cort helped her to get away in return for the money. Or part of it, in any case."

"Where did she go after San Diego?"

"That's going to be hard."

"What can I do to help?"

Sam thought about it. "I want you to evoke her memory for me. I want you to remember everything you can about her, her likes and dislikes, idiosyncrasies — anything you can remember, no matter how trivial. Anything that makes her stand out."

He did as she asked, painting a portrait so vivid, Sam felt an odd pang of jealousy and disappointment.

He's still in love with her, she thought. That or he's got one incredible memory.

"Sometimes a person can be traced through their habits," she explained. "Twenty years is a long time, and people change, but you know the saying."

"You make it sound like she was experienced at this kind of thing."

Sam shrugged. " 'Elaine Aldridge' may have been an assumed identity, too. She came into town, no friends, no living relatives, stayed to herself. You were the only person she was close to, and you've admitted your relationship was based mostly on sex." She paused. "Sorry, I didn't mean to be so blunt."

"That's okay." There was some reserve in his voice. A touch of defensiveness. It faded as he settled back and ran his hands through his hair.

Sam chided herself inwardly for feeling a surge of excitement at the gesture.

"What you're saying is true," Richard said. "Elaine didn't let anyone get to know her that well. Anything's possible. But what I'm getting at is — if she knew how to do all this, wouldn't she also know enough to change her habits?"

"Possibly."

"None of this helps to explain why she faked her own death."

"No, it doesn't. But if we find her, then we can just ask."

Richard frowned. "How would she have known to do all this? To change her identity? It must be hard."

"Twenty years ago?" Sam said with a laugh. "Hell, then it was even easier than it is *now*."

"Tell me."

"Why? Are you thinking of skipping out on me?"

"No. I'm just trying to work something out."

"All right. You go to the library, go through the old newspapers. Obituaries. Find someone who was born roughly the same date as yourself, someone who died very young. You don't want someone who left a lot of records, or someone with family still living in the area."

"Shit," he said. "The last couple of weeks before I broke up with Elaine, she was practically living in the library. She was planning this."

"You want me to go on?"

"Yeah. I have this image in my head of who and what Elaine was, and it looks like I've been doing nothing but kidding myself."

Sam was not oblivious to the pain in his voice. He evidently had feelings for the woman, even now. Perhaps he had entertained a fantasy of building a new life with her and their daughter. The thought made Sam angry. She suddenly felt used, and she wanted to hurt him.

What the hell are you thinking, Sam?

She didn't have a clue. These feelings were thoroughly unprofessional and she loathed herself for having them. She forced her anger down. He *was* using her.

He had hired her to do a job, not to fall in love.

Slow down. That's not what's happening here.

Maybe not. But she felt something for him. If these feelings continued, she would have to reevaluate her acceptance of this case.

"So," Sam went on, trying to hide the nervous edge in her voice, "once you have a name, you go to the Bureau of Vital Statistics and get that person's birth certificate."

"You can do that?"

"Sure, there's nothing to it. Anyone can get anyone else's birth certificate. I could get yours, you could get mine."

"Then what?"

"Well, now you have a name. So you have to start building a life. You can't get a job without a Social Security number, or credit cards, or much of anything else. So you have to get that."

"And you just walk into Social Security and ask for a card."

"No, it's a little more difficult. First thing you need is some kind of ID. So what you do is, you get a place to live. She had money, that shouldn't have been a problem for her. Remember, Norene Bloom said that Hilary Bartan paid cash for everything. She would have to get her phone, electricity, utilities, all hooked up. She would use the bills from those to establish residence, which is what she would show to the library to get a library card."

"What would she have needed a library card for?"

"Because a library card *is* ID. She would present that to Social Security and they'd give her a card."

"As easy as that."

"Well, the only problem she'd run into is explaining why she never had a Social Security number before.

That's not so hard. I could think of a dozen ways to get around that one." Her voice suddenly shifted to that of a teenaged debutante: "I've been out of the country. Daddy sent me to Oxford. Wasn't that just *dear* of him?"

Richard laughed. "You should be an actress."

"I have to be, doing this for a living. Anyway, with the Social Security number she could get bank accounts, credit cards, and a job. That's all there is to it."

Richard sighed. "I'm exhausted just thinking about it. How would she know to do all this?"

"Probably read about it in some book."

"Perfect." Richard put his hand over his mouth and valiantly attempted to stifle a yawn.

Sam grinned. "Am I keeping you up?"

"Sorry," he said sheepishly, then ran his hand over his sunburned cheeks. "Heat exhaustion, I think."

She reached over and patted his thigh. "Don't worry, you have permission to yawn."

"Thank you, but I'll try to be more gentlemanly."

Don't try too hard, she thought. Her mood darkened as she considered her next words. "I think you see where I'm leading."

"Cort knows more than he let on."

"Yeah. We're going to have to talk to him."

"Is there any way around going to him?"

"You could use your media contacts and make an open appeal to Elaine. Appear on the talk shows, give interviews."

"That would just scare her off."

"Then I don't see any other way, except running down other people who knew Elaine, people she might have worked with or been friends with. Someone who would have an idea where she would go, if things went bad."

"There wasn't anyone. That was part of the problem, she didn't really seem to have any life outside of her work and what we did together. You know, the whole cling-ing-vine syndrome."

Sam nodded. She had seen it many times before. "So what do you want to do?"

Richard sat back, thinking it over. "Let's go talk to the son of a bitch."

Chapter Seven

Dani left the campus library at ten minutes after nine in the evening. Attempting to study in her dorm room was nearly impossible, considering the noise level, and so she had sequestered herself in the library for the last five hours. Several volunteers had offered to walk her back to her dorm. On-campus rapes were up this year, and women were advised not to walk alone at night.

She had declined the escort. Her blood would protect her, should it come to that. Dani was walking down the library steps when she felt the warmth suddenly drain from her flesh. Noises drifted to her. Sirens. Sobs and wails. The confused murmur of a crowd.

The smell of blood.

Fear stabbed at her. Dani hurried across campus and saw the familiar glow of red and blue lights in the direction of her dorm. She reached the building and found three police cars and an ambulance driven onto the lawn. Uniformed officers held back a collection of students who had formed a ring around the crime scene barricades hastily erected by the officers. Dani felt the terror of the gathered students strike her like a fist, angrily pounding at the walls she had arduously built in her mind. Those walls had fallen yesterday afternoon, in the aftermath of the accident. She would not allow them to crumble now. Somehow she would stay in control.

Dani looked back to the dorm. The deadly silence the building radiated was incredibly disturbing. She had never experienced such a perfect quiet in her days at the university.

The red and blue flashing lights bathed her as she positioned herself at the periphery of the crowd, focusing beyond her need. The unmistakable scent of blood drifted to her from the building. She wetted her lips and tightly hugged her books to her breast. Voices sounded from inside. She heard the rickety sound of metal wheels.

"Coming out," a voice called.

The crowd, which had been enmeshed in whispers, fell silent as two emergency medical technicians emerged with a stretcher bearing the victim of tonight's attack. The body was zipped into a bag, it was impossible to tell if it was male or female. Several photographers burst from the crowd, greedily snapping shots of the corpse. Her mind flashed to the news footage from several years back of John Belushi's corpse being taken from his bungalow. Some things are private, you don't share them with the world. Vultures.

She felt a sudden loathing for the photographers; they reminded her of her own kind, leeching off the fear and desire of others to survive. Dani coiled her power and held it close. She was tempted to *do something* to the photographers, but she couldn't risk letting down the defensive barriers in her mind. The fear might overwhelm her and the demon might come out. Too many people were present and they had suffered enough.

"Two more inside," someone muttered.

Directly behind her, a familiar voice said, "Three this time. The worst ever."

Dani spun and was surprised to see the hardened face of Detective Sergeant Edward Pullman. That's right, she thought, he was a homicide detective.

Pullman placed his meaty hand on Dani's shoulder. Dani put her hand over his and gave it a firm squeeze. Scanning the faces in the crowd, Dani suddenly realized that she had not seen Nina. When Dani had left the dorm, her roommate had been curled up on her bed, happily listening to The Cure over her headphones as she worked on an assignment.

Dani had jostled her and asked her if she had plans for that evening. "No dress, no date, no desire," had been Nina's reply.

Dani's thoughts flashed back to a day several years earlier, when Sam had told Dani that her best friend Jami had been murdered. She and Jami had fought that day, and it had been over nothing. Jami had taken the bus home without Dani, and had begun the two-block stretch back to her house alone. That had been the last anyone had seen of the girl until her body had been found.

Dani had seen Jami again. She had seen the dead girl sitting in class, covered in blood, staring accusingly at her. It had only been after Dani had been abducted by the same killers and had killed them that Jami had left her alone.

Absently Dani realized that the corpses of Madison and Isabella had not appeared to her since the accident.

Another memory came to Dani. The day she first met Nina Chavez. The first thing that went through Dani's mind: Jami and Nina could have passed for sisters.

"Who were they?" Dani asked shakily.

"You know I can't tell you that," the fifty-four-year-old detective said. "Even if I was allowed, the bodies were pretty torn up."

"The Slasher?"

Edward frowned. "You know I can't—"

"Please."

"It looks that way."

Dani forced herself to remain calm. "The same kind of damage to the victims?"

"Yeah and the same problem with witnesses. No one heard anything, no one saw anything."

"That's impossible," Dani said. "These walls are like cardboard. You can hear people sneeze. What was the room number?"

Pullman gave her the number. It was on the same floor as the room Dani shared with Nina, two doors down. Carrie and Suzanne. But there had been a third body.

"Were they all female?" she asked.

"They were, yes."

She saw Lars and called him over. She asked if he had seen Nina. Her voice trembled as she spoke.

Lars, pale and shaky, said, "She went out with your cop friend. Brooks. The one who kept calling all the time."

"You're kidding," Dani said, wondering why Lars would bother making something like this up.

"It was the same guy who came around here looking for you last night. Said you were supposed to meet him at the Hellfire at seven, but you stood him up."

The message she had left at the club had apparently never gotten to him. She had tried to reach him twice that day and he had been out in the field both times. He must have called back when she had been at the library and reached Nina instead. She hadn't told Nina about the accident. Nina must have decided that if Dani had so little interest in Brooks that she would stand him up on their first date, he should be treated as fair game.

Dani's first thought was: *I'm going to kill that little bitch.* Then she snapped back to reality and nearly cried with relief.

Nina was alive!

She was about to thank Lars when, without warning, something brushed at the outer veil of her consciousness. Dani started and nearly dropped her books as she felt leathery wings slap against her thoughts, tiny razor-sharp claws slicing at her mind.

"Dani, are you all right?" Pullman asked.

Her heart was racing. Another of her kind was present, and it was utilizing its power.

"I have to get out of here," she said. Her tone was frantic, on the edge of hysteria.

"I gotta go, too," Lars said, and quickly vanished into the crowd.

Edward gently took Dani's arm. "Look, kid. I know this is upsetting. If you can hang on for a little while longer, I'll have someone drive you to your mother's place. You're not going to be sleeping here tonight, anyway."

"I'll be all right," Dani said, recalling their exchange from only a few minutes before. Pullman said that no one heard or saw anything. No one heard the screams, no one heard the frantic pleading for life.

That was not true. They *had* heard. Dozens, hundreds may have heard. But the killer had altered their perceptions of the event. He had made them think nothing unusual was happening when, in reality, three women were being killed. He had walked before them, entering the dorm, leaving it again, and had not allowed them to see him.

Dani broke from Pullman, assuring him that she would be fine, that he should get on with the task of finding the bastard who had done this. He nodded and went back to his men.

Something slammed into her hard, nearly rocking her from her feet. It took Dani a moment to realize that it had been a psychic barrage, not a physical one. A fellow student gingerly touched her shoulder and asked if she was all right. Dani smiled weakly and stumbled from him, to a gap in the crowd where she could see the opposite wall of spectators.

The murderer was one of her kind. Why had it never occurred to her before? It seemed so obvious now. The kills weren't enough for this one. He was present in the crowd, feeding from the devastating fear of the students, many of whom were shuddering, drenched with sweat. Dani could feel the thundering waves of fear radiating from the students. The killer was feeding from their emotions, then sending back what he didn't consume to raise their level of terror.

A sudden, terrible burst of pain exploded in Dani's mind. She had not been prepared for such a crude attack. The vampire had little finesse, but a great deal of power. As Dani attempted to recover, an image leaped into her mind:

The EMTs stop suddenly, and one of the stretcher's wheels catches on a rock. The stretcher overturns. They load the body back on, then unzip the bag to check the corpse.

It has Dani's face.

Dani forced the intruder away. Her vision returned, unclouded by hallucinations. She looked to the crowd once again, wondering which innocent-looking face housed the murderer. Most vampires were young when they were turned. Her prey could have been the anorexic computer hacker in the flannel shirt with the Metallica T-shirt or the perfectly coifed young man with the deep-set look of grief. The killer could have been anyone.

Suddenly her gaze fell upon a particular absence in the crowd, a point in which her vision would not properly focus. Dani felt as if she were staring at the blurred spot on a photograph. A figure was there, but she could tell nothing about it except that it was turned in her direction.

You've got to do something now, she thought. Hurry!

Dani reached out with her power, a bright, silver thread which traversed the distance separating her from the killer. She had been counting on the killer assuming she was weak and inexperienced. With any luck at all, it would let her into its mind, never guessing her ability until it was too late.

The vampire panicked and severed the thread before it reached him. Dani was surprised. The creature had reacted instinctively, swatting away her intrusion rather than allowing her access so that he could try to take control of her. Perhaps it had overfed and it was sluggish, unprepared to properly defend itself.

Most importantly, the vampire was afraid of her. It

had killed three people and had stayed behind to consume the pain, grief, and fear of the students, and it was afraid of *her!*

Could it sense that she had killed her own kind before? Had it branded her *Wildling?*

The thought filled her with rage. *So you're hungry, are you? You want fear? I'll give you fear, you greedy bastard. I'll give you so much you won't be able to tell mine from yours!*

Dani gathered her power and thought of a lesson Nina had shared from her acting classes, explaining the process of *sense memory:* Recall in vivid detail a traumatic incident in your life. Bring it all back, the smells, the tastes, the emotions. But don't give yourself over completely, not until you need it. Then become the moment. Let it wash over you. Feel all of it again, experience all of it as if it were happening to you that very moment, and react accordingly.

Dani chose her memory, then released it with her attack.

Dani raised the flamethrower. A torrent of flames snaked across the distance separating her from Isabella, engulfing the vampire. Isabella writhed, screaming in agony. She fell to the base of the stairs, clutching at herself, moaning in pain and despair. The flames wrapped around her without mercy.

From the crowd came a scream and a figure detached itself, stumbling away from the others. Miraculously, it had maintained its shielding, keeping Dani from seeing its true appearance. It ran, and several people turned to watch it. They regarded the figure strangely, as they were unable to gain a proper view of the retreating figure. Obviously, it was one of their own, overcome with grief. Others had departed in similar ways.

Dani circled around the crowd, the distant thunder of

the vampire's heart clamoring in her mind for attention. The creature had a few seconds' head start, but she would not lose its trail.

The figure darted through a walkway between two buildings. Dani followed, slow and relentless, giving the police and the other students no reason to become suspicious. There was nothing they could do anyway. She had no way of proving what she knew in her heart, that the blurred figure ahead was the murderer. The officers were armed. The vampire could have used its powers to force the officers to open fire on the crowd, on each other, and on Dani. She could still remember the mind-numbing pain and the liquid fire spreading through her body when she had been shot fourteen months earlier. Then she had survived, but now it would be different.

Dani came to the end of the alley and turned, dumping her books. The murderer was two hundred yards away, running hard. She hesitated.

Do you have any idea what you're doing, Dani? This thing has killed at least nine people. Maybe it's only sparing you because of your blood, it doesn't want to fight one of its own. If you push it, you might be number ten.

Dani ignored the voice of reason. This is what she needed, what she *craved*. She hurled herself into a dead run and was completely unprepared as a shape emerged from the shadows to her left, the rear entrance to another dorm building. Dani brought one hand up before her as she was struck in the face. She recoiled from the blow, her teeth clacking together, a silver tongue of fire reaching up into her brain. Tumbling to the ground in a heap, Dani forced her mind to move beyond the pain she felt. She registered the sound of footsteps retreating, heavy breathing, and felt the creature's fear. It wasn't just afraid of Dani, it was *terrified*.

Pulling herself into a sitting position, Dani realized what had occurred. Her prey had taken control of its own panic long enough to set a trap for Dani. It had caused Dani to see a mirage — the vampire fleeing in the distance — while it waited close by, in the shadows. Misdirection, the magician's favorite tool. Simple, but effective.

She wondered why it refrained from killing her when it had the chance. Perhaps because it didn't want to be branded a Wildling.

In her mind, she heard the demon. *A Wildling? You mean like* you, *dear heart? No, it wouldn't want to be that, because we know what happens to Wildlings, don't we? The Parliament comes for them. It comes and takes care of them.*

Choose your sides, Dani. Do it. If you want to be true to your own, then let it go!

Dani dragged herself to uncertain feet and ran after the vampire, wondering why it had not taken to the air. It could have escaped from her that way. She followed the creature to the outskirts of the university, beyond the lecture halls, through several narrow alleys and across a deserted field.

In the distance, she saw the violently churning waters of the deceptively named Tower Brook. Crossing the waters was the old stone bridge she had driven over countless times in the past. The bridge was one hundred yards in length, rising up slightly in the middle, where the drop to the waters below was one hundred feet. Once there had been a covered station in the middle of the bridge, but it had been declared a hazard and torn down, despite protests from preservation groups.

Dani was fifty feet behind the vampire when it stepped onto the bridge. Her lungs ached and her head throbbed. She made it to the bridge and collapsed, clutching at her stomach as she convulsed and a series of dry heaves passed through her.

Dani cursed herself. She had failed. Her human limitations had finally stopped her.

Incredibly, the vampire stopped and turned. Dani saw it as an amorphous blob, an ambulatory Rorschach test. She lashed out at the vampire with a single, powerful psychic blow, sending the monster into the dank basement where Dani had found herself several years ago, the prisoner of the two serial rapists and murderers who'd killed Jami. To Dani's eyes, the vampire's shape shrank down to a vague silhouette of a man, a shadow with arms, legs, and a head. The figure fell to its knees, clutching its head.

With a hoarse, defiant whisper, Dani picked herself up and launched herself at her enemy. The vampire had risen to its feet when Dani plowed into it, her hands wrapping around its dark neck. They fell back, the vampire's head striking the hard, cold surface of the bridge with a crack. Dani was carried forward by her momentum. She lost her hold on the vampire and rolled to a stop. Gasping, she turned and prepared herself for the vampire's attack.

The figure did not move, but it was not dead, Dani knew. The camouflaging technique it had utilized was still in effect. That would have faded if it had passed on.

The creature's head moved slightly, its body trembling as it tried to move. It turned over, falling flat on its stomach, and raised its head. Though Dani could not see its expression, the tilt of its head, the lean of its body

151

seemed to say, "Fine, you've got me. Now what do you intend to *do* with me?"

Dani suddenly realized that she had not thought this through. She was more than human, that much could not be argued. But she was less than this creature. She could beat it into the ground a thousand times, and it would eternally rise. She could shoot it through the heart or the head and it would make a joke and come after her. Dani had been certain that no human would stand a chance against her, but what chance did she have against a full vampire?

The creature was getting to its knees. Dani kicked out, slamming the heel of her boot into the side of its head. Pain shot through her leg on impact and the creature was rocked, but it did not fall. Dani slid behind the monster, cupping her hands together, and brought her fists down on the back of the creature's neck. It shuddered with the blow and dropped to its hands and knees.

Christ, what am I doing? Dani thought. I'm going to have to kill this thing to make it stop. Either keep it here until sunrise, so it'll burn, or go into its head and do to it what I did to Isabella — and even that didn't kill her, it just freed the beast in her blood.

Dani hesitated long enough for the vampire to reach back and take hold of her leg just above the ankle. It yanked hard and Dani fell flat, the nerves in her back exploding in protest and pain. She tried to free herself, but the vampire held her tight. It came around and Dani kicked at its face with her free leg. The vampire darted back and caught her other ankle. Rising suddenly, the vampire lifted Dani into the air by her ankles. Her hair cascaded down to cover her face and her hands scraped the ground.

She suddenly recalled rumors around school of how the first victims had been found, hung upside down, naked, gutted and skinned like meat at a butcher shop. That was how he was holding her. She tried to fight, her fists striking back at the dark shape of the vampire, but the strength of her blows was lessened by her position. The vampire approached the edge of the bridge, where a four-foot rail waited. Dani realized what the creature meant to do and she clawed at its legs, hoping to find a decent hold, but it shook her free, slamming her head into the metal rail. Brilliant white splinters of pain were driven into her skull. Before she could react, the vampire swung her over the rail and held her dangling over the side.

Jesus, I'm screwed.

The hands on Dani's ankles withdrew. She screamed as she fell, her hands groping blindly for the railing. Her right hand connected with the cold, rusty metal and closed over the rectangular bar. Her body tumbled over and she felt a sharp tug in her shoulder, followed by searing pain running down her arm. She swung forward, dangling by her fragile handhold, and thanked God that her fall had been stopped. Risking a look down, she saw the inky darkness of the waters spoiled by sparkling highlights from the moon; it made the waves look like razor blades, ready to cut her to pieces if she fell. But that was deceptive, she knew. From this height, the water would be hard as glass.

Dani reached out and grabbed hold of another bar with her free hand, then pulled herself up, her heart thundering. Every few seconds, she tightened with fear, expecting to see the vampire standing before her, waiting to shove her off, or drag her back and slash her throat. But the monster was not waiting for her above.

Dani hauled herself over the railing and collapsed on the bridge. Her legs were weak and unsteady as she tried to rise. She looked up and saw the dark figure standing on the other side of the bridge, staring at her. Suddenly it opened its hands and ran in her direction.

"Don't!" Dani screamed.

She heard the car approaching. Her shadow lengthened suddenly, as the glare of headlights stole across the bridge. Dani turned to see a dark four-door sedan racing toward her. There was no time to get out of the way. The headlights were blinding.

Dani grunted as the vampire tackled her, pinning her arms to her sides as they were both dragged over the railing, narrowly avoiding the oncoming car.

Dani's heart nearly stopped as she fell with the vampire to the freezing waters. She felt a rush of cold air upon her flesh and sensed how close they were to impacting with the surface, which now resembled shiny black marble.

Fly, you son of a bitch, she screamed in her head, but her lungs were filled with the sudden intake of breath and she could not make a sound as she continued to plunge.

A single image flashed into her mind instants before they hit the waters. Her mother getting the call to come down and identify Dani's body. *Mom, I'm sorry—*

They struck and Dani felt as if they had landed on concrete. At the last moment, the vampire had twisted, and had absorbed much of the blow himself. The waters churned around them, a white explosion of foam surrounding their bodies. Dani had the wind knocked out of her, and struggled for breath as she separated from the vampire and sank into the waters. The monster, still cloaked — therefore still alive — also plummeted into the murky waters and disappeared from view.

Dani had a momentary burst of panic as she struggled to regain use of her limbs. She was shaken by the impact, and every nerve in her body screamed out with pain, but she had not been incapacitated. Her arms and legs responded to her commands, and she was a dozen feet below the water before she transformed her legs into pistons and clawed her way back to the surface. She broke through and gulped wildly at the thin night air.

A terrible image came to her. The vampire hovering a few feet above her head, grinning as it finally revealed itself, then dropped down to sink her head below the surface and drown her. She looked up and it was not there. Surveying the waters, she saw no evidence that it had ever been there at all.

Dani considered searching for the monster under the currents, then recalled the power Yoshino and Isabella had displayed, the ability to transform their physiology and hide in shallow graves beneath the waters. If the monster was down there, it wouldn't come up until nightfall tomorrow, and by then, Dani could be ready for it.

She was about to start swimming for shore when something grabbed at her legs from below. She tried to fight, but it was too strong. With an anguished, frightened cry, Danielle Walthers was yanked beneath the surface. Bubbles rose in a burst and the waters churned violently for a time.

Then they were still.

Chapter Eight

Sam drove Richard to the address she had acquired for Robert Cort by virtue of forty minutes' worth of phone calls made earlier. She had targeted complexes known for cheap efficiencies and found him residing in The Sullivan—once known for the aspiring starlets who stayed there in the forties and fifties, many of whom went on to become major stars. The place had gone through a major decline in the sixties and seventies, but was saved from collapse by yuppie investors, who refurbished the complex in the eighties, giving it an exaggerated "old Hollywood" feel.

The Sullivan consisted of three two-story buildings which enclosed a center parking lot. The recession had killed the dreams of the investors, and now the apartments were headed toward a new and darker future as prostitutes and crack dealers had already begun to take up residence. Someone had smashed the heads from the ceramic pink flamingos lining the walk up to the Day-Glo office. Graffiti had been sprayed on all the walls, and a mural of the Rodney King beating had been painted on the side of the closest building.

Sam and Richard went to the apartment Cort had been renting. The place was dark, no one came to the door. The blinds were drawn.

"What do you think?" Richard asked.

Sam responded in a hushed voice. "He could be in there. I doubt it, though. You already gave him the money he wanted. Who in the hell would stay in a place like this after they picked up one hundred thousand cash?"

"You think he's gone."

"Yeah, but I'd still really love to get a look around at the place."

They turned from the door and were halfway down the stairs when an attractive black woman wearing casual clothes came running after them. "Hey!"

Sam and Richard turned. The woman held out a key. "You the brother?"

"Excuse me?" Richard said.

"Robert Cort. I live next door to him. He told me he was heading out of town for a while, but his brother might be stopping in. I was supposed to give him this key. So, are you his brother?"

"Yeah," Richard said automatically.

"Okay then," the woman said, tossing the key to Richard before she turned and walked away. Sam and Richard stared at each other with matching incredulous stares. They marched back upstairs and stopped before Cort's door.

"I'm going in first. I want you to wait here." She fished her car keys out of her purse and handed them to Richard. "If I'm not back at the door in sixty seconds, you run like hell, get the car, and use the cell phone to call 911."

"But—"

"Don't question me, just do it."

Richard nodded. Sam went ahead, keeping one hand in her purse. She unlocked the door with her left hand, pressing her body against the concrete frame next to the door. She turned the knob, then shoved the door open with her foot, keeping her body safely hidden behind the wall. A few seconds passed and she took a quick look inside the apartment, then slipped inside, easing the door shut behind herself.

Less than a minute later, the lights went on inside the apartment and Sam appeared in the doorway, motioning for Richard to come inside. The apartment was sparsely furnished and barely appeared lived in. Sam shut the door behind them.

"Okay, what's going on?" Richard asked.

"I'll explain later, after we get out of here. It doesn't matter that we were given a key, what we're doing isn't exactly legal. I want to make this in and out, real fast."

"So I should shut up and stay out of trouble."

"Right."

"I love it when you're bossy."

Sam shook her head and began her search. She was midway through the living room when the phone rang. Richard was sitting beside the phone, he reached for it without thinking.

She cried, "Don't—"

He lifted the receiver. "Hello? Hello? Anyone there?" He shook his head. "They hung up."

Sam turned from Richard, hoping that he hadn't seen the panic that had flooded through her. The moment the phone rang, she pictured a set of explosions going off. She had rigged a bomb exactly like that, once.

158

"We'd better hurry." Sam tossed the apartment as efficiently and neatly as possible, under the circumstances. She found an empty USAir ticket sleeve in the trash. No other personal items had been left behind. She quickly wiped the place down for prints and said, "Let's go."

They were outside the apartment, Sam locking it behind them, when Richard asked, "Shouldn't we give the key back to that woman? What if Cort's brother comes and—"

"Robert Cort doesn't have a brother," Sam said flatly. She stuck the key under the floor mat then motioned for Richard to follow. In moments they were back in Sam's car, heading for the highway.

"All right, now can I have some answers?" Richard asked. "And don't give me one of your, 'you must be fucking kidding' looks."

She did anyway.

"All I know about procedure in matters like this is what I've learned from the crap Seventh Heaven produces, and we both know that has nothing to do with reality."

"Point taken." They came to a light. Sam asked if Richard wanted to be taken back to the studio or dropped off at his hotel.

"I thought maybe we could go somewhere and talk."

"We'll talk on the way," Sam said as she followed the signs back to the highway.

"So tell me."

"First off, never trust providence. You were expected. That woman was paid off to give us the key." She took the USAir ticket sleeve out of her jacket pocket. "Cort wanted us to find this."

"He wants us to think he's left town?"

"Uh-huh. That, or he really has." She grabbed her cell phone and punched up Alex Wren's number on the speed dial. There had been a handful of people she had come to know during her brief employment at Halpern and Weiss, most notably the company's resident computer genius Alex Wren. After helping Sam fourteen months ago, Alex had come up with the idea of establishing a lucrative side business. Today, his service was on call to help her and other investigators break into the databases of literally hundreds of businesses and dozens of government branches.

After exchanging pleasantries, she asked Alex to find out if Robert Cort had taken any flights in the last month, or if he was booked for any upcoming trips. She then gave him the name and address of the woman next door to Cort—she had taken it from the mailboxes on the way out—and asked him to access the phone company's records and get a list of all calls made from her phone in the last hour, emphasizing the long distance numbers. They signed off.

"I'm really in the dark here," Richard said.

"Is there a chance that either Cort or Elaine would want to see you dead? Any reason you could think of?"

Shocked, Richard said, "Why would you ask that?"

"Cort blackmailed you for one hundred thousand dollars. That's a lot of money, admittedly, but not so much that it would cripple you financially, not so outrageous an amount that it would send you screaming to the police."

"So he wasn't being greedy. To most people, a hundred thousand dollars is a fortune."

"I agree, but he could have gotten more from you, couldn't he?"

160

"I suppose so."

"After he got the money, what did he do? He left town."

"We don't know that," Richard said.

"Don't we? I can just about guarantee what Alex is going to find out. The woman next door made a phone call to Robert Cort, telling him we were there. That hang up you answered? That was Cort verifying her story. All he needed to hear was your voice."

"You're just guessing."

"True. But let's say that I'm right. Cort left town. That's really unusual. Blackmailers rarely give up after their first taste. They're parasites. They attach themselves to you and never let go. They bleed you for all they think they can get out of you, then try for a little more."

"What does that have to do with Cort or Elaine wanting me dead?"

"Cort rented this place under his own name, making it easy for us to find the apartment. He paid the rent in advance, took steps to make sure we would get easy access, then left this laying around for us to find. This not only tells us to look at the airlines, it's telling us which one we should be paying attention to. He's leaving a trail he *expects* us to follow. Why would he do that? He was smart enough to vanish twenty years ago, leaving no trace. I have a hard time believing this man's intelligence spontaneously dropped that many I.Q. points."

Sam watched Richard's eyes. He wasn't exactly buying it. She had to find a way to make him understand. "My daughter used to absorb movies through her pores. A chunk of my paycheck was used for paying the rent of our local video shop in Tampa, or that's how it seemed at the time.

"There was a movie I watched with her called *The Parallax View*. Warren Beatty starred in it, playing a reporter who happens on a conspiracy — that's how I remember it, anyway. The bottom line is, he goes through the entire film thinking that he's solving this incredible mystery, but the truth is, he's being set up by the killers to take the blame for an assassination. They blow his head off in the last shot."

Richard nodded. "So you're saying that this is all some kind of setup. It's even possible that Cort's story about the child I had with Elaine is a lie."

"It could be. It feels to me as if we're being led, and if that's true, there has to be a reason."

They completed the drive in silence. A block before they reached the hotel, the cell phone rang. Sam listened patiently, hung up, then told Richard she should come up to the room with him.

Sam stood with a drink in her hand which she had barely touched. Richard's hotel room was located on the twentieth floor of the hotel. It was a suite, with a separate living area and two bedrooms. The furnishings were elegant and refined. Richard sat on the couch, watching Sam. She stared out at the view of the city from behind the glass door leading out to the terrace. The glittering lights of Los Angeles were deceptively soft and inviting.

"The call was made to a hotel in New Mexico," Sam said. "Alex has the hotel Cort's registered at. Again, under his own name, making it easy for us to find him. Or, at least, the next clue. The question is, do we go there and follow the bread crumbs, or do we sit tight, say 'fuck you, Robert Cort,' and wait for him to come to us?"

"What do you suggest?"

"We wait. When do you fly back to Italy?"

"Another week."

Sam turned away from the window and joined him on the couch. She set her all but untouched drink on the coffee table and kicked her shoes off before she curled her legs beneath her. "Then we give it another week. If Cort's going to make any kind of move, he's going to do it before you leave the country."

"Why? He could do it next time I come back, or call me direct in Florence."

"He could, but I don't think he will. I think he's impatient."

"Let's say this *is* a setup of some kind. He waits twenty years and now he's impatient?"

"People are like that. It's only in the movies that they always make sense. But if you want a rationale, try this one: The longer he waits, the less viable his threat seems."

"What would you do if you were me?"

"Hire a professional bodyguard. I could get recommendations for you."

"Even if you're right, it still doesn't mean they want me dead."

"No, it doesn't. I guess I'm just reactionary. Or paranoid. On the other hand, if he wanted to keep blackmailing you, it would have been easy. He could have dropped out of sight, then nailed you again whenever and wherever he wanted to. He had the advantage and he handed it away. That says to me that he has something else in mind."

163

She neglected to mention her other theory, that Cort was still in Los Angeles, and he was using an accomplice to create an alibi for him. Cort may have anticipated that Richard would have enlisted help from the private sector, and the elaborate trail may have been laid to draw Richard's "hired help" away from his side long enough for Cort to kill him.

Pretty fucking melodramatic, Sam, she cautioned herself. Yeah, and there's no such thing as vampires, either.

"What about you?" Richard asked. "Couldn't you be my bodyguard? You carry a gun, don't you?"

"Only when I think the situation warrants it," Sam said. That wasn't entirely a lie. She didn't take her gun with her when she showered. "Besides, there's more to it than carrying a gun, and I prefer not to take those kinds of jobs."

"Why?"

Sam looked away. She had a daughter. That was her standard response. A little girl who needed her. What would happen to Dani if she were killed? That argument had been valid when Dani was a child, but she was an adult now, fully capable of looking after herself.

She could not deny the swell of excitement racing through her at the thought of accepting this job. She had told her daughter that she understood the need to live on the edge, the rush that came from risking one's life. She hadn't realized until this moment how much she missed it.

Nevertheless, there was another, deeper reason for Sam to decline the assignment: She was starting to have feelings for him, and her emotions could make her sloppy. One error in judgment and they could both be dead. "I'm sorry, Richard. It wouldn't be appropriate."

A ragged breath escaped Richard. "The whole point, as I understand it, is not to tip off Cort that we know he's got other motives. If I hire some bruiser, I'm making a public statement. He's going to get the idea. But if I have a beautiful woman with me —"

"One whom the media is already familiar with, Richard. It would be just as obvious." She hesitated and downturned her eyes. "Thank you for the compliment."

"It's true. You're magnificent."

"Stop," she said, half laughing.

"I mean it. From the first time I saw you, I was blown away."

Sam's expression became hard. "Really, stop. I don't want this. I don't want this to go where it seems to be heading."

"And where's that?"

Involuntarily, Sam's gaze trailed toward the bedroom. She cursed herself inwardly as she caught his reaction.

"Richard, I have to leave, now." She started to get up and he stopped her by gently placing his hand on her arm.

"Please stay."

"I can't."

"Of course you can. It's a long drive back."

"Oh God," she said. "You can do better than that."

"Yeah, but I don't want to bullshit you, Sam. I've had a difficult time thinking about anything except making love to you from the first moment we met."

She hadn't expected him to be so brutally frank. He pulled her into his arms and she tried to think of something to say, some reason why they shouldn't do this, but her mind was blank. Drawing her close, Richard kissed her with an urgency that left them both gasping. They kissed again and his hands went exploring, delivering a tantalizing mixture of gentle caresses and rough fumbles and grabs.

Sam had allowed Richard to ease her jacket over her shoulders. He had unbuttoned her blouse and was about to slip it from her when she suddenly pulled away from him.

"No," she breathed, scrambling away from him.

"Tell me why not."

She thought of the operations she had endured and the scars that had been left. Her back was a mass of ruined skin. At least, that's the way it looked to her when she got her courage up and looked at it in the mirror.

"Because I'm, because it's—"

Ugly.

"I can't. I'm sorry, Richard. I didn't mean for this to happen."

"Yes, you did. We both did."

Sam suddenly realized that she was buttoning her shirt incorrectly. She gave up, stuffed it inside her skirt, and hurriedly put the jacket back on.

Biting his lip, Richard exhaled deeply. "If I let you walk out that door, I'm going to stay up all night, thinking about what would have happened if you had stayed. You know that we'll both regret it."

"Yeah, and maybe not now, but soon, and for the rest of our lives. Jesus, Richard, it's not some fucking movie, all right?"

"I know that."

She slipped her shoes back on and was on her feet, racing for the door.

He got there first and asked, "Can't you talk to me? Can't you tell me what's wrong?"

She wanted to tell him, but she knew it would sound foolish, and she knew he would say all the right words, do all the right things, but she couldn't face that moment of hesitation when he actually saw what she looked like. It was possible that he would surprise her and what she was afraid of would never happen, but she was unwilling to take that chance.

All you have to do is tell him, she chided herself, for Christ's sake, he's probably seen worse than a few scars. Still . . . her hesitation — her refusal — ran deeper than her fear over his reaction to her flaws. It was the scars he wouldn't be able to see that prevented her from staying with him.

She raised one hand indicating that he should give her some distance as she moved past him and opened the door. In her most measured, professional voice she said, "I will call you in the morning."

"Sam —"

In seconds she was out the door, into the hallway, standing before the elevators. She waited.

"You have to punch the button," Richard said from his open doorway, down the hall.

Sam turned in his direction and saw only the slowly closing door. She hit the button for the elevator and forced herself not to cry. That came later, after she reached her car.

On the long drive home, Sam called Richard's hotel and asked for his room. The call was answered on the third ring.

167

"Sam?" he asked.

"Yes." Her voice was icy, detached. "Here's how we're going to do it. I'll have a delivery service pick up your files and a detailed report first thing in the morning. If you like, I'll call around and line up someone to take over the investigation."

"Sam, we've all been hurt before. Don't do this. Let me in."

"That's not advisable at this time," she said, a vague tremor creeping into her voice. Before he could respond, she cut off the line. Seconds later, the cell phone rang again, but she ignored it.

Forty-five minutes later, she arrived at her home. There were no messages from Richard on her machine, as she feared there would be. A part of her was relieved. She sat alone in the living room, her eyes quickly adjusting to the darkness. She didn't move for almost an hour, nor did she think about anything in particular.

Finally, she considered turning on the television, catching up with the day's events, but she decided against it. She had just thrown away a client. That wasn't very bright. But what choice had she left herself?

She had acted improperly. It was one thing to have these impulses. She was human. It happened. But it was something else entirely to act upon them. She had always maintained a clearly defined line that separated the personal and the professional aspects of her life.

A life? You've got a life? You went out and got a life and you didn't tell me? Shame on you.

She thought of a conversation she had endured one night at the rehab center. Another patient, a woman, had come into her room and they had talked for a very long time. At the end of the conversation, the woman said, "Yeah, but what do you do? What do you do for yourself?"

Sam hadn't understood the question. She had explained that she had a career and she was raising a daughter. There wasn't *time* for anything else.

"You can't lie there and expect me to believe that you allow yourself to be strictly defined by the roles you've chosen in life. That's what you do, not who you are."

Sam had tried to think of one thing she had done for herself over the last nineteen years, one totally selfish thing, and she had been horrified to realize that she couldn't. There was the work, and there was Dani. She didn't need anything else. She didn't want anything else.

That night, she had made the decision that she would walk again. She would have her life back, no matter what hell she had to endure to get it.

Sam looked around at the darkened, empty living room. She had made it, she realized bitterly. She had set a goal for herself and she had attained it.

Picking herself up from the couch, Sam went into the bedroom, stripped to her panties, and walked into the bathroom, turning on the harsh lights. She pulled out the medicine cabinet door, angling the mirror on the door so that she was given a view of her back.

The scars were not that bad.

Turning off the light, Sam went to her bed. She thought about phoning Richard, but it was late and he would probably be asleep by now.

Yeah, right. Y'know, Walthers, you're a master at talking yourself out of what you really want. If you want him here, all you have to do is call him. You saw the way he looked at you. You know that even if he's pissed, he'll forget it by the time he gets here, or maybe you could make *him forget.*

She hugged her body, wondering what it would be like to share it with someone, even to share her life with someone.

Pick up the phone, make the call.

No, she thought. But soon, maybe. "And for the rest of our lives," she murmured.

A comforting warmth spread through her as she fell into a deep, dreamless sleep.

Chapter Nine

It happened as it might in a dream, or an elegantly crafted movie. Sam had been woken from her sleep by a pounding at the front door of her leased Beverly Hills home. Sunlight had been streaming into her bedroom. Her sheets and blankets were bunched into a heap at the foot of her bed. The terrible heat she had felt between her legs when she had sat on the couch with Richard the previous night had returned the moment she was awake. She didn't have to touch her panties to know they were soaked.

A part of her knew who was at the door. Another time and she might have pictured the police coming to tell her that her daughter had been in an accident, or worse, but such thoughts did not occur to her as she flung herself out of bed and hurried into the bathroom. A white terry cloth robe was thrown over the shower. She retrieved it deftly, caught a glimpse of herself in the mirror—hair everywhere, but looking pretty damn good anyway—and slipped it on, pulling the sash tight.

The knocking grew more furious. Sam left the bedroom, tore through the hallway, and was nearly out of breath as she crossed the living room and tore open the front door without even pausing to find out who was there.

Richard stood in the doorway, as she knew he would. He wore blue jeans, boots, and a black fishnet T-shirt which revealed his broad sculptured chest and powerful arms. The look in his eyes frightened and excited her, and she took a step back. He took that as an invitation and walked in purposefully, closing the door behind him.

Before Sam could say anything, Richard pulled her into his arms and covered her mouth with his own. Sam felt her body melt with his touch. He drew back and Sam allowed a slight gasp of protest to escape her. Her hands gently traced the contours of his face, and she was suddenly aware that with a single kiss, he had forced her to relinquish a promise, the terms of which were revealed in her eyes.

You can do anything to me. Anything you want.

She could not remember the last time she had been able to completely surrender herself. Greedily, she threw herself into his arms again, her lips parting, her tongue snaking into Richard's mouth. His hands traced the sides of her face, the pale, elegant stretch of her long neck, then fanned over her large breasts, covering them and caressing them through the white cloth.

"Hard," she whispered as she placed one of her hands over his and bore down on it, "harder."

He did not deny her. Fondling her roughly, Richard allowed his left hand to fasten on the sash at Sam's waist and pull it loose with a hard tug. The robe fell open and Richard repositioned his hands, closing over both her breasts, lifting them, kneading them, her painfully hard nipples pushing against his palms. He grabbed both nipples suddenly, twisting each of them so savagely that Sam threw her head back, screaming at the sudden burst of pain, exposing her throat, which he licked and bit lightly. Richard sank to one knee and pressed her breasts together. They were large enough that her nipples almost touched. His mouth went from one to the other, and he sucked at her sensitive flesh, attempting to force as much of one breast into his mouth, then he repeated the gesture with the other breast. Sam moaned and sighed with pleasure.

She felt as if she were sinking down into a deep, endless realm of pleasure when Richard rose from her breasts and kissed her hard on the lips, the gesture yet another promise, that what she had felt until now was nothing in comparison to what he would do to her soon. Her hands had traced the muscles of his chest, and were sliding down to his crotch when he spun her around and pulled the robe from her. She did not resist. He clutched at her from behind, alternately bringing startling peaks of pleasure and pain to her breasts as he kissed her neck and allowed her to twist slightly and return his kiss with her mouth.

She ground her ass into his crotch. "No fair," she hissed, "you're wearing clothes."

He smiled, drew closer, and brought her trembling hand to his lips. Before she could speak, he parted his lips and allowed one of her fingers to slide into his mouth. Sam gasped as he sucked hard on her finger, his tongue darting back and forth on the underside as he took it to its full length, his full lips closing over it with consummate skill as he eased it in and out, then allowed it to fall free as he took two other fingers and went to work on them. Her nipples became painfully erect and she felt a heat between her legs that nearly burned her.

Without warning, he pushed her hand down, sliding it over the front of her panties. "What are you—"

She cried out and he eased his fingers into the spaces between her own and forcefully manipulated the folds of her sex.

"Oh god, oh god, I'm so fucking wet," she moaned. *"Please."*

"What? Tell me what you want and I'll do it."

She shuddered and writhed as his fingers went to the exact perfect place, her thumb moving in circular motions over her clitoris. "Inside. Put them inside."

With her free hand she tugged her panties down and stepped out of them gingerly. Suddenly his fingers were inside her. She screamed again, buckling against him, and found that she could not believe the sensations building inside her. An orgasm welled in her.

"Want to see you," she murmured. "Want you to see."

He turned her roughly to the side, where the panels beside the window were covered in a long, thin mirror. She saw herself, naked, shuddering, Richard behind her, his face all but hidden by her wild dark hair.

"Watch yourself. Watch as it happens. I'll watch, too."

"No, I'm—"

"You're the most beautiful woman I've ever seen," he said breathily. "See yourself the way I see you."

She looked at her image in the mirror and her last

vestiges of self-restraint faded away. She watched her swaying, well-shaped breasts, stared in fascination at Richard's fingers delving inside her, and felt a good measure of appreciation for the years of hard labor she had put in to keep her body slender and well toned. Her muscles writhed, her body surged, and her gaze drifted to the reflection of her eyes and her open, gasping mouth.

"Beautiful," Richard said. "So very beautiful."

Her body took her over the brink. She clutched and screamed as the orgasm ripped through her, and somehow she focused her attention on the mirror, on the amazing, sexual creature panting and crying out, writhing and shuddering, trembling and releasing herself to abandon, giving herself fully, and felt for a moment that she was making love to this beautiful woman. A surge of triumph flooded through her as she watched this amazingly sensual woman shudder and come.

"Slow, slow down, stop," she said, her hands over Richard's, but he did not slow, he continued to inflict his meticulously choreographed performance, mixing pleasure and pain, and sending Sam into another screaming climax, which she watched with even greater appreciation. This time he allowed her to coast downward from her pleasure, kissing and touching her, murmuring into her ear that she was beautiful, the most beautiful woman he had ever known.

Turning, she shoved him back against the door, then pounced on him, ripping at his shirt, her hands clawing at his pants. "I want to taste you," she snarled. "Take these fucking things *off*."

Richard unbuckled his belt and was reaching for the

top button of his jeans when Sam batted his hands out of the way, dropped down before him, and tore them open, yanking hard at the zipper and pulling his pants down to midthigh. His sex sprung out at her. He hadn't worn underwear.

"Pretty fucking sure of yourself, huh?" Sam asked as she licked both of her hands then took him, running one slick hand then the other over his impressive, but not daunting length.

"You said—"

"Yeah?" she hissed, cupping one hand over him and working his sex furiously. He groaned and allowed his head to fall back against the door. "Something you want?"

"Said you wanted to"—he moaned "—wanted to taste—"

"Tell me what you want and I'll do it," Sam whispered, enjoying the momentary reversal.

"Taste me," he urged.

"Uh-huh," she said, opening her mouth and letting him slide between her lips. She ran her tongue over his silky, pulsing length, then pulled away, letting him ease from her mouth. "Tastes delicious. Too bad you only want me to taste, not to have."

"Have it," he said.

She licked the shaft, up one side, down the other, her hand never leaving him. "You sure?"

Grabbing her by the hair, he pulled her forward. Sam opened her mouth and allowed him to slide back in.

He groaned with pleasure. Sam placed her hands on the hard cheeks of his buttocks and worked her tongue over his shaft, her lips puckering in rapid motions, as she moved forward until he was entirely in her mouth, her lips pressing up against his pubic bone. Next she slowly withdrew, licking the length of him with side-to-side motions, while using her hands to caress him.

Suddenly he grabbed her. Holding her head in place, he thrust forward in a quick demanding rhythm of his own. "Fuck your face," he said. "Fuck your beautiful face."

Sam worked with her tongue and lips as he lived up to his promise. She had forgotten how much she loved this. But there was something she wanted more. Something she needed, right now.

She pulled away from him, her hand on his length. "I want you," she said, her eyes wild. "I want you in me."

"Then we can both have what we want."

Moving forward, she took him into her mouth once more, then withdrew, rising to her feet, and took a few unsteady steps backward. Leaning against the door, he pulled his shirt off, then his boots and pants.

"Do you have—" she began.

"Here," he said, digging into the rear pocket of his discarded jeans, withdrawing a package. Sam put her hands out as if she were a pitcher asking for the ball, and Richard tossed the small, silver package to her. She made a show of tearing it open with her teeth. The condom flew halfway across the room and she bit her lip in embarrassment, then raced him for it. It had fallen beside the couch. Sam picked it up, stroked Richard's length, then sat on the arm of the couch and slipped it over him. Standing before her, he leaned down and kissed her, then hooked his hands under her thighs.

"Wait, what are you doing?" she asked.

"Wrap your hands around my neck. Tight. Hold on."

"Are you serious?" she asked, then did as he said. He lifted her into the air and thrust forward, slipping inside her. She felt an explosion of sensations. A languorous sigh of satisfaction came from her as she sank down, then rose again. She smiled and increased the speed of her motions until she was wailing with pleasure, tossing her hair from side to side. He matched her every stroke, slamming into her with a passion that quickly brought her to the brink of another orgasm.

How fucking strong *is* this man? she wondered, amazed that he was still standing and not showing any strain as their bodies crashed together. He shifted his hands, cradling her ass with one hand as he brought the other around to her clitoris and began to manipulate her with the sureness he had displayed when he caressed her earlier.

Sam closed her eyes and screamed, an orgasm tearing through her in searing waves. She looked into his eyes and saw her pleasure reflected there. His sheer animal satisfaction at making her come triggered another series of smaller orgasms within her. Her gasps and whispers gave him cues and he eased her down, his knees bending as he lowered her to the floor and disengaged from her, turning her over.

She was panting, covered in sweat, when she drew her knees up and presented her long, elegant back to him. His hands closed over her round, firm ass and he leaned down to shove his face into her sex. Before long, she was crying out again, brought upward to the brink, then eased back.

Don't tease me, she thought. When he pulled away she suddenly thought of the scars lining her back from the surgery. She wanted to turn over, hide them, but he held her firmly and traced the line of each scar with his tongue, murmuring that it was her scars that made her complete beauty.

"Perfezione e solo perfezione se esso cicatrizzarsi," he breathed into her ear as he rose up over her body and eased his sex within her hot, wet depths. "Can you feel what you do to me?"

"Yes," she said, delighting in the slow, languorous motions as he plunged fully within her, then drew away to the brink. He reached around and clutched her swaying breasts, his motions becoming faster, more urgent, until he was scissoring in and out of her, causing her to scream again.

The doors to the home entertainment center were open, and in the television screen, she was able to see a dark, murky reflection of their bodies as she surrendered fully to the act, as making love to this man consumed her entire consciousness. He pulled her down, until they were laying side by side, but did not allow himself to separate from her. She raised one leg, hooking it back onto the cushions of the couch, and was able to see him moving within her. His face was once again hidden behind hers, a flash of blond hair, a hint of his burning eyes as he watched the reflection, too.

"Do you see what you are?" he asked.

She watched herself. She stared into the reflection of her face, once again saw the pleasure she received, and thought, an animal. Fucking. A beautiful animal, muscles covered in sweat. And somehow she was more than that. She was a god.

Turning away from her reflection, Sam twisted her upper body, felt a tinge of pain in her back and ignored it, then looked into his face as she said, "I'm yours."

With those words, Richard bucked wildly, releasing himself within her depths. She watched him come, his eyes fluttering, straining desperately to stay open, matching her piercing gaze. His frantic movements provoked another orgasm with her, and she cried out, then kissed him as the sensations became her world.

They eased down together, arms and legs entwined, and Sam attempted to catch her breath. Richard was still buried within her, and would occasionally push forward or back.

Sam's brow furrowed in amazement. She laughed and said, "You're still hard."

He nodded and pulled away from her. She spun around, taking his sex in her hands, removing the latex, and dropping it to the floor. She caressed and stroked him, and with a catlike grin she nodded toward the hallway. "Bedroom this time. I've got some more of those inside."

He glanced at the condom. "Pretty sure of yourself, weren't you?"

"Hopeful."

Sweeping her into his arms, he kissed her hard, then pulled away and said, "Me too."

They rose and walked hand in hand to the bedroom.

* * *

180

Sam rolled over, her every muscle sore and straining. Her eyes fluttered open and she smiled, feeling the heat of the midday sun upon her sweat-soaked flesh. After their third and final tumultuous bout of lovemaking, Richard and Sam had fallen into a deep slumber.

She had woken once, sometime earlier. Her first impulse had been to see if Richard had left, but he had lain beside her, on his back, his face relaxed in sleep, a slight smile playing across his features. The sheets had come down to their waists, and in the sunlight, she was able to view the light yellow curls of hair on his chest and his impressive build. He had the well-honed body of an athlete and the wicked, satisfied smile of a man lost in the dream of a lifetime. She wondered if it was about her.

She had risen from the bed, grateful that Richard was asleep. She hadn't wanted him to see her like this. Her hair was a mess, her breath was terrible, and she needed a shower. Sneaking away into the bathroom, she closed the door behind her and hoped that the shower would not wake him. He seemed so at peace, the sunlight washing over his body.

When she was through making herself perfect, or as close to perfect as she was going to get, she climbed back into bed with him and closed her eyes. Somehow, she felt so relaxed in his presence that she had fallen asleep again.

Awakened for the second time, she twisted, wanting to snuggle into his arms, and found that she was alone in bed. She sat up quickly, hoping he was in the bathroom. The door to the bathroom was open, the light was off.

"Richard?" she called, certain that her momentary anxiety would prove foundless. He was probably in the living room, fixing something for them to eat. She was ravenous. He probably was, too.

Sam rose from the bed, naked, and went through the hallway, to the living room, and looked outside before she even bothered checking the kitchen. The only car parked outside was her own.

"Son of a bitch," she muttered, falling against the door and crossing her arms over her heavy breasts. Though she knew she would find nothing at all, a part of her insisted that she check the entire house, hoping that he had left a note, at least.

Sam, you were so beautiful in the sunlight I couldn't bare to wake you. I'll be back soon. All my love, Richard.

Sure, she thought. Keep dreaming, sweetheart. You were just fucked raw in more ways than one.

There was, of course, no note. Her heart leapt into her mouth as she saw the message light blinking on the answering machine. Perhaps he had recorded a message. She played it back and found yet another telephone solicitation pitch.

"Son of a bitch," she said again as she retrieved her terry cloth robe from the floor beside the door, snatching up her panties, too. *"Son of a bitch!"*

Sam went to the living room, dropped into the couch, and curled herself up in a fetal position. She noticed that even the used condom they had left laying on the floor had been removed.

First thing you do is get rid of the evidence, she thought.

"Oh, goddamm it," she whispered, feeling tears well

up in her eyes. "I trusted you, goddamm it. I really did."

Realizing that she was bunching the panties in her fist, Sam frowned and hurled them across the room. "God, I'm so fucking stupid."

This time, the tears would not be denied. Sam cried into the pillows wedged tight into the corners of the couch, cursing herself for thinking this man would be different. She was smarter than this. What in the hell had she been thinking?

Eventually, she rose from the couch, went into her bathroom, and took a second shower. She no longer wanted to smell his Old Spice on her skin. Or was it Brut? She could have sworn he had worn Brut, but her skin and her bed had smelled of Old Spice. It didn't make a goddamn difference, she knew.

In the shower, she ran the water to scalding, then leapt inside, screaming as the water pelted her flesh, burning away the tender caresses, the tiny kisses, the reminders of her foolishness. After the shower she dressed in a pair of khaki shorts and one of her old Tampa Police sweatshirts. She wanted to call her friend Carlotta, in Tampa, but there it was three hours later. She would be at work.

What the hell time was it, anyway?

She checked and was surprised to see that it was only ten in the morning. It had seemed as if she and Richard had made love for countless hours. Apparently, that had not been the case.

"Son of a bitch," she said again, then went outside to retrieve the newspaper. She brought it inside and fixed herself an instant egg-sausage and cheese muffin in the microwave, along with a tall glass of Gatorade.

She had been looking forward to Richard's horrified expression when he learned about her breakfast habits. She had been looking forward to taking a drive with him, to going to the beach with him, or bowling, or shopping, or any of the things couples do. That had been ridiculous. There had been no promises made. All they had done was acknowledge that they had a mutual itch and scratching it had been great fun.

"SON OF A BITCH!" Sam shouted, hurling the paper across the room. It slammed into the bar, knocking over an unused decanter, which struck the carpeted floor and did not break. She rarely drank. On the other hand, she just might call up Edward Pullman later today and ask him if he was willing to see her drink him under the table that night. Nora would not approve, but she would come along to drive.

Reaching down to retrieve the newspaper, Sam caught part of the front page and felt her heart shrivel. With trembling hands, she tore the newspaper free of its see-through plastic sleeve and unfolded the front page.

The headline read: STUDENTS FOUND MURDERED AT LOCAL COLLEGE.

Sam stared at the photograph in mute fascination. A group of students watching as EMTs hauled a body out on a stretcher. The dorm building looked identical to the one in which Dani lived. The number above the door was the same. Sam forced down her panic and carefully read the article. The victims' names were being withheld, pending notification of the parents.

Dani's safe, she told herself. The police would have phoned last night if it had been her. Why hadn't Dani

184

called to warn Sam about this? She should have known this article would give her mother a heart attack.

Running to the phone, she dialed Dani's number. No one picked up. She hung up and dialed again, worried that she had made a mistake, and this time let it ring fifteen times before she disconnected the line and called the main number.

The R.A. picked up, sounding weary. She identified herself as Dani's mother and the young man told her that the police had prohibited him from giving out the names of the victims.

"Just tell me if my daughter is all right," Sam commanded.

"Yeah, sure, I guess. She wasn't one of the victims." He admitted that he hadn't seen Dani since last night. On Sam's insistence, he set down the phone and went to check her room. She wasn't there.

"Look, a lot of the kids were shaken up last night. Some of them didn't want to sleep here, after what happened, and they set up cots in the gym. Your daughter's probably there."

Sam asked the R.A. to have Dani phone her the instant he saw her. "You bet."

They hung up. Sam dialed Edward's precinct house, waited on hold for two minutes, then was put through.

"No, Sam, it wasn't her," Edward said in response to her question. He gave her the names of the victims, and that calmed Sam to a degree. "I was thinking of calling you last night, but when I found out that Dani had taken off, I assumed she was with you and you wouldn't want to be bothered."

185

She explained that Dani had not called, and that she was heading for the university to find her.

"I'm tied up on this one," Pullman said, "but if you don't have any luck, call me back and I'll see what I can do. Regs say we can't do a missing person for twenty-four hours, but I have some friends who are off duty and owe me a few favors."

She thanked him and hung up. Sam frantically searched for her purse, the journey taking her in a circle that led back to the living room floor, where she looked at the newspaper photo again, hoping to spot Dani as one of the grainy bystanders.

Instead, she found her attention drawn to a particular face in the crowd, a young, blond-haired girl who looked strangely familiar. Sam went to her case file on Richard Sterling and removed the photograph he had given to her of Elaine May Aldridge at age twenty.

The photographs were identical.

Chapter Ten

In the dream, she was flying. Dani exalted in the feel of the high, thin air and the gusts of wind blowing in her face and caressing her nude form. She rose higher, pierced the clouds, and flew directly into the sun, laughing and unafraid. The heat penetrated her flesh, reaching deep into her soul, allowing her to relax and be content to exist, to take pleasure in the moment, to *become* the moment. Her body melted away and she was one with the light, the speed of her flight increasing dramatically as she sailed through the air, the clouds whipping past.

Dani was awash with ecstasy, delighting in the perfect freedom of her flight, when the dream suddenly ended and she woke to a searing pain in her chest. Her panic subsided quickly. This had also happened the night of the accident. She had twisted too sharply to one side and had been rewarded with a bolt of agony that shocked her awake. Dani reminded herself of what the emergency room doctor had told her, the only injury she had sustained was a bruise where the seat belt had grabbed her, the discomfort would go away in a few weeks.

A part of her wanted to slip back into the waiting hands of the dream, but now that she was awake, her curiosity had taken hold. She looked around the small bedroom and realized it was meant for a child. The walls had been painted with an amusing, wraparound mural: bright, colorful animated images of life beneath the waters. On one wall, a blowfish was blowing a sax, on another, a tabby cat who might have been mistaken for a fish swam low, the air it held in its fat cheeks bloating its face and helping with its disguise as it advanced. The cat was eyeing a school of fish on the next wall, who were attending a grade school class. The fourth wall was behind her and she didn't have the energy to twist around. She got the general idea.

The furniture was solid oak, intricately carved with images from Lewis Carroll and J.R.R. Tolkien. She lay in a four-poster bed. The heads of the posts had been carved into the faces of Dorothy, the cowardly lion, and their friends.

Put 'em up. Put 'em up-up-up-up. . . .

Dani smiled and eased herself to a sitting position.

She looked over the side of the bed. The carpet was woven with images of strong women riding dragons. Turning slowly and carefully to one side, she saw the bright, powder-blue light of the afternoon sun streaming through the azure silk curtains. A dollhouse sat in the corner, and there was a closet half open, shrouded with shadows and secrets, which appeared to contain clothing and toys.

Dani put her hand to her chest and felt the soft cotton of her white sweatshirt. Raising one leg, she looked at the somewhat baggy pea green slacks which must have been slipped on her when she was unconscious. Her feet were bare and the covers where bunched at the foot of the bed.

She looked at the underwater mural and felt a chill. The last thing she could recall had been water pumping into her lungs as some force dragged her beneath the churning waters of Tower Brook. The cute little fish on the wall seemed to be looking at her as they might a meal they had been denied. She turned and looked at the final wall of the mural and was amused to recognize the cast of the *Fish Police* comic book. Inspector Gill wore his trenchcoat and was raising a drink to her.

The nightstand beside the bed held a clock radio, which gave the time as 2:29. Easing herself out of bed, Dani went to the window and parted the curtains. The residential street that greeted her led her to believe that she was in a fairly well-kept suburb of Los Angeles. The reason why she was there had been parked outside the window: A dark, four-door sedan. The same vehicle that had nearly taken her life on the bridge. The driver had come back.

She knew suddenly that she was not alone in the house.

A portable CD player with headphones lay on a chair beside the door, with a small stack of CDs. Dani registered the titles. Suzanne Ciani's *Neverland,* Clannad's *Past/Present,* Gounad's *Faust,* and Guns 'n' Roses' *Use Your Illusion.* Dani frowned at the last choice.

" 'November Rain' is the only song on there I listen to."

Dani turned sharply and felt pain shoot through her chest. Gasping for breath she sat down hard on the edge of the bed. The pain eased immediately and she looked up into the face of the girl who stood in the open doorway. A California blonde. Very cute.

"Generally, I think Axl Rose sounds like a gerbil caught in a steel press, but my mom died in November a few years back and it rained a lot that month. All the time."

"I'm sorry," Dani said, examining the girl more closely. Her eyes were sky-blue, the same startling shade as Bill Yoshino's eyes had been. Her face was heart-shaped, her lips blood-red and full. She looked about Dani's age, with a button nose and perfect cheekbones. Her beautiful blond hair—cut straight across her eyebrows—fell to elegantly curl around her creamy shoulders.

Her figure was not as generous as Dani's, but she was shapely, her white button-down halter top tied off below her breasts, her blue jeans tight enough to have been painted on. Her sandals revealed toenails that had been manicured professionally. Same with her hands. Her expression was forlorn, and her eyes revealed her shame and fear.

She had been the driver, Dani guessed.

"My name's Marissa Tomley." She extended her hand.

Dani gripped the head of the cowardly lion as she used the bedpost for support and lifted herself up. She took Marissa's hand. "Danielle Walthers. Call me Dani."

"Dani," Marissa repeated, but her tone was suddenly distant. She was looking at Dani's eyes as the light struck them from the window. They practically glowed with bright yellow fire.

Painfully aware of Marissa's curiosity, Dani turned her back to the light. "Why didn't you take me to the hospital?"

The girl shook her head. "I'm not sure. I was afraid."

"Afraid of what?" Dani asked. Her grip on the lion's head tightened. Her fingers dug into the wood.

Marissa was shaking as she said, "I didn't want to go to jail. It was stupid, it was really stupid, I know. But I worked as a lifeguard for three summers and I could tell you were going to be all right. I was hoping I could bring you here, take care of you, and we could talk about what happened."

Dani thought about it. As the driver of the sedan, she may not have seen the vampire. Maybe it had looked as if her car had simply swept Dani off the bridge.

Dani released her grip on the lion's head. "Do you have a phone? I need to call my mom and let her know that I'm all right. She's probably going crazy right now."

"Sure. Out in the hall." Marissa turned her back on Dani and led her through a narrow corridor, to a table with a black dial phone.

"So, is that your room?" Dani asked.

"It was, when I was a kid."

"Really? I like the mural."

Marissa laughed. "Yeah, it was fun sleeping there as a little kid."

Dani tensed slightly, but was certain that she had not given herself away. "You must have felt safe with Inspector Gill watching over you."

"Yeah," Melissa said brightly, "I really did."

Marissa lifted the phone and was turning as Dani struck her in the solor plexus, driving her to the floor. The girl's head connected with the edge of the phone table, and she slumped into unconsciousness. Dani knew Marissa was lying about the mural. The *Fish Police* didn't even exist when Marissa had been a little girl. There was only one person who would have cause to lie to her and bring her to a safe, neutral ground: her assailant from the previous night.

Dani had made the mistake of assuming that it had been a full vampire who had committed the campus slayings, when a powerful Initiate might well have committed the same acts. Dani didn't know why Marissa hadn't killed her. Maybe she was scared to kill one of her kind. Killing their own was the worst crime any member of their race could commit. Such an act carried the risk of being branded a Wildling, then being hunted, and slaughtered. Thankfully Dani's murder of Isabella had gone unnoticed. Maybe Marissa didn't want to take the same chance.

Dani yanked the phone cord out of the wall, rolled Marissa onto her back, and was about to tie her hands behind her when an explosion of pain burst in Dani's head, sending her sprawling against the wall.

Wait, please! a voice shouted in Dani's mind.

Marissa's voice.

Dani sat with her back against the wall, chest heaving. Marissa shook her head then sluggishly moved into a sitting position across from her.

"No more," Marissa said. "Please. I saved your life twice last night. I got you out of the way of that car, then I went back and kept you from drowning when the undertow had you. We can talk about this."

"The three people you killed at the dorm aren't going to be talking about anything, Marissa."

"That wasn't me," she pleaded.

"But it was you on the bridge. You were the one in the crowd, feeding off those people."

"Yes." Her eyes were wide, desperate.

"If you didn't do it, why did you run from me?"

"Because I thought you *had!"* Marissa snarled.

Dani stared at her blankly. "Why would you have thought that I killed those students?"

"I didn't know you, Dani."

Didn't know you. The words horrified Dani.

"And you still don't know *me*," Marissa said.

"You were inside my head."

Marissa nodded. "You were drowning. The undertow had you. I went back in the water to save you. I had to make you stop fighting. The more you fought, the better hold it had on you. I had to keep you down. I was afraid you would go after me again and we'd both die. Then it occurred to me, what the hell was I doing? If you had killed those kids, I was saving you so you could do it again. I had to know if it was you or not. If you had killed them."

"What would you have done if it was me?"

"I'd have let you drown."

Dani stared into Marissa's hard, unyielding eyes. "Yeah, I think you would have."

"But you didn't kill them. Your surface memories told me that. I knew where you were at the time of the killings, so I knew it wasn't you."

"All right," Dani said. "But that wasn't all you did."

Marissa lowered her gaze. "The driver of the car who almost hit you doubled back. I guess his conscience got the better of him. I found out where he lived, brought both of you back here."

"Where is he now?"

"In one of the other bedrooms. He won't be bothering us."

"Did you kill him?" Dani asked.

"No, God! I've never killed—that's right. I've got the unfair advantage. I *know* you didn't kill those kids, but you still don't know if I'm the one who did it."

"Like I said, you know a lot more about me than that, don't you?"

Marissa nodded. "I've never—I dunno, Dani. Until last night, I had never gotten that close to someone else who could do what I can do. There was one time, I was at the mall, late, when I was, I don't know how to put it, approached. This guy scared the living hell out of me. I got away from him, I'm not sure how. But I started doing things. Experimenting. I knew I had to be ready if I met another one. I had to be able to conceal myself."

"You did," Dani admitted. "I never even sensed you, and I was turned once."

"Until last night, I wouldn't have even known what that meant. I went back inside, Dani. Into your thoughts, your memories. I couldn't help myself. I had to know, I had to understand why I can do these things. What I am. Once I started, it was like a book I couldn't stop reading. I had to know everything."

"I hope you were entertained," Dani said bitterly, angered by the intrusion.

"I know about Antonius," Marissa said eagerly. "The centurion who thought he could become immortal by drinking the blood of Christ, and his punishment. I know that Lucifer forced Antonius to rise three days later, because if God could have a son on Earth, why shouldn't the devil? I know we're the children—"

"Shut the fuck up, will you?" Dani said, placing her hands to either side of her head. "You violated me, don't you understand that?"

Marissa's enthusiasm faded instantly. "Yes. I do. I know there's no way I can make up for what I've done, but I also know you need someone like me. I know your secrets. I know everything about you, about Bill Yoshino and Isabella. What they did to you."

"Stop it."

Marissa fell silent.

"You're right," Dani said finally. "You know everything about me and I don't know anything about you. There's only one way to change that."

"You'd have to come into my mind," Marissa said.

"Uh-huh."

"We'd have to trust each other."

"And we don't."

"That's not entirely true," Marissa said. "I know everything you've been through, Dani. I know what kind of person you are. I'd trust you with my life."

"If what you're telling me is true, you know what I did yesterday. At the accident."

"I don't understand it, but I know."

"There are things I can do to you from the inside."

"You don't have to threaten me. I understand."

"I don't think you do," Dani said. "You remember Jim Henson? The man who created the Muppets?"

"Of course."

"He died of endotoxin. We have something called ecoli that live in our gut. We can't live without them.

195

But if they get loose in the bloodstream, and they die there, they produce endotoxin. Your microcirculation breaks down. You die. It's insidious, Marissa. It breaks down the endothelium of your blood vessels and your blood vessels leak out into your tissues, your blood pressure drops and you die. It causes neurological damage, too, because you have to have this blood/brain barrier and it breaks that down.

"If you fuck with me, I can make that happen inside you. Because, for all I know, this is a trap. You killed those kids, and you're hoping that I'll believe you didn't because I don't want to risk going into your head, where I'll be vulnerable. So you get off. Or, I go in, and you ambush me. Because maybe you know it's the only way to kill me."

"Jesus," Marissa said. "Sam's right. You watch too many movies."

Dani flinched. The mention of her mother's name, the casual recitation of such intimate material made her want to harm the other girl.

Marissa's features softened as she realized her mistake. "I'm sorry. Your memories are still so vivid, I almost feel like they happened to me, instead of you."

"They didn't."

"I know." Marissa ran her hands through her full, blond hair. "How about this: There are these three women in an obstetrician's office. All pregnant."

Dani's brow furrowed. "What?"

"It's a joke. Just listen. Three women. One has black hair, the other's a redhead, the last one's a blonde. The black-haired woman pats her round little stomach and says, 'I know what the sex of my baby's going to be.' The other two women look at her. 'How

196

do you know that?' 'Well, when my husband and I conceived this baby, we did it in the missionary position. So that means we're going to have a boy.' The redhead shakes her head and says, 'When we did it, I was on top. So that means we're going to have a girl.' The blonde just looks at them and says, 'Does that mean I'm going to have a *litter?*' "

Dani tried to force down a laugh, but she found it impossible. The laughter bubbled up inside her and erupted as Marissa laughed with her. They rode it out and Dani, shaking her head, returned her gaze to Marissa. "That's pretty good."

"Because I'm a blonde, people expect me to be Patti Perkodan," Marissa said. She smiled, rolled her eyes, and tossed her head from side to side. "Hi! The birds are chirping, spring's here, and I'll be watching 'Wheel of Fortune' tonight just to see what Vanna's wearing."

"Brrruhrrr," Dani said with an exaggerated shudder. "You just made all the little hairs on my body stand up."

"Then I wear black on Valentine's Day and they really start noticing my attitude and they're like, Jesus, girl, how do you keep from killing yourself? Which hasn't been an unreasonable question, until lately."

Dani regarded her. "Let's do this. You know the rules."

Marissa nodded, closed her eyes, and leaned back. Dani remained watching her, until her consciousness blurred and the walls between them fell.

Dani was huddled on the floor of someone's bathroom. There was blood on the floor and on her hands.

Her blood.

No, that wasn't right. These weren't her memories. They belonged to Marissa. Dani turned her head toward the large mirror over the sink and saw that she was looking out through the eyes of Marissa as a child. The girl was terrified. She was experiencing her first period.

Marissa thought she was dying. She wanted to run screaming for Mommy, but something came to her, a force that rushed up and hammered her between the eyes. She tried to fight it, but she wasn't strong enough. At first she believed it was something outside herself, struggling to get in. Then she realized that it was something deep within, that wanted to get out.

For several moments, all Marissa knew was pain and confusion. The force inside kept pounding at her. The pain became acute. She was locked in the bathroom and the floor was slippery with blood. Rising to her feet, she fell and hit her head on the edge of the tub. Agony surged through her, then the pain went away, all of it. Something else moved through her, something she couldn't understand. Not at first.

Her mommy was home. She had her boyfriend over. Marissa's father died when she was ten. Mommy and her boyfriend were in Mommy's room, and Marissa *sort* of knew what was going on. She wasn't a kid anymore, or so she kept reminding her mother every chance she got. Now, lying alone in the bathroom, blood soaking in her nightdress, she wanted nothing more than to holler for her mommy like a scared five-year-old.

Suddenly she started to feel things she had never felt before. She was too excited to really be frightened.

Hands were on her. A mouth touched hers. She was alone, but she could feel it anyway. Someone was kissing her. Touching her. She was surprised, but she kind of liked it, at first. Then the hands got rough, they started touching her in places she didn't want anyone touching her, and pretty soon she could feel a man's *thing* near her, resting on her thigh, then it was in her hand, and she knew that in seconds it was maybe going somewhere else, so she *did something* about it.

Dani forced herself not to be dragged down by the tide of Marissa's emotions. She separated herself from Marissa's body and sat staring at the glassy-eyed litle girl, understanding with perfect clarity all that had occurred: Marissa's power had manifested, and it had allowed her to feel everything her mother's boyfriend was doing to her as they began to make love in the other room. But Marissa had only been a child, and she was unprepared for such feelings.

What did you do? Dani asked in the confines of Marissa's thoughts.

Marissa looked at Dani with her doe eyes. "Do I have to tell?"

No, Dani said, *you don't have to do anything. I'm just trying to understand. What did the police say?*

"When? What?"

When they took the body away.

The blond-haired girl was mortified. "I didn't kill him!"

Oh, Dani said, surprised. *All right.*

"No, I just . . . I made him take a cold shower, that's all. I mean, that's what they always said to do on TV, right? So that's what I did." Marissa hugged herself again.

Dani laughed. *How did you do that?*

Suddenly, Dani was inside Marissa once again. Together they climbed into the tub and put the shower on. The water was ice cold. Freezing. The girl wanted to wash it all away. The blood, and the feel of his hands and his tongue. She kept thinking of him, her anger swelling until she decided that she wanted him to feel this, too.

Removing herself from Marissa once again, Dani smiled. Even at that earlier age, Marissa had instinctively understood that she could not only receive these sensations, but send them, as well.

Did it make him stop?

The young Marissa was shivering as the icy water struck her full on. "Oh yeah," she said, shouting over the water. "He was sick for two days. Then, when he came over the next time, it didn't happen like that again. I stayed up the whole time, 'cause I was afraid if I went to sleep and they started up, I might have started feeling weird again."

So that was it?

"That was *nothing*. In school, it started getting really bad. I mean, I wasn't sleeping much, for a while. Not at home, anyway. Not when my mom had someone over. She was dating a couple of guys."

Dani nodded. "And in school?"

The bathroom fell away and a classroom formed around them. Dani sat in the chair beside Marissa, close to the rear of the classroom. The teacher had grayish-black hair. The students mostly paid attention, though a few, like Marissa, rested their heads.

Marissa's face was angled toward Dani. Her eyes opened and she said, "I started falling asleep in class.

That's when I knew I was right—it could happen when I was asleep. The first couple of times, it wasn't so bad. I had dreams, only they weren't really dreams, they were other people's memories and I was in them, like an actor, playing a part.

"I started finding out things about the other kids. Most of the kids I thought really had it going on, they were as messed up as I was. They had parents who treated them bad, problems in school, brothers and sisters who made their lives hell. The thing is, I didn't just *see* these things, I could *feel* what the people in my dreams were feeling. And it made *me* feel something, too. Especially when they got scared.

"They were scared all the time. Everyone was scared. When I took that in, it felt wonderful. It was like I had been hollow all my life, empty and waiting to get filled up, and here, all of a sudden, was a way I could make it better.

"I really liked it, Dani. I guess that makes me some kind of monster, doesn't it?"

No, Dani said. *No more than any of us. Go on, tell me the rest.*

"I started to look forward to it. And passing my classes was no problem, because if I concentrated really hard, I could get the other students to reveal whatever I needed to know, when I was dreaming. If I needed answers to homework, I could get them. The same with tests. I was smart enough to never copy anyone directly. I'd go into the heads of two or three of the top students and take kind of a sampling of all their work, then put things in my own words."

It didn't last, did it? Dani asked.

"No. One day, I was in their heads, and I came to

this boy. Paulie Wilson. I don't know how I missed him before. Maybe he had done such a good job of denying what was happening to him that I had been skating right past his nightmares, but this time they were right there and I fell into them."

What did you see?

"His parents were doing things to him. Making him do things with them, and with their friends. Sexual things. Disgusting things. I tried to get away from those memories, but they were so strong, and the fear was so intense, and the desire, too, 'cause I found that was almost as good, and I just couldn't get away. The best I could do was separate out. I made it so I wasn't a player, I wasn't seeing it and feeling it like I was one of them, doing it. But I could still feel his fear, and their desire. It was like a drug. I couldn't walk away from it. I tried."

Dani watched as Marissa's tears glistened in the glare of the overhead fluorescents. She wanted to reach over and wipe the child's tears away, but she restrained herself. The walls of this reality cracked apart, only for a second, and beyond the images of the classroom, Dani saw a bedroom that had been outfitted as a torture chamber, with a video camera set up before the bed. Two older men, naked with hairy backs, were leading a frightened teenager to the bed. The image vanished, the tears in the fabric of the dream landscape repaired themselves and Dani was relieved to find herself back in the classroom with the teenaged Marissa.

"I saw—it was so terrible," Marissa cried, "what they did to Paulie, what they said. I got so scared myself, I needed out. So I tried to get away. I was reaching out, I was looking for any way to escape. But I just made it worse. I started reaching the others in class, all the others. Their nightmares, their deepest fears, all of it came rushing in, *on top of* what I was already feeling."

Marissa turned and pointed out several students. "The prom queen who had been date raped and was certain she was going to have a kid. The boy on the school newspaper whose mother had been diagnosed with cancer. The bitchy girl in the back who was terrified of everything and had tried to kill herself twice, and was now convinced that the blood transfusion she had been given was tainted blood and was waiting to see if she tested positive for AIDS. Finally, I couldn't take it anymore. So I went deep."

What do you mean? Dani asked.

"I shut it all down. I did what our Miss Nancy used to tell us to do, I *just said no.*" Marissa smiled weakly. She was shuddering and Dani put her arm around the girl, rocking her back and forth. Reality became a blanket of darkness. The sights and sounds of the classroom faded. "I went into a coma. It lasted almost a week. That's how long it took for me to dig my way back out again."

Dani watched as the darkness lifted and they were in a hospital bed, Marissa dressed in hospital powder blues, Dani's arms still around her. Marissa pulled away and looked into Dani's face. "After that, I was scared as hell to go to sleep. The doctors hadn't been able to find anything wrong with me. They said it must have been a reaction to stress. I dunno, I guess they were right.

"Even though I was afraid, I had to go back to

sleep, eventually. It wasn't so bad. Somehow I had gotten control over it. I could block it out, I could shut it down whether I was asleep or awake."

The hospital room became a crowded high school corridor. Students jeered at Marissa as she walked down the hall with Dani beside her, others went to great effort to ignore her. Dani recalled this reaction. She had received it most of her high school "career."

"I went back to school and the kids treated me like I was a freak," Marissa said. "They thought I had a brain tumor or something.

"Paulie Wilson wasn't in school anymore. He had gone to the police and they arrested his parents. They found videotapes and still photos in the house. His parents were running a mail-order service. He was placed with the state authorities. I guess he couldn't take it anymore, either. Or maybe I couldn't take any more, and I made him turn them in. I'm really not sure."

They walked out of the school together and soon came to the shelter of a towering oak. They settled comfortably at the base of the tree, luxuriating in the warm sunlight filtering down through the cracks in the canopy of leaves above them.

Did you ever talk to anyone about this? Dani asked.

"There wasn't anybody, except my mom. I wanted to talk to her, but I didn't see how I could. My mom was like, the most practical person on the planet. She would have wanted me to see a psychiatrist. She was seeing one."

Did you ever think you were crazy?

"Every day! At least for a while there. Except—how could I have known about Paulie before everyone else?

That was the proof for me. That and knowing that I could do it again, any time I wanted. Eventually, I did. The kids at school were so terrible. One day I just wished I could be invisible. I just wanted to fade. Then all day, no one talked to me. No one seemed to notice I was even there. And when I tapped someone on the shoulder to ask them a question, they looked right at me and couldn't tell I was there.

"They got all cold and sweaty. They knew someone was there, but they couldn't see me, so they got really afraid, and it was all I could do to get the hell away from them before I started—"

Feeding, Dani said.

Marissa turned to her in mute horror. She swallowed hard and said, "That's what we do, isn't it?"

Dani nodded.

"Oh God," Marissa whispered.

It's all right, Dani said, wrapping her arms around Marissa and cradling her.

"It's not all right. You don't know why I was there."

The dorms, last night?

"Yeah."

It called to you, didn't it?

Marissa nodded.

The blood, the fear. It was too much and it called to you. The same thing almost happened to me.

"I started, y'know, feeding."

I remember. Dani noticed that Marissa's speech patterns were changing. When they had begun to speak, Marissa had sounded very much like Dani, strong, confident, sardonic. Perhaps she had acquired those traits from the time she had spent in Dani's thoughts, and now her true self was shining through.

205

"My mommy died, but she left me enough money that when I was old enough, I could go to college," Marissa said. "I came to Tower because it was what my mom wanted for me. She never had a real career, she never got a real education. Mostly, she waited tables all her life. I don't know where she got the money, but I was told it had been in the bank a long time, making interest. She always said she wanted me to have everything she didn't."

Marissa closed her eyes and rested her head against the tree, a beam of pure white sunlight engulfing her face.

What did you want to major in?

"My major? I hadn't decided yet. I'm not the same as you are, Dani. I've got all the drawbacks of an 'A' type personality, I just don't have the ambition to go with it. I mean, I worry about everything. Stupid things. Inconsequential things. What's the weather going to be like? Is my car going to start in the morning? I overanalyze everything. I spend days worrying over what someone meant by what they said, or what some look they gave me meant—"

But you have a way of getting around that.

"I know, but the more I do things, the more I feel different from everyone else. Before last night, it had been six months since I had looked into anyone's head, since I had fed off their feelings. I had convinced myself that it was over, that I wouldn't do this anymore, that it had all been a dream. But I was cracking up. I was sick all the time. The only time I'd feel better is when I was asleep. All I wanted to do was sleep all the time. When I was asleep I didn't have to think, didn't have to worry about all of this. Oh, God."

Dani allowed the dreamworld to fade as she withdrew from Marissa's mind. The girl was not the killer.

They were back in the corridor of the borrowed house, looking at each other from a distance that was only a few feet, but seemed much too far. Dani went to Marissa, placing her arms around the girl, who was sobbing.

"It's been terrible, Dani. I thought I was going crazy. My grades were going to hell, I'd wake up every morning with anxiety attacks, I couldn't focus, I was just so goddamned *afraid*. I've been afraid of everything."

"How do you feel now?" Dani asked, gently stroking Marissa's hair.

"When I'm with you, I don't feel afraid anymore, and I don't feel angry, and I don't feel like I have to be anything other than what I am. I don't feel alone."

"Yeah. Me, too." Dani held Marissa as she cried.

For a time, that was enough.

Chapter Eleven

Sam had spent hours at the campus and had been unable to turn up any trace of her daughter. Dani's rented car was parked in one of the lots near the dorm. It had been parked there overnight.

She had talked with Nina, Dani's roommate, who shamefully confessed that she had gone out with the man who had been attempting to romance Dani. Nina was worried that Dani may have found out and went somewhere to be alone.

Sam left Nina and spent time showing the newspaper article around. Though the campus killings had shaken everyone, identifying Marissa Tomley had taken practically no effort. With a few people, she used the photograph of Elaine. They were certain it was Marissa. She learned that no one had seen Marissa since last night. Her roommate had taken a hotel room somewhere off campus, it was possible that Marissa had gone with her.

Sam decided that she would delay sharing any of this with Richard until after she had a chance to interview Marissa and verify that Elaine **Aldridge had** been her mother. Once she did that, she would arrange a face-to-face meeting with Richard, the son of a bitch. She was willing to close out her involvement with him, but she wasn't willing to make it easy for him. Nevertheless, both of those events would have to wait until she caught up with Dani.

Sam spent the early part of the afternoon checking out the places Dani was known to frequent. Her daughter had left her car behind, but the cab companies had been forced to pull drivers back on duty to handle the number of calls from students who needed to get away from the university and were too shaken to drive. No one using Dani's name had hired a taxi, but the girl could have used another name. Showing photos to the drivers would have been pointless; if Dani had not wanted to be recognized, she would have used her power to ensure her anonymity. The time Sam spent phoning the local hotels proved equally frustrating and pointless.

She went to the Hellfire Club and found it closed, but the assistant manager spoke to her. He recognized Dani from Sam's wallet photo—a shot of Dani standing before the Karmann Ghia, doing a game-show hostess gesture—and commented that she normally dressed considerably wilder than the image portrayed.

The man's name was Lee Shawcross. He had dark hair, graying at the temples, and the tiniest waist Sam had ever seen on a man. Shawcross had not seen Dani at the club the previous night. He took her card, promised to phone if she stopped by that night, and gave Sam a pair of complementary passes. The steady stream of compliments and his forced, self-confident manner, indicated to Sam that he was interested in her. She played on that shamelessly, her overriding concern for her daughter overwhelming her desire to break the jaw of the next man who made a pass at her.

Outside the club, she phoned Ray Brooks. The man was extremely reticent at the beginning of their conversation, but his professional side emerged the moment Sam explained that Dani was missing. Brooks had not spoken to Dani.

Sam drove down to Venice Beach, scouring the area for her daughter. Dani had not been there. She went to several local breakfast and lunch hangouts, showed Dani's photograph, and received nothing but shrugs and blank stares.

By three o'clock that afternoon, Sam was forced to accept that if Dani had not wanted to be found, Sam's best efforts would be wasted. The familiar anxiety that had flooded through her years ago, when Sam and Dani had lived in Tampa and Sam came home to learn that her daughter had disappeared somewhere between the bus stop and their house, finally suffused Sam. She had been fighting off her fears, but she could deny them no longer.

Dani had no reason to hide herself away. She had not made contact with Sam because she had been unable to do so. She was someone's prisoner, she was hurt, or she was dead.

Sam returned to her car and called Edward Pullman. It took several minutes for him to come to the phone. Before he could say anything more than his name, Sam anxiously told him of the hours she had

210

spent fruitlessly searching for her daughter and asked if he could set his off-duty men on the search with her.

"Done," he said. "We'll coordinate from here. I'll have four guys here by the time you arrive. And there's something else you might want to know about. . . ."

Sam listened intently, then hung up. She drove back to the city, entered Pullman's precinct house, and fell into the man's comforting embrace. He led her to a small room, and through a window, she was able to see an adjoining interrogation room.

In the room, a man sat alone, his hands and ankles chained. He was swarthy, in his midtwenties, with wild, chestnut brown hair, a scruffy beard and mustache, and a lean but powerful physique. His features were long and hawklike, his lips thin and threatening.

"What's his name?" Sam asked.

Edward said, "Vince Calzaretti. Rich kid, believe it or not. Spends his time going up and down the coast. A drifter. We can place him at the murders last night and the first one, in San Diego. Given time, we might be able to get him for all of them."

"What does he say?" She was trying to be cold, detached, and it wasn't working. She shuddered.

"That he's guilty. And he has information we never released to the press."

"How did you find him?"

"He was sitting on a park bench in broad daylight. His clothes were soaked with blood. Forensics matches it to the victims."

"Did he put up any kind of fight?"

"He came willingly."

The door behind them opened. Ray Brooks entered and froze when he saw Sam. "Ms. Walthers."

"What is it, Ray?" Edward asked.

"They want to get started," Brooks said.

"Set it up."

Brooks nodded and exited the room.

"You're just in time for the confession," Edward said. "My guys are running late. If you want to stay and hear this —"

"I do."

The detective sergeant nodded. A silent agreement was made not to talk about what was on both their minds. Dani had vanished from the campus last night. The killer had not been apprehended until morning. There was a chance that his confession would include victims they hadn't anticipated, and Sam's daughter could be one of them.

They sat quietly in the viewing room as several officers brought in the necessary equipment to tape the confession. Calzaretti sat perfectly composed as the lights and the camera were set up. A stenographer pulled up a chair. Ray Brooks stood behind the thin, balding, Hispanic detective who questioned Calzaretti.

In moments, the bearded man was reciting a litany of evil, revealing in a rich, clear voice the exact manner in which he killed each of the victims. He gave names, dates, severity of wounds, and even acted out the way each of the women screamed and begged for mercy.

Sam watched the confession, her heart thundering as she listened to Calzaretti's words. As expected, he

212

named four women whose bodies had never been recovered.

Dani was not one of them. Sam grieved inwardly for the parents of the victims, but her own feelings of relief could not be denied. With the interrogator's next question, her sense of relief was turned to abject horror.

The Hispanic detective leaned forward and asked, "Why did you commit these terrible acts?"

Tensing, eyes wide with fear, Calzaretti said, "I can't talk about that."

Sam watched as sweat broke out on Calzaretti's brow. He began to shake. He looked like a theatrically trained actor who was suddenly being forced to improvise in the middle of the performance and was shocked to learn that he didn't have the ability.

"Don't ask me about that," Calzaretti mewled, tears welling up in his eyes as he rocked back and forth on his heels. His flesh had gone white, and he was gasping as if he were about to start hyperventilating. Calzaretti buried his head between his knees, his entire body shuddering as he began to weep.

Ray Brooks said, "Mister Calzaretti, are you on some form of medication?"

Calzaretti raised his head and laughed, tears running down his face. "Doctor, doctor, give me the news, I got a"—he paused, rolling his shoulders—"bad case, of loving you!"

"Okay, I think we should close this down," the Hispanic detective said.

"You can run, you can hide, but you can never get away," Calzaretti howled, tapping his forehead,

" 'cause it's up here, man. It's where no one can fucking get to it, you hear what I'm saying? Do ya? *Do ya!?*"

Sam watched through the glass as the Hispanic detective stared at Calzaretti with growing unease. This was not a performance. The man was genuinely terrified. He went to the window, where Pullman sat beside Sam, and said, "I think we should call someone."

Calzaretti burst into motion, rising to his feet and overturning the table. "Don't make me, I'm begging you! Please. You don't know what's inside of me. Oh God, *please!*"

Brooks surged forward. "Mr. Calzaretti—"

"You don't know what it's like, having it inside you, a ticking bomb, tick-tick-tick—"

The Hispanic detective was on his feet, coming at Calzaretti from the other side, when the confessed murderer suddenly doubled over and dropped to his knees, clamping his hands and arms over his face.

"Jesus!" Ray shouted. "He's going into some kind of convulsion. Call an ambulance!"

Inside the viewing room, an ashen-faced Edward Pullman reached for the phone and barked a series of orders. Then he rose to his feet and burst from the room. Sam followed. They entered the interrogation room in time to see Brooks kneeling beside Calzaretti, attempting to gently pry the man's hands away from his face. Calzaretti shook violently, his arms locked firmly in place as his head twisted back and forth. He threw himself back, landing flat on the floor.

As Calzaretti's head struck, his hands and arms fell from his face, allowing a thin stream of blood to spout

214

from his lips as something slithered out of his mouth. Sam felt as if she were going to throw up as, in her mind, the object on the floor suddenly registered as the man's tongue, which he had just bitten off. The room started to spin, but she forced herself to maintain her crumbling hold on consciousness. She had seen worse than this before, but in those cases, she had been prepared for violence. Calzaretti's seizure and his self-inflicted wound had startled her.

Calzaretti started to make sounds that might have been screams, but they were strangled, anguished cries. His hands curled into claws and he plunged them toward his eyes. Brooks managed to catch one of his hands in time, but the other savagely found its mark, gouging the eye from its socket.

"What's this son of a bitch on!?" Ray screamed, crouching on top of Calzaretti, holding back his hand while the Hispanic detective vainly attempted to catch the free one. Calzaretti's face was a mass of gore. The man was attempting to peel the flesh from his skull.

Edward ran to the fallen man, fell to his knees, and took hold of Calzaretti's flailing hand, holding it tight in both of his. Sam knelt beside Edward, lending her strength. The man squirmed, his body rising up into a bow, as he sent Brooks sprawling away from him. Calzaretti's breath hitched several times and he collapsed, unmoving, to the floor, the strength vanishing from his limbs as if a cord had been torn from the wall.

He was dead. Sam looked at the gory mass of the dead man's face, then caught sight of the dazed, horrified look each of the officers shared. Brooks moved forward, tearing open the man's shirt, attempting to restore his vital signs. The Hispanic detective assisted him, as Sam and Edward watched, knowing their efforts would be futile.

Sam realized that she was trembling. She flinched as Edward placed his hand on her shoulder.

"I need to get out of here," he said. "Get me to the door."

She almost smiled. His thinly veiled attempt at chivalry might have angered her under other circumstances. Pullman did not need her help. He assumed she needed his and this was the only way she would accept it.

Guiding the older man to the hallway, Sam sat down beside him on a bench. They held hands for a moment, trying to decide exactly what in the hell had just happened, when suddenly her beeper went off, causing both of them to jump.

Snatching the beeper from her waistband, Sam felt her heart leap as she recognized the phone number. The call had been made from Dani's dorm room. She raced to the nearest phone, dialed the number, and exploded with relief as she heard her daughter's voice on the other end of the phone.

"Stay where you are, baby," Sam said. "I'll be right there."

Marissa had never been happier in her life. She had finally found someone with whom she could share her private fears, her hidden desires, and not feel ashamed, or monstrous for her feelings. After they had gotten over the initial shock of their mutual discovery, Dani and Marissa had taken control of the dark, four-door sedan's owner, and had him drive them back to the campus. It was a simple matter for Dani to erase the events of the previous evening from the man's mind and substitute memories of a drinking binge, an event with which the driver was not unfamiliar.

Marissa had watched Dani in amazement. The girl's control over her abilities was absolute. Marissa reached out with her own power, studying the manner in which Dani worked her personal magic, and had felt proud to consider this strong young woman a friend. Dani had gone back to her room, where she would call her mother.

Marissa collected a message from the front desk before going up to her own room. Once she arrived there, and found her roommate missing—as usual—Marissa tossed the message to the side of the phone and began to rifle through her clothing. Dani had promised that tonight would be a special night for both of them. She wasn't exactly sure what Dani had in mind, and the mystery thrilled and delighted her.

After going through all of her clothes, mixing and matching, worriedly trying on several outfits, Marissa had settled for a frilly white blouse, a shiny black broach over the top button, a black leather miniskirt, black lace stockings, and an elegant but functional pair of black shoes.

Finally, she returned to the phone message, stared at the name in confusion, debated with herself for a moment, then decided to call the number. A man answered the phone. He spoke in a wondrous, gentle voice, and he told her things that she had never believed she would hear in her entire life.

She hung up the phone, trembling, and immediately dialed Dani's number. The line was busy. Marissa waited a few seconds, redialed, and received the same results. She considered going over to Dani's room, but she was shaking, all she could think about were the words of the stranger who was not a stranger at all. She was trembling with nervous anticipation. Dani might want to come along. That would spoil everything. Marissa wanted—no, she *needed* to see this man alone, to use her power to reach into his mind and find out if his claims were true. After that, she and Dani would have the rest of their lives to party all over town, or whatever it was Dani had in mind.

She knew she should leave a note for Dani, but she had no idea how she could explain the amazing thing that had just occurred. Stopping at her door, she took one of her markers and jotted a quick message on the erasable board outside her door. She looked at what she had written, smiled, and threw the marker on her bed.

Dani would understand. She was Marissa's friend, she would be happy for her when she knew the truth of today's phone call, and the meeting she was hurrying toward.

In her agitated state, in-town traffic was especially hard to take. Marissa felt as if a hoard of butterflies had been loosed within her gut, and the ridiculous image made her laugh and relax slightly. Her hands gripped the wheel so fiercely she was afraid she might twist it out of shape.

Finally she arrived at the address the man had given her. The door to his place opened and she knew the moment she looked into his eyes that this man was her father; she didn't need to use her power to verify what she could feel in her heart. She threw herself into his arms and pressed her head against his chest. His heart was thundering as loudly as her own. As he led her inside and shut the door behind them, the ever quickening staccato of his heart would not leave her ears, though she was no longer pressed up against his chest. The living room was darkened.

"I've been waiting for you for so very long," he said as he kissed her forehead and reached down to stroke her long, lustrous hair. "I've been searching for you. I thought I'd never find you."

"I'm here, Daddy," she said, suddenly embarrassed by the perhaps too familiar and childish name. Her concern evaporated instantly as she felt a soothing cloud descend upon her mind, erasing her every concern.

That was when it occurred to her: This man *was* her father. Her true father.

The man whose blood ran in her veins.

Inhuman blood.

She looked up sharply, expecting to see him transform into some hideous creature. But his soft, gentle expression never changed and she relaxed instantly. The increasing rhythm of his heart, a triphammer out of control, filled her with a glorious excitement she was only vaguely aware he was projecting into her mind.

"I need you to trust me," he said. "I know that's difficult. You don't even know me."

He touched her arms, tentatively at first, then with a reassurance that made her legs turn to water. He lifted her up and carried her to the couch, where he laid her down with the tenderness he might display with the most precious object in the world.

"There is a world you've never known," he said in his rich, melodic voice. "A world to which you are entitled, where you will be the storybook princess you always imagined you would be, but you will need no one to rescue you, because you will be stronger than any mortal who might desire you. You are flesh of my flesh, blood of my blood. Release what's in your heart. Become true to yourself."

Marissa stared into his eyes. "I want to. But I'm afraid."

He took her hand and brought it to his lips. She felt a startling electric shock at the initial contact, which eased and became a languorous pleasure that ran deeper than any sensual act she had ever experienced, that touched her heart and her soul.

"Come with me, my darling daughter," he said sweetly, "the best is yet to be."

"I will," she said without hesitation. She shuddered as he leaned down, kissing her cheek, then her neck. Somehow her broach had been removed and the top few buttons of her blouse were undone. She couldn't remember how that had happened. It didn't really matter.

Twin fiery explosions flared from the pale flesh of

her neck, and she gripped her father's hand with enough force to shatter the bones of a human hand. He did not seem to mind. The pain she felt vanished instantly, and the room transformed into an amazing collection of Day-Glo, psychedelic colors.

Soon the beating of their hearts was in perfect synch, and they both relaxed, the rhythm easing until Marissa could once again hear sounds other than the pounding of her frantic heart. She was surprised to hear another pounding, fists on a door, shouting.

"What?" Marissa asked groggily, the blood haze she had experienced leaving her disoriented. "What's that?"

"A guest," her father said as he pulled away from her. "Someone I want you to meet."

Marissa clutched at her father, terrified by the thought of being parted from him. She was only vaguely aware of the blood smeared across his face and the throbbing pain above her throat. A new sensation rose up and dominated all that had come before it:

She was starving. Ravenous. Marissa did not know which she needed more, the love and approval of her father, or the exquisite fear that rushed to her from behind the locked bathroom near the front door. The look in her father's eyes told her all she needed to know: There was prey to be had and he would join her in the feast.

Never in her life had she felt so comfortable, so at ease. She had tried so desperately to fight the darkness within her, and now she realized that she had been struggling for no reason. This was natural. For the first time she felt thoroughly unafraid.

He helped her to stand, and together they walked across the carpeted floor, steadily and reverently, as if they were going down the aisle and he were about to give her away. They stopped before the locked door, grinning at each other as they saw the way the wood shuddered under the blows from the other side. The lock had been reversed.

"Open it," he said. "Consider it your coming-out gift."

She opened the door and, using one hand, hurled back the screaming, terrified human who attempted to bolt to freedom, then pulled her lips back in a smile that was made all the more ferocious by the pair of long, razor-sharp incisors that had suddenly sprung from their housings.

Marissa hauled the human from the bathroom and threw her prey across the room. The prey crashed into a glass table, which shattered under the impact.

Her father beside her, Marissa laughed and went forward to unwrap her gift.

Chapter Twelve

Sam took her daughter into her arms and held her close. She had returned to the campus and met Dani in her room. Dani had been alone.

"Where in the name of God were you?" Sam finally asked, the words verging on the edge of hysteria.

Dani told her mother all that had occurred from the moment she left the college library. She explained that she had sensed the being she believed to be the murderer, how it made sense that one of their kind was the most likely suspect. The golden-eyed teenager told of her fight on the bridge with the shadow-creature, who later turned out to be Marissa.

Sam became pale. "Marissa Tomley?"

Dani nodded, and confirmed Marissa's identity from the photograph and news article Sam carried.

Her legs turning to water, Sam sat down on the edge of Dani's bed.

"Mom?"

"Marissa's an Initiate," Sam said softly, her mind making impossible connections. "Where is she now? I need to talk to her."

"I took her back to her room. We were planning on going out later. Girl's night out. You know. Just a couple of white chick vampires out on the town." Dani smiled weakly. She thought of the long nights of initiation Bill Yoshino and Isabella had subjected her to, making her believe that her power was a glorious and natural thing, while they taught her their ways and honed her skills. She had planned to give Marissa an education tonight, one in which the girl would learn to accept herself for what she was, and perhaps find a way not to loathe the power she had been given. They were going to visit the charity hospitals, and Dani was going to teach Marissa how to use her power to heal, rather than destroy.

"Take me to her," Sam said. "Please, honey. It's important."

Dani nodded. She had thrown on a pair of Spandex running shorts cut off at midthigh, an electric pink halter top, and her best leather jacket.

"You're wearing that?" Sam asked, suddenly recalling the words of the thin man at the Hellfire Club.

"Uh-huh." Dani pulled her sunglasses from the pocket of her leather jacket and tossed her long, wild hair behind her. The bathroom door was open and from the corner of her eye, Dani was able to see the reflection of two dark women in the mirror over the sink. Both were covered in blood. They were smiling.

Dani shuttered the image by sliding her sunglasses on. She turned away and nudged her mother's arm. "Let's go."

They left Dani's room and walked across the street, to Marissa's dorm. Sam hesitated before the door to

224

Marissa's room.

"What's the matter?" Dani asked.

"The room numbers," Sam said. "They run exactly the same as in your building."

"So?"

"The room where the students were killed last night," Sam said as she pointed at the placard which read 330, "was this one, only in the other building."

Dani felt her heart thundering. From the end of the corridor, beyond her mother, she caught another glimpse of Madison and Isabella as they turned a corridor and vanished.

On the door's erasable pad, a message had been scrawled. It read:

I'LL BE *BACK*.

Beneath it was a happy face and the letter "M." The door was not locked. Sam knocked, received no reply, then went inside. Clothes were strewn everywhere. The room was empty. A quick search revealed a crumpled phone message laying next to the phone. Sam opened the pink scrap of paper and drew in a sharp breath as she read the number.

"Oh Jesus," she said, clamping her hand over her mouth. Her first instinct was to hide what she had just learned from Dani, to find a way to talk Dani into coming away with her and never returning to the university, but that would never happen. Her daughter was an adult. She deserved to be treated as such.

"Mom?" Dani asked.

"I think your friend's in trouble," Sam said. "I'll explain on the drive."

In moments they were in the Rover, Sam revealing

the details of her various encounters with Richard Sterling, who had been led to believe that he was Marissa's father. Sam finally understood that they had both been used.

"It was Cort," Sam explained. "It was him all along. *He* was Marissa's father."

"You mean her real father?"

"Yeah," Sam said. "Cort was another fucking vampire. I guess that bastard Yoshino wasn't kidding when he said that L.A. was crawling with his kind."

"But—girls are the outcasts. Vampires want sons, not daughters. Why didn't Cort just kill Marissa and her mother twenty years ago? And why would he be coming back for her now?"

"I don't know why Cort wants Marissa, honey," Sam said. "I think Cort has been using Richard to help him find Marissa by making him believe that Marissa was his own daughter. Maybe because Cort couldn't come looking for her in the daylight—but Richard could. The only thing I care about is that Marissa knows about you. If Cort gets to her—"

Dani hugged herself. The secret. Dani had helped her mother destroy a vampire pack. Dani would be branded Wildling. Others of her kind would come after her for the death of Isabella.

The late afternoon traffic was difficult to cut through, and Sam knew that if she first went home, as she wanted to, it might be too late to stop what she feared had already begun. The harsh sunlight seemed to taunt them, flaring brighter than it had all day just before it would vanish completely. Deep streaks of pink and amber sliced across the sky as they pulled into the parking garage of Richard Sterling's hotel.

As they rode the elevator to Richard's floor, Sam drove a fresh clip into her Beretta 9mm automatic. Dani had been very quiet. She knew, as her mother had known, that they had to get Marissa and Richard away from the hotel before Cort rose and found them.

The elevator doors opened and Dani immediately felt an intense wave of need rush through her.

"She's here," Dani said in a breathy whisper. "Marissa's here and something's happening."

"What? What's happening?"

Dani hurried out of the elevator, her mother at her side. Sam had already told her the room number. Dani felt her power coil within her, the all-too-familiar surge of her blood thirst practically overwhelming her. Channeling her anger into a sudden, inhuman burst of strength, Dani threw herself against the locked door and shattered the lock. The door swung inward and she was greeted by a sight that sickened her.

Three figures were on the floor, before the couch. The glass table had been shattered. Glistening shards of blood-stained glass covered the floor. A cleaning woman lay on her back, her throat torn open, her rib cage burst apart, her heart sitting on the floor beside her. Dani did not have to look up to know that splatters of blood leaked down from the ceiling. Crouching over the dead woman was Marissa, covered in the woman's blood. Her eyes blazed unnaturally, her bloody canines stretched from the housing of her upper jaw. Her teeth were jagged, razor-sharp. The girl's long fingers had been transformed into talons.

This is what I was missing, Dani thought. This is what I wanted to be. Jesus.

Sam entered the room behind her daughter and saw the man who knelt behind Marissa, his canines buried in her exposed throat. He detached his fangs from his daughter's throat and turned to stare at Sam without emotion. He was still wearing the outfit he had worn when he arrived at her door that morning.

"This isn't possible," Sam whispered.

Richard Sterling placed a comforting hand on Marissa's shoulder and she went back to lapping at the bloody remains of the corpse. The windows were covered over with sheets of thick black canvas.

"Hello, Sam. Good to see you. I'm sorry I couldn't stay around before." He ran his hand over his black, fish net T-shirt. His muscular chest was moist with blood. "I guess you can see now why I had to run off in a hurry. I mean, the last thing I would want to do is be rude to—"

Before he could finish, Sam raised the 9mm, aimed it at the windows, and curled her finger over the trigger. A sudden burst of liquid fire exploded in her brain and she stumbled back, into Dani's arms.

She could not fire.

Richard shook his head with a sorrowful laugh. "You really don't understand what's going on here, do you?"

Dani tore the gun from her mother's hand and tried to fire. Pain lanced through her and suddenly she could not remain standing. Sam caught her daughter and gently lowered her to the floor.

"You're smarter than that, little vampire," Richard

said. "In fact, you're brilliant. I considered you for a time, but you're Wildling. You're tainted. You're too strong willed. With you, there'd be no guarantees." He looked down at Marissa. "Flesh of my flesh. Blood of my blood. That was the only way to go, difficult as it was to find my little girl."

"What in the fuck are you talking about, you son of a bitch?" Sam cried.

"Oh yeah," Richard said. "That's right, you don't watch the kind of movies I make. Not often, anyway."

"This isn't a movie," she said, recalling the last time she had said those words to him. She suddenly felt very tired. "I trusted you."

"I know that, Samantha. And I appreciate it. Really, I do."

She looked at him coldly, cutting glances to her daughter, whose head lolled back and forth as she struggled to retain consciousness. He had called her Samantha, the name she loathed.

"I really am sorry it had to happen this way, Samantha. It wasn't the way I had planned it." Richard hesitated. He seemed perfectly composed, as if he were the subject of an interview. "You must have questions."

Jesus, Sam thought. He really does think it's a movie. Some goddamned "B" movie, and this is the part where he stands there and tells his victims everything before he kills them.

"You're partially correct," Richard said.

Sam stared at his glacier-blue eyes. Her body was trembling. She had trusted this man. She had given herself to him, placed her heart in his hands, and he had ripped it to shreds without hesitation. He had entered her body, and, apparently, her mind.

She thought of a conversation which had taken place months earlier. Dani had phoned her in the middle of the night, in tears, begging Sam to pick her up. Sam had brought her home and they had talked for hours. Dani had admitted she was afraid of never finding the kind of love she'd shared, however briefly, with Bill Yoshino.

Bill Yoshino lied to you. He raped you. He made you think he loved you, but he didn't.

No.

You have to come to terms with this.

I wanted it. Don't you understand that? I wanted it, I needed it, all he did was show me the part of myself I've always hidden away. The part I keep boxed in tight now.

She had understood her daughter's struggle only too well. Sam had felt violated by Eugene, the man she had divorced twenty years ago. He had used her in every conceivable way and because of the scars he had left upon her, she had been unable—or perhaps simply unwilling—to trust again.

Bill Yoshino raped you.

And Richard Sterling raped me, Sam thought bitterly. He was in control of everything I felt, right from the beginning.

"Ridiculous," the vampire said, shocking her from her thoughts, which she could not hide from him. "Nothing's really changed, Samantha. We've just let down the masks. That's the way relationships are."

"We don't have a relationship, you bastard."

Crouched beside Richard, the snarling, blood-soaked creature who had been Marissa looked up at

Sam, eyeing her the way a well-trained attack dog might view a threat to its master. Sam found it difficult to reconcile the murderous creation before her in the terms Dani had used to describe the girl less than an hour before:

She's so scared, so fragile, like a porcelain doll. She's so damn innocent.

Richard stroked her hair and Marissa relaxed. "You see that? She doesn't know me. She doesn't even know herself anymore. But she'd die for me. You can't get loyalty like that except from your own flesh."

"Do me a favor, Richard. If you're going to do something, get it the fuck over with. I'm really tired of listening to your bullshit."

He shook his head. "You really don't understand. I have no intention of hurting you, or your daughter. If I had wanted to do that, I could have by now. I don't think either of you have a clear idea of what you're dealing with. I'm an Immortal. My daughter is now an Immortal, and she is *also* my thrall. Your Dani is powerful, I'll grant you that. But compared to us, she's nothing, and compared to her, you're even less."

Sam remained silent. She refused to give him what he wanted, the chance to act out the villain's final scene, just like one of the bad guys from one of his movies. A sudden, twisting pain reached into her skull and she gasped as the walls of her resistance were demolished by Richard's power.

"I saw you," Sam said, hating herself for her every word. "In daylight. Twice, I saw you."

"No, you didn't."

"At lunch, that first day—"

231

"I was inside the hotel. There were no windows in the hall, the elevator was sealed, and the restaurant was also windowless. I can move around during the day as long as I avoid sunlight. That's why I chose this hotel, why I selected this room. I had one of my assistants check it out for me in advance."

He glanced at the dead cleaning woman on the floor. "This bitch opened the shades while I was asleep in the bathtub. I heard the phone ring and went outside. That's how I got my instant suntan. I've been saving her for something special."

Sam struggled with the burning pain that forced the questions she was attempting to bury to come to the forefront of her thoughts. She tried to resist, considering the satisfaction she would be denying him, but she could not.

"You produce movies," she said, unable to stop herself. "That means you have to visit sets during the day. You have to take meetings. You've been photographed."

"I'm pretty high up in the Net. That gives me some rights and privileges."

"I don't understand."

"Do you have any idea how many of my kind exist in your world? Do you actually believe that we don't talk to each other? That we don't try to help each other?"

To Sam, the concept of vampires working together, pooling resources, was both starkly ridiculous and frightening. She thought of the luxurious Malibu beach house that Yoshino and Isabella had used. Her initial assumption had been that the vampires had murdered the true owners, but not before a transfer of their assets had been arranged. When she investigated her suspicions, she learned that the house had been under the ownership of a dummy corporation which she could not trace any further. It had been Yoshino's way of keeping his name from documentation, she had assumed, but she now realized it was possible that the house could have been owned by someone else, by others of Yoshino's kind.

She thought of the photos on the walls in the memory room. Celebrities in the movie business, actors, producers, columnists from many decades. Sam had assumed that all vampires were parasites.

That the vampires had *organized*, and that their organization was somehow tied to the entertainment industry, made perverse sense to Sam.

Richard was continuing to glean her thoughts. "Yoshino was a comer. He told your daughter about a script he had written that was making the rounds. That was true. If he had kept his love for fun and games under control, he might have become a player, instead of becoming dead. By the way, the cabal actually believed the story you made up for the press. That's why there hasn't been any repercussions. And as long as you and your daughter play fair with me, there won't be any. Fuck with me, and I'll let the Parliament know what I've learned. You don't want to know what they do to Wildlings, like your precious daughter."

"Wildlings are vampires who kill their own kind," Sam said. "That means you're Wildling, too.

"No," he said.

"You killed those students. You killed the girl they found in the alley."

"They were Initiates, not Immortals, and they were only *women*."

"That means they don't count?"

"Exactly so."

Sam brought her rage under control.

"Some of your victims were male."

"Human males. Innocents, if such a thing really exists, but useful in diverting attention."

Sam hesitated, thinking of what Norene Bloom, the woman at the hotel where Elaine Aldridge had gone after she had faked her death, had told her. "Why did you kill Kimmie Bloom?"

A smile spread across Richard's face. "I remember her. She was pitiful."

"Why did you kill her?"

"The better question is why did I help Elaine to fake her own death," Richard said.

"All right," Sam said.

"I wanted a son. I was able to sense that the child she had conceived was a girl. You may have already gathered from the way you found your daughter exactly how much regard we Immortals have for women."

"None at all, as far as I can tell," Sam said.

"And why should we? Antonius, the first of our kind, understood the truth. Human women have some value. They can carry our heirs. But female Immortals? They can't bear our children, they can't perform any function that gives them intrinsic value—though they can be intriguing lovers."

Sam shuddered. The society of Immortals objectified women in exactly the same way as their human counterparts. Whores and—what had Richard called his daughter—thralls. Nothing else.

"You never answered the question," Sam said.

"About Elaine? I had considered leaving her. I had considered killing her. She had failed me. I was so angry the night I learned she was carrying a daughter that I told her everything, and I gave her a display of my talents, so that she knew I wasn't bullshitting her. I scared her so badly it was a miracle she didn't lose the child.

"Somehow, I got out of our apartment and Cort was waiting for me. I decided to go back and kill her, and would have, too, if it hadn't been for Cort.

"He had been a *helper* to me. We need them. Imagine what your life would be like if you couldn't step out into the sun. Nothing's ever open. Then you get daylight savings time half the year and you're in for a really frustrating experience.

"Cort was there, and he was in love with her. He convinced me that even a female could one day prove useful to me. I had been a movie fanatic, even then. The whole thing sounded like a Hitchcock film. I loved those. It was exciting. But there was still the question of Elaine, and her fragile condition.

"I considered using my power to erase the unpleasant memories, but I knew that she had been traumatized far too deeply. She wouldn't have survived the 'surgery,' so to speak. Bob Cort came up with another plan. He had been a friend to Elaine. He went to her that night, and as he expected, she told him about me.

235

"She also told him about the money she had."

"The twenty thousand dollars."

"Yes."

"That had been a bribe. She had been in love with a boy from a wealthy family. The family did not approve of her, and eventually, she came to realize that he would never marry her over the wishes of his family. He met someone else, someone more suited to his social position, and eventually offered her the money to help her get started somewhere else. She told him that she wasn't his whore. She didn't want his money. But he was insistent. Finally she became so angry, she took the money, with some vague scheme of using the 'bribe' to publicly humiliate her ex-boyfriend and his family.

"She moved to Los Angeles, made Xeroxes of the check, and deposited the money in her account. Eventually, her anger dimmed, and when she learned that she was pregnant, and the trouble she was in, she decided she could put the money to better use. Cort helped her with this. He came up with the idea of faking their deaths, then going somewhere that I wouldn't know about. Of course, she had no idea that he was working for me.

"The plan had been that he would keep track of her for me. That way, if I ever came back for the child, I would have no problem finding her. Unfortunately, it didn't work out that way."

"Cort really wanted to get away."

"Oh, he wanted to. I knew that. I expected that. I took out insurance in that likelihood. But I'll get to that. Faking the accident was a simple matter. I could still affect Elaine's perceptions, influence her decisions, without hurting her. It was my little pushes that made her go along with Cort's plan.

"I drove the car into the water, then found our witnesses and planted the false memories in their heads. It was all very simple, very tidy."

"Elaine Aldridge became 'Hilary Bartan' of San Diego," said Sam. "Her next-door neighbor was Kimmie Bloom. A woman you killed."

"I had been out of the country. I hadn't read my correspondence from Cort. If I had, I would have known that Elaine had moved. I wanted to see my daughter. The Bloom girl was living next door. The walls were thin. She heard Cort and Elaine arguing, heard their talk of our kind. She stopped me when I left Elaine's apartment. I was furious, looking for someone upon whom I could vent my anger.

"She thought I could bite her on the neck and turn her into an Immortal. She had seen too many movies. I went into her apartment and played with her for a time. Then I disposed of her."

Sam thought of the wounds Norene had described. Five piercing wounds, which the coroner had taken for knives. Then she thought of the vampire, Isabella, in her transformation, her hands transformed into talons.

"You also killed the witnesses to the accident."

"Of course. Wouldn't you have done the same, in my position?"

Sam gave him no answer. Instead, she asked, "Why did you kill the students?"

"I was trying to find my daughter. Elaine found cor-

237

respondence that Bob was preparing for me. A report. She took Marissa and vanished. The girl was only two. I had lost interest in the situation. I stopped checking on the validity of what Cort had been telling me, I assumed that he would be so terrified that he would never lie to me. It seemed that he was even more terrified of telling me the truth.

"I suffered some reversals. Not in the dealings that your society recognizes, but in mine. I remembered my daughter, and decided that I finally had a use for her. I went to the place Cort said she could be found, and learned that he had been lying to me all those years."

"Is Cort alive?"

Richard smiled. "You had the good fortune of being present when Vince Calzaretti made his confession, one of several instructions I gave him. Let's just say that Cort passed away under similar circumstances."

"You went to the dorm last night, before you came to me."

"Killing arouses me."

Sam squeezed her eyes shut. "I could understand if you had seen the photograph in the paper, but that came after. You already knew where Marissa was living."

Richard shrugged. "You're going to be offended."

"And that matters to you?"

"Well. The truth is, I hired two other investigators. They had considerably more information than you had."

Sam's lips curled up in disgust. "Why did you even *bother* hiring me?"

"I told you that the Parliament believed the story you gave the press about Yoshino's death. I didn't. I knew too much about his movements. He knew something about mine. It was in my best interest to learn the truth. All it took was being in the same room with you, once, about a month ago, and I learned everything. Unless you're of our kind, you won't know that we're in your head if we don't want you to know."

"You still could have turned us in. That was your duty, wasn't it?"

"I suppose. But I became intrigued by you. Let's just say I wanted to get to know you better. But I still haven't answered your earlier question. You said that you saw me in the daylight on two separate occasions. I've explained the first. I was indoors, shielded. But that leaves our little session this morning, doesn't it?"

Sam watched him, her heart brimming with hatred. Richard snapped his fingers and suddenly the room was suffused with daylight. He snapped them again and again, as if he were throwing a light switch. The room was bright and airy, filled with light one second, then protected by the dark curtains Sam had wanted to blow apart with her Beretta.

"As you know—" He stopped himself and laughed. "Do you know how many times I have to read scripts with dialogue that starts with 'as you know?' You're right, Samantha. It's rubbing off on me. I mean, if you know something already, why should I bother telling you?"

Sam nodded. She understood perfectly. Dani had this power. It was granted to each of her kind, whether they were Initiates or full vampires. Another memory

239

of the troubled times she and her daughter had shared months earlier came to her. Dani had saved a man from a group of street punks. She had made them see her as someone else, a man:

"It's easy for me, y'know?" Dani had said viciously.

Suddenly, she had not been Dani anymore. Without warning, she had transformed into a perfect replica of Sam.

"Don't you do that to me!" Sam had cried, grabbing her daughter by the shoulders. The illusion shrank away, leaving only Dani. The girl's lower lip had begun to tremble and tears had welled in the corners of her eyes.

Richard had done the exact same thing to her. He had altered her perceptions. He had lied to her.

"I could let you figure out all of it," Richard said. "But as you've gathered, this is *fun* for me. I always wanted to play this scene with someone."

"Then finish it," Sam said, looking at the dark curtains. She understood that while his words were true, he was entertaining himself with his string of revelations, delighting in the deepening expression of betrayal on Sam's face, there was another reason for him to drag this out. He was stalling until night had fallen outside, until it was safe for him to start conducting his true business, whatever that might be.

"The Net has several branches. Some of them hire out to the humans for quick cash. Mostly, our resources stay among ourselves. We have a casting department that you wouldn't believe."

"Casting department?"

"You wanted to know how I handle appearances during the day. It's simple. For people in my position, the Net finds body doubles. They secure them, deliver

240

them, and I program them. They know everything they have to know to take my place when it's either impossible or simply inconvenient for me to appear in person.

"Of course, they age, and the stress wears them out fairly quickly. I know you could make the argument that they're human beings, but that's exactly the point. They're only humans. They're expendable."

"Don't you feel anything?"

"Toward them? No. No more than I would feel guilty about throwing away disposable contact lenses. But you are a totally different matter."

"Why?"

"When we were together, I sensed your strength. I knew that you would be a perfect—"

Suddenly, before Richard could finish his statement, Marissa burst into motion, launching herself at Sam. Marissa's talons swept forward, and her maw opened wide, revealing her collection of razor-sharp teeth.

In Sam's arms, Dani suddenly came to life, her golden eyes flashing open. She vaulted at Marissa, tackling the girl and sending her back against the wall. A painting fell, crashing to the floor beside them. Sam understood that her daughter had been feigning unconsciousness, and had been using her power to appear nearly lifeless while she listened and waited for an opening.

Though she was heartsick as she watched her daughter hold back the creature that had been Marissa, she knew that she could not afford to hesitate. She dropped to her knees and snatched an object from the floor, a small black cigarette lighter that had been thrown from the cleaning woman's pocket along with several other items. She cut her hand on the broken glass and ignored the sudden sting of pain. She had considered picking up the Beretta and once again attempting to blow out the dark curtains, but a glance at her watch had told her that night had fallen outside.

Darting to the bathroom closest to the door, Sam snatched an aerosol can of hair spray from the counter. She heard a crash in the other room and emerged from the bathroom with the lighter held before her, the aerosol can behind it.

She was surprised to see Richard dragging Marissa off Dani. The girl's legs kicked high in the air and Richard nearly lost his balance as he attempted to control the monster he had sired. Sam ran forward, pressed the release on the aerosol can and flicked the lighter at the same moment. A tongue of flame reached forward. Richard tossed Marissa from him and turned away from the flame. It seared his arm and part of his back, then he turned and slapped the items from Sam's hands, the force sending her back. She stumbled over the cleaning woman's corpse, fell to moist, blood-soaked carpeting, and reached for her gun.

Sam knew that the only permanent means of destroying the vampires were fire and sunlight. She had shot Isabella twice in the head and had splattered her midsection with a shotgun, and the woman had regenerated. But the initial shock of the bodily damage had more than once been enough to put the vampires down for brief periods, and if she could disable them long enough, she could take advantage of their condition and burn them.

She turned over, bringing the weapon up, and felt a bolt of agony pierce her. Her finger tried to close over the trigger, but she felt a sharp pain at the base of her skull and fell back, paralyzed. Her worst nightmare had suddenly become reality. Images of waking up after her countless operations, certain each time that she would never be able to move again, rushed into her. The fear became overwhelming, she could not force it down.

Across the room, Richard, Marissa, and Dani had been struck by the startling force of Sam's distress. Dani recalled the threat she had made against Marissa earlier that day. She coiled her power and attempted to reach into Richard's mind, hoping to leap past his consciousness before he had a chance to fight back. She would use her power to alter his physiology, to inflict the type of damage that perhaps even a vampire's inhuman body chemistry could not fight.

She did not make it.

At the first brush of contact, Richard struck out with his power. The pain sent her sprawling. She stumbled across the room and fell beside her mother. Turning, she saw that Richard's face was beet red, his jaws tightly set, the veins in his forehead and neck throbbing and pronounced. Beside him, Marissa sat in a crouch, her taloned hands ripping out tufts of fabric from the rug. Dani attempted to find some trace of the confused, frightened young girl she had known earlier that day, a girl who had risked her own life to save Dani. All that seemed to remain was an animal,

243

the same primal creature that Isabella had been reduced to moments before Dani had turned the flame-thrower on her.

For an instant, Marissa's eyes softened, and an expression of sheer agony was painted upon her face. Dani suddenly heard Richard's voice, though he was not speaking.

Marissa, listen to me. I am your father. You are of my blood. You will do as I say and you will leave the woman alone!

With a scream of absolute anguish, Marissa leaped forward. Dani fought the numbing effects of Richard's power, ignored the burning fear she had felt from her mother, and slammed into Marissa. They were driven back with such force that they crashed into the window separating them from the lanai. The glass exploded outward as Marissa's back connected first with the black curtain that had been hooked in place, then with the glass. Dani's attack had driven the breath from the blonde. The curtain fell upon them and Marissa became wild, ripping and clawing at the fabric, which had been thick enough to spare them any lacerations from the broken glass.

Dani screamed as Marissa's talons raked her arm, causing an explosion of pain. Realizing that it could just as easily have been her throat which had been slashed in Marissa's frenzy, Dani attempted to grab hold of Marissa's wrists. The girl rose up suddenly and Dani lost her grip. The shredded black curtain fell from them, and Dani lashed out with a flat-handed jab to the girl's solar plexus. The blow, which should have paralyzed Marissa, only served to anger her more. Marissa grabbed Dani's hair, slammed her face against the lanai wall, then dragged her to the railing.

Dani was fighting off the effects of the blow to her head, feeling a warm trickle of blood falling into her eyes, when she saw the sparkling lights of the city stretched out before her. Night had engulfed Los Angeles, a sight Dani had found beautiful so many times before. She felt a cool breeze lift her hair as Marissa hauled her high overhead. Dani's view suddenly became dizzying as she saw the lights twist into a tunnel and suddenly she was looking down at the ground twenty stories below.

An explosion sounded and Marissa stiffened. Dani screamed as Marissa teetered forward and dropped her over the edge, into the night.

Chapter Thirteen

Dani's hand shot out, grasping Marissa's arm. The girl toppled forward, over the ledge, and together they plunged toward the street. Last night, they had performed this same act, tumbling together toward death. Then, they had survived. Marissa had still been human. She had wanted to save Dani from danger. Tonight, Marissa had wanted to kill both Dani and her adopted mother, Sam.

Dani had glimpsed the bright red splotch on Marissa's back, wetter and more vibrant than the bloodstains from her murder of the cleaning woman. The sound she had heard was unmistakably the Beretta. A single shot had been squeezed off. Marissa had been hit. A human might have been killed by the wound, but Marissa had merely been startled.

They were twisting, pirouetting in midair, clutching at one another. Marissa's hands were human once more, her wolflike incisors had shrunk into their housings, and her eyes were wide with fear. Dani saw a lanai rush up at her, two women standing at the edge, sipping drinks which they raised.

Madison and Isabella. Both women were smiling invitingly.

Jesus, God, Dani thought, maybe I should let it happen, maybe I should—

Then she thought of her mother, left alone in the suite with Richard and she began to claw at the railings that flew past. They weren't close enough to reach.

Suddenly, Marissa began to struggle in Dani's arms. They were turning, spinning wildly, catching dizzying glimpses of the mirrored surface of the office building across the street, the streets in the far distance, the cars that seemed to be growing as the women plummeted, and the building's face—alternating views of solid wall and more lanais. Another couple, real this time, not a hallucination, saw them and shouted in surprise.

Dani felt a presence in her mind, chanting her name.

Marissa.

The human girl within the creature had not been destroyed, her mind had retreated from the horror of what had been done to her. She had been forced to embrace her heritage, given no choice but to become what she feared and loathed the most.

Dani could barely breathe. Her heart was thundering and she tried to force her fear away. They had so little time. Dani reached out with her silver thread and eased into the girl's mind.

Marissa, listen to me! You can save—

Suddenly they struck the side of the building and nearly lost their grip on each other. They were bounced out farther from the building, and Dani saw that they would land away from the curb, in the street.

Trying desperately to calm herself, Dani glimpsed Marissa's surface thoughts and realized that the girl was overwhelmed by self-loathing and wanted to die. Dani had felt the same way once, but death was not the answer. The struggle for humanity could be fought and won. Dani had proven that. She was not going to allow Marissa to throw both their lives away.

Dani thought of a single, calming image, an image she had seen only in her dreams for the past fourteen months. She forced Marissa to understand what it was like to fly, to allow her body to transform into something which could defy the laws of nature and reality. Dani's dreams of taking flight, of rising into the silvery clouds and then above them suffused Marissa.

It's for you, Dani whispered invitingly, *all for you. Take it, don't be afraid. There's no reason. I won't let you be hurt. Hurry now, Marissa. Hurry, sweetheart, and take it for both our sakes!*

Dani felt Marissa's hand, once again a talon, rake across the side of her face, tearing open a deep, bloody gash. Her eyes flashed opened in surprise and she saw that they were within a hundred feet of the ground, speeding toward the hood of a Federal Express truck. The driver was looking up at them, mouth agape, his clipboard sitting on the pavement, where he had dropped it. Four or five other onlookers were staring at them.

God, no, please!

248

The roar that had been in her ears changed suddenly, and she felt an impossible sensation, as if it had become the previous night once again and they had struck the surface of the waters. She felt a horrible tearing, as if her every muscle was being ripped apart. The pain eased at the same time as their rate of descent. Dani saw that they had veered off, though they were spiraling toward another point on the street, their heads aimed toward the grill of a red Topaz. They lifted up suddenly and Dani felt her long, flowing hair being pushed back against her skull as she came within inches of having her brains splattered against the hot metal of the oncoming car. Rising above several cars, Dani shuddered and cried as she felt the cool evening winds. She looked into Marissa's face and saw that the blonde was crying, and her tears were blood-red streaks arcing down her cheeks.

Dani was surprised as Marissa instinctively spread her power before her, altering the perceptions of any humans who had seen them, or any who might see them now. Their memories of the event would be no more substantial than if they had noticed a hint of movement at the periphery of their visions, then turned to see there was nothing there at all.

Dani pulled back with her silver thread, disengaging herself from Marissa, the effort and the shock of all that had happened leaving her drained.

She was unaware as Marissa carried them far from the hotel, into the depths of L.A.'s underside.

* * *

"I'm impressed. Genuinely impressed," Richard said as he walked over to Sam and took the Beretta from her hand. "I honestly didn't think that was possible."

Sam sat up, staring in shock at the broken window. There had only been one time in her life when she had focused so much of her will in a single instant. She had found Dani as an infant, abandoned beside a garbage dumpster, and she had raced the little girl to the hospital. By the time she got there, the baby was no longer breathing. Sam had been willing to die in that single instant if the child could live. When she had seen the young, blond-haired vampire lift her daughter over her head, she knew that Dani had only one chance.

Somehow, she had overcome her paralysis, clutched the gun, and fired a single shot that should have pierced the space between the blonde's shoulder blades and instead missed the spine altogether. She had prayed that Marissa would fall back, dropping Dani behind her, into the lanai. That would have been the normal response, the human response. But Marissa was not human, she had been turned by her father.

Sam had watched helplessly as Dani fell over the railing, taking Marissa with her. Richard had once again exerted control over her, and had stood by patiently, watching her with a wan smile. He checked his watch, shrugged, then walked to Sam and knelt before her.

"Well now," Richard said, "shall we see how it all turned out?"

He held out his hand and Sam felt herself slowly rise. She despised being under his control, her every movement his to command. They walked, holding hands like lovers, to the lanai, where he made her stop before she could look over the railing.

"Isn't this pretty?" he asked, making a wide, sweeping gesture with his hand. "The city at night. The lights. The sounds. Everything's alive."

Sam was shaking.

Richard smiled. "Go on and look."

Turning, she looked over the railing and saw a typical street scene far below. Sam felt herself relax instantly. Dani and Marissa were not there.

"I guess I try too hard to be a showman," Richard said. "In some acts, there's nothing like that final few seconds of tension, when you think you're going to see how something turns out, then you have to wait a little longer. Delayed gratification. I read a study on it, once. Nothing like it."

Her body tensed once more and she found her head angling toward him, her gaze shifting away from the street. The force that had been controlling her movements, the power that originated in Richard's mind, eased slightly, but only enough to allow her to speak. She could not ever raise her hand against him.

"You bastard," she said, "you could have gone after them."

"Of course," he admitted wistfully. "I thought about it. Then I decided that if my daughter couldn't save herself from something this minor, then she wasn't worthy of the gift I had given her. And she never would be strong enough to follow the script I've been writing for her."

"Dani might have died, too."

"That would have been regrettable, at least for your sake," he said calmly.

I'm going to see you burn, Richard Sterling, Sam thought, but at this moment, the threat would have been an empty one, and she did not want to give him the satisfaction of hearing her say the words.

He winked at her. Her thoughts were still open to him.

"You're wondering where they've gone. That's a reasonable concern. But don't worry. I can find Marissa. My blood is in her. Distance is meaningless."

"That wasn't the case before."

Richard frowned. "She wasn't an Immortal then. She's going to be happy being on her own for a little while, but it won't last. She's going to want to be near me, she's going to feel the need. I can wait for it."

"Your daughter won't be fully turned until she makes a kill on her own."

"That's true."

"And it has to happen within three days, or you'll lose her. I saw what was in her eyes. She hates you. She hates what you've made her become."

"Part of her feels that way. Part of her loves it. We'll see which is stronger. As for her second meal, she *does* have your daughter. But I wouldn't worry about it. There's plenty of fresh meat out there. She'll find something that intrigues her. Or she'll die."

"Don't give me that shit. Yoshino tried to put that idea in Dani's head. She had the choice of going on as one of you and she refused."

"I know."

"She didn't die. She went back to being human."

"She's not human, *Samantha*. She never has been, and never will be. Your daughter can deny what she is for as long as she wants, but she could always be turned again, and this time she may make a different decision. But that's not what we're talking about. I mentioned Vince Calzaretti before. He was working for me, though he didn't sign on until last night. I had a very busy night, as you may have gathered.

"You should be happy. I mean, there is an up side to all of this. By being present at Calzaretti's confession, you've helped to save a human life. I mentioned the people I have on duty through the Net. My happy little worker bees. My body doubles."

"Yes."

"I had been thinking that I would send for one of them. That way I could give you a demonstration of a technique I've mastered. It's called an Azrael Block. Have you ever heard of such a thing?"

Sam tried to keep her mind blank, insisting on giving him no reaction. Despite her best efforts, a wave of fear raced from her.

He closed his eyes and inhaled as if he were sampling a new and delicious wine. "That was good, Samantha."

"Stop calling me that."

His eyes became hard. "You're a *woman*. You shouldn't be going around with a man's name. If I wanted to, I'd cure you of that little problem. I could make you respond in any way I choose. I could make you *come* every time I called you Samantha. I could make you a slave to it. So don't fucking argue just because I want the woman in my life to show a little decorum and allow herself to be addressed properly by her man."

She wondered how long he had hated women.

"Longer than you could imagine," he said. "But not all women, just those who don't show proper respect. I know this is a much different age from when I was brought up. And you don't want to *know* how long ago that was. I knew the world was going to go to hell when the church loosened up all those restrictions. Now anything goes. The world's a nightmare for people who want some decency in their lives."

She stared at him incredulously. "What in God's name are you talking about?"

Richard smiled. "I'm sorry. Now I'm the one who's making speeches."

Sam thought of how tolerant and gentle he had seemed in his office the other night, when she had been talking about the archaic manner in which women were still perceived. He must have been writhing inside. The thought pleased her.

With a sigh, Richard said, "You don't have to know any of this. What you do have to know is what happens if you defy me. What you saw this afternoon, at the confession, was my work. I knew that I had been sloppy on several of my kills. I was getting depressed. I didn't care about proper form. That's not like me. I found Vince, put into his head what

254

he needed to know to make a confession, then gave him an extra added bonus for his hard work."

"The Azrael Block."

"Yes. I can make the trigger take any form I choose. A response to a certain question, or a slip in proper behavior—whatever. What's important is that I placed one of those in Marissa's head. Tick-tick-tick. She either kills in three days, or she dies. There is no other option for her."

"Does she understand that?"

"Yes. She does. But now we have to talk about what you understand. And what I've placed in you." Richard set her hands on his shoulders and drew her into an embrace. She felt sickened by his touch.

"I hate you," she whispered.

"I know. That makes it all the better. I've given you two gifts, Samantha. They complement each other. One of them is an Azrael Block of your very own. The other is the reason for such measures."

She tensed, but could not pull away.

"I had pictured another way of telling you this. A candlelit dinner, perhaps. A cruise on my company's yacht. But I really can't wait."

He pulled back so that he was staring into her eyes.

"You see, you are going to be the mother of my second child. . . ."

Chapter Fourteen

Marissa had been frightened when Dani withdrew from her mind, but the sheer exhilaration she felt at flying over the streets outweighed her fear. Though it was difficult to form rational, coherent thoughts, she had learned a great deal from the time she had spent in Dani's mind the previous night, and she knew secrecy was of paramount importance. She reached out with her power — which had never been so strong, she could not even have *imagined* it being so strong — and blanketed the streets below her, altering the perceptions of any who might have looked up and seen her as she carried Dani in her arms.

Where can we go? Marissa had asked in the soft, delicate corridors of Dani's mind. *We need a safe place.*

The images that had assailed Marissa were of no use: She could not take them to Samantha Walthers's house. Venice Beach, come morning, would be deadly for her. The Malibu beach house had been placed on the market six months ago and was now under renovations by the new owners.

Suddenly, an image of people laughing and moving to unheard rhythms beneath deep, strobing red and blue lights came to her. She saw high, arching cathedral walls with glaring spotlights. Blazing red doors. Blinking neon signs.

The Hellfire Club.

No, she could not go there. Too many people. Too much life. Too much *temptation*.

There were other places. Similar places. She had read about one which had recently been closed. With a degree of effort, she was able to recall the article, and with it, the address of the club.

The streets were teeming with life. Marissa could sense the fear and desire that swept the triple-X district, where glittering, gaudy lights pulsed and pounded and signs in storefront windows made vulgar promises to an eager clientele. She wanted nothing more than to stop and taste the human delicacies that were strewn below her. The men and women who were not satisfied at home, who needed to satiate their dark sexual urges with strangers, or attempt to exorcise them with fantasies packaged in magazines and videos. The hawks who were always on the lookout for new talent.

The predators and the prey.

Marissa knew on which side of the equation she now belonged. A wave of conflicting emotions swept over her. Her hungers had been sated. Without trying at all, she could picture the look of absolute horror on the cleaning woman's face, she could feel the pulse of the woman's quickening heart as death fast approached, and she could delight in the exquisite fear she culled from the woman as she bathed herself in the woman's blood.

The thoughts made her shudder. She was a human girl. She knew that she should have been repulsed by what she had done, but she was not. It had been thrilling, a near-perfect sensual experience. Nevertheless, she wanted to be away from the humans.

Marissa found the two-story building that housed the club. The owner had been busted for allowing a production company to use the club as a location for adult videos and there were padlocks on all the doors. Marissa circled around to the rear entrance, set Dani on the ground, then snapped the padlocks without effort. The door refused to give easily and Marissa slammed at the cold metal hard enough to leave an impression of her hand. There was no doorknob. Taking a few steps back, she slammed into the door with her shoulder and the door jumped off its hinges.

Marissa stared in shock as the door teetered for a moment, then fell back and slammed to the darkened interior of the club.

"Damn," she said giddily, "and I don't even work out."

She retrieved Dani and carried her inside, setting her down near the doorway. The light from the club's small rear parking lot filtered in through the open doorway and illuminated the backroom. The place was a skeletal husk. The red carpeting was filthy, except in certain areas, where large items had left perfectly clean rectangles and squares. She pictured amplifiers and other equipment. Scraps of paper had been left with bits of tape on the wall. Holes indicated where other missing items had been nailed. Marissa wondered if the police had confiscated the club's assets, or if the owners had sent people to remove their belongings. In either case, it seemed to be a perfect hiding place; no one was coming back here any time soon.

She found a fuse box on the wall and threw several breakers. A dull purple luminescence filled the room accompanied by a slight hum. She looked up and saw several neon sculptures hanging from the ceiling. Closing the panel, Marissa stepped away and crouched before the door she had ripped from its hinges. She lifted it, amused by how light it felt—though she knew most humans would not be able to lift it at all—and set it against the doorway, blocking the view of the casual passerby, who might cut through the parking lot or use it as a make-out spot.

She saw the door to a small, adjoining bathroom, and went inside. It was very cramped. She flicked on the light and stripped off her halter top. Slowly she turned to look at her back. She saw a mass of bubbling flesh which shocked her, and a small black object that was emerging from the puckered flesh.

A bullet.

The instant before she had toppled from the window, she had felt something slam into her upper back. A searing pain, a trickle of red-hot liquid stealing down her spine; then her world had been consumed by her imminent death, and her sudden discovery of flight.

She watched in fascination as the flattened bullet

was ejected from her back. It fell into the sink where it sailed the outer perimeter in descending spirals then vanished down the open mouth of the drain. Looking back to her regenerating skin, Marissa felt weak. She turned away from the mirror and stumbled out of the bathroom.

Dani was stirring. Her arm had been slashed and it was bleeding. The side of her face had also been scarred. Blood suffused her wild, long hair, reducing it to a tangled mass. Her breathing was even. Marissa watched the steady rise and fall of her chest.

This woman, Marissa thought, this woman I can trust.

Gently, Marissa eased the torn leather jacket from Dani's shoulders. The girl winced and moaned slightly from the pain in her arm. She examined Dani's wounded arm and was relieved to see that no arteries had been severed. There was some blood loss, however, and Dani was pale and shaky.

Marissa slipped Dani's jacket over her bare chest and zipped it up halfway. She felt extremely comforted in the jacket. Rising, she walked into the bathroom, found her discarded shirt, and ripped it into long strips. She ran the water, dabbed several strips, and brought them back to the floor, where Dani lay. After cleaning the blood from Dani's arm and face, she created a makeshift bandage with a section of cloth and used another strip to tie it in place around Dani's arm.

Staring down at the scratches she had left on Dani's face, Marissa realized that they were still bleeding slightly. The call of her blood slammed into her without warning, and she suddenly found herself leaning down, licking the blood from Dani's face. She heard Dani's moans, but she ignored them. The need had welled up inside her and she felt a fiery knot of desire being slowly loosed, the desire not to be alone, the desire to restore the friendship she had attained with Dani earlier that day, then lost because of the animalistic blood haze that had consumed her.

My blood, she thought. My blood can heal her. And it can make her like me. I can turn her.

Most importantly, it would get her away from the Walthers woman, her father's brood mare. She had been able to sense the life within Walthers instantly, she knew what her father had done.

It wasn't fair, it wasn't right!

She had been the one he was looking for. How could he want *another* child?

All she could think about was savaging the woman and destroying the life that was growing within her. Her father had used his power to hold her back; he had made his choice between Marissa and the new child. He could walk into the sunlight and burn for all she cared.

When he had first turned her, she had understood his plans for her, and she would have went along with anything he told her to do. But when she sensed the life he had created in Dani's adopted mother, the world had become a fireball of anger and unreason. She had only fully returned to herself after Dani had helped her to see that her life had value, that they must live.

She looked down at Dani's body. The girl had been wearing an electric pink halter top, black Spandex shorts that went to midthigh, and black leather boots that rose a few inches above the ankle.

Tentatively, slowly giving in to a hunger and a need quite unlike what she had felt earlier, when her father had reached into her mind and released her primal desire for blood, terror, and death, Marissa eased her tongue away from the slight furrows she had caused in Dani's deeply tanned flesh and flicked the tip of her tongue at Dani's slightly parted lips. Dani groaned deeply and Marissa slipped her tongue deep into her mouth, reaching up to caress her breasts with her hands.

She could feel Dani's heart beginning to race. The blood-need came upon Marissa once again and she became one with the distant thunder of Dani's heart, the crashing river of blood coursing through her veins, and the young woman's quickening pulse. Marissa gathered her power and reached out, easing her desire into Dani's mind as she felt her razor-sharp canines extend from their housings. She unzipped the jacket, slid down the front of Dani's halter to expose her breasts, and took the woman into an embrace as she kissed her greedily, their bare breasts pressed together, Marissa's nipples hard and straining. She thought of the memories she experienced when she had been in Dani's mind, the time Dani had shared with Isabella, what they had almost become.

"Be mine," Marissa whispered. "Be with me forever, sister-love."

Kissing her way down to Dani's throat, Marissa opened her mouth wide and eased the tips of her fangs into Dani's neck. Suddenly, an icy dagger of pain shot through Marissa's skull and she was driven back and away from Dani. She fell to the carpeted floor, screaming in pain, and saw Dani rising to her knees.

"That's not what I want," Dani snarled. "How dare you come near me like that!"

Marissa raised her hands in shock. She wanted to explain how wonderful it would be for them, how they would fly through the nights skies together and never be apart. They would each be there for one another, they would be each other's strength, and they would not have to be afraid to be weak in front of each other. They would love and they would cherish their every waking moment together, they would be sisters and they would be lovers in the night.

Coiling her power, Marissa prepared to send her message of love, desire, and happiness into Dani's mind. But the dark-haired girl had sensed the sudden rise within Marissa, and had believed that Marissa was about to launch an attack against her. In her mind, Marissa stepped back with her power and opened herself fully, baring herself to Dani in an attempt to show she meant no harm, that she had only love in her heart for the girl.

A blinding flash of agony exploded in Marissa's mind as the psychic barrage Dani had launched struck Marissa full on.

Marissa saw the endless line of victims she would

take throughout her inhuman life, she felt the horror and violation of each killing she would perform as if she were the victim, seeing herself through their eyes. When she registered the faces of the victims, she understood that she knew each of them. They had been friends from childhood, teachers, counselors, those she had admired or wanted to be close to, and finally, she saw her mother, Elaine, covered in blood, backing away, screaming in fear and loathing.

There's a price! a voice shouted inside her head. *There's a price that's too high, Marissa. Far too high!*

The images faded and Marissa found herself staring into Dani's blazing gold eyes. They, too, were filled with loathing.

Unable to stand the sight of Dani's disgust for what she had become, Marissa ran for the door, hurled it to one side, and ran screaming into the night.

Dani tried to stand, but her legs would not cooperate. She had to phone someone, she needed to get help for her mother, who had been left at the hotel with Sterling. The retaliation against Marissa had practically left her drained, and she collapsed on the floor, her hand falling on a spot of blood. She felt a sharp sting in her neck where Marissa's fangs had bitten into her flesh and she covered the wound, thoughts of blood loss and infection racing through her mind.

My daughter, the doctor.

Her mother's voice, cutting through the delirium that had threatened to engulf her. She had to be strong, she had to find a way to get help for her mother. Reaching out with her silver thread, Dani found that she could make only the most fleeting contact with the minds of those who passed before the deserted nightclub. If she had not been so drained, she could have taken one of them, and forced them to make the call for her.

Pullman. She would call Edward Pullman. He had taken Sam into his heart as if she were his own daughter, he would not hesitate to help her.

Crying out in frustration, she realized that it was no use, she was too weak. She surveyed the room and saw the shadow of a telephone on the wall, from behind the open door to the bathroom. She began to crawl and soon she had covered the first dozen feet. In moments she was before the door, reaching up for the knob, hoping it would give her enough support as she attempted to pull herself to a standing position. She was on one knee, about to bring her other leg up, when the darkness closed over her like a fist, and she fell to the floor.

She would not get up again that night.

Marissa was trembling, standing before a street sign at the corner of a busy intersection. She could not catch her breath. Tears reached down her cheeks. How could Dani have rejected her? They had been in one another's minds. They had seen each other's secrets. She knew that Dani had fought

265

the blood-need, had even named it the demon and had treated it like another entity within herself. That had been wrong.

Marissa knew, she understood what she was, and how unavoidable a union between herself and her need would eventually prove. Her father, may he rot in Hell, had taught her that in the course of a few hours.

Marissa understood Dani's hatred of her condition. Dani had been stronger than she had been, she had been able to throw off the call of her blood, or at least gain some semblance of control. Marissa did not have that choice, and the images Dani had pushed into her head had been hateful and vicious.

There would always be victims for their kind. That was unavoidable.

Suddenly, a car screeched to a halt before Marissa and she heard a man's rough voice shout, "How much, bitch?"

She looked up at him sharply, and became aware that she had not bothered to once again zip up the front on the leather jacket she had taken from Dani. Her breasts were partially revealed. He thought she was a whore, a filthy, human *whore*.

The car that had stopped was a brown Duster. The driver was a thin black man whose age was not readily apparent, as his face was covered by a thick mustache and beard, and a red knit cap had been pulled to an inch of his bushy eyebrows. He wore dark glasses. The man beside him, leaning out of the passenger side door, was a white man in his early twenties, Italian, with spiky hair and a goatee.

He wore a pea-green army jacket, ripped strategically.

The man had continued to issue a steady stream of obscene questions, but Marissa had moved her gaze from him and directed it to the intersection. The Duster was stopped at the light, heading eastbound. The north and southbound traffic was thick and practically impenetrable.

"Drive," Marissa commanded, effortlessly projecting the demand with her power.

"Lickety-split," the black man behind the wheel said as he floored the Duster.

"Jesus Christ, waitaminute!" the man with the goatee screamed as he was hurled back into his seat. The tires of the Duster squealed and the car shot forward. The car made it past two lanes of southbound traffic before a tractor trailer hit it full on, demolishing the driver's side of the vehicle, then sending it pinwheeling into the first of the northbound lanes, where a gray Toyota jackknifed and struck two cars off to its left. Several cars attempted to stop behind the tractor trailer, but it was too late for them. Within seconds, the intersection was a steaming mass of twisted wreckage, with more than a dozen cars damaged or destroyed.

Marissa delighted in the rush of fear and agony that had greeted her as the collisions had occurred. She stood for a moment, shaking with pleasure, all thoughts of her father's betrayal and Dani's disturbing choice swept away. The indescribable pleasure she felt made her want to experience more.

With a laugh, she zipped the stolen jacket halfway

267

up, then turned and strutted across the street, luxuriating in the pain and death she had caused with a single use of her power. She wondered how much more of this delicious fear she could inspire if she truly worked at it.

Tonight, she decided, she would find out.

Chapter Fifteen

Marissa was in love with the night. She felt the glory of the darkness encompass her like a lover as she walked through one of the worst neighborhoods she had ever visited. The marquees above adult theaters proudly proclaimed the titles of triple-XXX films, and posters for such video releases as *Edward Penishands* and the infamous *Nurse Nancy*—the film that helped to bury Pee Wee Herman's career in Florida—were plastered everywhere she turned, along with advertisements for 900 numbers.

The men and women who walked past her either gazed at her with open desire or made a point of downturning their eyes when they approached. It made no difference to Marissa. She could feel the intense need radiated by nearly everyone who walked this stretch. Marissa was surprised that the most succulent emotions sometimes came from the whores and the dealers. Many of the prostitutes, both male and female, lived in a constant state of terror. They were afraid of taking that final ride with a lunatic who would slit their throat or force them to have unprotected sex.

The drug addicts also proved to be an amusing distraction. At random, she would reach into their minds and bodies, either sending their need out of control or plunging them into withdrawal. No one would stop and examine the users who would fall to the ground, writhing in agony because of Marissa's touch.

She hated them, and deep down, she knew the reason why, though she would not admit it to herself.

Suddenly, a handsome, square-jawed Latino who was dressed like a lawyer stepped out of a white convertible which had pulled up to the curb a dozen yards from Marissa. He carried a briefcase. His watch was a Rolex. Designer sunglasses covered his eyes. A nearby street light cast highlights on his rich, thick black hair, which had been stylishly groomed. His fingernails appeared to have been manicured.

The man approached a poorly dressed, overweight hawker who was extolling the virtues of a porn house that was so new, the unlit sign for the previous business to occupy the space, MOM AND POP'S ALL-AMERICAN DELI, still sat above the door.

The Lawyer, as Marissa thought of him, spoke with the overweight man for a few moments then looked away in disgust.

"Jesus," the Lawyer spat. "Get him for me."

The overweight man nodded sharply, addressing the Lawyer as "sir," and vanished into the porn house. The handsome Latino glanced at his watch, then looked back to the convertible. Several men sat inside. The Lawyer shook his head and frowned. One of the men in the car curled his fingers and thumb, forming an O, and jerked his hand back and forth several times. Laughter sounded from the car. The Lawyer shook his head and turned away.

Marissa stopped when she was within a dozen feet of the Lawyer and leaned against a wall. She could easily have looked into his mind and gained all of his secrets, but she was in the mood to play, and that would make it far too easy.

Spreading her psychic cloak before her, she ensured that no one would see her. She could walk up to them, slap them, and her image would continue to be mentally erased from their perceptions. Maintaining the shield took practically no effort, and so she walked close to the Lawyer and examined him more fully. She delighted in the angles of his chiseled face, and was intrigued by the chain that held the briefcase to his wrist.

She wondered if her suspicions about the briefcase were correct. Images from espionage novels entered her head. She saw the Lawyer slide the briefcase across a long boardroom table, then leap to the floor as the man he had handed it to was blown apart, either by a gun on a springload device, or some form of explosive. Resisting the temptation to peer into his mind and learn the answers she leaned over and gently planted her tongue in the man's ear.

He darted back in alarm, clamping his hand over his ear, looking around to see what had touched him. He looked in Marissa's direction and saw nothing. She could not help but experience his sudden rush of fear, and she was impressed by how quickly he regained control of himself.

Before she could come up with a new game to play,

the overweight hawker appeared, and he wasn't alone. A man in his early twenties wearing black leather pants, boots, and a black silk shirt with several necklaces came out, giggling, stoned. His features revealed that he was related to the Lawyer, who thanked the overweight man, jammed a hundred-dollar bill in the man's pocket, then grabbed the younger man's arm and steered him to the white car. The door sprang open and the Lawyer tossed the younger man inside.

"You can be so fucking worthless, do you know that? I don't know why *he* fucking puts up with you, I really don't," the Lawyer said.

"Come on, Ramon," the younger man said. "It's no big deal."

"Bobby, just shut up, all right?"

The younger man nodded.

Ramon, the Lawyer, nodded to the driver and said, "Get us the hell out of here."

Marissa did not hesitate as the white car pulled into traffic. She spread her arms wide and lifted herself into the night, but this time it wasn't quite so easy. Flying over the white car, determined to follow it to its destination, Marissa began to feel tired and drained, and the strength that had suffused her slowly slipped away. When they reached their first light, Marissa dropped to the ground gracelessly and tore open the driver's side door of the car behind the white convertible. She allowed the man behind the wheel to see her.

"What are you doing in *my* car?" she asked the driver, lashing out with her power.

Bucking in the seat, he cried, "I'm sorry, ma'am, I'm sorry!"

He undid his seat belt, got out of the car, and closed the door after Marissa was inside. The light changed and he wandered into traffic, inspiring several angry car horns to flare. The white convertible was in motion again, and Marissa followed it closely, using her power to force the passengers in it to ignore the presence of the blue Probe that was practically glued to its bumper.

Thirty minutes later, after reaching a somewhat more affluent part of the city, the convertible pulled up to an exclusive gym with valet parking. Marissa parked across the street. She watched as Ramon, Bobby, and two other men got out of the car. The two men she hadn't seen previously were identical twins, with stocky builds and matching salt-and-pepper hair. They carried themselves with the professional demeanor of bodyguards, or well-trained dog soldiers.

Marissa left the Probe and entered the health club, effortlessly shielding her presence. The building was three stories high, with smoked-glass windows that allowed a casual observer to see the unmistakable forms of men and women working out, promoting the club while protecting the privacy of its members. She had worked at a Bally's for several weeks and had been forced to quit because of the incredibly strong desire she encountered from the male *and* female clientele. Tonight, she reveled in those sensations, although they were not directed at her.

Marissa caught up with Ramon, Bobby, and the guards as they were being shown into one of the private workout rooms on the third floor. She slipped inside as the doors were being shut. Suddenly, she became concerned that this room would be lined with mirrored walls and ceilings. Though the men she trailed would not have been able to see her directly, her reflection would have been plain to them. Instead the room was lined in black vinyl and there was only a single large mirror in the center of the room. Marissa's fear dissipated.

She was surrounded by gleaming weights, Stair-Masters, Nautilus machines, and a half-dozen workout benches and steps. A dozen men stood in the workout room, which was thirty square feet. Marissa recognized four of them as the men she had followed inside. Of the remaining eight, only one was dressed in workout clothes. He was in his late forties, short, with a barrel chest. His arms, legs, and neck were tree trunks. He wore a pair of white shorts, white Nikes with matching socks, and fingerless weightlifting gloves. The man's head was a jar with short, graying hair, piercing deep blue eyes, and a menacing scowl. His body was covered in tattoos, so many that Marissa could only make out a spattering of images as the man curled a set of hand weights as Ramon spoke to him—or spoke at him, to be more precise. If the man was listening, he gave no indication. Marissa watched as a python seemed to slither across the tattooed man's arm, its jaws opening and closing over a tattooed eight ball.

Surrounding the tattooed man were a brace of bodyguards, all of whom somehow managed not to sweat, despite their dark suits. The bulges in their jackets betrayed their guns. Marissa understood the reason for the vinyl covering: Soundproofing, in the events of shots being fired. She wondered how many men had been shot in this room, and once again resisted the temptation to use her power and learn the answers. She looked to Ramon, who sat on the edge of a workout bench across from the tattooed man and folded his hands over the briefcase, which rested in his lap.

"Mister Coska, our network exists to bring you the finest quality merchandise," Ramon said in his most lawyerly voice. "We have a reputation to maintain. Someone's been spreading bad products on the streets. And this *someone* has gone out of their way to make it look like it was me, which in turn reflects badly on you."

Ramon opened the briefcase. It was filled with cash. "I would like to make this offering as a show of friendship and loyalty. Even though I am the victim in these circumstances, I know that your reputation has also suffered, and I wish to make amends—"

"Shut up," Coska said as he turned his gaze to Bobby, who was nervously shifting his weight from one foot to the other. "Is he shitting me?"

"No way, Fred," Bobby said.

Marissa smiled. She understood why Coska insisted on having Bobby with Ramon: He could read Bobby. The young man was a walking polygraph.

Coska finally turned his menacing gaze on Ramon. "Here's how it is. This buys you one week. If you can't get this shit straightened out by the end of that time, I'm shutting you down. I've been through this kind of thing before, we all have. But you need to be able to handle your own affairs before they come around and start making trouble for your benefactors. Does that make sense to you?"

Marissa watched Ramon's eyes. He was perfectly composed, but she could feel the searing waves of fear leaping from him.

"Of course, Mister Coska. That's very generous."

"Tell me about it."

Marissa sensed that the meeting was at an end, and she was not satisfied with its conclusion. She had been correct about these people, they *were* involved in the drug trade, and in her eyes, that made them like her father, who had forced her to become a slave to her own addiction when all she wanted in the world was to be free, or to be dead. There was freedom in death. Only thoughts of Dani kept her from finding a fiery end for herself.

Turning her gaze to Bobby, she considered that she still hadn't looked into any of their minds, she hadn't learned even the answer to the mystery that Ramon and Coska had discussed: Had Ramon made a mistake that he was trying to hide, or was he the victim of his rivals?

Another idea came to her, and she decided that truth was meaningless, she had another agenda in mind. She crouched in the corner, behind a heavy weight machine, and reached out to Bobby's mind. She planted images there, visions of Ramon meeting with a group of perhaps two dozen men, giving them precise instructions.

Suddenly, Bobby leaped to his feet and hollered, "It's a setup! Mister Coska, he's gonna try to kill you, he's got men all around this building, he's got people inside here who are gonna fucking blow you to pieces—"

Ramon grabbed Bobby by his silk shirt and slapped him with the back of his hand. His lawyerly demeanor faded as he snarled, "What the fuck are you talking about? What are you trying to do? They should have drowned you at birth you stinking little—"

A hand weight caught Ramon on the side of the head. He snapped back, a thin stream of blood arcing into the air. Several men drew their weapons, including Ramon's salt-and-pepper-haired dog soldiers. They were not the first to fire. One of Coska's men shot one of the twins in the throat just as the twin's finger closed over the trigger of his automatic. The other twin began firing, placing a bullet in Coska's arm, through the eye of the snake tattoo. The spray of bullets struck flesh, killing two of Coska's men, wounding three others, while several slugs of metal were imbedded in the weight benches or ricocheted against the hard steel of the machinery.

The wounded, dying twin was on his knees, clutching at his throat. His brother suddenly jerked spasmodically as a hail of bullets stitched across his chest and another shot entered his forehead and caused the back of his skull to explode. Both twins fell to the floor at precisely the same moment.

From her hiding place, Marissa clamped her hand over her mouth, barely restraining her bubbling laughter. The rush of exquisite fear that she took from the dying men had put her in a state of near-sexual frenzy. The more she tasted, the more she desired.

Coska looked at Ramon, who was on his hands and

knees, attempting to rise, and Bobby, who was forced to sink down to a workout bench because his legs would no longer support him. Blood running down his arm, Coska shifted the hand weight from his wounded arm to his free one and said, "How many?"

"It's bullshit," Ramon said. "There's no one out there!"

Frowning, Coska raised the weight and brought it down squarely on Ramon's back. The man let out a cry of pain and surprise then flattened to the floor. Coska stepped on his wrist and brought the weight down on Ramon's hand. Ramon screamed as the crunch of bones being pulverized filled the air.

"How many?"

"He's lying, he's lying," Ramon cried.

"Fuck this shit," Coska said, slamming the weight on the back of Ramon's head again and again until the man's bloody form ceased to twitch.

"Bobby, you're gonna be more reasonable," Coska said.

The younger man shook his head. "You know it, yes, sir, Mister Coska."

"I thought I told you to call me Fred."

"I'm sorry, Fred. Yeah, of course, Fred."

"So *you* tell me how many men he's got here, where they're positioned, what they're waiting for. You tell me."

From behind the workout station, Marissa coiled her power, brushed Bobby's mind, and obscured the details of the false memories she had planted there.

When Bobby was unable to answer Coska's question, the tattooed man went to work on him with the weights. His death was long and terrible.

Marissa allowed the drama she had created to unfold, but she felt empty when it was over. The hollow feeling in her breast quickly changed to anger. When she heard Coska tell his men to "haul the trash" she exploded in a rage, reaching out with her power to burrow deep into Coska's mind.

He looked down and saw a large black shape partially detach itself from his arm. The snake, whose right eye was a gory mass, opened its maw and spoke to him. It told him what he needed to know, it gave the face of his betrayer.

"It's you!" Coska said, snatching a weapon from one of his men and opening fire on him. His guards were so stunned that by the time they were able to react, Coska had whirled, screaming an obscenity, and shot two more of his men.

As they raised their weapons, disbelief slowing their responses, Coska continued to fire until he was the only one left alive in the room.

The only one other than Marissa.

She came to him, rising into the air like a dark angel, the blood calling to her, her need screaming for release, though she knew that when she killed again, she would retain this form forever. Opening her arms, she allowed her razorsharp canines to sprout from their housings.

Coska looked at her, the madness she had inspired within him suddenly vanishing. He nodded, closed his eyes, and placed the gun on the underside of his jaw.

"No!" Marissa screamed, but it was too late. The explosion blew out the back on the tattooed man's head. She caught him before his body fell and sank her teeth into his neck, but the blood was already cooling, and the life was gone from him. Her hands transformed into talons and she tore at his throat and chest, savaging him the way she had mauled the cleaning woman earlier that day.

When she had looked at Coska, moments before he killed himself, she had seen not his face, but the face of her father, the grinning, confident face of the man who had destroyed her life.

The blood was sour, but it dulled her need, allowing her reason to return.

She suddenly realized where she was and what she had done. Covering her face with her hands, she began to cry.

What in God's name had she been thinking? Why did she do this? So many people had died and it was her fault.

A hand closed over her shoulder and she cried out at the incredible burst of sensations that raced through her, a comforting wave of pleasure that made her shake. She looked up and saw one of Coska's men. He was young, with sandy blond hair that fell in a wave over his brow, helping to obscure his slight receding hairline. His features were angular, vaguely Austrian, and his eyes were black, with only a few slivers of gray. His white shirt was bloodstained.

She knew instantly that he was one of her kind. He had been powerful enough to shield his presence from her, though they had been in the same room.

"We have to get out of here," he said in a voice that was loving, gentle, and kind. "Take my hand, I won't hurt you."

"I should stay," she said, "I should wait for morning."

"No," he said. "Be with me tonight. If you want, there's a skylight in my apartment. I keep it there so I can at least look at the light. Don't make any decisions until morning."

"All right," she said, realizing that she didn't even know his name. She half expected him to suddenly tell her, to reveal that he had been in her mind, that he was doing to her what her father had done to her, but that was not the case. He had not violated her the way Sterling had.

"I'm Timothy Fairfax," he said, holding out his hand to her. She took it, surprised by his gentlemanly manners, and told him that she was Marissa.

She held his hand as he led her out of the bloody room.

After they had left the club, Timothy using his power to disguise them as they made their exit, they took the car Marissa had stolen and drove for fifteen minutes, heading back in the direction from which Marissa had come. They were close to the Third Street Festival grounds, and Timothy suggested that they deposit the car in a garage and leave it.

They walked several blocks and came to a one-story brick building a few doors down from a comedy club. Marissa had been to the club before, and would have loved to have stopped there, but she knew that she had been around enough humans for tonight, and she wanted to spend time with this man, to learn his secrets.

They entered a small hallway and encountered a door to their right and a short flight of steps directly before them. Marissa looked up and saw the glass skylight Timothy had mentioned. It wasn't actually in his apartment, but in the morning, the square of light would strike just before the steel door to his sanctuary. They would be able to see it with the door open.

"Who owns the first floor?" she asked.

"I do," he said as he led her to the basement door and unlocked a series of dead bolts. "I really don't use it for anything important, but it helps appearances."

He opened the door and motioned for her to go inside. She stepped into the darkness and he threw the light switch by the door. His basement apartment was an elegantly furnished flat. The floor was black marble, with beautifully crafted Oriental rugs thrown near the living area and his sizable four-poster bed. His furniture was wood with black trim and gold handles. Oriental images were glazed into the surface of the wood. Bookshelves lined the wall. An expensive home entertainment center complete with a laser disk, ceiling-mounted projector, and a screen that would descend by remote control, made up the living room. He had a bar and a kitchen. The door to the bathroom was half open, revealing a black marble shower and a gold-lined mirror.

"Would you like anything?" he asked.

"My sanity," she said, trembling. He took her into his arms and held her in a warm, comforting embrace, rocking her slightly.

"It's hell in the beginning, I know," he whispered into her ear. "It gets better. You learn to trust."

"*Who* do you learn to trust?" she asked, her entire body quivering.

"Yourself." He pulled away from her and looked into her eyes. "That's the major battle. You have to know that what you're doing is right for you."

"What I did tonight was terrible," she cried. "It wasn't human."

"Why should it be, when that's not what we are?" He caressed the side of her face. "I can show you things. I can teach you. I can be a true friend to you, Marissa. Do you want that?"

"I don't know."

"You don't have to make any decisions now. The offer is there. You're going to need a place to stay, a safe place. That can be with me, for as long as you want. There's no one in my life. There hasn't been for a long time."

He leaned down and kissed her. "I'm going to take a shower and change. Unless you'd like to, first?"

"That's fine," Marissa said, stunned by how calm the evening had become after the explosion of violence at the spa. The blood of the dead man, Coska, lazily drifted within her, and a part of her was saddened that the kill had been so unsatisfying. She had not expected the man to have the strength to defy her.

Marissa listened to the rapidly shifting patterns of water for a time, then stripped off her clothing and joined Timothy in the shower. His body was lean and muscular, and his sex came instantly to attention when she stepped into the shower with him. They washed one another, pausing for the occasional kiss or caress, and toweled each other off as they went to his bed and lay down in each other's arms.

"What were you doing there, tonight?" she asked, deciding to enjoy the freedom of acting as a human — a being without the power to look into the mind of another.

Timothy sighed. "I don't believe in the traditional ways. There are things we have to do if we're going to survive. We can't avoid that."

"You mean we have to *kill*," she said, already feeling her hunger rising up inside her.

"Not as often as you would think. The newly turned need blood, a great deal of blood, but the hunger gets easier to live with. I haven't made a kill in two months."

"I don't understand, how do you survive?"

He smiled. "Look at me, Marissa."

She did as he asked.

"How old would you say I am?"

"Twenty. Twenty-one."

"I fought for the North," he said.

She looked away and pressed her head against his chest, allowing him to caress her damp hair. "How many people have you killed?"

"Thousands."

Swallowing hard, she said, "How many do you regret killing?"

"Only the first. She loved me. The bastard who turned me, my father, told me the old legends were true, that I could make her one of our kind. I wanted her with me for all eternity. I didn't think I could face

284

existing for so long without her. I went to her and I told her everything. She was shocked at first, I had to prove it to her. Once she believed, she allowed me to take her. But the hunger was too much for me. I became an animal. When it was over, my father was behind me, laughing at his little joke."

"Was he the second you killed?"

"No," he said quickly. "I would have, but I wasn't strong enough. He said that I was weak, that I had too much of the human in me, and that I would be a disgrace to him. I've never seen him since. All the others after her, all those I killed—they needed killing."

Marissa swallowed hard, considering his words. "What you said before, about not following the 'traditional ways.' What did you mean by that?"

"Most of our kind, the unschooled, anyway, find a human to provide for them. They choose someone wealthy and they become whatever that person needs. They take their fear, their desire, and when they have no further use for their host, or they get bored, they kill them. I prefer to live my own life. Making money is easy. Over the past year I've developed a hell of a reputation as a bodyguard."

"I ruined that for you. Your client's dead."

"It doesn't matter."

"What are you going to do?"

"I have enough money to last me for a few years. Maybe I'll just spend some time with you."

Marissa hugged him even tighter. "You don't know me. You don't know anything about me."

"I know you're frightened."

285

"Yes."

"And I know I want to make the fear go away. I want to chase away all your demons."

"Why?" she asked.

"Because we're the same. I sense it."

Marissa thought of Dani, the friend she needed so desperately, who had turned away from her, who would never willingly embrace her blood heritage again, and who would have hated Marissa if she had been successful in forcing it upon her.

"You could have stopped me at the spa," she said, "you could have—"

"Did you want to be stopped?"

"No."

"Did you find what you were after?"

She kissed his chest. "Yes."

Timothy pulled her up, kissed her hard on the mouth, and opened his mind to her, allowing her to experience his secrets. He did not object when she kept her mind closed to him, but gave her body without hesitation. Plunging his tongue into her mouth, he caressed her breasts then his mouth worked its way down until he was ravenously consuming her sex. She lay back on the bed, moaning and crying with pleasure. Her body began to feel incredibly light, as if strong arms had lifted her up from the bed. Eyes opening wide, Marissa noticed the proximity of the ceiling and bucked wildly, crying out as she realized that both she and Timothy were making love in midair. The knowledge pushed her over the edge and she rode out the first of many shattering orgasms she would enjoy that night.

She could not believe what he was doing to her. "This is wonderful," she whispered. "I want you, too."

Swimming gracefully through the air, Timothy arced his body around to reach her. Marissa caressed his length, then eased him into her mouth as he continued to make love to her with his tongue. Marissa felt not only the pleasure she was receiving from Timothy, but also the wracking waves of ecstasy he was experiencing from her ministrations.

Soon, while they continued to levitate above the bed, Timothy entered her and they strained against each other, changing positions with a matchless grace. She was overwhelmed by the passion with which he drove himself inside her, and the dual sets of pleasure she was receiving from their coupling.

Several hours passed before either of them touched the ground.

"There it is," Timothy said. "If that's what you really want."

Marissa stared at the glowing, blue-white shaft of light. Morning had finally come and it had brought both the piercing white light visible from the open doorway of Timothy's sanctuary, and the deadening need to fall into a deep, dreamless sleep and allow her body to restore itself after the tumultuous night she had experienced.

Timothy and Marissa stood in the sweaty afterglow of their unworldly sex, Marissa standing behind Timothy, her hands wrapped around his chest as she peered at the light from over his shoulder.

"Yeah," she said wistfully, "there it is."

"I can't look at it for too long, but I try to see it every day."

"Are you happy, Timothy?"

"Very."

She kissed his neck from behind, running her hands through his hair, when suddenly she yanked his head back, brought her taloned hand around in a sweeping motion, and sliced through the meat and bone of his neck, severing his head in a single, swift motion. She caught his body as it fell, leaning in as she opened her mouth and swallowed from the geyser of blood spaying up from the wound. From the corner of her eye she saw the lips of Timothy's severed head moving, forming a soundless word:

Wildling.

She ripped the heart from his body, then kicked the dead flesh forward, into the waiting pool of light. Biting down hard on the vampire's heart she sucked what blood was left in it then tossed it into the light with a laugh. She watched as the flesh sizzled, smoked, and burned. There was no doubt in her mind that by nightfall, nothing would remain of the corpse.

Marissa prepared to hurl Timothy's head onto the pyre. She would see it burn, then she would walk into the light. She hesitated, considering the pain she would endure, then took a step forward and stopped dead.

She could not do it.

Screaming in frustration she turned back to the apartment and hurled Timothy's severed head inside. He was just like the others. Worse. When they had made love, he had opened his mind to her, swearing that he was telling her everything. But he had known what would upset her, he had known exactly what sides of himself to put on display. In the moment of his orgasm, he had lost control for the briefest of seconds and she had been able to glimpse the truth.

In his inhuman lifetime, he had fathered six children. Five had been females. He had killed the mothers and the babies that were growing inside them. The sixth had been a son, who had died from a fall when he was six. That was ten years ago. He had sworn that he would never try again, but Marissa could tell that eventually he would take another human female, and when he did that, his infatuation with her would be at an end, unless he could make her love him so much that she would care for the child.

They were all the same.

How many people have you killed?

Thousands. They needed killing.

Who was he to make that judgment? He was not a part of human society. He was a predator. She had been moved to inspire the deaths of Ramon, Coska, and their soldiers because they reminded her of her father. They preyed on weakness. They offered dreams and fantasies to get their victims hooked, then pulled their prey into a choke hold from which they could never escape. But Marissa had been unwilling to look beneath the surface of each man. Some might have been fathers, devoted husbands; some may have been forced into the life they were leading, and may have loathed what they had become. Redemption was possible for them.

They were human.

Those of her kind had made a conscious decision. To live, they would kill. A few might make the moral distinctions Timothy made, but even he had not hesitated to kill five women who had been pregnant with his daughters. He had no remorse over those killings, only a deep rooted frustration because he had not been given a son. Some of her kind might have been turned by force, the way she had been turned, but they had a clear choice also. They could walk into the light. Kill themselves, or face death at the hands of one like her.

Dani had been right to refuse the gift Marissa had offered. Though Dani continued to torture herself for the murders she had committed, she had ultimately made the correct choice, and she had been working toward finding a way to use her powers to help others, not to prey upon them.

Marissa turned back and looked at the light. She had taken a second life, though it had been one of her own kind. The pressure she had felt in her skull had eased, the *death thing* that her father had placed in her head vanishing now that she had become an Immortal.

But she was not going to be like him. Dani had wanted to help Marissa, and she had accomplished her task. Marissa had done something decent. She had taken from the world one of her kind, saving human lives. That should have been enough to give her the strength to walk into the light. Only by killing herself could she ensure that she would not change her mind and become what her father wished her to become.

She considered what his plan for her had been and noted the bitter irony. He had rivals among the Immortals. He had wished to kill them and gain their power. She would have been his weapon, flesh of his flesh, blood of his blood, placed under familiar compulsion to kill for him without hesitation or fear of the consequences.

Marissa looked at the light once again. A few steps, a moment of burning pain, then it would be over. But there was still so much she could accomplish. If Dani could overcome her blood-need, then Marissa could follow her example and stay true to the decision she had made this day.

She would kill Immortals, with Dani's help.

And Richard Sterling would be one of the first.

Chapter Sixteen

Sam sat on the floor of the living room, staring at the brilliant white sunlight filtering in through the open window. Her back was sore, her muscles screaming, but she could not move and she could not speak. Her hopes that the shot she had fired the previous night had been heard, and that help might arrive, had vanished as time had passed. Though he had been distracted, Sterling had apparently managed to blanket the area with his power and alter the perceptions of any who may have heard the single explosion of the Beretta.

When Sam had fought the vampire pack for control of her daughter's soul, fourteen months ago, she had been blessed with the advantage of surprise. Until last night, she had not confronted one of the monsters when they were ready for her, and she had learned that her decades of physical training and her skills with weaponry were not enough. She would have to find a way to damage this bastard, and for that, she would have to go deep into herself.

Richard had given her some time to do exactly that. After they had come in from the lanai, he had commanded her to watch as he took a butcher knife, which he had stolen from the movie studio and savaged the corpse of the cleaning woman. When he was done, he splattered Sam with the woman's blood, then placed the knife in her hand. She had tried to stab him with it, but the lancing pain in her head had returned.

He leaned in, kissed her hard on the mouth, and practically breathed the words, *"La donna e un sesso superiore."*

It had been such a short time before when he had said those words to her under much different circumstances.

Women are the superior sex.

Richard had begun to laugh and found that he could not stop. He apologized over and over, not really meaning it, and finally got around to commanding her to sit against the opposite wall, the knife clutched in her hand. Suddenly, she felt his presence in her head, a cold, weighty thing. It was a violation she could never fully revenge herself for, though she would certainly try at the first opening. The presence retreated, but it had left something in her thoughts. She felt unclean as she listened to the words Richard had placed in her head, a short scene from a script he had written that he expected her to recite when the proper moment arrived. It was like listening to a terrible song that you could not chase out of your thoughts. She thought of the "confessed murderer" whose death she had witnessed. Richard had programmed him, too, and he had been unable to fight the violation.

There was a difference, of course. Though Sam had been placed under an irresistible compulsion, she would not die after she had spoken the words he had given her. Richard claimed that he had given her a child. He wanted her alive to bear the child, and he would want her alive to care for the infant and its special needs. Her knowledge of their kind would make her an ideal parent, at least until the child was old enough to be turned by Richard.

She had only one weapon to use against him. He had placed the Azrael Block in her head. If she violated his conditioning, she would die the way Calzaretti had died, or perhaps by an even worse method.

The thought, taken on its own terms, had both frightened and delighted her. "I'm not afraid of dying, and if I die, your child dies."

He shrugged. "Then I'll make another child. And you'll have taken an innocent life, just to be defiant. I really despise nineties women. It was much better a century ago. And besides, what makes you think my little gift is there to harm you? It's to *keep you* from harming yourself. Or the child."

Jesus, she thought, and struggled to keep her fear under control. She watched him frown. He had been expecting a healthy serving of terror to feast upon after that revelation. He was not going to get it.

A thought had flashed into her mind. "You used protection," she said. "When we fucked, you used a condom."

He went to her and slapped her across the face. "We did not *fuck*. We made love. There is a child growing inside you that is the product of how we felt when we made love. Get used to that thought. I will not have you show disrespect to me, or to our child in that way."

It wasn't until later, when he was gone, that she allowed herself to wonder why he did not simply program

294

her to become the woman he wanted. Perhaps he had no idea what he wanted.

But while he was there, he explained that the condom had been an illusion. That was why it was no longer on the floor the morning after they had been together.

"You could have made this so simple," she said. "Why didn't you?"

"I told you, Samantha, I crave entertainment. After as many years as I've been through, I've found that it gets harder and harder to keep myself amused."

He left her then, and she had been frozen ever since, unable to look away from the bloody, savaged remains of the cleaning woman, unable to release her grip on the knife.

Now it was morning, and the stench was becoming unbearable. But Sam could not move from the floor. She was paralyzed.

The dead woman's name tag had read *Irene Wallis*. Sam wondered if this woman had a family who was looking for her, or if she had been alone. She was evidently part of the morning cleaning crew. Richard had forced her to come back, in uniform, on her off hours, so that he could revenge himself against her.

He was not all powerful, he was not invulnerable, and the incident with Irene Wallis proved that he was not above making stupid mistakes. Sam clung to that knowledge, holding it close as the hours stretched on and she tried to examine all that he had said, to understand, in his terms, the man's motivation. He had been raving the night before, his personality shifting so rapidly Sam could hardly keep up. It was as if he had worn so many masks in his existence that even he was no longer certain which of his faces was the real one. Or perhaps he had seen too many of his own movies, and he was a slave to the senseless melodrama he dished out to the willing public.

One way or the other, Sam sensed that he had an underlying agenda, one he was not going to share unless he was forced to do so. If she could use her skills as a detective to find his weakness, to learn his secrets, then she might have a true weapon to use against him.

Sam was shocked from her thoughts by the sound of the door opening. The morning cleaning crew had arrived. A tall, thin, blond woman entered the room and let out a scream as she saw the blood and the remains of her murdered coworker.

The paralysis that had chained Sam to her position on the floor suddenly lifted. She tried to stand, as she was supposed to in Richard's script, but he had not thought about how sore she would be, the way her muscles would be locked up after sitting for so long in the same position, struggling against her own body to somehow move.

"It's her own fault!" Sam heard herself screaming. "She shouldn't have been coming on to *my Richard*. If she had kept her hands to herself, I wouldn't have done it. But I'm glad. I killed her and I'm glad!"

Sam's hand sprung open and she dropped the knife. She felt a dizzying surge of relief. Those terribly composed words had been swimming around in her head for so many hours that she thought she would go insane if she wasn't able to rid herself of them. She tried to ignore the hysterical wails of the thin blond cleaning woman as she rose and worked out her sore muscles.

Richard had explained that he was going to be very busy for the next several months, and he did not want to have to worry about where to find her. By forcing her to confess to Irene Wallis's killing, she would be put away safely in prison until he was ready to retrieve her.

But Richard had made another mistake, Sam realized as she watched the screaming woman who had come to the room expecting another long and boring day. He had told Sam that she must confess to the killing, which she had done. He did not say that she had to wait around for the police to come get her.

Retrieving the knife, Sam slipped the weapon inside the waistband of her khaki shorts and pulled her sweatshirt over it. Forcing herself to stay calm, she walked past the cleaning woman and grabbed her bag where it lay near the door. She snatched a large white towel from the woman's cart and wrapped it around her face, leaving only enough room for her to see her way to the end of the hall as she passed five witnesses who had been roused by the screams, then made it to the elevators.

Running as best she could down two flights of stairs, Sam emerged on the eighteenth floor and took the elevator to the second floor. It went nonstop. She was not seen. Sam got out on the second floor and took the stairs once again, grateful that there was a door leading directly to the parking lot. In moments she was in her car, driving back to her leased home in Beverly Hills.

She burst through the front door, hoping to find Dani waiting. The house was empty. She checked her answering machine and shouted an obscenity as she saw that there had been no messages left.

She knew that she could not stay here. Even if she were extremely lucky and she had left no prints in the apartment, the cleaning woman might be able to identify her. Other witnesses may have seen Sam and Dani enter the hotel, and her visits with Richard to the restaurant, to the movie set, and to Cort's apartment, had made her extremely visible. By nightfall, when the police caught up with Richard to question him about the killing in his room, he would be surprised that she had not been captured, and he would either give the authorities her name, constructing some new elaborate scenario, or he would come looking for her.

Walking into her bedroom, she paused to look at herself, then stripped, showered, and slipped into a pair of jeans, a tank top, and a dark blue shirt she tied beneath her breasts. She had purchased a Kevlar bulletproof vest a few months ago, and had convinced Dani to help her smuggle out the collection of weapons that she had stored in the basement of the Malibu house.

The weapons, which she had scrupulously maintained, were now stored in a small room to the rear of the house. She hauled the boxes containing the weapons out, opened them to make sure she was packed with enough ammunition, then carried them to the Rover. She went back inside, fixed enough provisions to last her several days, and collected three changes of clothes. When she finally finished loading up the car, she took one last look at the Beverly Hills home, then drove away, hoping to find some trace of her daughter.

Chapter Seventeen

Dani woke in the deserted club to find that night had once again fallen. She could feel the marks Marissa had left on her skin. Though she had stopped Marissa before the girl could share blood with her, something had occurred between them that had haunted her dreams as she had lay sleeping, her body recovering from the shock that had been inflicted upon it.

Be mine, Marissa had whispered. *Be with me forever, sister love.*

They had nearly become lovers, and there had been a part of her that had responded to Marissa's cold touch, a part of her that had wanted to once again leap into the night skies, to taste the blood of humans, to be an Immortal.

Dani scrambled into the bathroom and became ill. When she was certain that the dry heaves had passed, Dani flicked on the light and looked at herself in the mirror. The scars on her arm and on her face had nearly healed. She had wondered why she had been able to use her power to heal others when she apparently could not heal herself. Now she had an answer. She had been denying her heritage, she had been attempting to be human, and she had not allowed her power to work in her own behalf.

She recalled the story her mother had told of Tory, the Initiate who had been turned and had reverted. Her mother had claimed that Tory had flown for short bursts, and that she displayed more power than any normal Initiate.

Dani heard a rustling from the backroom and walked out to see a figure standing in the open doorway. She recognized the leather jacket with the ripped sleeve first, then saw the gleaming mass of blond hair and the startling, malicious smile that had been etched upon Marissa's face. The girl carried a cloth bag in her hand with something that appeared to have the rough proportions of a bowling ball.

"Hi, hon," Marissa said. "I'm back. Miss me?"

Dani shuddered as she looked at her friend. She could see that the young woman standing before her was not the ravening beast she had confronted in Richard Sterling's hotel room, the creature that had wanted so desperately to kill Dani's mother, and had nearly killed Dani. The feral hatred remained, but it had been coupled with a wary intelligence, and a jaded, tired sensibility.

"I've got something for you," Marissa said.

"Oh? What's that?" Dani asked, wondering if it would do more harm than good to raise the psychic walls she had learned to build during the long months after Isabella's death. If Marissa could see her thoughts, the girl might revert to her animal state. All Dani wanted in the world was to find out what had happened to her mother back at Sterling's hotel. Were she to suggest it, were she to even *think* about it, Marissa might go insane. But she could not keep her thoughts away from the subject for long. So far, Marissa had not delved into Dani's mind. Perhaps it would stay that way.

"I brought you a present," Marissa said, making a sharp motion with her hand that caused a heavy object to fly from the sack she carried and roll across the floor, to land at Dani's feet.

Dani gasped as she saw the severed, bloody head of a man, his features twisted in surprise and rage. His razor-sharp canines had dug into his lower jaw, propping his mouth open. His lips were pulled back, and his eyes were wide.

"What do you think?" Marissa asked, allowing a ragged breath to escape her as she nervously rang her hands. Her need for approval was palatable.

"Who was he?" Dani asked.

"Does it matter?"

Dani was silent.

"His name was Timothy. He was amusing. Then he stopped being amusing. I had to punish him."

Averting her gaze from the head, Dani said, "Did he try to hurt you?"

"He was a monster," she said sharply. "He was just like all the others. Not like you and me. He doesn't understand what it's like to be a human being. He deserved everything he got."

"All right," Dani said, carefully noting Marissa's reference to both herself and Dani as human beings, a statement that could not be further from the truth. "What do you want to do now?"

"I thought we'd hang out. Hit some clubs. Real ones, not like this place."

Dani nodded. Though she was not looking down at the severed head, she could feel some of its hairs brushing against her ankle. She swallowed hard. "Are you sure tonight's a good night for that?"

"Why wouldn't it be?"

"I thought we might take it easy tonight. I'm not really feeling up to a lot of excitement."

Marissa curled her hands into fists. "Do *not* fucking patronize me! We both know what's going on here. I'm going on a hunt. I'd like for you to come with me." Her expression softened. "I *need* you to come with me."

The muscles in Dani's face tightened. "I'm not going to help you kill anyone."

Rubbing at her temples, Marissa said, "Don't you get it? Look at what I brought you."

Dani felt the fluttering of Marissa's power at the outposts of her conscious thoughts. She did as Marissa commanded and the fluttering ceased, Marissa had pulled away.

"How can you stand there and tell me that it's wrong to want to kill these fucking things?" Marissa asked. "You know what they are. You know from experience the way they twist everything, the way they lie to you, the way they hurt you and betray you and make you love them for it."

Dani understood that Marissa was not only talking about her father, who had forced her to become what she hated and feared the most, but other people throughout her life who had hurt her. She was half insane with anger and a need for vengeance that was as all-consuming as Dani's need had been when she had been fully turned.

Looking into the eyes of the dead vampire at her feet, Dani wondered if murdering one of her own kind would constitute a valid second kill. Marissa had only slain one human, as far as Dani knew. If there was a chance of reclaiming Marissa's humanity, Dani meant to help her.

But what would she do about her mother? What *could* she do? If she told Marissa that she wanted to contact her mother, to ensure that her mother was safe, and perhaps enlist her help in their hunt, Marissa might be pushed over the edge. Dani knew that. Even now, her momentary hesitation was causing Marissa to become suspicious.

She thought of what it had been like when she had been turned and the *pack* had taken her to places that were filled with prey. She barely had been able to control herself. Perhaps there was a way to use Marissa's preoccupation with the murder of their own kind to Dani's advantage.

"It could be dangerous," Dani said.

"Not as long as we're *pure*," Marissa said with a cruel laugh. "Virgin white."

"I don't understand."

"So long as they don't get any farther into our heads than we want them to go, they won't be expecting what we're going to do with them. That little piece of shit at your feet certainly wasn't."

"But I'm not as strong as you are," Dani said. "You might be able to fool them, that doesn't mean I can. And if they make me, they'll know all about you."

"So you won't come with me?"

"That's not what I'm saying."

"Then let's go."

"Wait. What if we find more than one? What if we come up against an entire pack?"

"We'll avoid them. I'm only interested in doing one at a time. At least for now."

"Marissa, we've got more important things to worry

about."

In exasperation, Marissa said, "Like *what?*"

"Where will you go when the sun comes up? You know that the sun will kill you."

"Of course I do." She pointed at the corpse. "I watched the rest of this sleazy little bastard fry to a crisp in the light. And now that he's dead, he won't be needing his place. He didn't have any friends. No humans, none of our kind. It will be a perfect place to hide."

Dani had exhausted her cache of objections. "How are we going to do this?"

Marissa smiled and came forward, raising her hands. Dani managed not to shudder as Marissa took her face in both her hands.

"That's where you come in, my darling," Marissa said. "You are going to be the *bait.*"

The line outside the Hellfire Club extended for half a block. Beautiful people with perfect hair and the latest styles stood silently on line, filled with hope that they would be allowed in tonight, and fear that they would have to face the humiliation of being denied.

Dani and Marissa approached the blood-red door of the reconverted church which housed the Hellfire Club and did not stop as a dark-haired man with a perfect body and smoldering eyes looked at them. One touch of Dani's power and they were walking past the man, who held the door open for them, over the objections of those who had waited outside for longer than they would care to admit. Dani paused for a second to read the words that had been scrawled in black spray paint across the door.

"Abandon all hope, ye who enter here."

She had been to the club many times before, and she had always smirked at those words. Tonight, she prayed they would not prove to be prophetic.

The inner chamber of the club was designed to resemble a near cousin to the Black Lodge set from "Twin Peaks." Strobing lights flickered in corners, while steady beams fell upon the man behind the check-in booth. Red leather couches lined the chamber, along with several doorways sporting red silk curtains. Odd shapes could be seen through the curtains, people moving, writhing. Throbbing dance music filled their ears.

"What's your pleasure?" asked the dark man behind the counter. "The dance hall of the dead? The Marquis deSade—"

"We'll take the full treatment," Dani said, barely looking at the man. "And you'll pay for it out of your own pocket. How does that sound to you?"

Before he could object, Dani lashed out with her silver thread, stimulating the pleasure centers of his brain, snaking through his physiology to bring him instantly to the edge of an orgasm. His legs buckled and he had to clutch the counter for support.

"Yes," he said, unable to resist.

Dani held out her hand, continuing to look away from the attendant. She did not want to see his face. She hated doing this to an innocent stranger, but she had to prove to Marissa that she was going along with the girl's plan.

The attendant took Dani's hand and used a silver hand unit to stamp the space beneath her knuckles with a bar code that had the image of a cloven hoof chipped away within its stringent lines.

"Her, too," Dani said, nodding at Marissa, who held her hand out and made a "kiss kiss" motion as the attendant stamped it.

Pulling Marissa away from the entranced man, Dani led her through the center curtain, and they entered a sprawling vista of fear and desire. The central dance hall was packed with elbow-to-elbow humanity.

Prey.

Dani felt a sudden urge to release the demon that resided in her breast, to launch herself into the swelling crowd of humans and become one with their overriding desire. But she could not allow that to happen. Tonight, of all nights, she had to remain in control of her own hungers, her wanton desires.

The wood planks of the dance floor had been painted red, along with the walls and the tiers of the second floor, where people looked down at the dancers. Stalactites hung from the ceiling, pointing downward like twisted, disease-ridden fingers singling particular dancers out for damnation. Plaster creations rose from the walls, sculptures of dancers writhing in agony or ecstasy, depending on the way the light hit them. Smoke suffused the dance hall, making the illusion of a random level of Dante's hell all the more apparent.

There was a bar where the altar had once been, and several pews lined the wall, allowing a lucky few to sit out a dance or two. There were a half-dozen specialty rooms in all, two branching off the dance hall to the left on the first floor, a third on the right. The fourth room on the first floor was the business office. The setup was identical on the second floor, except that one of the four spaces had been set aside for rest rooms.

The corridors between the rooms were designed to

appear cavernous, though the floor was perfectly smooth and level to ensure that none of the patrons slipped and fell.

Dani turned to Marissa and asked her a question. It was nearly impossible to hear over the thunderous sound of the music, which made Dani's eardrums rattle. Marissa shouted for her to repeat herself.

"Let's dance!" Dani cried, taking Marissa's hand and dragging her onto the dance floor, where they nudged and elbowed a spot for themselves. Dani had loved to dance, though she had only learned of her gift when the *pack* had released all her hidden talents. Marissa's feral confidence did not slip, and she joined Dani, matching her every motion as they lost themselves in the dance, their gazes locked except when they performed full turns.

The point had been for them to blend in, but their sharp, sensual movements were already attracting the attention of several men, none of whom seemed to be of their race. Dani brushed off the casual advances of the humans with her power, though neither woman had been able to resist sampling the sumptuous waves of desire each man radiated as they attempted to win a dance and perhaps a night of passion.

Marissa had told Dani that she would trust her for all the casual uses of the power they shared. Marissa was busy shielding her vampiric nature from any of their kind they might encounter. Dani would be the one to lure them in. They would see her as they might see any Initiate, vulnerable, easily bent to their particular needs. When they had taken Dani to their sanctuaries, Marissa, who would follow at a discreet distance, would take them before Dani could come to any harm.

Though the club was packed with hundreds of people, there were no others of their kind that Dani could sense. She did not bother to tell Marissa this. Marissa was slowly becoming overwhelmed by the proximity of so much humanity, so much innocent blood. Her movements, graceful as ever, had become separate from Dani's. Her eyes fluttered and half closed as she threw her head back and allowed herself to taste the desire that suffused the entire club.

Marissa gasped, her eyes rolling back into her head, and suddenly she was transported. Dani watched her, and continued her own dance steps, occasionally allowing a human to cut between Marissa and herself, until soon Marissa was swallowed up by the crowd.

Dani knew that she could not allow Marissa to remain on her own for long. Though the young woman had sworn that her taste for blood would extend only to fellow Immortals, her animal nature might once again rise to the fore. Dani estimated that she had about enough time to get to a phone, make a single call, and hurry back.

Cutting glances over her shoulder to where she had last seen Marissa, Dani did not see the couple she was about to collide with until she plowed into them, nearly knocking the tall, thin, dark-haired woman from her feet. Dani recovered quickly, her hand finding the arm of the falling woman and immediately steadying her.

"Nina," Dani said in surprise. The man with her was Ray Brooks.

"Omigod!" Nina said, looking at Ray, then Dani. "Honey, sweetie, I can explain—"

Dani felt her lip curl up. She had not even thought about what it would be like to see Nina and Ray together. Her immediate instinct was to dismiss the situation—for God's sake, she certainly had more important matters that needed her attention—but she could not control the sudden rush of anger that flooded into her. Ray was the only man she had been attracted to in a very long time. First circumstances, then Nina, had robbed Dani of her chance to experience even one evening with the man, even one chance to find some intimacy and affection.

Then she thought of her mother, and Richard Sterling, and decided that perhaps she was indeed better off.

"Have a nice life," Dani said, brushing past her roommate and the handsome, off-duty police officer, who could not meet Dani's gaze.

"Dani, wait!" Nina called, chasing after her golden-eyed friend, who quickly disappeared behind one of the red curtains. Nina brushed the fabric aside and caught sight of Dani, shoving two people out of the way as she caught up with Dani at the foot of the stairs.

Dani turned as she felt Nina's hand on her shoulder.

"Just give me thirty seconds, I can explain," Nina said loudly, the explosive sounds of the dance floor following them into the corridors, muted only slightly by the distance.

Shuddering, Dani spun on her roommate, eyes blazing as she said, "I don't have time for this, go back and enjoy tonight, forget I was ever here!" and used her power to push the message deep into Nina's mind.

The tall, Spanish woman turned and went back to the dance room without another word.

Dani felt horrible that she had let her petty angers spiral out of control, causing her to do the one thing she promised she would never do—use her abilities against someone she considered a friend. She raced up the stairs, knowing that she could not give herself over to self-indulgence of remorse for what she had done. There would be time for that later, and time to also make amends. But now her time was running out.

The pay phone was in use and five other people were waiting for it. Dani once again reached out with her power, causing each of the people on line to suddenly change their minds about making a call. She snatched the quarter from the hand of one of those who had been on line, and went to the pay phone, which was located just outside the deSade room. The sounds of whips snapping through the air and people gasping as they watched trained professionals perform for them drifted to Dani as she dialed the number of her mother's beeper. She punched in the main number of the club, then hung up the phone, praying her mother would decide to drive immediately to the club when she dialed the main number. She had been shielding her thoughts concerning her mother as best she could, and knew that Marissa would be able to read her worries instantly the moment they were once again in contact.

The voice of the demon spoke in her head: *What if she's not wearing the beeper, Dani? What if she gets here too late? What are you going to do then? And what if she can't come to you, Dani? What if she's dead?*

There was nothing else she could do. Dani bit her lip. That wasn't true. There was one other thing she could do, though it would be risky as hell.

She drew a deep breath. Samantha Walthers would have died for her in the basement of the Malibu beach house, fourteen months earlier. Sam was her *mother.* It would be worth the risk.

310

Heading toward the stairs, she approached the door to the Caligula Suite and heard the sounds of dancers grunting and making horse sounds. Images of the play *Equus* leaped into her mind as she quickly passed by the private Den of Debauchery.

Heading downstairs, hurrying through the hellish crimson corridors, Dani entered the dance floor and tried to find Marissa. If she had used her powers, she could have instantly singled out the blond-haired vampire. But she needed to find another, first.

Snaking through the crowd, Dani found Ray and Nina. They were dancing very close, their bodies grinding together. Dani lashed out with her power, instilling in the young, dark-haired police officer a single, tightly focused burst of information that would disperse within his mind over the course of the next few minutes. First he would feel an urge to leave the club, then a compulsion to call Edward Pullman and enlist his aid in finding and helping Samantha Walthers.

She moved on, searching through the crowd until she came to the bar. Marissa was nowhere in sight.

Suddenly, Dani nearly doubled over as she felt a white-hot burst of sheer terror cut through her. She understood in that instant the horrible mistake she had made.

By the time she once again reached the foot of the stairs, the screaming had already begun.

Chapter Eighteen

Dani found Marissa crouched over her kill near the open doorway of the second-floor rest rooms. Her hands had been transformed into bloody, gore-drenched talons, and her razor-sharp canines glistened in the pinkish-red glow of the muted overhead lights. More than a dozen people were trapped in the hallway behind her, too terrified to pass her. Behind Dani, people were screaming and running for the stairwells.

The man Marissa had slain had not been of their kind; he had been a human. Whatever chance there might have been to save Marissa's soul had been extinguished. Dani tentatively reached out with her power, hoping to calm Marissa and lead her out of the club. There was a brief instant of contact, then Marissa batted away Dani's silver thread in a sharp, feral motion.

From the momentary glimpse Dani received of Marissa's thoughts, she knew what had happened, and she knew that it had been her fault. She never should have left Marissa alone in the crowded club, humanity pressing in on her at every side. Marissa's memories played before Dani as if she were watching a scene from a movie:

Dani was gone. Marissa could sense it. She had gotten lost in the sensual haze of so much fear, desire, and need, that she had lost sight of her friend.

Panic seized Marissa, and it spread from her in concentric rings, seeping into the crowd, causing the humans to radiate even more anxiety. Marissa attempted to control herself, but the fear was too much for her. She lapped at the petty dreads of the humans around her, consuming their fears until she was intoxicated with pleasure.

Her hunger did not vanish. It seemed that she could not be sated. The more she consumed, the more she desired.

With every shred of her strength, she attempted to cling to one thought:

Dani.

Her friend would not have left her in this place. That meant Dani had not been given a choice. Someone had taken her. Another of their kind, a filthy Immortal, had entered the club and Marissa had been caught unaware. Dani was not an Immortal, she would not be able to resist the compulsion one of their kind could place on her.

Swimming up from the haze of wondrous fear that had engulfed her, Marissa was beginning to shove her way forward, through the crowd, when suddenly she felt one of their kind using its power. The sudden, angry lashing of a vampire forcing a human under its power.

Dani realized suddenly that it had been her Marissa had sensed, when she had used her power on Nina.

The Immortal was close, Marissa sensed. She combed the dance floor, attempting in vain to control her own terror. If one of their kind were to harm Dani, Marissa would never forgive her-

self. She had forced Dani to come along with her, she had been the one who had needed Dani so desperately.

Marissa went through dens on the first floor, careful to rely on her mortal senses. She did not want the Immortal who had taken Dani to know that he was being stalked. She was in the Byronic Hall when she felt the surge of power once again. The vampire was close, and that meant the creature had not taken Dani from the building. There was still a chance to rescue her friend.

Vaulting up the stairs, Marissa combed the dens of the second floor, but she did not find Dani.

Instead she saw the powerfully built blond-haired man with glacier-blue eyes and reddish, sunburned skin.

Sterling.

Her father.

He had found them, and he had taken Dani or had one of his underlings perform that duty once he had broken her will. Marissa's fear turned to excitement. Carefully shielding herself, she followed her father at a discreet distance. She knew that she would have only one chance to surprise the man, and she would not allow that opportunity to slip away from her.

Following Richard Sterling, Marissa was surprised as she saw him walk into the men's room. Was he meeting someone there? Who else would he be looking for?

She saw a man leading a woman from the men's room. They were awash in the wicked afterglow of human sex, the skin of their faces and necks beaded with sweat.

Marissa followed Sterling inside. She found him near the sink, washing his face. There were a half-dozen men waiting for one of the stalls or the urinals lining the wall, another seven or eight keeping them occupied.

Launching herself forward, Marissa slammed her father's head against the glass. There was a cry of surprise, a sharp splintering crack, and a splatter of blood that filled in the

314

spider's web of cracks Sterling's head had created in the glass.

Before the Immortal could recover, Marissa hurled him forward, toward the door leading to the corridor. He issued a quick, surprised curse, then tumbled through the doorway and came to a stop on his stomach. He attempted to rise, one hand over his bloody, lacerated forehead, and Marissa leaped upon him, slamming his head against the hard wood floor.

Sterling had no time to rise again as Marissa reached out with her power, plunging her psychic knives into his mind. She had to know what he had done with Dani before she could kill him.

What she encountered in his mind confused and angered her. She found the memories of a man named Laurence Hilliard, a professional actor who had just been approached about appearing on a soap opera. Hilliard was married, and his wife was expecting their first child. They didn't have the money to undergo the tests to learn the baby's sex, and money had been a major concern.

His job at the Hellfire Club, as one of the dancers in the Caligula Suite, had just come to an end. He had come here tonight to collect his last paycheck and say goodbye to his friends who would continue at the club.

"No!" Marissa had screamed, unwilling to accept this tangle of lies. Sterling had been trying to confuse her, he was desperate to once again take control of her mind. She could not allow it.

Her razor-sharp teeth had ripped from their housings and her hands had transformed into talons as rage became her entire world. She pulled Sterling up by his hair and sank her canines into his throat, jerking savagely to sever the wildly pulsing artery she encountered. A spray of blood struck the far wall, droplets splattering on several of the humans who watched Marissa and Sterling in horrid fascination.

She plunged her talons into his chest, tearing through his silk shirt as she pierced his heart with her rapierlike fingers, shred-

315

ding the pumping organ without hesitation, without mercy. Marissa took his blood into her, lapping at it greedily, when the first pangs of remorse settled onto her.

Sterling was dead.

She would not be able to learn what he had done with Dani. She had failed her friend. Her anger escalating, Marissa tore into the corpse a second time, cracking open its rib cage as she wailed in rage.

It should not have been this easy, she suddenly realized. Her father had the powers of a god. Even with the advantage of surprise, his death should have been much more trying, and the compulsion he had left in her mind had also not been broken.

She looked down into the face of the dead man and saw that he was not Richard Sterling, he was not even an Immortal.

She threw her head back and screamed.

Dani shuddered, separating herself from the memory. She looked once again at her friend, who crouched like a wild animal about to spring, the blood caking her pale features, the gore dripping from her talons. The humans surrounding them provided a solid wall of fear that had numbed Marissa's reason. Dani could feel the blood-need rise within her. The pungent scents of the kill made her tremble, the sight of so much blood, enough to sicken any human, made her inadvertently lick her lips, which had suddenly become hard and dry.

Then she saw Madison and Isabella standing in the crowd, also soaked with blood, and the sight gave her the strength to force down her own inhuman need and maintain control of her thoughts. She wanted desperately to reach out with her power and alter the perceptions of the witnesses in the crowd, but she knew that the slightest use of her abilities would shatter the walls she had hastily erected in her mind and allow the darkness and the evil of her blood to come rushing in.

"Do you know who I am?" Dani said as she cautiously approached her friend. The blond-haired vampire made a single, sharp feral motion with her head and did not take her gaze from Dani's golden eyes. "Then you know I would never mean you harm. I won't go away. I won't desert you. But we can't stay here. It's dangerous."

Marissa regarded Dani warily, her body tense, her muscles coiled. A terrible smile appeared on her face and she said, "Dangerous? To whom?"

Dani took another step forward and stopped suddenly as Marissa brought her talons to her lips and allowed one of the long, porcelain knives that had been her fingers to slide between her lips lasciviously as she licked it clean. Dani knew that dozens of people had seen Marissa and had escaped the upper floor of the club. They would be hysterical, they would not understand, they would not believe what they had seen. Their memories would be of the wild, animallike creature Marissa had become, not the human girl she had appeared to be when she first entered the Hellfire. With any luck at all, they would not be able to give a competent description of her.

Dani looked at the monster before her and tried to understand why she didn't turn and try to get away herself. Marissa was beyond saving. At Marissa's feet was the corpse of an innocent man. Dani could blame herself all she wanted for the man's death, but she did not take his life. Suddenly, she heard the voice of the demon:

You killed Madison. She was your friend and she died begging you for her life. You could have chosen not to harm her, but instead you tore out her throat and sank your teeth into her still beating heart.

Is that any different from what happened here tonight?

Dani brought herself another step closer to Marissa, and knelt before her. "People will be here soon. We have to leave."

"No," Marissa said in a low, deep voice. "We're not going anywhere. I like it here, Dani. I've got everything I need."

Turning suddenly to the small crowd of witnesses pressed in the hallway behind her, Marissa said, "In fact, I think we should have a little party."

Dani felt her flesh become cold. She remembered what it had been like when she had been turned, how she had regarded humans as meat, succulent prey and nothing else.

"You have to let them go," Dani said, attempting to quell the fear that was rising inside her. She had no idea what Marissa might do with the witnesses, but in the girl's current state, she could savage them all before her reason returned to her. Dani did not want even more deaths on her conscience.

"I don't *have* to do anything," Marissa said. "You know what I am." Her lips curled in disgust. "I can make anything happen. Anything at all."

"They're human, for God's sake. They're not like your father. They're not like us. Please, if you won't come with me, then at least let them go."

"And you'll stay with me? No matter what?"

"I will, Marissa. I will."

Marissa turned and looked at the humans. Except for the sound of hysterical sobbing, they had been near silent. Marissa's power had ensured this. She scanned

318

their faces, delighting in the expressions of abject terror she found.

Looking away from them, Marissa gazed into Dani's golden eyes and said, "I still think I deserve a party. A coming-out party. I never had that. I never had the pretty dresses, the friends, the gifts."

Marissa looked down at the bloody corpse before her. "I suppose now I never will."

Quaking uncontrollably, Marissa squeezed her eyes shut and snarled, "Get them out of here, Dani. Get them the hell out of here before I change my mind."

Dani nodded and went to the hostages.

Chapter Nineteen

Sam had been driving through the streets of Los Angeles for hours. She knew that her daughter could be anywhere, alive or dead, and the knowledge had driven her half insane. Her radio had been tuned to the police band. The constant squawking intermingled with bursts of static and dead silence had set her nerves jangling.

Images of Marissa leaping for her throat rushed through Sam, reminding her of the last few seconds of life the vampire Isabella had endured before Dani had burned her. If Marissa's reason had been destroyed, if she were nothing but an animal, Dani would have almost no chance against her.

No, Sam reminded herself. The creature had not only saved itself after plummeting from the twentieth-story window, some instinct had been awakened in it that had also caused it to protect Dani, just as it had the night before.

A few moments ago, a communication had come over the police band. A detective radioing that he was on his way to interview another of the staff members at the Olympiad.

Sam had read about the slaughter at the Olympiad's Spa the previous night. The lack of witnesses to the event, despite the number of people present at the spa, had caused Sam to wonder if the creature who had taken her daughter was involved.

Her beeper went off, causing her to jump in her seat and force herself to remain calm. Pulling it from her waistband, Sam stopped at a light, checked the number, and did not recognize it at first. Easing the Rover into the parking lot of an all-night supermarket, Sam took her cell phone from the glove compartment and dialed the number from her pager.

"Hellfire Club," a man answered.

Shawcross, she thought. The assistant manager. He must have seen Dani. Sam asked for the man and was told he was unavailable.

"Could he have called me in the last few minutes?"

"Not a chance. He and the owner have been in conference for the last hour."

Sam hung up, dropping the cell phone to her seat, and felt a comforting wave wash over her. Dani had to have been the one who made the call.

Her sense of well-being vanished as she pulled out of the parking lot, drove as quickly as she could, understanding that she must avoid being stopped by the police, then suddenly heard the first of the reports erupt from the police band.

A victim had been slain at the Hellfire Club. The perpetrator was still on the premises, holding hostages.

Sam was twenty minutes from the club. She raced through the streets, cutting off drivers, taking detours, running lights, and made it to the general area of the Hellfire in fifteen minutes. When she arrived there, the scene she encountered chilled her. A half-dozen police cars were already present. Wailing sirens and flashing blue and red lights filled the night. The SWAT team had already arrived.

The red doors of the club were open, and police were attempting to control the stampede of people who were rocketing from the reconverted church. Sam saw a young woman with red hair trip on the stairs leading down from the door and scream as another woman slammed the point of her high-heel shoe into the woman's hand. The police pulled the injured woman out of harm's way, but from the shouts inside the club, Sam guessed that there were dozens of others who had been trampled.

Anxiously watching the faces of the people attempting to leave the club, Sam hoped to glimpse her daughter's face, though she knew her hope was not a realistic one. Dani might have already left this place, and if she were using her power, even Sam would see her as someone else.

Suddenly, she felt a strange tugging, an unnatural force that caused her to tremble and sweat. A voice inside her head rose up in her and shouted, *Your daughter's dead, they're going to find her in pieces!*

Sam tensed her entire body, then relaxed her muscle groups from her toes up, until she allowed a ragged breath to escape her. She took a few more deep breaths and knew that she had been correct: Marissa was here. It was her power that Sam had felt, a nebulous cloud of panic snaking its tendrils outward from the club.

A pair of spotlights struck the ground and Sam looked up, suddenly registering the pair of police helicopters which had come upon the scene. The steady beating of their blades reached down to her as she parked the Rover behind the hastily erected police barricades and considered the weaponry she had brought with her, including the over the shoulder flamethrower she had purchased illegally. She had to get inside the building before the police had a chance to seal it off. She was already carrying the twin to the Beretta 9mm Richard had taken from the room, and a satchel containing several flayers—explosive devices that would send shrapnel everywhere. That might be enough, but if Marissa had developed the power of her father, Sam's only hope was to hit the girl hard and fast, to destroy her before she was even aware of the threat she faced.

Hurrying from the Rover, Sam threw the satchel over her shoulder and cut anxious glances to the rushing crowd leaving the club. She didn't have much time. Her options were to merge with the crowd and make her way inside, through the cloud of human chaos that was congealing around the main entrance, or to take advantage of the momentary distraction being offered to the police and find another way into the building.

A pair of headlights suddenly flared in her direction, brilliant white light engulfing her. Her instinct was to run, but she knew if she called attention to herself, she would run the risk of being stopped before she got into the building, where she was certain her baby was being held by a monster.

The lights dimmed and a car door opened. The car was a deep blue Mitsubishi with a flasher sitting on the dash. Detective Sergeant Edward Pullman emerged from the backseat, accompanied by two other men. One was the Hispanic detective from the interrogation the previous day, the other was a young, wiry man with streaked gray hair.

"Sam?" he asked.

"Jesus," she whispered. This couldn't be happening. Not now. Her thoughts instantly flashed on the screaming cleaning woman who had heard Sam's confession earlier that day, who would be able to give a perfect description of her. Even without the witness, the police had enough to place her at the scene of the killing. There would have been at least one full set of prints that she left behind. And if all else failed, there was always Richard, who would have told the story in such a way that Sam would have been the prime suspect.

She had been taking precautions all day to avoid places where she would be recognized and had switched the plates on her Rover twice that day with those of other vehicles that could be mistaken for her own. Edward would have become aware of the manhunt for her, and probably would have taken charge.

Now he was standing before her, about to place her under arrest. Sam wondered if she would be able to put all three men down, disabling them quickly and cleanly, before they could take her. The thought of harming her friend was abhorrent to her, but she had to place her daughter's welfare first. There was a stiffness in her back, and the network of scars left there seemed to burn as a reminder that she was not what she had once been.

The best way would be to draw the Beretta, but if one of the other cops saw the weapon, they might take her down. She could not die here, not until her baby was safe and the bastard who had violated her was dead.

"What's going on, Sam?" he asked. "First I get a bunch of phone calls at my house from that crazy bastard Ray Brooks about you being in some kind of danger — that's what my wife said anyway — and now I find you in the middle of this. So, what is this? What's going on?"

Edward Pullman ran his hand over the soft white patch of hair that stubbornly refused to go down over his scalp. He frowned, looking past her.

She nearly laughed, the white hot panic that had been filling her brimming over in her mind. *What's going on? Oh, I can tell ya, no big deal. I was raped by a vampire and my daughter might be killed by the bastard's daughter at any moment, or by one of your men when they try to take the monster down. That's about it, nothing much beyond that. Just a typical day.*

Oh, that and the fact that you're going to have to arrest me. I almost forgot about that.

"We've got a real crisis," he said, shaking his head. "Do you have a reason for being here? If not, you know the drill."

He knows I'm armed, she thought. He wants me to relax so his people can take me down easily.

From the corner of her eye, she saw that the crowd leaving the Hellfire Club was thinning. She would have to get away from them now, there was no other choice.

Sam rubbed at her neck with her right hand, ready to slide it inside her jacket and yank the Beretta from its holster.

Without warning, Edward suddenly made a gesture and said, "Richard, Lee, you guys go on without me. Tell the officer in charge that I'm here."

The two police officers followed their orders without hesitation. They walked past her, Sam bracing for their attack, but they made no move against her. She heard their footsteps on the street as they went to the other units and wondered what Edward's plan had been. Perhaps they would come back, with others. If it was necessary, she would take Edward as a hostage until she was able to get into the club.

"Sam, will you at least say something?" Edward asked.

"I didn't do it," she said finally.

"Didn't do what?" he asked. "What, are you getting paranoid on me, Sam?"

Her hand inched closer to her open jacket and the gun waiting inside. For all she knew, either of Edward's men might have doubled back and was coming up from behind her. She did not hear their footsteps, but if they were half as agile as she was, she would not. She did not dare turn and look. The detective sergeant before her may have been in his fifties, but she had played racquetball with him, had seen him in the gym sparring with men half his age and laying them out with a single, powerful blow. All he would need was a momentary opening, a wavering of her gaze, and he would be upon her.

Over the last year, this man had been like a father to her. During that time she had come to depend on him, to perhaps even love him. But she knew that if it came to it, he would put his professional responsibility first. If she felt even a breath of displaced air behind her, she would dive past Edward, draw her weapon on the roll, and come up behind him.

Sam tensed, preparing for what seemed to be the inevitable. "Edward, we're friends. We both know what's going on."

Edward's gaze became hard. "Sam, I love you. I'm telling you this as if you were my own. Shit or get off the pot. I have a situation to deal with here."

"For God's sake, Edward," she said, feeling her heart slowly break as her fingers crept closer to the weapon. "I didn't kill that woman."

"What woman?"

"The one in Richard Sterling's hotel room."

"Of course you didn't. Louise Simmons did. She confessed to the whole thing this afternoon, after she smoked Sterling."

Sam's hand fell away. "Say that again."

"She killed the cleaning woman then went over to Sterling's office. He keeps a spare bed over there. She soaked it with gasoline and set him on fire around eleven thirty this morning. Then she just sat there and waited. By the time someone smelled the smoke and got into there — I'll tell you, it was a weird place, no windows — there wasn't a hell of a lot left of him. What does this have to do with you?"

"I—"

"Sam, I can't do this now. I'm sorry. I've got people being held on the second floor. I've got to keep things quiet until the hostage negotiator gets here."

He walked briskly away, leaving Sam to turn and watch him go. Neither of his men was anywhere near. No one was even looking in her direction, except for the crowds of onlookers, many of whom had been inside the club, who were gathering outside the barricades.

Richard Sterling was dead and someone *else* had confessed not only to his murder, but also to that of the cleaning woman.

That was impossible. The compulsion she felt would have lifted — or would it? Could it survive his death? The only specific programming that she had been under was to avoid harming the fetus he had placed in her. That, of course, could also be a lie. She didn't feel pregnant. She had spent hours driving any such thought from her mind.

327

She had one child. Dani. And Dani was not safe.

Thoughts of what Edward had said when he first saw her returned. Ray Brooks had been calling Edward's house, attempting to warn him of some danger she was in. He couldn't have known that she was in trouble unless someone told him — namely Dani. She searched the sea of faces gathered outside the club and saw Brooks arguing with Nina Chavez, Dani's roommate. His hands were on her arms and he seemed desperate to convince her of something. The lithe, beautiful Spanish woman pulled herself from Brooks' grasp and punched him in the mouth. He stared at her incredulously as she stormed off.

Sam was about to go after Brooks when she heard a crash and an explosion of shattered glass. She looked up to see a man's body explode from one of the second floor, plate glass windows. The body sailed through the air and struck the pavement before a pair of startled officers.

"Go! Now!" voices shouted.

Sam looked at the club in horror, suddenly realizing that the SWAT team was being deployed. She watched as eight men wearing vests and riot gear, carrying high-powered weapons flooded in through the front door. Officers had been stationed around the perimeter of the building.

"Oh God," she whispered. This was wrong, all wrong. No one was following procedure. They were rushing blindly into the heart of the situation, with no finesse, no preparation.

The panic which had struck her when she first arrived on the scene gripped her again. It was Marissa. The vampire's power was growing to novalike proportions, infecting the minds of the officers.

An image flashed into Sam's mind. She was lying on her bed, completely paralyzed, while Marissa slashed at Dani with her talons, tearing her apart as she screamed and begged for Sam to do something—do *anything*—but all Sam could do was watch.

Without hesitation, Sam vaulted over the barricades, ran to the closest police cruiser, got behind the wheel, and cranked the ignition. Drawing a deep breath, she backed up, then put the vehicle in drive and floored it as she heard the startled cries of the police officers. She barreled down the street, avoiding two other police cars parked near the curb, and made a sharp right. The cruiser bucked as she pushed it over the curb and aimed it for the stairs, leaning down on the horn. A cry burst from her lips that was only barely audible over the blare of her car horn, and she felt the cruiser's tires take each step. The top of her head slammed into the roof. Suddenly the partially opened red doors loomed before her and she saw the guards who had been stationed there leap to either side. The grill of the cruiser slammed against the doors with a jarring impact that tore the right door from its hinges, causing it to slam against the front windshield and crack the glass as the other door was whipped back inside.

Suddenly, she was inside. The cruiser arced to the right, slamming into a wall, and Sam was thrown in her seat as the vehicle was jammed to a stop. Hurling the cruiser in neutral, Sam opened her door, kept a firm hold on her satchel, and left the cruiser.

The counter to the left was empty, and the low, atmospheric lighting made Sam feel that she had indeed entered Hell as she heard footsteps. At least one team of SWAT members was coming back to investigate the crash. Sam leaped the counter, landing hard, and knew that she had to become one with the shadows as she heard the first two SWAT members arrive from a nearby staircase.

Dani could no longer think of anything to say to Marissa. She had tried to reawaken the humanity within the girl, but after allowing Dani to free the witnesses, Marissa had entered a frantic state which had culminated in her lifting the corpse of the human she had slain and hurling it from one of the stained-glass windows.

"He's not coming!" she cried. "He's not fucking coming, the bastard! The bastard!"

A spotlight swept over the shattered window, its beam reaching into the long corridor like a probing finger that immediately retreated. Dani could hear the activity outside and knew that the police would soon be entering the club. She had been waiting for an opportunity to use her power, hoping that she could subdue Marissa, but even if that were possible, what would happen to her friend? If the police managed to hold her until morning, Marissa would die screaming in the sunlight.

"Where are you!" she shouted. "Where?"

Dani stood near the closed door to the Caligula Suite, watching helplessly as Marissa cried out repeatedly for her father. She had been certain that he would come for her, and she would be able to end his life before her own was snuffed out.

When the footsteps sounded on the stairs, Dani could feel the animal need and desire well up in Marissa. The proximity of humans was again beginning to cloud the girl's thoughts, and her frustration over her inability to confront her father had grown to frightening proportions.

"Marissa, please, they're coming!" Dani shouted. She watched the blond-haired vampire turn in her direction, and for the briefest of moments, Dani saw the frightened young girl she had first spoken to the day before. Then a hard, murderous expression twisted Marissa's features into an ugly, contorted mask of rage.

Dani knew that she should run, that she should find a place to hide before it was too late, but she could not accept that there was nothing left that she could do for Marissa. Somewhere inside the bestial shell into which her flesh had been transformed was the young girl who wanted to be a fairy-tale princess, who wanted nothing more than to be lost in fantasies and perhaps one day create them for others.

This last revelation had come in Dani's dreams, after she had fought off Marissa's attempt to turn her, and the thought had haunted her. Marissa had been so unsure of herself, so self-condemning, that she had been unwilling to admit her true desire to anyone, especially herself. Dani had been able to picture Marissa sitting in a sunlit studio, working on children's books, sharing the dreams she had known since childhood, and perhaps giving some lonely child like herself the courage to go on and realize that one day she could become everything she ever wanted to be, and fulfill her every dream.

It had been that thought that Dani had clung to, that thought that had made Dani stay with Marissa, despite the danger.

Marissa stood only a few feet away, and the beam of light from one of the helicopters struck her full on. Her hands were still talons, and she raked them across her own face and neck, creating bloody furrows.

The little girl had grown up, and instead of realizing her dreams, she had become one with her nightmares.

Dani knew that all she had to do was take a few steps back, run into the room behind her and hide herself as the officers were forced to confront Marissa, but she could not bring herself to do it. A moment before the first of the officers appeared, Dani scrambled to Marissa. Dani turned her back on the girl and pulled Marissa's talons near her throat.

"Don't fire!" Dani screamed, wondering how coherent a story the officers had managed to glean from the witnesses whose release Dani had helped to secure. "Please, for God's sake, don't fire!"

The first pair of officers appeared, their weapons leveled. Though their faces were obscured by their faceplates, Dani could tell from the sudden, jerky motions, so unlike the normal pantherlike smoothness of those who had gone through such rigorous training, that the men were shocked by the sight of Marissa. Dani knew that Marissa's talons would look like knives to the officers, knives poised to rip out Dani's throat.

"Please!" Dani screamed.

"Let her go," the first man said though a radio box in his armament that made his voice sound tinny, robotic. The shapes of other officers in shock gear were visible behind the first pair. One was smaller, perhaps a woman, though it was impossible to tell for sure. They advanced, filling out the corridor, six officers strong.

Until now, Marissa had been pliant, either amused by Dani's ploy, or too disinterested to object to the scenario Dani was attempting to create. The spotlight from one of the helicopters swept over the window once again, the light striking Dani and Marissa full on. When it passed, Marissa slowly closed her taloned hands over Dani's wrists and gently lowered them. She gave Dani a hug from behind, rocking back and forth slightly.

"Are you afraid of me?" Marissa asked the officers. "Do you have any idea what it's like to really be afraid? To know that no matter what you did, you were going to fail, you were going to let someone down, or betray them? Do you know what that feels like? I can show you. I can show you that and so much more. . . ."

Dani could feel Marissa's power slowly easing from her, reaching across the short distance in the hall to engulf the officers like a dark, nebulous cloud. The sensation reached Dani's mind, and she was only barely able to force away the leathery, fluttering wings of Marissa's terrible power. Even the slightest brush caused Dani to gasp and witness a frightening vision of her mother giving birth with only Richard Sterling in attendance, the man reaching into Sam with his razor-sharp, taloned hands, butchering her as he withdrew the child he had planted there, so many months before.

The nightmarish image made Dani shudder and pull herself away from Marissa, who did not attempt to hold her back. She stumbled to the door of the Caligula Suite, knocking it open with her back. She felt a cold rush of air against the side of her face and saw a blood-red cloud of smoke rush into the hallway from the room, accompanied by flashes of laser light and blinding strobes. The golden-eyed young woman looked back to the officers who were each experiencing their private hells courtesy of Marissa's power.

Dani did not want to feel the overwhelming sensual rush of fear that left the officers, but she could not withstand the assault of images cascading from them. The taste of the fear woven deep into the fabric of those memories made her grasp the doorway for support. She looked to the shattered window at the end of the hall and wished that she could fly through that window, fly from the maddening chaos that had become her life.

A flash of red grazed her vision and she heard a short, explosive burst of gunfire as a hail of splinters were ripped away from the door beside her head, cutting into the skin of her face.

She turned back sharply to the officers and saw that they were no longer in control. Marissa was walking forward, arms spread wide, her talons glistening with her own blood.

"No!" Dani cried, rising above the hailstorm of fear that Marissa had inspired to reach out with her own power, plunging deeply into Marissa's exposed thoughts as she forced the girl to confront her own hidden desire, the gentle, peaceful life she had secretly coveted but never dared to dream she could attain.

It's not too late, Dani whispered in Marissa's mind as she eased images of Marissa sitting in her imaginary studio, rainbow-colored dragons and friendly princesses lining the walls, stacks of fan letters written by young hands sitting beside her.

Despite what's happened, we can still go back. I'll help you Marissa. I'll be with you. You can control this. Don't let it control you.

Suddenly, another of the officers began to scream and opened fire on one of his comrades. The gunfire shocked Dani from Marissa's mind, but she saw that her words and her power had achieved the desired effect. Marissa seemed dazed, confused, and totally human.

Dani took Marissa's hand and was about to lead her to the stairs, when another handful of officers appeared at the head of the stairs. The rolling cloud of dry ice from the Caligula Suite suffused the hallway, and the explosion of panic that Marissa had inspired in the first group of SWAT members had not lessened. One of the men turned his gun on the officer closest to the head of the stairs and fired. The faceplate of the man shattered and he was flung back. Another officer fired blindly, wounding another of the new arrivals.

Dani pulled Marissa into the open doorway of the Caligula Suite, where a cloud of vapors engulfed them. From what glimpses Dani was able to attain of the room's interior, Dani felt as if she had walked into a film set. Statues of the gods to whom the Romans prayed lined the far wall, including one of the mad emperor, Gaius Caligula, the fourth Roman emperor, who had declared himself a living god. The floor was slippery, and the dry ice which pumped relentlessly from the vents near the floor clogged the room. Before them lay a throne and a small courtyard with a sparkling fountain that spouted red wine, though it looked like blood. A false tree had been erected and a series of ankle and wrist bracelets had been installed on its surface, pulleys with thin, dangling cords hanging from its low hanging branches. The audience seating was arranged like a small theater, with tiers of marble benches.

Dani knew that most of what she saw was an illusion, cheap materials substituting for the real thing, but at a glance, through the smoky red haze, the strobing hot lights, and the incongruous snaking laser lights, the setting was enough to make her believe she had been transported to another time and place.

Slamming the doors behind them, Dani was looking for a lock when the first of the bullets came ripping through the door. She grabbed Marissa and dove away from the door and the hailstorm of bullets that quickly cut the door to pieces.

Coiling her power, Dani lashed out, attempting to instill in the minds of the half-insane police officers a fear of what was inside this room.

It's death here. A charnel house.

Dani pushed forward with images she desperately prayed would keep them back: *Hundreds laying dead in the room, the floors slippery with blood, the walls splattered with blood; dozens of gunmen lined up before the doors, prepared to cut the officers to pieces; a hospital ward with dozens of children playing innocently, children who would die if the officers came in, guns blaring.*

The first of the officers burst through the remains of the doors, the madness that Marissa had inspired within the armed men overriding any compulsion Dani could now place them under. Dani took Marissa's hand and dragged her to the heart of the set. She saw the red flash of the officers' laser sights and pulled Marissa behind the sacrifice tree as the first staccato burst of gunfire tore into the prop, which had been constructed with an iron skeleton.

A handful of armed men entered the Caligula Suite behind the first. Dani projected images of Marissa at either end of the room. Several of the officers saw the apparitions and believed them to be real. They took positions and opened fire as more armed men flooded into the room.

Though Dani had never attended a performance in this particular Den of Debauchery, she had seen others, and she knew that the performers often appeared and vanished at will, meaning there were hidden doors, and possible routes of escape. She looked up to the lighting grid above them, then touched Marissa's arm. Marissa looked at her with a dazed, little girl expression.

We're going to have to fly, Marissa. You're going to have to help me, Dani said within the confines of Marissa's mind.

Suddenly a pair of officers appeared around the side of the set, leveling their weapons at the two women. Dani sprung forward, shoving the first officer's gun up and back, so that its weight shattered his faceplate and slammed into his skull, causing him to reel back. She sensed the man beside her was about to fire on Marissa and she kicked at his weapon, averting the deadly spray of bullets. Snatching the gun from him, Dani grabbed him by his heavily reinforced vest and threw him over the throne a few feet away. His head struck the rear of the throne and he collapsed.

The fog within the room seemed to be congealing. There was a control booth somewhere for this production, and whoever had been in it when Marissa's powers had gone out of control had left the settings on maximum when he left the station. Only the sweeping lights, strobing to give the movements of everyone in the room a jerky, unreal appearance, helped to cut through the buffeting clouds of dry ice.

A figure suddenly emerged from the rolling crimson clouds before Dani and Marissa. Another officer dressed in riot gear, weapon leveled. Two more appeared on either side, flanking him.

"Honey, get down!" a voice screamed.

Dani recognized the voice of her mother and did as she commanded, dragging Marissa to the floor. There was a sudden explosion off to Dani's left and she heard what sounded like dozens of guns firing at once. From the periphery of her vision, she saw pinwheels of light bursting through the pinkish-red fog and saw the officers divert their attention and begin to fire.

My mother's alive, Dani thought. *Alive!*

Suddenly, she felt Marissa's hands upon her. There was a roughness to her touch as the vampire grabbed Dani by the waist and kicked off from the floor.

"No, Marissa!" Dani screamed. "We can't leave her! We can't leave her again!"

But it was too late to reason with the blond-haired vampire. Marissa and Dani rose into the air, lifting up in a weak motion, their bodies pirouetting, changing positions, first leaving Dani exposed to the guns of the officers, then Marissa. Dani saw the officer in the middle raise his gun. She reached out with her power, piercing beyond the veil of his conscious thoughts, and released a flood of endorphins in his system. The unexpected, temporary high made his legs buckle and he lowered his weapon, firing instead at the floor. The men on either side of them leaped away in terror.

As Dani withdrew from the officer's mind, she saw the manner in which she and Marissa had been perceived. The officer had been chanting in his mind, *Fear is the enemy. Kill the fear.*

Marissa had been the maker of the terror each man had experienced, and nearly all of them were certain that their hearts would stop, their brains explode if the fear didn't end. Dani had felt the thundering of the man's heart and had wondered if perhaps they were right.

Dani and Marissa made it to the lighting grid, which Dani saw was secured to a series of wooden rafters, when suddenly Dani saw another officer burst through the cloud beneath them and raise his weapon. The rising couple suddenly reversed positions and Marissa screamed as a bullet tore through her shoulder, lodging somewhere deep inside. Blood flew from the wound and suddenly their ascent failed.

Dani grasped at one of the rafters, curling her arm around it as she hooked her free arm around Marissa's waist. The vampire seemed to weigh little more than a child, her body having transformed to achieve the miracle of flight, though her strength had not lessened. Dani looked down, wondering why the officer had not fired a second shot, then saw her mother crouched over the man, who lay flat on the floor, his arms spread before him.

"Marissa, you have to help me!" Dani shouted as they dangled above the room, a perfect target for all the other hunters in the room. "Please!"

Automatic weapons fire sounded from below. Another officer, shooting at shadows. Dani looked down and saw her mother crouching behind the fountain, digging into her shoulder bag for another weapon she could use to distract the officers without harming them.

Dani knew that beneath each impersonal faceplate, beneath the body armor each man or woman in the room wore, was a human being with a history and a desire to protect, just like her mother. Their minds had been tampered with, their desires warped, but that had not been their fault and they did not deserve to die for it.

Looking down, Dani saw an officer suddenly burst from the crimson cloud, a spotlight revealing him. He was in a deadshot position to Sam's side, his finger on the trigger of his weapon. Before Dani could act, another man exploded from the cloud, but this man did not wear armor or a faceplate. Dani could see his face clearly.

It was Ray Brooks.

With a scream, Brooks threw himself between Sam and the officer, who fired a half-dozen shots into the officer's back. As he fell, Sam whipped around with her Beretta, firing three times into the chest of the officer. The bullets drove the man back and he fell to the floor seconds after Brooks, whose back was a red, bloody mass.

Dani had placed him under the compulsion to help her mother. He must have seen her come back inside the club and had reinterpreted the programming she had given him. She wondered how many innocents would die because of her.

Another pair of officers appeared and Sam fired twice at each of them, the bullets slamming into their chests, where the impact would not kill them, because of their Kevlar vests, but it would crack some ribs or bruise their hearts, stopping them.

"Dani, get the hell out of here!" Sam screamed. "I'll make it out! Go!"

Above, Dani watched as Marissa's eyes suddenly flashed open, her body recuperating from the trauma caused by the bullet she had taken. She saw Sam, and with a last, sudden burst of flight, lifted herself high into the rafters, breaking from Dani in the process. Her initial rise caused Dani to flip over the top of the support beam, her feet striking a blazing white spotlight and shattering it. Dani fell into the next rectangular pocket of empty space between the wood and metal grid. She tried to anchor her feet on the next support beam over, but the impact of her legs on the beam rattled her and she suddenly found herself falling. Reaching out in desperation,

Dani grabbed for the beam she had been holding before and felt her fingers close over it. There was a sharp pain in her shoulders as her fall was arrested, and she swung in a pendulous motion above the room.

"DANI!" Sam shouted from below as she fired the Beretta half a dozen more times.

Dani caught sight of an officer with a shotgun aimed at her. With a cry of agony she pulled herself up, vaulting up and over the wooden rafter as the shotgun exploded. She felt the rush of air from the pellets and heard them cut the support beam beside her in two. She landed on the intersection of two cross beams, and barely had time to catch her breath before she felt cold hands descend on her and drag her upward, beyond the lighting grid, beyond the rafters, with such force that she didn't even have time to scream.

Sam had not been spared the agonizing effects of Marissa's powers, but she had been subjected to the worst horrors of her life in the past few days, and she was able to focus past the madness which had affected the others. The mental disciplines she had practiced with Dani had helped her to focus the sum total of her being on a single goal, saving the life of her daughter.

When she saw Dani disappear into the rafters she knew that her daughter was somewhere that the officers crowding this room would not be able to follow, and that meant she was safe from them. But the vampire was there with Dani, and its actions were unpredictable.

Sam fired two more shots with her Beretta, knew that her clip had run out, and slammed the weapon into its holster as she dragged a .45 from her bag. The splinter weapons she had brought might have killed the officers, the same with the shotgun. She knew they were not acting on their own desires, they had been driven into a killing frenzy by the vampire who was still exerting some form of control upon Dani.

Sam fired the .45 at another pair of officers, then began to retreat toward the doorway from which she had emerged. She knew from her last visit to the club that there were a series of crawl spaces and hallways snaking around the various suites; the schematic was posted on the wall of the office into which she had been shown by Lee Shawcross.

If the officers had been in their right minds, they would have immediately deployed men to these positions, but the vampire's power had reduced their ability to reason and impaired their judgment. Sam checked her safety, saw the small door she had propped open, and scrambled back a few feet.

Suddenly, Sam felt an arm close over her neck. She was in a choke hold. The fog had obscured one of the officers, and he had moved in to take her down. Sam did not try to peel the man's arms from her throat. That would have wasted precious seconds. Instead, she aimed the .45 back, toward the officer's leg, and fired twice.

She felt him buckle upon the impact of each bullet, but he did not let go. Numbness spread through her, and before she could fire the weapon again, her body surrendered to the choke hold. The sights and sounds of the flash zone faded and the darkness overwhelmed her.

For a time, she felt absolutely nothing. Then, as if a switch had been thrown, she found herself instantly aware. She was lying on her side in the bushes at the rear of the Hellfire Club, clutching at her throat, coughing.

She saw the bloody leg of the officer first. With a strength she knew she should not possess after her ordeal, Sam spun and kicked at the man. She could not allow herself to be captured.

He darted out of the way, moving so quickly that he practically vanished from one spot and reappeared in the next. Sam reached for her weapons bag and found that it was gone. The shotgun she had worn had been stripped from her, along with the Beretta.

Rising to her feet, Sam tried to run from the man, but a familiar, icy finger of pain stabbed into her skull, causing her to fall to her knees. A heavy boot connected with her shoulder, driving her face forward, into the dirt. A rough hand reached down, turning her onto her back. Sam was not surprised when the officer removed his faceplate and she saw the suntanned flesh and the glacier-blue eyes of Richard Sterling.

She thought of what Edward Pullman had told her: Another woman had confessed to the killing of the cleaning woman, the same woman who had burned Richard Sterling to death later that morning.

Sensing her thoughts, Richard smiled and said, "I'm not the only one of my kind whose capable of making a mistake. The bitch-queen's handmaiden roasted the wrong man. She found my current substitute, my daytime human, and killed him instead of me."

Sam nodded, wondering who he meant by the "bitch queen."

"That's not important, Samantha. What is important is that we're together, though, this is going to have to be quality time, because there's a lot I have to do tonight."

"You could go fuck yourself," she said amicably.

He slapped her, making her head whip around, then

he laughed and said, "Sorry, honey, I have a lot on my mind. I guess I'm just tense. If things weren't so busy, I'd suggest you help me work some of it out. It wouldn't take much to get you on your knees, now would it?"

Sam was silent. She would not give him what he needed, her defiance so that he could put her in her place. Nor was she giving him the rapt attention he so desired. She was there, she could not break away from him in her body, but she would not hand to him the sanctity of her thoughts.

"Things have changed since last night. 'Richard Sterling' is dead. His company is already being picked over, his assets frozen. What I've worked for the last twenty years has just been blown to hell.

"The upside to what's happened is that I no longer have to be so fucking clandestine. The first move's been made against me. That means I'm free and clear to start the war. The only problem is, I have some unfinished projects. You're one of them."

He reached down, placing his hands on either side of her face, and kissed her hard on the mouth. His power knifed into her mind, and she attempted to fight him, but he was too strong.

When he pulled away, Sam understood the terms of the conditioning he had placed in her. His words echoed in her mind. The command had been simple, clean, and direct:

One year from this night, you will return to this place at ten o'clock in the evening. You will bring my child with you. If I am not here, you will wait until midnight. If I do not arrive then, you will return every week until I come for you.

She saw Richard smiling at her and wanted more than anything in the world to kill him then and there.

344

"As much as I enjoy theatrics, *Samantha,* you have always been the one to point out that things work differently in real life than they do in the movies. I suppose I should have listened to you. A man should always listen to his beloved."

He winked and retreated into the shadows, melding with them and vanishing from view, leaving Sam to rise from the ground. Her rage over the casual violations Richard performed upon her was brimming over. Suddenly she heard the harsh beating of blades slicing through the air and turned in time to see the pair of helicopters suddenly begin to fly above the club, their spotlights sweeping the roof.

She thought of her daughter, trapped with Richard Sterling's monstrous daughter, and the sight filled her heart with fear.

Chapter Twenty

Dani had no time to react when she felt Marissa's hands upon her, carrying her high into the arched ceiling of the club. An explosion of gunfire had sounded and suddenly they were rocketing toward a trapdoor leading to the roof. Marissa struck the door first, her body splintering the wood. She dragged Dani with her, and the murky, oppressive darkness of the club vanished as they erupted into the cool night sky.

Marissa arced through the air, describing strange and beautiful patterns, and Dani clung to her, a part of her reveling in the sensation of flying free, without the cumbersome shell of machinery surrounding her.

"I'm a little pissed," Marissa said as she suddenly shoved Dani away from her. Dani cried out as she fell, though they were only a few yards from the club's roof. The high, arching roof had several flat areas for workmen. Dani fell on one of these, an angry fist of pain lashing at the back of her head as she connected, then lay still.

Dani shuddered as she saw Marissa hover near her, flitting above and around her. Perversely, Dani saw her as a bloodstained Tinkerbell, laughing and darting through the air. "Dani, I've tried to be your friend. I've tried everything I could to make us sisters, real sisters. But I don't think that's possible anymore."

Dani looked at Marissa's face. The girl's eyes were blazing, her razor-sharp canines had extended, and her hands had transformed once more into talons. The light Dani had forced into Marissa had been overcome by the darkness in her blood, the hunger and the need that Dani would also feel for the rest of her life.

"We're not the same," Marissa said as she stopped and laid out flat in the air, facing Dani. Marissa rested her face in her hand and poked her elbows into midair, as if for support. "I wanted to be like you. I thought if I was able to kill the others, I would get your approval. You want to help humans. You want to *be* human. Maybe you can still do that. I can't.

"What you did to me was wrong, Dani. You tried to make me think I could be human again. You tried to make me care about the things I used to care about. But that can't happen. My priorities have *changed*.

"I wanted you to change with me. I wanted you to help me and be at my side. But that's not going to happen. I see that now. I—"

Suddenly, both of the police helicopters rose above the level of the roof and shined their spotlights on Dani and Marissa. A wide, malicious smile appeared on Marissa's face as she turned in midair to face the closest of the machines. The side door was open and a sniper wearing a seat mount came into view, his feet dangling over the edge.

Dani could feel the sniper's fear, which erupted at the sight of Marissa hanging in midair like a wraith, an inhuman visitation. Suddenly she felt the brush of Marissa's power as the vampire eased her thoughts into Dani's mind. Their words would have been eaten by the roar of the helicopter's engines and the steady chopping sounds of its blades slicing through the night air.

Maybe I was all wrong about you, Dani. Maybe you were just trying to give me a gift. I can do the same for you.

Marissa reached down and grabbed Dani's hand, hauling her from the rooftop perch. Dani screamed and kicked as she saw the collection of police cars in the street almost three stories below. Suddenly they were racing toward the sniper, who had been paralyzed by Marissa's power, unable to fire upon her. Marissa's talons raked through the heavy supports that held the sniper in place, material that stretched over his torso. Her knifelike fingers bit deep and the man screamed as a cloud of blood rose from his stomach.

Marissa grabbed the man by the collar and hurled him from the helicopter, where he tumbled to the ground, his spine shattering as he impacted with the hood of a police car. Marissa threw Dani into the front seat of the helicopter, beside the pilot, then allowed herself to fall away as she sailed around the outer hull of the helicopter, flying low enough under the rotor blades to avoid being swept up into their pull. Tearing off the door to the pilot's seat, Marissa sliced through the frightened pilot's restraints, then looked over to Dani.

"You said you wanted to fly," Marissa said with a cruel, brutal laugh. "So fly!"

Before Dani could object, Marissa grabbed at the man's shoulders and yanked him from the pilot's seat. Together they fell away, into the night, as if they were parachuting from a high altitude. The chopper pitched forward and down, plunging toward the office building across the street from the Hellfire Club. Dani leaped into the pilot's seat, her hands shooting forward and grasping the controls as she felt the momentum of the craft building.

The door beside her and the rear side door were both open, sucking in air. Marissa had sliced apart the restrains and so Dani could not secure herself in the pilot's seat, she had to rely on the inhuman strength of her legs to hold her as she wedged herself in tight.

She grabbed hold of the pitch controls, repeating her training in her mind as she attempted to force her panic away. The craft was a Hughes 500 Jet Helicopter, with speeds of up to one hundred and fifty miles per hour. She gripped the collective pitch control in her left hand. It would give her altitude. The cyclic, in her right hand, controlled her direction. The helicopter was sailing toward its destruction, in seconds it would crash. Dani adjusted the cyclic, banking away from the glass windows of the office building as she used the collective to lift the helicopter up, out of its collision path with the building.

Suddenly the second police helicopter arced into view, and Dani could see Marissa with one hand on the landing skids, using her power to guide the second craft into her way. The pilot that she had taken with her was gone. Dani assumed that Marissa had allowed the man to fall to his death.

A freezing blast of fear uncoiled in Dani's stomach, and she veered the helicopter she commanded into the direction from which the oncoming craft had come, banking hard as she wondered if the glittering lights of Los Angeles and the startled faces of the officers in the opposing craft would be the last sights she ever beheld.

Dani felt hard gusts of air buffet her helicopter as it passed close to the police chopper, but managed to avoid a collision. Suddenly she was clear of the other craft, rising above the streets, anxious to fly as far away as she possibly could. She had to find a safe place to land the helicopter, then get back to the club. Her mother was still there, and Dani could not abandon her.

Gasping, Dani suddenly felt cold, shadowy hands snake inside her mind, seizing her will. She banked the helicopter, bringing it back around to hover over the roped-off stretch of street before the Hellfire Club, where the other police helicopter also waited. Dani saw Marissa flying in gentle, lazy circles around the other helicopter. Marissa began to perform elegant figure eights, using her will to force the pilot of the opposing chopper and Dani to slowly bring their crafts closer together. With each circle Marissa made of the helicopters, the distance between them rapidly dissipated.

Marissa passed before Dani's window, a catlike, satisfied grin on her face as she took a slight bow. Then she faltered slightly, and for an instant Dani was once again in control. Before she could pilot the helicopter away, Marissa's power slammed down on her again, making her vision dim, her perceptions blur. Dani struggled to burn through the haze that was descending on her, then she saw the reason for the sudden lethargy that Marissa had inflicted upon her:

Marissa was crying and she had not wanted Dani to know it. The human girl within her was still alive, though her blood had risen and had attempted to destroy the humanity, warmth, and love that Marissa's mother had instilled in her.

Dani saw Marissa mouth the words, "I'm sorry" and suddenly Dani was once again in control. Before she could take advantage of Marissa's momentary surge of compassion, Dani saw Marissa turn suddenly and saw the girl's mouth open wide in a scream.

Turning in the direction of Marissa's gaze, Dani saw a figure who cleanly sliced through the air, sailing directly for Marissa.

It was her father, Richard Sterling. He was wearing the blue uniform of a SWAT member, including the Kevlar vest.

"Christ," Dani whispered. She felt the man suddenly, a cold, detached figure whose full concentration was centered on a single task: He had come here tonight as an executioner.

He must have known; he must have sensed that she had gone Wildling, that she would no longer be suitable for the purpose he had created her to fulfill.

Dani saw Sterling ignore both helicopters as he arced through the air. He approached his daughter, talons curled, his mouth a collection of razor-sharp teeth. Marissa stared at him in fear, then her expression changed. The feral smile returned, and she swung around to greet the man.

Marissa had only a few seconds before her father was upon her. She waited until he was close enough to strike, and she dove suddenly, launching herself out of his path as she coiled her power.

Dani was able to guess what Marissa planned, and she steepened the pitch of the blades, causing the helicopter to rise straight up. The scene below her dwindled, as if she were looking down at illustrations in a book, and Dani was once again tempted to arc away with the helicopter, to leave father and daughter to whatever end they could arrange for one another, but she had an interest in this. She knew that neither she nor her mother would ever be safe so long as Richard Sterling was alive.

Dani watched as Sterling made another run at his daughter, and this time Marissa allowed him to come close enough to draw blood. Dani could see that it was the only way the girl had to feint and draw her father close to the second helicopter.

Suddenly, the police chopper banked and the sniper who sat in the open doorway of the helicopter opened fire on Sterling. The vampire's body jerked half a dozen times in the air as the bullets cut through him, then he lashed out with his power — Dani could feel it even from this distance, a searing flash within her mind — and the sniper suddenly turned his weapon on himself, jamming the rifle under his jaw as he blew off the top of his head. The helicopter suddenly veered off course, arcing down and away from the figure who hung shakily over the city.

From her vantage, Dani could not see if the bullets had been taken by Sterling's vest, or if the sniper had aimed at the vampire's head. Marissa did not allow Sterling time to recover from his wounds. She was upon him immediately, her taloned hands plunging toward his head. He backflipped, avoiding her blow, and sailed away from her. Marissa raced after him, and together they flew from the area of the club.

Dani looked over her seat, saw the black box containing the additional weaponry from the sniper who had been assigned to this helicopter, and reached back, flipping open the box to see an AK-47, fully loaded, waiting. Putting her knee against the collective, she snatched the gun and eased off the safety. Suddenly she saw the remaining police helicopter follow in pursuit, and Dani knew that Marissa would not hesitate to sacrifice the pilot of the craft if it gave her an advantage over her father.

Drawing a sharp breath, Dani manipulated the controls and followed the flashing lights of the police helicopter. She understood why Sterling had fled. His body would need time to recover from whatever wounds he had received. But flying had been difficult for the vampires, or so Dani had been led to believe. She had been told that it was a pleasure best reserved for the moments after a kill.

Marissa had killed tonight, and had taken the blood of her victim. Sterling wore the uniform of a SWAT member. He had probably slaughtered that man and perhaps several others during the chaos.

For a moment, Dani looked out at the lights of the city and remembered what it had been like to fly of her own accord. Those memories had kept her alive on the long nights after she had made her decision to embrace her humanity, and they had also tortured her when they had invaded her dreams, reminding her when she woke of all she had lost. On those mornings she would lie in bed, allowing the precious sunlight and its wondrous, comforting warmth to force away her fears and her regrets.

Marissa would never again walk in the light. Dani looked at the lights of the craft before her and wondered if *she* would live to see the first pale streaks of morning light.

They had passed through the city, flying over a suburban stretch, and reached Echo Park. Dani had been here once before, but only briefly. The area beneath them had houses on its small hills, and they were approaching Echo Park Lake and the park surrounding it. She recalled that Echo Park was a neighborhood in transition, with a large population of newly arrived Hispanics. The architecture was very old, with Victorian-style houses. It reminded Dani of the Tampa neighborhood her mother had lived in when she found Dani.

They were over the park, which Dani prayed would be deserted at this hour. The Hughes 500 carried three hundred and sixty pounds of fuel, fully loaded. The craft Dani piloted was two-thirds full. She assumed the opposing Hughes would be at least half full, perhaps more. If Marissa allowed the helicopter to crash into a building, or a private residence, the explosion would be hellish.

"Let's do this," Dani whispered. She put her knee against the collective as she held the automatic out the window as she increased her speed, burned past the pursuing helicopter, and came into visual range of Marissa and her father. Marissa was several yards behind Sterling, making Dani wonder if he was leading her to a particular destination, or if his wounds had truly been this severe.

She saw the vampire look up in surprise as her helicopter appeared over him and she fired several times. He snapped away, but not before one of the bullets ripped across his cheek, fracturing the bone. Dani saw Marissa come upon him as she piloted the Hughes on, describing an arc over the lake below. The helicopter still piloted by the police followed her. Dani had no idea if the man in the other chopper was following by his own will, or that of Marissa.

She saw Marissa and Richard fighting directly above the lake. He swept out with his talons, creating a deep, bloody gash in her arm and upper chest, and even from a distance, Dani could feel the psychic blows that each was delivering.

Dani had wondered why Sterling had not used his impressive mental powers against her, and she now realized that he had been busy maintaining his shields against his daughter, whose animalistic hatred of him was far more powerful than his desire to sweep away the evidence of an experiment that had achieved disappointing results.

Richard flung Marissa away from him, but not before her talon raked across his face, leaving a bloody cloud in the air. Dani saw Marissa flounder and fall away, and she prayed that the girl would guess Dani's plan in time.

Jamming the automatic back in its case, Dani used both hands on the controls of the Hughes and piloted the craft on a direct course for Richard Sterling. The vampire looked up sharply, attempted to use his power against Dani, and shuddered as Marissa launched another attack against his mind, a torrent of undiluted hatred barreling into him.

Dani was upon him in seconds, dropping the altitude as she approached so that she could use the whipping blades of the helicopter as a weapon. Sterling seemed to understand Dani's intent and he allowed his body to fall like a stone.

He was almost too late. The suction from the blades

caught his light body and buffeted him like a rag doll, and he crashed against the front window of the Hughes, leaving a spider's web of cracks as he fell away. She heard a thud on one of the landing skis and felt the chopper tip slightly.

Dani looked over in shock to see that Marissa had sent the second helicopter on a collision course. The buffeting came again.

Sterling was hanging on to the landing ski.

Dani pulled up suddenly, panic suffusing her, and nearly lost control of the helicopter. She heard a sudden clank, as if a grappling hook had been slammed down on the open doorway beside her, and saw Sterling's face as he lifted himself up. Dani registered the proximity of the second helicopter. It was speeding toward her on a direct trajectory. Marissa had hoped to crash the helicopters together, and use the fireball to incinerate her father.

"Hello, little vampire," Richard said with a mock-paternal smile.

The convex dome of the opposing helicopter's front window loomed before her. Dani banked off, but she felt Marissa's power grazing her thoughts. The chopper before her matched her every movement.

They were about to collide when Richard Sterling leaped into the helicopter, his talons aimed at Dani's throat.

Sam had been surprised to find her bag, still filled with her weaponry, laying in the bushes a few feet away. Sterling had left it as a joke, as a display of his superiority. Sam grabbed the bag and circled around the club to find Edward Pullman sitting on the ground, his back against the passenger door of a police cruiser. He was as dazed as the other officers and the hundreds of witnesses in the crowd. Even Sam had a difficult time sorting out exactly what had occurred. The sweeping waves of disorientation and confusion had left memories of chaos and death in their wake, but not comprehension. There were no reasons for what had happened, no easy answers.

Two crews from local news stations had arrived on the scene. Their equipment had been destroyed, the tapes removed from their recorders, and each one of them was rolling on the ground, huddled in fetal positions as they sobbed and babbled incoherently. More of Sterling's work.

Sam understood that it had not only been Marissa's power causing the scene to escalate out of control, Richard had also helped. If Sam had not been present in the club, and in terrible danger, he might have confronted his daughter before she was able to take to the night skies.

"The helicopters," Sam said, the words nearly catching in her throat. "What happened to the helicopters?"

"They went down," the detective sergeant said in a hollow voice. "They crashed in Echo Park Lake. We've got units heading there now."

Sam broke from him and ran back to her Range Rover. She dug her hand into her pocket, brought out her car keys, and nearly screamed as she saw three figures suddenly appear in the reflection from the driver's side window. She turned, gasped as she saw the face of the woman before her, and plunged her hand into the bag. She was stopped with a firm but gentle touch. A surge of reassurance passed through Sam as she heard a haunting, melodic voice whisper in her mind:

It's all right. We're friends. We've come to help.

Sam shuddered. She knew that no matter what she did, the woman and the two men flanking her would be upon Sam the instant she tried to fight them or escape. They were too close, and, she sensed, too powerful.

The woman's eyes were black with flecks of crimson. Her beautiful dark hair fell about her shoulders in sumptuous waves, and her luminous European features made her appear otherworldly. Her diamond earrings sparkled, even in the dim street light. She wore a long, black leather trench coat, pulled tight, and black leather boots. Though she looked very young, certainly less than thirty, Sam sensed from the woman's bearing that she was much older.

The man to her right had hard, set, Scandinavian features. He was handsome, with a wild mane of blond hair. His eyes were glacier blue, like Richard's. The other man had auburn hair, regal features, and a slightly more rugged build. Both men were dressed in designer-original suits, and both stared at Sam impassively.

All three were vampires.

The woman held her hand out to Sam. "Would you like me to drive? It might make it easier. . . ."

Dani was amazed to find herself alive. The last few seconds before impact were a blur in her memory. She felt Sterling's hands upon her, then felt herself being flung from the opposite side of the helicopter. There had been a horrible, grinding sound, a tearing of metal

358

that seemed to rip through her skull, and an explosion that seared her as if she had been close to the heart of the sun. Then she had been falling, plunging into the waters as chunks of metal, some larger than her, sliced into the water around her, striking like shrapnel. One ripped across her back, but the furrow it made had been very light. There was a tumultuous churning as the two helicopters which had been fused together upon impact struck the waters, then Dani had felt strong hands on her, dragging her to shore. Suddenly she broke the surface of the waters, took a lungful of air, and cried out as she was heaved upon a bed of rocks. Her hands went up instinctively to protect her face, but she groaned in pain as she struck the flat stones.

Turning, Dani saw Richard Sterling standing over her. Marissa was nowhere near. Dani could not even sense her. The girl's plan had failed, and she had run away, frightened of the power swelling within her father, despite his many wounds.

Dani tried to rise, but Sterling lashed out at her with his power, sending her sprawling back. Instinctively, she knew what she had to do, though the thought sickened her.

Richard came forward, grasping her face with his hand, digging his thumb and powerful fingers into the hollows beneath her cheekbones. Dani could sense that he was holding himself back. If it had been his desire, he could have pulverized her jaw with his grip. She knew that he had saved her life for a reason.

Staring into his glacier-blue eyes, so like the eyes of Bill Yoshino, the young man who had betrayed her and taken her innocence both in body and soul, Dani allowed her fears to consume her. The terrors of her entire lifetime coalesced into a boiling mass, and at the core of her fears was the snarling face of Richard Sterling. The vampire's features changed to reveal an expression of wonderment and triumph as he feasted upon her private horrors, gaining strength and pleasure with each new delicacy he took from her. But even this wasn't enough.

You know what I've done to your mother, don't you? Richard asked in a taunting, demonic voice. *She's carrying my child. She will come to me in one year with the baby. The outcome of that meeting, whether she lives or dies, is up to you. You must kill my daughter. You're the only one she trusts, the only one who can get close to her.*

Kill her for me, or in one year's time, when I return for Samantha Walthers, I will take her child, and perhaps her life. Or do you think it might be more entertaining to leave her alive and perfectly sane inside her head, while her body displays all the symptoms of the insanity that destroyed her own mother? Better yet, I could leave her paralyzed, unable to move, unable to do anything but remember.

I can do any of these things, little vampire. I can do any damned thing I want. It's a wonderful feeling, little vampire. A shame you'll never feel it.

Dani had felt her consciousness, her identity, her soul, slipping away, the defensive walls she never let down crumbling beneath the onslaught of Sterling's power. She had allowed this only once before in her life, this complete submission and surrender of her identity, and that had been when Bill Yoshino had taken her, and had forced her to release the demon that had been inside her. She had loved him. She had been willing to give him anything, to do anything to win his love, even deny the feelings she had in her heart for a woman who had saved her as an infant, who had given her life to Dani, and had loved her beyond all reason.

Sam was the one person whom Dani loved above all others; the one person for whom she would gladly die to protect.

Suddenly, for a fraction of an instant, Danielle Walthers ceased to exist and the demon rose up. Richard Sterling tried to pull away with his power, but it was too late, he had become too intoxicated with the fear he believed that he had inspired, and he had allowed a fraction of his own defenses to fall away, creating a slight opening into which the demonic, hateful thing that had once been a human girl slip through.

Sterling tried to recoil, tried to gather his power, but it was too late. The demon was within him now, and it did not reason, it did not care. It lived only to kill, only to consume — a parasite that would eat him away from the inside.

Richard Sterling began to scream.

Sam sat in the passenger seat of the Rover, her heart racing as she stared at the porcelain-skinned woman who drove the vehicle at more than one hundred miles an hour. In the backseat, the two male vampires sat serenely, their eyes closed, their hands on their knees. Sam could sense flashes of their power, images of the streets ahead being reflected back from the perceptions of other drivers or those humans on the streets.

Cars sped out of their way before them, keeping the way clear at all times. When they approached red lights, the dark-eyed woman did not slow. The traffic which should have been an impenetrable wall would suddenly ease, tires squealing as drivers braked at their own green lights, freeing the intersection for the passing car. The vampires were using their power to control dozens of humans at will.

Sam had never conceived of beings with such power.

The woman beside her turned to Sam and said, "You know what we are, don't you? And who I am? Your daughter's told you everything, I know she has."

"Don't be so sure," Sam said.

The woman did not bother to look back at the road, which frightened Sam. They passed through an intersection, barreling through yet another red light, and suddenly changed lanes. The woman did not look away from Sam.

"No one's going to hurt you. No one's going to hurt you ever again," the woman said. "You have my word on that."

"I don't think that's something you can promise."

"You'd be surprised what's in my power, Sam. Very surprised. There's very little about your situation that I don't know. And there's very little that I can't make happen. I've already helped you once. If it weren't for me, you'd be in jail right now, or running from the police."

"Instead another innocent woman is there."

The vampire shook her head. "The woman you mention is under my employ. She's an Initiate, like your daughter, but she wants to become an Immortal. Our lawyers will make an insanity plea, and we will ensure that the judge goes along with it. She will spend a few years under psychiatric care, and then we will secure her release. In return for this, she will be granted sizable privileges."

"You make it sound like it was a business deal."

"It was. A simple trade. I have another trade to discuss with you. If you're interested in hearing it."

"Do I have a choice?"

The woman's dark eyes became hard. "There are always choices, Sam. It's merely a question of making the right one."

Sam nodded. As the Rover sped beyond the city, driving through the residential district that separated Sam from her daughter, she listened to what the woman proposed.

As awareness returned to Dani, she suddenly understood what it had been like for Marissa, and more importantly, what Isabella had felt in her final moments before Dani had destroyed her. Until this moment, Dani had been certain that she had murdered Isabella; she now realized that she had truly performed an act of mercy by burning the woman's flesh and releasing her from her torment.

The demon that was her blood heritage had savaged Richard Sterling from within, attacking his mind, preying upon his weaknesses. Dani now understood his obsession. He had been a turncoat British officer who played a major role in the American Revolution. In retribution, his English family, a wife and two children, died when his house was burned. Since that time he had been trying, without success, to recreate that family. By tricking Dani into slaying Marissa, he assumed that she would be so overcome with blood lust that he would be able to turn her. She would become his surrogate daughter, fulfilling the role Marissa was too insane to handle. Sam would be his wife, their son the successor he had always dreamed of having.

That dream would never become a reality. Dani was still within his mind, and he was struggling, fighting for his life. The demon had done all it could. It had plunged Richard back to relive his darkest memories, it had forced him to feel the agony and the fear that had nearly destroyed him when his family had been killed.

She saw the woman who had come to Richard on the night he had planned to end his life, the vampire who had made love with him, who had forced him to surrender his grief. She had taken him on a wild odyssey that had climaxed when she had released his every hunger and desire, when she had woken his blood and made him an Immortal. When Dani had gazed upon that woman's face, she thought she might scream.

It was Isabella.

On that night, he had lost his ability to recall what it had been to love. He had been desperate to recover that feeling, but it had been placed out of his reach. He knew that it was there, but it would never again be his, the evil he had given himself to preventing him from ever knowing such love again.

His frustration, his anger, had churned within him, and after decades of pain, he came to loathe the woman who had done this to him rather than let him die. He made the decision that he would one day make her pay, even if it took a century or more before that occurred.

The demon had tormented Richard, slicing away at his fragile weakness, but it had sensed that Richard's many years of living with the pain would prove stronger than anything the demon could do to him.

Dani knew that she could not afford to allow her

compassion to keep her from her task. Sterling would never allow her to live after what she had done. She could already feel his power growing, and the fear she had given him earlier was returning to her at his urging.

You said you'd die for her, a voice whispered in Dani's mind. *It's the only way. You're too weak. He'll push you out of his mind soon. You know what you have to do. If you wait, he'll have you.*

Dani did not hesitate. Using her power, she leaped beyond Sterling's conscious mind and used her knowledge and skill to attack his inhuman physiology. She stimulated the mast cells within his body, releasing a deadly burst of histamine, sending his body spiraling into anaphylactic shock. His trachea swelled closed and he was unable to breathe.

For a moment, she was able to see through the eyes of her body, and the sight gave her some encouragement. Richard had collapsed on his back, his body bucking as he lashed out and pulverized the rocks near him. Dani lay on her side, just out of his reach, unable to move.

She could sense his vast healing abilities begin to fight the abuse she was heaping upon his system. Dani attacked several blood vessels within his brain, causing them to bubble and clot, and finally to burst. Pushing with all her strength she activated his sympathetic nervous system, pushing up his heart rate and contractibility, causing peripheral vaso constriction and clamping down the arterials so the pressure in the aorta and the pressure going to his brain would cause another aneurism.

Sterling's brain suddenly ceased to function, but he did not die. There was something else within him, a

365

presence that went beyond the body, beyond the brain, and would not release its hold on life.

Dani once again found herself staring out of her human eyes, watching the still form of Richard Sterling. She would not relinquish her hold on him.

This is murder, she thought. An execution, exactly the same as what he had planned to do with Marissa.

How can you do this, Dani? How can you live with the knowledge that you've done this?

She thought of her mother and silenced the pleading voice in her mind. She would do anything, become anything, to protect the woman.

Sterling's eyes flashed open and Dani screamed as he launched himself at her, his power gnawing at the silver thread that connected them. Dani grasped at his wrists, holding back his taloned hands, which had been poised to tear open her throat, and she pushed against him with her power, stimulating Richard's parasympathetic ephrans, the vegas nerves which traveled down his carotid arteries and innervated the viscera, practically the entire body cavity.

Her attempt to inspire Vegal Escape succeeded. Sterling's heart stopped and he shuddered, looking down at her as his face went pale and she jammed his taloned hands deep into his own chest, then yanked them apart, causing his body to quake and fall away as a geyser of blood shot into the air.

Dani scrambled away from him, tripped on a stone, then shouted as she felt his cold hand close over her leg.

Little vampire, he whispered in her mind.

Then he yanked her toward him, his power slamming into her, shredding the bond that had allowed her to inflict such damage upon his body and his mind.

Dani had never endured such horrible pain in her life. He caused her to feel everything she had done to him. The shock made her want to pull away, to retreat so deeply within her mind that she might never return, but he would not allow this.

Struggling to his feet, Sterling lifted Dani by her throat and yanked his right hand back, preparing to thrust it toward her chest and rip out her heart.

Sam gripped the open window of the Range Rover, her hair whipping behind her, as she looked anxiously ahead. The woman beside her expertly navigated through the lanes of Echo Park, the male vampires having launched themselves through the back windows and taken to the air above them.

They had not spoken for several minutes. There was nothing left for them to say. Sam had no idea what she might expect to find when they finally arrived at the park, but she had been thankful that they had managed to get there before the police and rescue units.

Her daughter was not dead. She had been attempting to convince herself of that fact from the moment she heard Edward Pullman tell her that the choppers had gone down. Sam wondered how they knew that; had someone seen it happen?

The woman beside her told her that she had briefly entered the detective sergeant's mind, and she had learned that the pilot of one of the crafts had left his radio open. His screams and the sound of the midair collision had been unmistakable.

Suddenly the cover of trees vanished and the lake was before them. Flaming debris was scattered along the shore, and in its midst stood Richard Sterling, holding Dani high in the air. He looked sharply in their direction, and Sam realized that the vampires had been using their power to shield their presence from him.

Sam caught a glimpse of the woman's face and registered genuine surprise and distress. By cloaking themselves from Richard, ensuring that he did not run when he sensed their presence, the vampires had been unable to rely on anything but their human senses. They had not known that Dani was in such danger.

The woman next to Sam made a sharp turn and braked the vehicle, leaving Sam with a clear shot. Sam heard the screams of the male vampires who rushed toward Sterling, but they would arrive too late. His hand had already begun to scissor forward, his knifelike fingers about to pierce Dani's chest.

Sam had begun to aim the second the Rover stopped. She squeezed off three shots and saw Sterling's hand explode inches away from her daughter's chest. He screamed, raising the blood-spouting stump to his face, and Sam was able to see the gory mass of his chest.

The first of the male vampires who had been flying reconnaissance—the one with short auburn hair—dropped from the sky and snatched Dani away from Richard. Sterling's talons dug furrows in her chest, but she was alive and away from him. The second vampire—the Nordic man—descended on Richard, and was surprised as Richard darted away, slashing with his remaining talon. The Nordic vampire clutched at his throat, which had exploded in a cloud of blood, and struck the ground hard.

Sam was out of the Rover and the woman beside her screamed Richard's name. He whirled on her in an animal frenzy, lashing out with his power. She shuddered, but whatever pain he caused her did not stop her from advancing on him. Suddenly he swiveled in the direction of the auburn-haired vampire who had just set Dani on the ground.

Sam was nearly upon Richard, her hand drawing out the small, black, hand-held flamethrower from her weapons bag. She was about to pull the trigger and send a tongue of flame reaching out at the man's head when the woman cried for her to stop.

Suddenly, no one moved, and Richard Sterling smiled.

In Sam's mind, a lightning-quick burst of information stabbed into her, images of the link Dani had formed with Richard, the link that she believed to be severed, though it was not. He didn't have to touch her to use her as a hostage. He didn't have to be anywhere near her to kill her. All he had to do was maintain the link, weaving their nervous systems together, and whatever damage his immortal, nearly indestructible body might endure, Dani's mortal form would also suffer.

"You should have let me die when you had the chance, Alyana," Richard said to the woman.

"I won't make that mistake again," the vampire replied as she squeezed her eyes shut and curled her lips into a grimace.

Sam saw Dani quake in the arms of the auburn-haired vampire, then lay still. "What are you doing?"

"Burn him," Alyana said.

In the distance, sirens began to wail.

Sam felt a powerful, invisible force close around her hand, but she fought it off. If she burned Richard, Dani would also burn.

"No," Alyana said, "it's in me now. Do it. Trust me, please!"

"She's lying," Richard said. "I'll take your daughter, there's nothing you can do."

Looking at the expression of forced confidence of Richard Sterling's face, the sensitive smile that he had employed when they first met, Sam wanted nothing more than to set the man on fire and watch him die. But how could she be certain? The vampires had no reason to care about Dani, despite their promises, despite the deal that had been struck.

"Sam, you've got to believe me!" Richard cried, stiffening suddenly as he realized his mistake.

Sam. He called her Sam. Not *Samantha*. In that instant she knew he was full of shit.

Without another moment's hesitation, Sam squeezed the trigger of the hand-held unit she carried and allowed a burning streak of flame to explode, engulfing the vampire's head and shoulders. He turned, screaming, and Alyana fell to her knees, shuddering and crying out with the pain. Sam pulled her weapon and emptied the clip into Richard Sterling's head. The corpse fell to the ground, its movements at an end.

Alyana fell back, her flesh red, her eyes wide. Sam holstered the weapon with shaking hands, then ran to her daughter. Dani was alive, reason slowly returning to her eyes.

"We're all right, baby. We're safe. He's gone."

Dani folded herself into Sam's arms.

The auburn-haired vampire had been looking in the direction of the sirens, which lessened suddenly. "They'll go deeper into the park, away from here. By the time they start wondering what the hell they're doing, we'll be gone."

From the rocks near the shore, among the still flaming debris, the blond-haired, Nordic vampire rose, his neck a bubbling white mass. Alyana was also on her feet, walking toward Sam and Dani.

Dani stared at the woman incredulously. "Isabella?"

As Alyana came closer, Dani realized that it was not Isabella. Isabella was dead. But she knew why this woman seemed strangely familiar. Dani had seen her before, during the last few moments of Isabella's life, when the vampire's private memories had been laid out for her.

This was the vampire who had turned Isabella. The woman who had loved Isabella like a daughter, but had pulled away from her when the child had desired its freedom.

There was something else that Dani had learned about Alyana from her glimpse into Isabella's past. Alyana belonged to the Parliament.

"It's over, isn't it?" Dani asked.

Sam lowered her eyes. "No, honey. There's still Marissa. . . ."

Chapter Twenty-one

The terms of the agreement Sam had made with Alyana, contingent on Dani's approval, rang in Dani's mind as she walked through the park, the cool night breeze playing across the deeply tanned skin of her face. Three nights had passed since Richard Sterling's death. In that time, two Immortals had been slain in San Diego, Marissa's hometown. Their bodies had been hung in Balboa Park, strung upside down from low-hanging branches, handcuffs securing their severed heads to their dangling wrists through punctures made between the teeth and jaws.

The park was overrun by transients at night and desperate young vampires often sought prey there. It was impossible to learn if the victims had been murdered in the park or brought there afterward. Other vampires had found the bodies; the human authorities were blissfully unaware.

Alyana had explained her interest in Marissa as a strictly professional concern. Members of the Parliament were often charged with the recovery and destruction of Wildlings. Dani knew that wasn't Alyana's only motivation. Alyana was the Immortal who had turned Isabella and had considered Isabella her daughter.

Even after they had parted, Alyana had watched over Isabella, helping the woman whenever necessary. The Malibu beach house had belonged to one of Alyana's many corporations and had been leased to Yoshino without Isabella's knowledge.

Yoshino had no qualms about taking "gifts" from anyone. He had known that Alyana and Sterling were rivals, and that a war would one day erupt between them. By remaining friendly to both sides, he had attempted to ensure his own future.

The day after Sterling's death, Sam had gone to the obstetrician, who confirmed her pregnancy. An odd transformation had taken place in the woman. Though it was now possible for her to have Sterling's child removed from her, she had refused to make that decision. Sam explained later that she had been overcome by thoughts of Dani as an infant. They had never encountered Dani's biological parents. The vampire who had impregnated Dani's birth mother could have been as startlingly evil as Richard Sterling.

Dani had fought against her blood heritage and won. This child, this life growing within her, deserved the same chance.

An hour after nightfall, a knock had come at their door. Alyana and her partners appeared, dressed elegantly, as always. They brought an offering of a very rare wine, which Sam refused.

"We should toast to our partnership," the auburn-haired vampire had said. His name was Johannas.

The flaxen-haired man sitting beside him was Marley.

Dani knew that her mother loathed these creatures, despite their assistance the night before. Alyana had spoken slowly and carefully to Dani, as if she were addressing a child. Dani had expected Alyana to hate her because she had killed Isabella.

Alyana revealed that she had shared those feelings, and had, in fact, learned through her spies in Sterling's network of the truth behind Isabella's demise and had planned to take suitable revenge. The visions Dani had suffered of Madison and Isabella had been the result of Alyana's presence, as Alyana had been near Dani many times and had taken Dani's secrets without her knowledge.

When Alyana saw the results the visions had on Dani, she had been confused, and had, over the course of time, come to regard Dani as something of a goddaughter. Isabella had loved Dani. Many of Isabella's memories lived in Dani's mind. Though Alyana could have taken them from Dani, the girl's life was the last link Alyana had to Isabella, hence the deal Alyana had proposed.

Securing the capture of a Wildling was never an easy task. Every night Marissa lived, another of their kind was at risk. The more highly placed vampires, those in the Net, had received information on Marissa and would report any sightings of the young woman. Enough of Marissa's intelligence had remained to make her a greater threat than some of the creatures they had been forced to put down in the past, monsters who had been reduced to a primal, animal intelligence and basic, murderous impulses.

Catching a Wildling was sometimes as simple as offering the proper bait. Alyana knew from what she had culled from Dani's mind that Marissa continued to possess a depth of feeling for Dani that would never allow her to harm her friend, no matter how deeply she was driven by the dark impulses inside her.

Dani knew that was a calculated guess, at best. Provided Alyana was correct, there were no guarantees that the vampire she might encounter would be the same Marissa she had last seen — and even then Marissa had come close to harming Dani on several occasions. Alyana had promised that Dani would be in no real danger, and perhaps it was true that Alyana and her companions could keep Dani from harm. They were incredibly powerful. Dani felt a slight tremor rising up within her whenever they were near, a slight buzz of excitement, an intoxication that allowed her to be more relaxed, more confident than she might have been otherwise. But beneath Alyana's soothing tone was a hard, cruel, businesslike edge. They didn't need Dani for this. They could easily have taken Marissa on their own.

This was Dani's penance, her punishment for choosing her human mother, Sam, instead of Isabella. Alyana could have killed Dani at any time, if that had been what she wanted. Instead, she had chosen to allow Dani to live. She had to justify that decision in her own eyes, and possibly those of the other members of the Parliament. Dani blamed herself for failing Marissa, for not somehow forcing the girl to display the strength that Dani's mother had brought out in her. Knowing that Marissa had been destroyed would be terrible for Dani, but taking a part in her destruction, perhaps killing the girl herself, would be a sobering and unforgettable lesson.

Walking through the long, dark stretches of the park, Dani considered that she had never been particularly religious. Her mind had not been made up on the subject of God and Lucifer, though she had been told that the blood of Christ and the fallen angel ran in her veins. If she believed in God and an afterlife, then she would also have to believe in Hell, and that was not a concept she wished to confront this night.

There was one hell in which Dani could easily believe: The hell Marissa now faced. The joyous human girl within her was not dead, it was trapped in a shell of cruelty and corruption. Dani had agreed to Alyana's plan not only to save her own life — as she understood the penalty for refusing the agreement — but also to free Marissa. She wanted to give her friend the choice of ending her existence with mercy, without pain, rather than dying like an animal, hunted down and destroyed, dying in agony and terror at the hands of an impersonal executioner.

Sam had remained at the hotel with Marley, the flaxen-haired vampire, who seemed content to sit and stare at nothing at all. Alyana explained that Marley had recently read Mallory's *Le Morte D'Arthur* and often enjoyed reciting the entire two-volume text back in his head.

Sam had not wanted to be left behind, but Marissa could sense the presence of Richard's child within her. Sam accepted this, but Dani could feel her mother's fear for her when she left.

Now Dani walked through Balboa Park, and the uncharitable thought that had come to her when she first learned the name of the park returned to her now. Sylvester Stallone, shoulders hunched over, approaching Talia Shire:

Yo, Adrienne! Ya wanna see my turtle?

The thought nearly made her smile. The park itself was beautiful, with old-style Spanish-Moorish buildings mixed with slightly newer, Californian-styled architecture. She had passed several ornately designed buildings with red tiles and sculpted stucco in floral and fruit shapes, many of which had been designed as temporary structures during the various expositions which had been held here.

She had walked the length of the park several times tonight, passing through El Prado, the courtyard and walkway, and had gone through the central museum district, sometimes following the pathways forking off to other attractions. There were canopies of trees and lit patches of open-spaced grass.

Dani heard the time as the one-hundred-valve carillon in the California Tower tolled the hour. Statues of prominent Californian historic figures stood at the base of the two-hundred-foot tower, which possessed a blue tile dome. The Museum of Man, an anthropological museum, sat beneath the California Tower.

One o'clock. Nothing.

She had been spreading her power before her, causing the many transients who might have taken her for prey to feel a numbing fear when she passed by, and avoid her at all costs. The brief tremors of terror they radiated filled her with a comforting warmth.

377

Dani was on the approach to the Organ Pavilion, a huge, open-air theater with covered walkways that spread from the stagelike wings, when she heard a small stone skip along the ground behind her and strike the heel of her boot. Spinning in alarm, Dani saw a tall, long-haired man wearing a cardigan sweater, ivory slacks, and dockers. His gold watch caught the moonlight, as did the rims of his round, stylish glasses. In the light, his hair appeared honey-blond, and his beard was scruffy, but not unattractive. The man's eyes were green and piercing, and his features were thinly sculpted, but handsome. He stood with his hands in his pockets, shuffling his weight from one foot to another.

The man was unquestionably an Immortal, one Dani had never encountered before. Alyana and Johannas promised that they would be close to Dani at all times, utilizing their power to keep themselves hidden from the senses of even the most powerful of their kind.

"You shouldn't be alone here at night," he said. "It's dangerous. Especially now."

Her heart nearly leaped from her chest, and she allowed her fear to flow freely, hoping to disarm the man by giving him the same false sense of superiority that Richard had so eagerly desired.

The vampire ignored her fear.

Dani stared at him in confusion and wonder.

"It's impolite," he said, cocking his head slightly to the side, like a wolf. "My name's Dean."

"Dani," she replied.

"Sounds like we'd make a good couple, doesn't it?"

378

"I don't know," she said coyly. "I barely know you."

He nodded. "Why are you here?"

"Is that important?"

"It is if you're here for the same thing I'm after."

"What's that?"

He smiled, shrugging. "You know how it works. If I have to tell you, you don't deserve to know."

Dani felt a genuine chill. She had not sensed the presence of her kind at all this night and that had not surprised her. A message to stay away at all costs had been left in this place for two nights running. He had come for the same reason she had, to find the Wildling, and bring it down. He assumed the Parliament would reward him.

"You should get out of here," Dani said. "Now. It's not safe."

"I know. That's what I keep telling you."

Stupid, overconfident bastard, she thought. She knew that if she talked to him long enough, Alyana or Johannas would soon appear and put the fear of death in him. From looking into the auburn-haired vampire's face, she knew that he had perfected that expression.

"I think we both want the same thing," he said softly. "The blood of the Ancients. The only way to get it is to prove yourself. That's what I intend to do."

"Fine. Just do it without me."

"You want it, too," he said. "I can feel it."

"I want you to leave, that's all."

"It's *not* going to come after you. You won't make a satisfying meal for it."

"I really think you should go."

He sighed. "If you think that's best."

"I do."

Nodding, he turned his back on her, took a few steps, then, with a motion that was almost a blur, pulled up his sweater with one hand and reached for something with the other as he whirled back on Dani. She saw a glint of metal, something in his hand, and the holster that had been taped around his waist, beneath the sweater.

A flare gun, she realized. Jesus, he thinks it's me!

His finger was closing on the trigger, and Dani was already diving away, though she had nowhere to run, no place to find shelter, when his hand suddenly jerked away from her direction and his chest exploded in a mass of gore. Dani saw a white talon emerge from his chest as the flare gun was ripped from his hand. The figure that had appeared behind him was swathed in shadows.

They killed him, Dani thought, panic rushing through her. Then she realized her mistake, and a clean white fear burned in her mind. She watched Dean fall to the ground, shuddering. He was on his knees, attempting to rise, but his head was jerked back suddenly, and the talon sliced through his neck, severing his head.

The shadows engulfing the figure parted and Dani saw that it was Marissa. She felt sickened as she watched Marissa open her mouth and swallow greedily at the spraying geyser of blood.

For the briefest of moments, Marissa would be vulnerable. Dani expected Alyana and Johannas to appear behind Marissa at any moment.

Now, damn it, she thought, what are you waiting for?

They did not reveal themselves. She wondered if something had happened to them, or if they had lost her. That seemed impossible. Her mother had described the trick Marley and Johannas had performed on the drive over. The Parliament was composed of the oldest and most powerful of the vampires.

Another reason for their reticence occurred to Dani. In one hundred years, a thousand years, this night would mean nothing to them. Not unless they made it interesting.

It was up to Dani. They wanted her to do it.

The flare gun lay a few feet from Dani. There was a chance she could reach it, immolate Marissa, and use her power to spare the young woman the agony of her death.

Dani chose to remain perfectly still.

Alyana and Johannas could take Marissa if they so desired. Dani could not stop them. But she would not destroy the girl as if she were an animal. Dani was human, and that was beyond what they could expect of her.

For an instant, Dani saw the figures of Madison and Isabella standing behind Marissa. They were no longer covered in blood. The two women held hands, smiled at Dani, then vanished.

She knew that she would never see them again.

She was free.

Suddenly, Marissa looked up from her kill. She allowed the body to fall away from her as she rose to her feet and licked at the blood on her hands. The young woman was dressed in Dani's leather jacket, which had been zipped all the way up, black blue jeans, black boots.

"Where is he?" Marissa snarled.

Dani felt her sudden sense of well being vanish. "Who?"

"My father," Marissa said, covering the distance separating her from Dani so quickly that Dani barely saw her move. Marissa slammed Dani to the ground, her razor-sharp canines glinting in the soft orange glow of the street lights.

"Marissa—"

"He's here, goddamn it. Tell me!"

"You're wrong. You have to listen to me. Please!"

"Why?" she asked, her eyes blazing. "Because you're my *friend?*"

"Yes."

Marissa's laugh was hollow. "And you want to help me."

"I do."

"Huh. That's good. Because I want to help you, too, Dani." Marissa placed her talon in Dani's face, the razor-sharp tips of her porcelain fingers centimeters away from Dani's eyes. "That's why I'm going to give you about ten seconds to see things my way. Because if you don't, you won't be seeing anything, ever again. . . ."

Chapter Twenty-two

"Marissa, your father is dead. Richard Sterling is *dead*."

The vampire frowned deeply, her talon wavering for a moment. "And you want me to look into your head, don't you? So that I can see for myself that you're telling the truth?"

"It's safe for you, Marissa. I won't try to hurt you. I won't do anything to you. You can trust—"

"Bullshit!" Marissa said, snapping Dani's head back on the walkway. "That's what he'd *expect* me to do. You're expendable. He'd put a trap in your head."

"God," Dani whispered.

"I know he's out here," Marissa said. "Do you think I'm a fucking moron? I knew he'd hear about the killings. I knew he'd come after me. And when I saw him save both of you from the crash, I knew you were going to end up his dog."

"He burned to death," Dani said. "I saw it happen."

"In the crash?"

"No, after. He wanted to do just what you said. I fought him. I thought I could kill him, but I couldn't.

He was about to kill me when my mother came. She burned him."

Marissa withdrew her talons. *"You* might actually believe that. It makes sense, that's what he would do."

"Please—"

Pulling away from her, Marissa raised her hand, which was human once more, and motioned for silence. Dani nodded, and slowly moved into a sitting position. Marissa crouched beside her.

"It's pretty here," Marissa said as she looked out on the round outdoor stage in the near distance. "My mom used to take me here during the day. We'd go to the del Coronado sometimes, too. She used to work there. Ever go to the Del?"

"No," Dani said, wondering where the others were hiding, if they intended to wait all night. Perhaps that was their plan. To keep Marissa there until the sun rose.

They might have the power to accomplish such a task. Dani's only advantage, the only weapon she had, was that Marissa was unwilling to go into her mind, and that meant she did not know about Alyana and Johannas.

"The Del is gorgeous," Marissa said, her tone softening. "It looks like a gingerbread castle. I loved being there. They filmed *Some Like it Hot* there. You know that movie, don't you? All you used to watch was old movies."

"I've seen it. You're right. The Del is beautiful."

"The people who worked at the Del? They treated me like a princess. That's what they all called me. I think when I was a little kid, and my mom worked at the Del, I think that was the only time I was completely happy, that I felt really safe. Do you understand?"

"Yes."

"Do you have a place like that?"

Dani swallowed hard and touched her chest. "In here."

"Your mother. What she feels for you. That's what helps you survive. I knew that before. When I was inside your thoughts that night."

"Yes."

Marissa put her hand around Dani's shoulder and drew her close. "Richard Sterling is alive. He made you think you saw him die, that's all. He knew if you were doing something for all the right reasons, or thought you were, you'd go along with it."

"That's not true."

"Hush," Marissa said, rocking her slightly.

Dani squeezed her eyes shut. She had to find a way to convince Marissa that her father was dead. If Marissa could believe that, she might be willing to stop the killings.

That wouldn't be enough, Dani knew. The Parliament wanted her dead. They had no interest in her personal redemption.

"Daughter!" a man called.

Marissa and Dani both spun at the sound. Dani's heart nearly exploded at the sight before her. Less than one hundred yards behind them stood Richard Sterling, cradling Samantha Walthers in his arms.

385

"No," Dani whispered, trying to make sense of what she was seeing. Marissa couldn't have been right. Dani had seen Richard die. It had not been an illusion.

"Come with me, little vampires," Sterling said in his mocking tone. "The best is yet to be!"

The words had been calculated to send Marissa into an explosion of mindless rage, and they achieved that effect. Sterling rose into the air and gently fell back, as if he were totally relaxed. The night winds seemed to guide him, blowing him back along the path as a small cloud of delicate leaves brushed against the eucalyptus trees.

Marissa turned away from Dani with a scream of primal hatred. Understanding came to Dani as Marissa was about to launch herself into the air in pursuit. The golden-eyed young woman snatched the flare gun from the ground and raised it. Before she could pull the trigger, Marissa whirled and slapped it from her hand. Throbbing pain exploded in Dani's hand but she managed to restrain a scream.

"You're so fucking anxious to protect my father and his broodmare, are you?" Marissa cried. "Then maybe you should come with us!"

"Marissa, it's a trap. That's not your father and it's not my mother. Your father is—"

Dani recoiled as Marissa slapped her, the blow sending her to the ground, where she struck her head. Dazed and powerless to resist, Dani felt herself being hauled up and thrown over Marissa's shoulder. Suddenly they lifted into the cool night air and in moments they were following the winding path "Sterling" had taken with his prisoner. Dani's receding view of the park told her where they were headed:

The tower.

Dani reached out with her power, tentatively brushing at the outer walls of Marissa's consciousness, just as she had the first night they met. Once again, Marissa pushed her away, but this time she did it with the power of a god, not an untrained child.

They slowed and Marissa allowed them to sink to the ground. She set Dani down and the golden-eyed young woman saw that they were before the ornate and stunningly beautiful tower, which looked like a vast cathedral. The building had been sealed off to the public for decades, but there was a small rear entrance to allow servicemen inside.

Marissa placed her finger to her lips and said, "We're going to have to be vewwwy, vewwwy quiet. It's wabbit season!"

Dani shuddered as Marissa took her hand and dragged her around the side of the building. She pictured Alyana or Johannas closing on them from either side of the building, or from above. It had been them, posing as Sterling and her mother. Dani knew that now.

"Marissa," Dani begged, "what if you're right? What if it is Sterling?"

"I know it is."

"And if you're right, you know what he can do. You know there isn't any way to fight him."

"I don't want to fight him," Marissa said with a

slight laugh. "I just want to kill him."

They turned the last corner and stood facing the open service door.

"Marissa, it's not too late," Dani pleaded.

"Yes, it is," Marissa said as she dragged Dani toward the swell of darkness that waited beyond the narrow doorway.

Samantha Walthers stood in the darkness of the second-floor landing of the clock tower. Marley seemed to be enmeshed in a particularly amusing passage from *Le Morte D'Arthur*, or so the slight smile that came to his lips indicated.

The vampires had lied to Sam and her daughter, but Sam had expected that. They had not been satisfied that Marissa would be drawn by the lone presence of Dani. They wanted her to have a taste of Richard Sterling, to feel him near. The child growing within Sam would be an irresistible lure, the vampires had wagered, and the presence of Samantha Walthers would guarantee her daughter's actions.

Sam thought of the innocent life within her. Richard Sterling was dead. He had no hold on this child. The vampires had told Sam that she carried a son, and Sam knew that in their culture, a male child was considered an object of reverence. The females, those like Dani and Marissa, were often killed or tossed off.

It would be different for the males. They would not be raised in ignorance of their blood, their traditions.

Sterling had promised to be quite involved in the raising of his son, and Sam had no doubt this would have been true, had he lived.

Sam had deduced another reason why sons were so precious to the vampires: These were cursed creatures, and their ability to sire male children was apparently limited. Each male child was a triumph.

That meant they wouldn't let her go when this was over. Earlier that night, she had heard Marley and Johannas arguing, though they had sat quietly and had made no movements. It was their thoughts she had overheard, their rage allowing their carelessness for a few damning seconds.

I have seniority, Marley had bellowed. *Alyana and I have been together for one hundred and ten years! You've served her half that long!*

But I am the favored, Johannas had countered. *And I have never betrayed her.*

I was young. I have paid for that mistake.

And perhaps our lady has forgiven you. We will have our answer in time. I trust her to make the proper choice, and will abide without complaint.

The child should be mine! Marley screamed.

In a way, Johannas had said, *it will belong to us all.*

The conversation had ended abruptly, and Sam had made no indication that she had heard any of it. She was a human and did not share in their godlike abilities. They had no reason to believe she had learned their true plans, and so they had not bothered to reach into her mind and remove the knowledge they had accidentally given her.

But Sam had known that eventually they would enter her thoughts, and so she had taken steps to protect herself. Dani's account of Richard Sterling's final moments, the agony in his mind, had given her the key. For most of the vampires, love was an emotion they could no longer feel, though they could recreate the hollow memory of it, rebuild the façades, the trappings. It tortured them, and so they ignored it, avoided it at any cost.

Taking what she had learned, Sam had blanketed the memory within the most cherished recollections that she and her daughter had shared, including the final moment when Dani had turned her back on her blood for love of the values Sam had raised her to respect, and for love of her mother, who would have gladly died for her.

Sam had compartmentalized her thoughts, and taken great pains to focus only on the present, even when she had performed another task of which the vampires were still completely unaware.

Suddenly, footsteps sounded from below. Dani and Marissa had entered the tower. They were upon the winding staircase leading to the second floor, where decades old clutter, old unmarked crates, and the heavy bells and machineries of the old clock sat within the domed building. There were small windows nearby, with glass panes.

Marissa appeared at the head of the stairs, Dani behind her. They stopped as they saw the Nordic vampire standing beside Sam.

"It's over, little vampire," Marley said, speaking in

Richard Sterling's voice, utilizing the phase the dead man had given his daughter and all of her kind.

Hands fell upon Dani and Marissa's backs, sending them sprawling forward. Two figures materialized at the landing, cutting off their path of retreat: Alyana and Johannas.

Dani had been stunned to see her mother. "Mom, are you okay?"

"I'm fine," Sam said. "Don't worry, honey, we're both going to be fine."

Taking a step in Sam's direction, Dani was stopped by Marissa, who reached out and grasped her arm.

"Which one is he?" Marissa asked, her need for vengeance rolling from her in crashing, molten waves of hatred and desire.

"What are you talking about?" Dani asked.

"Goddamn it, you tell me right now!" Marissa screamed.

Alyana shook her head. "She still doesn't believe it, Dani. She thinks Sterling's alive. She thinks he's using his power to play a shell game. One of us is him, the others are either humans or other vampires who work for him. She even suspects your mother. I doubt that she will hesitate to act for long, and if she chooses your mother, we may not be able to stop her in time."

Sam watched the anguish in her daughter's face and wished she could tell her that Alyana was lying, that they would not allow harm to come to Sam, they wanted the baby she was carrying. But she would only get one chance to act, and they would paralyze her if they had any reason to suspect what she had done.

"Tell me, Dani," Marissa said, her fury consuming her.

Dani knew that the vampires would not wait for long. They had wanted to trap Marissa in a confined space, and drawing her to the tower had been a simple matter.

"It's up to you, now," Alyana said as she looked into Dani's eyes. "You know what you have to do."

Marissa's grip on Dani's arm tightened. *"Tell me— "*

Tears suddenly welling in her eyes, Dani lashed out with her power, sending her silver thread into Marissa's mind like a thin, piercing stiletto. She reached Marissa's most vulnerable memories, those of Elaine, Marissa's mother, and burned past Marissa's defenses. She had known that Marissa was becoming disoriented, confused, and frightened, and that if she did not seize upon this opening, one of the others would.

Elaine Aldridge and Richard Sterling sat at the edge of Echo Park Lake, amid the flaming wreckage of the helicopters. They were dressed in white summer clothes, sitting upon elegantly carved ivory chairs, a white table between them. An umbrella protected them from the sunlight that sought to burn off the harsh morning haze rising from the waters of the lake, mingling with the gray billowing clouds of smoke from the twisted machinery.

They raised their glasses in a toast.

"Oh dear," Richard said as the umbrella suddenly caught fire and disintegrated into ashes. Sunlight fell upon Richard Sterling and his flesh burst into flames.

"Sweetheart, should I get you something?" Elaine asked, but

392

it was Elaine no longer. The woman's features had smoothed and become those of Marissa.

"I'm sorry darling," Richard said in a partially bemused, but ultimately quite sad and resigned voice. A fireball was engulfing him, causing his flesh to melt, his features to blur. "This is quite embarrassing. I suppose I really must leave you."

He rose from the table, and so did Marissa. Richard leaned in, kissing the air beside her face. She did not flinch as her hair was singed.

"Tah!" she said.

Richard's aristocratic demeanor had already fallen away as he stumbled to the ground, a gun suddenly leveled at his head and emptied as he went down and did not move again, the flames transforming his remains into a charred, skeletal mass.

Dani recoiled as Marissa thrust her out of her head, then backed away, sobbing with grief. She knew that Marissa finally believed her father was dead. The vampire's only regret was that he had not died at her hands, as she had planned.

"Who are these people?" Marissa asked, unable to look at any of them.

Dani turned to Alyana. "Leave her with me. It's going to be all right, now."

"We can't do that," Johannas said. "That's not the way the Law works. She's killed her own kind. She's Wildling. She has to die."

"He's right," Alyana said.

"What about Sterling? He was an Immortal."

"That was self-defense. He gave us no choice."

Several yards away, Sam allowed her hands to slip into the long, deep pockets of her jacket. She bit her

393

lip, tensed her shoulders, and allowed her concern for her daughter's life to suffuse her, making her a distasteful prospect for the casual inspection one of the vampires might have been tempted to perform.

"You're all like him, aren't you?" Marissa asked in a low, frightened voice. "And I'm like him, too!"

Dani went to her. "Marissa—"

"I don't want to be this," Marissa hissed, her fear blossoming out of control. "Oh God, Dani, help me, I don't want to be this!"

Marissa screamed as her hands transformed into talons and she began to slice at the front of her own jacket. The jacket parted, revealing a small carry-all strapped to her waist.

This time, unlike those fatal four seconds before Dani's car crash, time did appear to slow. Understanding crashed down upon Dani as Marissa's talons tore a small gap in the travel pouch, revealing a series of shell casings wired together and filled with plastic explosives. Marissa's talons struck a small switch which had been exposed.

A red light flashed twice on the explosive device.

Dani was not the only one to realize what was about to happen. A surge of panic passed through each of the vampires. Their godlike power would not protect them from what was about to happen. Fear laid open their thoughts to Dani. Suddenly she knew what her mother had known, that while Alyana may have meant to hold true to her promises to Dani, she had made other promises to her companions. Sam's child, Dani's brother, would be raised as one of the vampires, raised to become something perhaps worse than Richard Sterling.

The light on Marissa's belt flashed once more. Dani could smell the incendiary device. Marissa had talked of the del Coronado. Near it was a military base. It would have been very easy for Marissa to have found a man from the base who was at the Del or in town. Marissa would have overpowered his will, forced him to construct what she would need and bring it to her. She had known that she could not take Richard Sterling except through the methods she had gleaned from Dani's mind: Surprising the vampires, taking them down hard and fast, and without mercy.

Marissa had meant to bring her father into an embrace, ignite the device, and destroy them both in a fiery explosion. Now there was nowhere for Marissa to go. She was crying and begging Dani for release.

This was the girl, the human girl who Dani had first met, the girl who had saved Dani's life. Dani made a decision and prayed it would be the right one. She grabbed at the belt and pushed down the red release, yanking the belt and the device from Marissa. A terrible agony flashed into her mind, the gift of the vampires who knew what she was about to do. They were too late to stop her. Dani's body was in motion. She hurled the explosive near the stairwell, where Alyana and Johannas stood. Johannas took Alyana, hurled her toward the stairs, and the device exploded.

There was a blinding white flash and suddenly the tower thundered and the walls rocked. The roar in the confined space deafened Dani. She felt her perceptions blur and received only a chaotic jumble of images, concrete, mortar, and steel were caught up in a whirlwind, spreading through the room like shrapnel. The walls burst apart and the oncoming wall of shrapnel raced toward Dani and Marissa, and was about to slice them apart, when the great metal bell came crashing down before them, shielding them even as the walls cracked open and gave way.

The thunderous vibrations suddenly stopped. Dani felt a ringing in her ears. She could not find her equilibrium, she could not stand. A single thought raced through her mind: Her mother. Had her mother survived?

Crawling through the smoking wreckage, Dani saw shadows moving and looked up to see beams from the ceiling swing back and forth in a pendulous motion. She made her away around the outer edge of the bell, which had been wedged into the huge gap in the floor, so that it hung between the two floors.

She found her mother laying beneath the bloody remains of the vampire Marley, who had turned and used his body to shield Sam from harm, as Dani had wagered he would. The protection of the male child was paramount to these creatures. They never would have taken Sam to the tower if they had believed there was any chance she might be harmed.

Sam rose slowly, twisting and pulling herself away from Marley's corpse. Dani helped her, and quickly examined her. There were no visible wounds, and Dani reached out with her power to ensure that her mother had not sustained internal injuries. She had been terrified that her mother might have paid the cost of her actions.

Dani sensed an odd presence, and realized that it was the child Sam bore. She expected to feel some trace of Richard Sterling, some vestige of the inhuman taint which he had left the child as his legacy, but there was nothing except the tiniest flare of life, innocent and pure.

Sam's lips moved, but Dani could not hear what the woman was saying. She didn't have to. She could sense the concern in Sam's mind for her daughter. Laughing, Dani took her mother into an embrace and began to cry.

I'm fine, she whispered in her mother's thoughts. *We're both going to be fine. I love you.*

Dani withdrew her silver thread. Suddenly she felt the leathery wings of Marissa's power as they brushed the outer walls of her consciousness. Dani looked up and saw Marissa standing behind them, her hands and face awash in blood from the wounds she had made in her stomach.

Dani did not resist as Marissa eased her thoughts into her mind:

I'm so scared, Dani. I want to die. But will you be there? Will you help me?

Dani reached up and took Marissa's hand. *I will, Marissa. I will. . . .*

They reached the del Coronado with several hours left before sunrise, parked the Range Rover, and went inside. Escape from the park had been a simple matter. Marissa had flown first Dani, then Sam, from the ruined clock tower, then helped to shield them from the perceptions of the humans who came to pick through the wreckage, or stare in shock at the devastation.

Along the way, Marissa had insisted that they make two stops. They parked across the street from an exclusive dress shop as Marissa broke in and stole dresses in each of their sizes. Dani waited outside, using her power to warp the perceptions of any humans who might see the car or any of the participants in the break-in. Later, they stopped at an all-night family restaurant, went into the ladies room, cleaned themselves off, and changed.

Marissa had chosen bright, summery dresses, off-the-shoulder whites and pastels. Sam had taken the small object from the long pockets of her jacket and slipped it into the matching bag Marissa had given her. It had been the military-style flayer, a device that she had taped onto a kitchen knife and wrapped in a towel when she had been in the hotel room the vampires had rented. They had thought it was amusing to let Sam keep her weapons bag, and they knew it gave her a sense of security. Richard Sterling had said that she should have been an actress. He had not been far off in his appraisal. Though she had not needed the flayer thus far, she was not entirely sold on Marissa's willingness to sacrifice herself, and she worried that their night of confrontations was far from at an end.

Marissa had spoken incessantly, though Dani had

barely been able to discern a sound. Dani knew that her own healing powers would fully restore her hearing, and she had already taken steps to erase the ringing from her mother's ears. By the time they reached the Del, conversation was once again possible.

"I love it here," Marissa said, getting out of the car.

Sam had allowed Dani to drive, she was in no condition for the task. The hotel was brightly lit and had all the fairy-tale qualities that Dani had expected from the brief glimpses she had received of the place in Marissa's thoughts. They went inside, passed through the lobby without raising any attention, and went to the patio, where they sat looking up at the stars.

Dani had sensed the struggle in Marissa. The woman had sated the blood-need within her, and her obsession with killing Richard Sterling no longer had a focus. The part of her that had learned to love the hunt and the kill was not going to be easily convinced that she should walk into the light come morning.

Marissa was utilizing her power, altering the perceptions of the workers on staff this late and any visitors to the hotel who might come upon them. Of course it was perfectly natural that they come around and bring drinks for Lady Marissa and her guests, and that they smile warmly and bow graciously to the newcomers.

When they were alone, Marissa turned to Dani and said, "What I told you about my mother passing away in November, when it was raining? That was true. I don't know what made me think about it, it's just that—I don't know, I keep having this perverse thought: What if it suddenly starts raining tonight? That would be pretty terrible, wouldn't it?"

Dani took Marissa's hand. She saw the way the girl's lower lips had begun to tremble, and she squeezed Marissa's hand reassuringly.

"You know, if I thought, if I knew, that I could be just like this, then maybe it would be okay." Marissa shrugged. "Remember what you put into my head? That picture of me working in my studio at night, and all the pretty pictures and the letters from kids? I really like kids. I wanted a sister when I was growing up, but my mother said she would never have any more children. She couldn't. Something had been done to her.

"Anyway, I was thinking, maybe I could still do that. If I could be just like this. Just the way you see me now. Why isn't that possible, Dani?"

Dani bit her lip hard. She knew that it might have been easier on all of them if she had not removed the device from Marissa's waist. She could have grabbed Marissa and thrown her toward the others. Instead she had chosen to save her.

It had been the human girl she had saved, the terrified human girl who was sitting beside her now.

"If things could be like that, then it would work out, wouldn't it?" Marissa asked.

"Yes," Dani said gently. "If they could be like that."

"I just want to go back and do it all over again," Marissa cried.

"So do I, honey," Dani said.

Marissa shuddered. Her gaze became hard as she

looked to Sam. "I'm sorry for what I did to you." She hesitated. "I want to say that it wasn't me, but it was a part of me. I can still feel it inside me. Promise me you won't let it have me again. No matter what I say, no matter what I do. If it gets me again—"

"It won't," Sam said, finally understanding Dani's loyalty to this girl. "You have my word on that."

"Let's go down to the beach," Marissa said. "It's prettiest down there."

They went to the shoreline and looked out at the moonlight sparkling on the waters. They could see Point Loma, a small peninsula of land housing a beautiful lighthouse. At night, Point Loma was closed, locked behind gates, as it resided on land owned by the military. A ferry was docked nearby to take travelers across the waters.

"My mom and I used to take that ferry all the time," Marissa said. She shuddered as an echo of the killing frenzy that had so often suffused her returned. "She wanted so much for me. She had so much ambition, she thought I could get everything right, everything she got wrong. When I was accepted at college, she said I was going to become something better than she could ever dream of becoming." Marissa laughed hollowly. "Thank God she never saw me like this."

"She still would have loved you," Sam said.

"Not after—"

"She would have," Sam said firmly. "No matter what."

Marissa nodded. "Thank you."

They sat together in silence, watching the sky.

There was nothing left for them to say. When the first pale streaks of blue appeared at the horizon, Marissa's chest began to heave.

"I can't do this," she said, scrambling back. "It's too horrible. I can't—"

Dani eased her power into Marissa's mind, attempting to spread a blanket of comforting warmth over the girl.

Marissa, you're not alone.

In her mind, Marissa was screaming, *I didn't want this, I didn't ask for this, not for any of this. I was supposed to have my whole life, I was supposed to get old, why can't I have that, oh Jesus, why?*

Dani knew what she had to do. She reached beneath Marissa's surface thoughts and took full control of her mind. She caused Marissa to see herself in ten years, having graduated from college and attained her masters. Marissa was working with troubled children, helping them to free themselves from the monsters and demons that plagued them. At night, Marissa saw herself going home to the man she loved, eating a meal he had prepared for her, and making love with him the entire evening. On weekends, she saw herself in her studio, working on fairy tales for lonely children, those who were so much like the way she had once been.

Five years later, ten years, and Marissa and her husband were living in a bigger house, one they shared with their two adopted children. The walls of Marissa's studios were lined with letters and drawings from children, and Marissa allowed her own children to help her in the work.

The bright delicate dream suddenly turned. Dani felt another presence enter the fantasy landscape she had created for Marissa, a presence that had been so dark and filled with hatred that Dani knew it must be the animal that had been mercifully quiet until now, the murderous thing that also lived within Marissa, and could feel the ravages that Marissa's body had begun to endure.

Dani fought against it, as she had the demon within her own blood, but it quickly overpowered her, and the dream became a nightmare:

Marissa was working in her studio, a beautiful, glass-enshrouded addition to their house, when she heard a roar from outside and looked up to see the rear of the family van she had recently purchased loom up and suddenly crash through the far wall. She screamed as glass flew at her and her two children, attempting to shield them with her own body.

The driver's side door opened, and a dark man with a ruined face got out. His hands were talons, his mouth opened wide to reveal a maw of jagged, razor-sharp teeth. He stepped through the shattered frame of the door, advancing on Marissa and the children with blinding speed. Marissa had no time to object as the dark man tore both children from her, lifting them up by their throats.

"For me?" Richard Sterling asked. "Honey, you shouldn't have!"

There was a sudden explosion of fear within Marissa's thoughts that shocked Dani out of her friend's mind. Suddenly she became aware of her physical surroundings, saw the sun rising over the waters, and felt the cool fresh air of the night being burnt away. She turned to Marissa, and realized the mistake she had made:

The source of her nightmare had not been the animal within her, clawing at her for survival. The man from the dream was standing before Dani, holding Marissa in what Dani knew would be an unbreakable embrace. Marissa's arms were pinned to her sides, and her legs kicked out at the creature who had made her a prisoner, but the monster only laughed.

It was Marley.

Standing off to the side of Marissa and her captor were Sam and Alyana. The female vampire had placed the tip of her right talon against Sam's throat, and she gazed at Dani with the cold, unforgiving stare of a business executive who had chosen a course of action and would proceed no matter the cost.

"Johannas is dead," Alyana said. "I would have died, if not for his sacrifice. Marley will recover, given time."

Dani looked at the man. The long leather jacket he wore covered most of his body, but his head revealed the flayed, bubbling flesh, the streaks of bone, the single remaining eye, and the raw, exposed muscles fused to his trembling jaw. He did not look at her. He was enjoying the sight of the screaming young woman in his arms.

Dani could feel the warmth of the sunlight on her hands and face. Alyana and Marley may have wanted revenge, but they could not be willing to sacrifice themselves to the light to get it. There were endless

404

nights stretched before them. Dani could not understand why they were not running away in terror from the light.

Marissa's skin had begun to sizzle. The hairs on her arms had burst into flame and she howled in agony, tears welling in her eyes as she looked to Dani for help, for mercy.

Alyana poked at the flesh beneath Samantha Walthers's jaw. "Go anywhere near her and I'll rip the woman's head off."

"You'll kill the baby."

"It's Sterling's child. His son. He could be a threat to me one day. I don't care if he dies. And don't worry about the humans. I've had them used against me as weapons far too many times. They won't come near this place until we're through."

Marissa's screams ripped through Dani's mind and heart. If she attempted to alleviate Marissa's agony, as she had promised to do, Alyana might well kill her mother.

Around them, the sun was rising high, its heat growing stronger. Marissa's hair caught on fire.

"Dani, please!" Marissa screamed.

Alyana was not burning. Neither was Marley.

"The blood of the Ancients," Alyana said, as if those words would explain the impossible sight of the full vampires standing in sunlight, ignoring its deadly effects, which were tearing Marissa apart.

Dani looked to her mother.

"Do it," Sam said. "She's going to kill both of us anyway."

Alyana shook her head. "Marissa dies one way or the other, Dani. You and your mother could live. This is a test of loyalty. Do you even understand the *concept* of loyalty?"

Dani looked to Marissa. She was shrieking hysterically, her fangs bursting from their housings, her hands transforming into talons that raked her own burning flesh. The sundress Marissa wore caught on fire and Marley threw her down, the proximity of the flames beginning to alarm him.

"You should have let her die in the tower," Alyana said. "You should have never betrayed me. I wouldn't have betrayed you."

Marissa writhed on the ground, and Dani could sense that the human girl she had tried so desperately to protect from harm had retreated. Dragging herself to her feet, Marissa leaped into the air, flying in the direction of the cool, redeeming waters. Marley leaped up and caught her leg as she passed overhead, and hurled her down to the ground. The crack of bones shattering joined with the sizzling hiss of meat as Marissa covered her face with her hands, which exploded into flame.

Dani knew that she could not violate Alyana's orders and burrow into Marissa's mind without risking the woman's retaliation upon Sam, but there was something else that was in her power. The vampires had not been using their powers to control her or Sam, because they would have been forced to drop their walls of defense against feeling the intense pain Marissa suffered, the same walls Dani had subconsciously erected. But they were training their defenses against Marissa, not Dani, and they were not completely shielded, because they were taking some degree of pleasure from the waves of fear exploding from Marissa.

Dani opened herself to the agony Marissa was experiencing, allowing the pain to flood into her so that she shared the exquisite torture. Dani fell to her knees, her body quaking, and before Alyana could defend herself, Dani lashed out and loosed the full effects of Marissa's dying torment upon Alyana, who buckled and allowed Sam to slip away from her.

Marley advanced on Sam, but this time he was obviously not interested in being her protector. He had seen the weapon Sam had pulled from her bag, and knew that she was going to plunge it into Alyana's flesh. He saw the blade of the knife attached to it glinting in the fires of morning and he went for her.

Sam heard him move behind her, knew that she would not reach Alyana in time, and spun, burying the knife deep in Marley's throat. She threw the small switch on the side of the flayer, then dove away from the vampire, rolling in the direction of her daughter.

Making a gagging sound, Marley looked to Alyana, an expression of surprise and betrayal masking his features. He grasped at the weapon as an explosion of razor sharp steel fragments detonated, turning his neck and most of his head into a bloody red cloud. Scraps of metal flew through the air, though their velocity had been eased by the resistance they had found in Marley's inhuman flesh. Sam shouted as several small bits of metal sliced across her left arm and side, one the size of a bullet piercing her arm and flying out the other side. Alyana had attempted to rise into the air, but several shreds of metal had struck her, too.

Dani turned suddenly to Marissa, who was little more than a slowly moving, burning husk, and leaped into her mind. She moved past the cowering, dying animal that had been Marissa's blood legacy, and found the human girl who had been her friend. Removing the memories of the pain Marissa had endured, Dani gently eased Marissa back to the time when she had been happiest, when her mother had worked at the hotel, and the attendants had treated her like a princess in the most wonderful fairy tale she could ever conceive.

Goodbye, Marissa, Dani whispered as she felt Marissa's consciousness dim, her life racing away. *Goodbye.*

Dani suddenly found herself back on the shore, being cradled in her mother's arms. Marissa was dead. Alyana stood before them. Dani thought of the expression which had appeared on Marley's face before his death, and realized what had occurred.

Alyana smiled. "I told you, loyalty is everything to me. When I set up a deal, I don't change the rules."

"You *let* me go," Sam said.

"Of course."

"Why?"

"Ask your daughter. She knows."

"It was their idea," Dani said. "Johannas and Marley. They were planning on taking my brother."

"Yes," Alyana said. "They felt they were entitled. The only question was which of them would get the child. They were planning on putting that question to me, as I was an impartial third party." She shuddered with anger. *"I was running dogs like them a millennium ago!"*

Sam and her daughter watched the vampire. The sun had fully risen, and its effects were only now beginning to show on the woman.

"I could kill both of you so easily," Alyana said. "I could cut open your minds and make you feel pain such as you've never dreamed possible." She came forward and knelt on one knee before Dani. "I meant what I told you before, Dani. So long as you live, a part of my daughter, Isabella, remains alive. It's out of respect to you that I'm going to let the human and the seed within her live.

"I forgive you for what you've done. It was no less than I would expect my daughter to have done for me. But remember what has happened here today. Remember that you tried to defy me, and your friend died screaming.

"Most of all, remember *this.*"

Dani was startled as Alyana leaned in and took her face in her hands, gently kissing her lips. She felt a gentle burst of pleasure in her mind, then the slow unraveling of the message Alyana had imparted to her brain, a message that was for Dani alone:

Others of our kind may not be so forgiving. I will do what I can, but there are no guarantees that I can keep the truth of what has happened from the other members of the Parliament.

409

They may come for you one day, and if they do, I will be powerless to stop them.

Take care, little one. Vanish and be safe. It will comfort me to know that somewhere you are alive, and that a part of my daughter is alive within you.

Dani watched the vampire back away, turn, and walk in the direction of the hotel. Then she looked to her mother and said, "We'd better get the hell out of here. . . ."

Epilogue

It was a bright morning. Sam squinted in the glaring sunlight, which had once been a source of comfort to her. She had been certain that so long as there was daylight, *their kind* were powerless.

But that was no longer the case. Apparently, that had never been the entire truth for a few of the vampires, the oldest and most powerful of their kind. Dani had told Sam of something Isabella had said to her: For their kind, with age came power.

Sam had known that the vampires sometimes fed one another, and that the blood of the more powerful could sometimes carry their strength.

The blood of the Ancients.

Shaking her head, Sam decided that she did not want to think about it any longer. She had finished with the banks yesterday, transferring what funds she was not taking with her to offshore numbered accounts. This morning, the Rover was fully packed with all they could safely carry. The rest they would acquire as they went along.

She thought of Edward Pullman and felt a tug of sadness. Dani had gone to him and used her power upon him, making him believe that Sam was moving back to Tampa, and would probably not be in touch again. He was not to contact her. It pained her to deceive him, but she could not afford to have him or anyone else come after her family.

Dani had returned to campus and withdrew from her courses, citing a similar story. She said goodbye to her professors and the friends she had made on campus. Nina had cried when she saw Dani, the tears she had been unable to shed over the death of Ray Brooks suddenly released. Dani had also found it impossible to weep for the man, though she had helped to cause his death, and that had frightened her. Even as she took Nina in her arms with a compassionate, but mechanical embrace, Dani felt absolutely nothing. She knew that when the feelings struck, they would be terrible.

Presently, Dani was locking the house up. The girl did not bother to look back at it.

"Let's go," she said in her cool, unemotional voice.

"Sure," Sam said, enjoying the chance to rest for a while.

An hour later they picked up Jimmy Hawkins at a coffee shop in downtown Los Angeles. He had one overnight bag and a knapsack.

"Traveling light?" Sam asked as she threw his belongings in the back.

"The only way *to* travel."

Dani had been very quiet. She had barely spoken to

Hawkins, though it had been her idea to contact the EMT, who had been present when Dani had performed her "miracle" during the highway crash. They had met again several days ago, and he had agreed to help without hesitation.

"You understand that what you're doing for us is dangerous," Sam said as Dani pulled out of the diner's parking lot, and drove in the direction of the highway.

"I do," he said. "I understand the risks perfectly. I don't mind." That had been the same answer he had given during their first meeting. "Besides, all I'm doing is taking you part of the way. You're on your own after that. It wouldn't be safe for any of us if the demons chasing after you made the connection between us, and if they did, it's best I can only take *them* part of the way."

"That's right," Sam said. "It's for the best."

They took the roads heading east, eventually leaving California, and were passing through the strange, twisted landscapes of Arizona well into the afternoon. Dani pulled the Rover into a rest area, where only a few trucks and other vehicles had stopped. All three left the Rover and stretched their sore, tired muscles. Dani went around to the back and opened their cooler.

"Why are you doing this?" Sam asked Hawkins once again.

The Native American shrugged. "I dunno. Guilt, maybe. I came to Los Angeles because I wanted to learn more about medicine, I wanted to do something for my people, help them whether they wanted it or not. I was just being selfish, because when I went back, it was never to stay, and when I was here, I learned what I had to learn to get by. I don't have the gift your daughter has. Even if she didn't come from the old ones, even if she didn't have her blessings, she would be able to give a lot to whatever tribe you end up with.

"The man I'm taking you to, he's a scholar. He has a private library that can teach you about many tribes." Hawkins tapped his head. "Then there's always what he has up here."

Dani came around and handed each of them cool drinks. They sipped at them slowly. The heat was unbelievable.

"Of course, this man, he's going to tell you things that you think aren't real, stories about the old gods, and the skinwalkers, and the places that no one goes to anymore, because of the ghosts. You'd better listen to those stories, too."

Sam nodded. Two years ago, she never would have believed in such fantasies. Today, she was willing to listen to anything. Dani placed her hand on her mother's shoulder, touching her gently.

"Look over there," Hawkins said. "See those rocks in the distance, that outgrowth, with the ledge? The whites called that place Satan's Hammer. There's a little trail beneath it that hardly anyone ever takes, and those who do always come to harm soon after.

"We know the place is cursed. The caves over there are the resting place of evil spirits. You might be considered a skinwalker if you were to stay there. The

414

people would ask if you were not afraid to lay with demons."

Sam laughed bitterly. "It's a little late for that."

Hawkins nodded. "You must not answer his questions like that. He would be shocked. He would ask you, doesn't anything make you afraid?"

"Afraid?" Sam looked away from him and thought of her daughter, and the son she would one day have, the child growing within her. So much could go wrong. She could lose them both. "Yeah, there are things that make me afraid."

Dani sensed her mother's unease, and she folded herself into the woman's arms.

"It's all right, Mom," Dani said, gently stroking Sam's back. She looked to Hawkins. "I know what I'd tell him."

"What's that?" he asked.

Dani looked out at the horizon, where the sun was already starting to swell. She pictured the sunset, the blood-red orb sinking over the horizon, and the onset of darkness. "I'd tell him there are *better things* to be afraid of. . . ."

They stood watching the sun for a few minutes, then returned to their car and headed back on the main road, driving into the blinding sunlight.